Alternative Liberties

Also from B Cubed Press

Alternative Truths

More Alternative Truths: Tales from the Resistance

Alternative Theology

Alternative Apocalypse

Stories for the Thoughtful Young

Poems for the Thoughtful Young

Space Force

Alternative War

Alternative Deathiness

Spawn of War and Deathiness

The Protest Diaries

Alternative Holidays

Holiday Leftovers

Post Roe Alternatives

Madam President

Southern Truths

Alternative Liberties

Edited by
K.G. Anderson, Lou J. Berger, Debora Godfrey,
Cliff Winnig, Irene Radford and
Bob Brown

Cover Design
Jay O'Connell

Published by

B Cubed Press
Kiona, WA

All rights reserved.
Copyright © 2025 B Cubed Press
Interior Design (e-book) Bob Brown
Interior Design (print) Bob Brown
Cover Design Jay O'Connell
Print ISBN: 978-1-949476-47-7
Electronic ISBN: 978-1-949476-48-4
First Printing 2025
First Electronic Edition 2025

Alternative Liberties

Copyright

Foreword © 2024 Cliff Winnig
Turns Out, It Was Cancer After All © 2024 Jim Wright
Art as Resistance © 2024 Andrew L. Roberts
Just One Vote © 2024 Louise Marley
Diminished Horizons © 2024 Adam-Troy Castro
C.A.R.E. © 2024 Mark Rivett
A Day in the Life of a Freedom Fighter © 2024 Joseph Nettles
Seen and Not Heard © 2024 Tera Schreiber
Little Boxes © 2024 Jacy Morris
Yo Mike Johnson, Answer your Phone © 2024 Merv Sims
The Big Fat Double-Take © 2024 Paula Hammond
A Better President © 2024 Brenda Cooper
In Real Time © 2024 C T Walbridge
Unwanted Visitors © 2024 K.G Anderson
Preacher Feature © 2024 Mike Adamson
The Sylvia Rivera School for Wayward Queers © 2024 Voss Foster
Suka-blat © 2024 Robert Walton
Doubleplusbad © 2024 Juleigh Howard-Hobson
A Place Before the Storm © 2024 William Kingsley
Ms. Drake's Lesson © 2024 Lou J Berger
The American Holocaust: A History © 2024 Louise Marley
So Many Reasons to Despair © 2024 Akua Lezli Hope
Animal Control © 2024 Jonathan Erman
Sanitation Day © 2024 DP Sellers
To my granddaughter, about to be born © 2024 Debora Godfrey
Not Civilized Yet © 2024 Nancy Jane Moore
The Hoal Book © 2024 Chaz Osburn
Death of the God Emperor of the Universe © 2024 Elizabeth Ann Scarborough
Moctezuma's Rescue © 2024 Loren Davidson

Alternative Liberties

Legacy © 2024 Larry Hodges
US History in DeSoto County © 2024 Jason P. Burnham
Three Patriotic Witches © 2024 Susan Murrie Macdonald
NeighborHelp © 2024 Earl T. Roske
Weaponized Genealogy © 2024 Tom Easton
It's already happened © 2024 Stephanie L. Weippert
Sivilized World © 2024 Elwin Cotman
Smart Squirrel © 2024 Kurt Newton
ad regum victorem © 2024 Andrew L. Roberts
Drink It © 2024 Stuart Hardy
Who's in Stall Number One © 2024 Amy Ivery Wolf
"The Terrific Leader" © 2018 Harry Turtledove
Brown Eyes © 2024 Ell Rodman
Tricentennial Blues © 2024 Jenna Hanan Moore
So Gallantly Livestreaming © 2024 Don Bisdorf
Best Pocalypse Now © 2024 C. A. Chesse
Priorities, ©2024, Pearl Sims
Afterword © 2024 David Gerrold

Foreword

We always remember the moment we learned of a great tragedy. For people of certain ages, to recall the JFK assassination, the explosion of Space Shuttle Challenger, or 9/11 is to recall where you were when you heard the news.

When Trump won a second term, I was with friends and colleagues on the B Cubed podcast, doing special election night coverage. The Democrats' defeat rolled over us like a train wreck in slow motion, and I rolled through all the stages of grief.

But from the ashes of that night rose the phoenix of this anthology: a counter to Trump's promise of retribution and revenge, a light against the rising dark.

The brave writers herein clearly love the United States of America: maybe not the America that was, certainly not the America that is about to be, but the *promise* of America. Give us your tired, your poor, your huddled masses, and we'll give them liberty and justice for all.

Science fiction has satirized the present, imagined dystopian futures, and offered visions of decency that could be. In this volume you'll find all three. You'll also

Alternative Liberties

find smart, passionate essays and a sprinkling of poems. Some truths can only be told in verse, after all.

With this book, we take a cue from Emma Lazarus and, like Lady Liberty, lift our lamp beside the golden door. Let these works—full of creativity, determination, and courage—light your way and inspire you.

Together, we'll build an America worthy of its long-delayed promise.

—Cliff Winnig, January 2025

Alternative Liberties

Table of Contents

Foreword *Cliff Winnig*	i
Turns Out, It Was Cancer After All *Jim Wright*	1
Art as Resistance *Andrew L. Roberts*	9
Just One Vote *Louise Marley*	11
Diminished Horizons *Adam-Troy Castro*	17
C.A.R.E. *Mark Rivett*	45
A Day in the Life of a Freedom Fighter *Joseph Nettles*	55
Seen and Not Heard *Tera Schreiber*	63
Little Boxes *Jacy Morris*	75
Yo, Mike Johnson, Answer Your Phone... *Merv Sims*	85
The Big Fat Double-Take *Paula Hammond*	87
A Better President *Brenda Cooper*	95
In Real-Time *C T Walbridge*	109
Unwanted Visitors *K.G. Anderson*	113
Preacher Feature *Mike Adamson*	121
The Sylvia Rivera School for Wayward Queers *Voss Foster*	133
Suka-blat *Robert Walton*	145

Alternative Liberties

Doubleplusbad — 151
Juleigh Howard-Hobson

A Place Before the Storm — 153
William Kingsley

Ms. Drake's Lesson — 159
Lou J Berger

The American Holocaust: A History — 167
Louise Marley

So Many Reasons to Despair — 175
Akua Lezli Hope

Animal Control — 177
Jonathan Erman

Sanitation Day — 185
DP Sellers

To my granddaughter, about to be born — 195
Debora Godfrey

Not Civilized Yet — 199
Nancy Jane Moore

The Hoal Book — 201
Chaz Osburn

Death of the God Emperor of the Universe — 213
Elizabeth Ann Scarborough

Moctezuma's Rescue — 219
Loren Davidson

Legacy — 229
Larry Hodges

US History in DeSoto County — 235
Jason P. Burnham

Three Patriotic Witches — 243
Susan Murrie Macdonald

NeighborHelp — 247
Earl T. Roske

Weaponized Genealogy — 261
Tom Easton

It's Already Happened — 267
Stephanie L. Weippert

Sivilized World — 269
Elwin Cotman

Smart Squirrel — 279

Alternative Liberties

Kurt Newton
ad regum victorem — 287
Andrew L. Roberts
Drink it — 289
Stuart Hardy
Who's in Stall Number One — 295
Amy Ivery Wolf
"The Terrific Leader" — 301
Harry Turtledove
Brown Eyes — 307
Ell Rodman
Tricentennial Blues — 315
Jenna Hanan Moore
So Gallantly Livestreaming — 325
Don Bisdorf
Best Pocalypse Now — 337
C. A. Chesse
Priorities — 339
Pearl Sims
Afterward — 343
David Gerrold
About the Authors — 349
About B Cubed Press — 361

Alternative Liberties

Turns Out, It Was Cancer After All

Jim Wright

Last year I spent three months waiting to see if I had cancer or not.

The doctors were all pretty sure I had it. And it was going to be the kind that I probably wouldn't survive. Then, they were finally able to complete a test and I woke up from the procedure and... didn't have cancer. Just totally didn't have it. "You can go," the doctor said. "We don't need to see you again for ten years."

It took me a week to even process the relief.

I'm not sure I still have.

As I noted on Threads, much of the day after the 2024 election felt a lot like that three months.

I was hoping for a similar outcome.

Hoping I'd wake up and all would be well. But...

Well, now we know who's who.

Now we know who our real friends and allies are. And who isn't.

I was going to ask: So, what was it this time?

What's the excuse this time?

Was it the price of eggs?

Cost of gas at the pump?

Wait, wait, she didn't have any ground game in swing states wah wah wah?

Hated her laugh?

No, it's Gaza? Yeah, it's Gaza isn't it?

What's the excuse this time?

But, you know what? It turns out I honestly don't care. I mean, when it's terminal cancer, do you really care how you caught it?

I don't care what the excuse is this time around and ultimately, it doesn't matter anyway. Every single thing lefties claim they care about? In the end, none of it mattered enough.

And now, we've lost it all.

Donald Trump will decide our fate.

What? What's that?

Oh, we'll fight, will we? It's not over! We...

Yeah, save it.

Just fucking save it, I'm not interested. The cancer is too far along.

You personally? Sure, you might have cared enough, but it turns out a lot of those we thought were on our side, those we thought would stand up for their own rights, just... didn't. Not only didn't, but they appear to have thrown their lot in with Trump and are willing to let Elon Musk, Laura Loomer, RFK Jr, and the local Preacher Man run their lives. A lot of those women I saw in line yesterday? Apparently they *did* vote away their own rights.

No, no, I'm not blaming women.

I blame Americans, all of us. That's who I blame.

I'm saying everyone knew what the stakes were, there was a record turnout and somehow 20 million *less* Americans voted this time and so we decided to reelect a twice-impeached serial rapist

Alternative Liberties

currently out on bail for more than twenty felony convictions.

Why? I don't know. The reason doesn't much matter now anyway, does it?

You again? What now? Trump is going to what now?

LOL. No. Trump isn't going to jail. You can forget that pipe dream. Those who prosecuted Trump? Odds are, *they'll be the ones* going to prison.

Merrick Garland? You tell me he had to go slow, etc. Well, he went slow and I'm not a lawyer but I goddamn well know politics and I fucking told you so for whatever that's worth. Merrick Garland might have been *right*, but he still failed us worse and just as deliberately as any Benedict Arnold. Slow. Fuck me.

Oh, and all those MAGA insurrectionists Garland *did* lock up?

They're free on Jan 20, 2025. With a full pardon. Because if we didn't lock up the guy who led the insurrection, well, then nothing else matters and everything Garland *actually* accomplished is totally moot, erased, never happened, the guy might as well have never existed. He's a nebbish, history won't even remember his name.

And again, I did tell you so.

I told you so, but I was just pissing into the wind.

You already knew.

You knew.

I have to laugh at those this morning saying "well, at least we passed abortion protection in..."

Oh stop. That's the one legitimately funny bit today. Oh, you passed abortion protection and you're gonna put it in your state constitution? Hardee har har. Yeah. Trump and these pinched faced religious nuts are going to enact a national abortion ban, yes they are, and whatever your silly little state constitution says means exactly fuck all. What are you gonna do? Appeal it to

Alternative Liberties

the Supreme Court? LOL. But hey, take what joy you can this morning, I guess. Laugh it up. You might not get a lot of chances for humor in the future. We're going to see measles, polio, mumps, and the flu ravage our population again. Preventable diseases that were conquered decades ago are going to kill, blind, sterilize, and maim our kids again. Me? I'm getting old, I probably won't survive whatever mismanaged pandemic comes next, unless horse dewormer up your ass actually does work this time.

They're going to drill and mine our national parks and frack our water.

They're going to tear down the wind turbines and solar panels and cook the planet.

They're going to turn the military loose on us and damn posse comitatus. The law and Constitution only matter when you elect people who respect it.

They're going to ban same sex marriage and lock up LGBTQ people as insane, just like the Germans did back in the 1930s, or worse.

They'll round and deport 20 million people and it's going to leave such a massive hole in our economy that we might never recover, but Elon says you'll be fine after a couple of years of hardship. My dear old mom used to say: you can get used to hanging if you hang long enough. We're about to find out just how true that is.

Healthcare? Social Security? Gone. Hope you got plenty of savings to support you in your old age. What's that? Oh. Well, maybe you can sell a kidney then.

They're going to impose tariffs, give tax breaks to billionaires, give Trump direct control of the Fed and Elon control of everything else, and utterly destroy the economy.

The billionaires won't suffer, but you damn sure are going to.

They're going to put guns in every school right next to mandatory Jesus.

Alternative Liberties

However bad you think it's going to be, it'll be worse.

But, you knew that.

Oh sure, eventually, a decade or so down the road, after the recession and the wars and the riots and the violence, just like those who voted for the Third Reich, those who voted for Trump are gonna get screwed by the very rapist they helped elect.

And, you know, I just don't care about that either.

Sure, they'll have it coming, but if I'm still around to witness their comeuppance (an unlikely event to be sure, but maybe I'll get lucky. If you can call living in that world luck) I'll feel neither joy at their misery nor sympathy for their suffering. Fuck 'em.

See, we're all going to get screwed right alongside them, the undeserving and the guilty alike, The Good and The Bad Germans both.

Not just us, but all our friends too.

The war in Ukraine is over, Putin won on election night. NATO and Europe are next.

The war in Gaza isn't over and won't be for a while, but the outcome is inevitable now. But hey, at least you have your principles, right?

Taiwan? South Korea? Oh well. So sorry. Sucks to be you.

If it's any consolation, it's gonna suck to be us too.

But again, you *knew* this.

I'm not telling you anything you didn't already know.

We all knew, but for a lot of lefties yesterday, well... here we are.

Yeah, yeah, I know, I know. You're mad at me now for saying so.

Be mad. It'll keep you warm when the power goes out.

I wish you were mad enough yesterday to show up.

And so here we are.

Alternative Liberties

Trump isn't just going to be president again. He's going to be quite literally a dictator because there is absolutely *nothing* to hold him back this time. We handed him the White House, the Court, the Legislature, and total immunity. It's not just this latest election, it's all the ones that came before too.

You need to face what that means.

He's going to take revenge on us. He's going to do what he said he would do. He's going to destroy everything you love. You knew that, and it wasn't enough. You're going to have to face it.

Trump is going to burn down the world and maybe that's what it'll finally take.

That's what the far left progressives shouted at me back in 2016: burn it all down. Burn it all down.

Burn it all down. Burning it all down isn't the moral high ground, it's just arson and people die in a fire, but again here we are and careful what you wish for. Because now it is all going to burn and I hope those who started this fire get everything they've got coming to them. And who knows, maybe they're right. Maybe when we're squatting in the ruins, covered in ash, maybe then it'll be enough to get you to show the fuck up. Or not.

What should you do? What should any of us do?

I don't know.

I don't know. I'm out of ideas.

I'm old. I'm tired. I'm worn out from this fight. More, I'm worn out from sounding the alarm and watching it fall on deaf ears.

What to do?

Flee maybe. Get out while you can, if there's some place that'll take people who didn't give enough of a fuck about their own fate to change it when they had the chance. Hopefully Europe won't turn away desperate Americans fleeing fascism like we did to the Jews fleeing

Germany back in the 1930's. But, hey, if they do, well, you can't really blame them can you?

But, again, again, and again, you knew all this.

Yes, you did. And now? Grim? Depressing? Panic attack? You *knew* it would come to this if you didn't show up. And it wasn't enough. Why? Why wasn't it enough? What's the excuse this time? Like I said above, I don't know and I don't care, but I'm sure we're going to hear all about it anyway and why those of us who actually did care, who sounded the alarm claxon over and over, and who actually did show up are somehow to blame.

See you in the camps.

I'll be the guy drinking prison wine with Hillary.

Alternative Liberties

Alternative Liberties

Art as Resistance

Andrew L. Roberts

Resistance may be futile
but resistance is all I have
Four years of Donald Trump
has created a deep resistance
in my flesh
the very mention of him
gives me hives
But art is my inoculation now
and crafted verse of searing words
the vaccination against his infection
Art is my resistance
Art is our resistance
Hear me now
you artists, authors, essayists, and poets
Art is our resistance
our words, our paint, our songs will be
our swords and shields
our bandages and our comfort

Alternative Liberties

Do what you do and resist for those
without the means to resist
Do not render yourselves futile
Art be our resistance.

Just One Vote

Louise Marley

The flames towered high against the night sky, red and hot and fierce, dancing this way and that against the faint stars. They crackled and smoked, threatening to burst out of the firepit. Lila grew too warm, watching, and had to step back. She was already burning, with anger and with resentment. She was hot to do some damage.

She was doing damage, of course. As she stood with baby Alice in her arms, she watched a pile of comics catch a spark and begin to burn. A stack of paperback novels had already been devoured. A pair of fishing boots softened and sagged, and she shifted her position to save Alice from breathing the rank burned-rubber smell as the boots succumbed to the heat. A fishing pole and tackle box beneath them were already blackened and bent. Lila knew she would be picking up garbage cans full of hunks of ruined metal and blobs of melted plastic out of the ashes when this was over.

Alternative Liberties

If she hadn't been holding Alice, she might have cheered when the golf clubs began to char, and the canvas bag holding them grew red spots here and there. They were new, those clubs, and expensive. They wouldn't burn, but no one would ever swing them again.

She was aware the fire was too big for the firepit, and she braced for the sounds of fire engines racing into their neighborhood. Instead, her neighbor Suzanne wriggled through the fence that separated their houses and trotted toward her, carrying a fire extinguisher.

"Lila! What's going on? Your bonfire is..." She stopped, and stared at the firepit, where the golf clubs were gradually blackening. "Are those Rocky's clubs? Where's Toby?"

"With my mother." Toby, at four, might have interfered with this operation. He loved those comics, as did his father.

"Lila," Suzanne said, her eyes growing wide with alarm. "What's going on? Does Rocky know you're doing this?" She set the fire extinguisher on the ground. It wasn't needed, as the flames had begun to subside.

The smell of burning canvas joined the scent of melting rubber. Lila wrinkled her nose as she turned to Suzanne. "Stinks, doesn't it? And no, Rocky doesn't know." With relish, she added, "It's a surprise."

"Surprise?" Suzanne blinked. "That you're burning his golf clubs?"

"Yes. Well, trying to."

Suzanne turned to gaze in obvious confusion at the mess of the clubs and the bag and the boots. As the fire died down, other things already destroyed in the fire appeared. There were baseball hats, their insignias gone forever. There were the dissolving remains of a styrofoam cooler, the wreck of an aluminum folding chair, and a half-consumed Coors beer sign with most of its letters gone. In the middle of everything a pile of shirts and jackets and jeans smoked steadily.

Alternative Liberties

"Lila," Suzanne breathed. "You burned Rocky's *clothes*?"

"Well, again, I tried. They don't burn very well. Most of these things don't. Even with fire starter poured over them." She pointed to the empty Sterno can on the ground near the firepit.

"But—his *clothes*?"

"Not all of them." Alice stirred, and Lila shifted her to the opposite shoulder, cupping her little head with her hand, and snuggling her close. "He still has that fucking tee shirt. He was wearing it when he left the house today."

"Tee shirt," Suzanne said.

"You know the one. You saw it at the barbecue over the weekend."

"Oh," her neighbor breathed. "Oh, yes. That one." She put her hands on her hips, surveying the detritus beneath the collapsing flames. "Wow, Lila. You must be really mad."

Lila turned away from the fire, gazing across the yard at the driveway where, very soon, Rocky would appear. Her voice was tight and low. "Mad doesn't cover it, Suzanne. I'm furious. Raging. Murderous."

"But, Lila—over a tee shirt?"

Lila looked into Suzanne's face, and Suzanne recoiled at the expression in her eyes. "It was one step over the line, Suzanne. One step too far." She turned back to the fire, watching it eat up the last of what would burn, char and stain what wouldn't. "It was the ballot."

"Wh-what? What ballot?"

"My ballot. My vote."

"What about it?"

Lila drew a shuddery breath, feeling her rage begin to subside just as the flames were doing. "The kids were

Alternative Liberties

sick with that virus everyone had, and I couldn't leave them, so I gave Rocky my ballot to mail."

"But the election was three weeks ago."

"I know." Lila breathed in again, more steadily this time. The pile of ruined belongings made her feel better. Much better. Better than she had all day. "I went out to his truck last night for his travel mug to give it a good wash, because he never thinks of it. I found my ballot, stuffed in that little nylon trash bag he carries. Just folded in half and stuffed in there, like junk mail."

Suzanne raised her eyebrows. "Uh-oh."

"I took it in the house, and when I showed it to him, he said he forgot. I asked him about his own ballot, and he said he filled it out and mailed it at work. But he 'forgot' to mail mine."

"Lila, I don't think—"

Lila turned an icy gaze on her neighbor. "You don't think he did it on purpose?"

"I mean—it's just one vote—"

Lila's rage began to grow again, like a hot spot in a dying fire. "One vote? *One vote?* Who did you vote for, Suzanne?"

Suzanne's gaze shifted sideways, away from Lila's. "Well. Um. I didn't."

"Didn't what?"

Suzanne stared at the ground. "Didn't vote."

"You didn't vote? Are you kidding me? Women *died* so you could vote!"

Suzanne lifted her head, and said in a defensive tone, "Well, Lila, I'm sorry, but it's not like it would have made a difference."

Lila squeezed Alice too tightly, and the baby began to snivel. She made herself relax her arms, but her jaw was still tight, and her voice was like gravel. "Every vote makes a difference. And this was mine. *Mine!*"

"He said he forgot—"

"He didn't forget! He knew I voted differently from him, and by 'forgetting' he doubled the value of his. That means not only was my vote not counted, his got twice the weight it should. Don't you see that?"

"Well, I guess I do, but..."

"And then there was the tee shirt."

"Oh." Suzanne bit her lip. "Oh, I see. The one that said—how does it go—'Your body, my...'"

Lila interrupted, her voice so tight it hurt. "That one. I want to burn that, too."

"But you can't, since he's wearing—"

"You don't think so?"

"Well, how could you? I mean—"

"He'll come home eventually." Lila exhaled, a long, noisy breath. She watched the last of the fire flicker and begin to go out, taking with it the crumbs of Rocky's treasured comics, the lurid covers of his paperback collection.

"He won't let you have it," Suzanne said grimly. "Not after he sees all this."

"He might not have a choice. Do you think he sleeps in it?" Lila grinned at her neighbor, coldly, deliberately showing her teeth. "Even if he does, it's going to be burned. Wherever it is. I have another can of fire starter."

Alternative Liberties

Diminished Horizons

Adam-Troy Castro

About three years and two genocides in, they finally got around to me. My crimes, even as defined by them, were minor. Nobody thought that I'd been involved in insurrection against the administration. I hadn't ever picked up a gun, hadn't ever thrown a stone, had only once or twice, in my personal stone age, participated in a demonstration.

But I'd been vocal. I'd condemned the President's positions, written at length on the many crimes attributed to him, including fraud, and treason, and multiple rapes. That my writings had mostly been online and directed to people who mostly believed the same thing made me low priority, made me think that I could survive and continue to live my little life as long as I kept my head down. This does not make me a hero. This makes me a small and frightened human being. Three years in, millions had died and I could only hope that I was too small for them to worry about.

Alternative Liberties

Then a man knocked on the door and asked to come in. It was one of those asks that carries with it an order. I said yes and he came in, sat on my best chair, surveyed what he saw on my bookshelves and on my walls, and then sniffed at some of the fantasy-related art I had collected in my decades of genre writing.

"I have to admit," he said, looking at some of my book covers, "that this strikes me as pretty sick stuff, overall." He did not say that of any of my horror covers. He was referring in chief to a woman in form-fitting black looking up at a dragon. Fantasy, I have found, is frightening to people who cannot process it, and this is the weapon we used to have against people who once upon a time thought it should be repressed and eradicated: the people who once went after *Dungeons and Dragons,* for instance. Unclean! Demented! Kill it before it breeds! This man saw a woman with a dragon and processed that I was not just a dangerous radical but a twisted, verminous human being, intent on polluting the minds of children. My Bob Eggleton painting of a spaceship floating over a herd of alien creatures struck him the same way; my sofa cover showing, of all things, Jack Skellington, the singing hero of a children's film called *The Nightmare Before Christmas,* was "morbid." And I was left thinking that if these benign things were too much to win his approval, and he had power, I was in trouble.

His name was Donzmann. He had brown teeth, a smoker's complexion, and canine jowls, the kind that you suspect of flapping whenever he shook his head vigorously. He was calm and polite, but cruelty seemed baked within him; his casual conversation about my belongings reminded me of an old movie about, among other things, a wealthy British twit who, in the 1930s, invited some representatives of Nazi Germany to his estate. In the film, one of his guests quietly explored his

Alternative Liberties

halls, taking notes on his art, clearly inventorying it for the near future when England would belong to his masters and all the treasures could be removed from the walls and shipped home. I had no illusions that any of my art or books struck my visitor as valuable enough to be claimed as loot. But it was all grist for his pending condemnation of me and any consequences he was already planning.

It was a civil conversation. My Australian Shepherds, Hammett and Chandler, positioned themselves between myself and the intruder, not growling but clearly reading that I was afraid of this man and that I needed to be protected from him. What I needed, I thought, was for people to have been willing to vote for a woman candidate over a man whose credentials involved decades of robbing his contractors blind, but it was way too late for that.

I would always remember one mildly disapproving question. "Chandler? As in the guy from *Friends?* That was close to pornographic."

In an earlier age I would have told him that this was crazy. "No. Never even saw the show. Chandler as in the guy who wrote *The Big Sleep.*"

"What is that? A movie?"

"Yes," I said, "eventually."

"Are you mocking me, sir?"

"No." But I must have been, because I felt the mild frisson of a reader's sense of superiority.

He took a note.

Then he put down his pen and told me that I had been tried *in absentia* and that, as a minor offender, I had been sentenced to six years of house arrest. During this time, I would be prohibited from posting anything online, or writing anything for publication. That was unnecessary, as I had stopped writing forever on the

Alternative Liberties

day the President issued the order that criticism of him, current or past, was sedition.

I would not be allowed any contact with my friends or relatives. That was redundant as my wife had died and my siblings had fled the country, and some friends and the only relatives who remained were in-laws who had had been estranged from me before the new order.

What other associates and friends I still had had collapsed into their own bubbles of safety, unwilling to risk any associations that could result in their own trials *in absentia*. I would not be allowed to venture more than twenty steps from my home. That was redundant, as I already lived on a pension and, these days, had most of my groceries delivered.

That I would be denied engagement with society would not be hardship; this was the society that had voted him in, after all, and had cooperated with his mass arrests and his deportations and his mass executions, and had decided that he was the ordained messenger of a God who was no longer a God of love, but of terror.

The so-called civilization around me was one I no longer wanted any part of. I would have left the country if I could, but so many safe havens around the world were either just as bad, or tired of admitting refugee Americans unless they were rich. My exile was already internal, and I didn't expect to live the mandated six years. So I told Donzmann that I understood.

Maybe I invited the rest by failing to hide my subtle expression of triumph. Maybe my failure to gnash and wail indicated victory of some sort. The President's minions were the kind of people who assumed defiance even when they were facing compliance, and maybe they took it as seriously as those who merely wore the red baseball caps did while rioting for him.

But Donzmann scowled. His gaze rested on the big portrait of my late wife. He said, "Who's she?"

Alternative Liberties

I answered simply that she was my wife.

He said, "And *where* is she?"

I said she was gone and had been for a long time.

He asked me if I could prove that.

I said that I had no idea where her death certificate was, having endured multiple moves in the time since, but that her departure was a matter of public record and that the Federal Government probably still had the resources to confirm it without my help.

He said, "Did she concur with you?"

I said that we had been married for twenty years and that of course she didn't. "On some things," I said. The weak joke appeared to irritate him.

Another of my home's wall decorations was a print of the vintage poster for CASABLANCA, the one with Bogey holding a gun as the faces of Ingrid Bergman, Paul Henreid, and Peter Lorre float around him like helium balloons. It existed alongside other classical movie posters, including the ones for SEVEN SAMURAI and BRIDE OF FRANKENSTEIN and LAWRENCE OF ARABIA.

These, too, sustained me. I had been vocal, in my life, about how CASABLANCA, and SAMURAI in particular, were among the essential movies, the ones that told vital truths, of living as a commendable human being in times of unbearable evil, of singing the Marseillaise when the Nazis were dominating the piano. The posters surrounded the image of my smiling wife as if I'd intended them as commentary, but I'd never intended any resonance.

They were art I had, and they were art I *needed*, if only in memory, because I'd more or less committed the movies to permanent residence in my skull. It still hurt when Donzmann finished his questions, rose from his chair, and plucked the CASABLANCA poster off the wall. He said, "You will also not be permitted subversive

Alternative Liberties

materials," and I knew enough to not protest, given the President's now fully-confessed love of Der Fuhrer's leadership style.

I said, "I understand." The phrase "I understand" had long ago occurred to me as inherently irritating to these people. It was not defiant and it was not compliant, but was, instead, an acknowledgment that incoming information had been received and processed.

"I understand" is, in the absence of any other options for rebellion, a deep offense in that it communicated what it had to sans commentary. It offered no easy on-ramps for further punishment. But they feel it, or at least I like to think they do, and maybe this made it the wrong thing to say, planting fresh loathing in the system. I don't know. But it was what I said and it was what he left with, a blueprint to move on, to keep the pressure up until I was finally hurt enough to scream.

They gave me no trouble with groceries. They even helped to arrange for the deliveries to be regular and without input from me, beyond the already-established precedent. The first delivery was only missing my regular vice, ice cream sandwiches. I was sorry about that, but did not fill out the part of the form that asked for complaints. I signed my name, put everything away, and for weeks lived a constrained life that was not all that different from my prior one. I read my books, played with Hammett and Chandler and, from time to time, stepped out onto the front porch, well within my truncated borders, and enjoyed two things that the bastards had not taken from me: sunlight and fresh air.

The dogs stayed inside, which bothered them, but it was necessary because, if either one decided to run— an unlikelihood given their respective ages— I would not have been able to chase them. They would shit on the paper, and I would dispose of it afterward.

Alternative Liberties

For a while, I actually enjoyed my internal exile. It was not devoid of the sadness and dread of a world gone mad, but there is a pleasure to be had in being under the unimpeded sky, in breathing air that my lungs could not identify by pollutants, of seeing squirrels and birds and the occasional lost butterfly, though butterflies were rare and soon gone.

Peace of that sort is often a temporary pause for unwanted thought, and I welcomed that, too, because the alternative was to think of everything I had lost, everyone who was gone, and all the crimes that were still ongoing just outside the bubble where I was permitted to exist. Sometimes I fantasized about happy alternate worlds where my wife was still alive, or where my siblings had not fled to other shores, or where I somehow developed superpowers and was able to swoop down from the sky, bloodlessly beat up the bad guys, and restore justice to the world.

The final confrontation with the President was infinitely more satisfying than that old Kirby drawing of Captain America decking Hitler, and I do not say that it felt real, because it did not, but because it was a thing that was satisfying to imagine, balm for a mind that had, on the printed page, imagined any number of worlds that were worse than this one, that offered no bland escapism for the reader. But I could escape within those fantasies, for a minute or an hour, and then I could smile as a squirrel ran across my spotty, unwatered lawn.

When it got to be too much, I went inside and turned on one of the few channels that still showed old entertainment, channels that were not engaged, 24/7, in whipping the audience into compliance via fresh heights of outrage. By choice, I did not watch the news because I knew the only news that was still aired was that which had, of late, turned to images of the leader's

Alternative Liberties

smiling face, radiating shafts of light, interspersed with bulletins that did not inform the audience of what was happening, but seemed to wander around the periphery, providing rancid clues.

There was another war, that was certain. There was another ethnic cleansing taking place in another American city, that was certain. Shots had been fired, that was certain. And all of this left a fresh roiling bubble of tension in my gut, and the dogs would sense this and, whining with the infinite compassion of canines who could sense fear, they would join me on the couch to let me know that they were here to protect me.

This went on even after Hammett failed to wake one morning. Chandler discovered him, and so I was spared the heartbreak of a living dog forever looking for one for had been put down at the vet, because dogs are not stupid about life's most important things. He processed that his sibling and lifelong companion was gone and, though in grief, understood that he was not alone and that his duty was to ensure that I was not alone.

This is one grand secret of the world: even in dystopias there are dogs, and dogs are never corrupt.

In the wake of Hammett's departure, I tried to read but managed to do very little of that. My mind was still too disordered by grief for the comforts of prose. But that is a service that book spines provide for those who are not currently reading. The printed title and byline still provide a flashback to the *experience* of reading, and so I found myself, in my wanderings through my house, briefly smiling at the encounters with my old friends *Dombey and Son, The Three Musketeers, The Postman Always Rings Twice, Flowers for Algernon,* and *Memos from Purgatory*. The relationships I had had with them had flowered in the past and were still very much alive.

Alternative Liberties

Some days I left the house, though, of course, not to go anywhere. I could not do that. I could only stand within my mandated radius, sometimes sitting on a folding chair. Sometimes, this was a comfort, even in those cases where I could barely remember plot points. Other times I heard wailing sirens and coughed from whiffs of tear gas. Once, I heard sustained rifle fire. But this too ended. I cared, and I tasted despair, but I could not grasp the implied horrors. I was alive, but paralyzed.

There were months of this.

Then the erasures began.

"I'm sorry this took so long," Donzmann said.

He had returned to my home, greeted me politely, and once again taken up residence in my favorite chair. He insisted on small talk first.

What was up with me, he asked.

Nothing, I said truthfully.

Keeping out of trouble?

Yes.

Things like that. So rote they felt scripted.

Then came the apology for taking so long. It was bureaucracy, he said. After the purges, with all the experienced people being replaced by loyalists who needed to learn the job in hand. It was going to be perfect, eventually, but there were growing pains. Important business had to be put off.

"Now," Donzmann said, "it's time to start the next phase. You had to know more was coming, yes?"

"Yes," I said, and something in my voice made Chandler whine.

He had a list of outlawed writers he intended to prune from my shelves. "That's the thing," he mourned. "So many books are written by malcontents, people who see the world not as it is but as it should be. We never should have bothered with most of them. They cause trouble. So many of your stories are downright

Alternative Liberties

schizophrenic in that they portray worlds that don't exist, and never *could* exist; fantasies, which are for masturbators in basements, or woke literature, which is the source of all the problems. If we had some guarantee that the volumes you have could be prevented from going anywhere but the landfill once you died, we could indulge you in your unhealthy obsessions, but there are children out there, and unstable individuals who might turn violent when exposed to them. This is removing a contagion while we have a chance. You understand that, don't you?"

I repeated the fuck-you for the powerless: "I understand."

Donzmann explained that they knew this would be painful for me and that they were really doing what was best by not allowing me to keep the volumes that were outlawed in libraries and that, in some cases, came with criminal penalties. I could get in trouble. Or I could be "further demented" by perusal of things like *Slaughterhouse-Five*. In this world that the President had made, all that it took to permanently criminalize a book were five hundred complaints, nationwide, and that was easy to achieve with organized groups that managed that number with as many as twenty novels a day.

"That's a great convenience," he said. "I don't even have to read them."

"I understand."

His men came in. I won't go so far as to say that they all looked like him. They were a diverse group, some fit, some fat, one a grizzled old veteran and one a kid still in his teens, different from one another but still comfortably within the hard boundary of being white men. They all looked at me the same way, as a degenerate who needed to be deprived of degenerate things.

Alternative Liberties

It was not hard to imagine their understanding that, just before their arrival, I had been doing perverted and unclean things and that I would go back to them the instant they left.

They took my Library of America hardcovers. They took the revised *Lies My Teacher Told Me,* by James W. Loewen. They took anything that reeked of horror. They took Ursula Le Guin, one of them pronouncing it "Goo-In." They took Octavia Butler. They were, unfortunately, experts on which books were written by homosexuals and which had treated homosexual characters in any empathetic way. It was something they were aware of without ever reading past the title page. They took delight in calling such books *pornography.*

They deprived me of Clive Barker, of William S. Burroughs, and of Patricia Highsmith. And, when they were done taking all that, and formed a mound on my lawn with them, Donzmann told them to take the books with my own name on them, including the four that were tie-ins to a favorite superhero. They took my short story collections, the novels and the scattered works of nonfiction, and one that was a memoir of three earlier bad years and how I'd survived them, all rendered as sinful by the attachment of my name. I did not tell them that, in taking these, they were taking my life, but they had to know this because the scouring was designed to inflict maximum pain.

It reminded me of an incident from my teens, when my father had decided that comic books were bad and that my collection had to go. It had been my job, while subjected to his anger and scorn, to carry armfuls from my bedroom closet and dump them into a trash can half-full of water, all while weeping and sobbing and telling him I hated him. It was still an element of my complicated feelings about him, even now; but he was a complicated man and the pure sadism of his edict was inextricably connected to memories that communicated only love and the pain of his loss.

Donzmann and the others were not so complicated. I had no feelings of love toward them or their master, a man who, by my reckoning, communicated no good qualities whatsoever: no life philosophy beyond punishing as many people as possible in a manner as cruel as possible.

And it must have hurt my father, that time and all the other times I said I hated him. With Donzmann, with the President, the point was to make me feel impotent in my hatred, and the hatred was something that fulfilled them, that confirmed the efficiency of their work. Doing things that were worthy of hatred was their job description.

Donzmann said, "The place looks cleaner."

"It looks soulless and sterile."

"*I* don't have any books. Are you saying my home looks sterile?"

"I haven't been to your house. I don't know what it looks like." *It probably looks as sterile as hell, you fuck.* But I couldn't say that because it wouldn't have done any good.

After a moment he said, "The thing about books is that they just gather dust. There's no point in keeping them around, unless you read them right away and then get rid of them. The ones we took were just a collection of delusions and degeneracies, written by the diseased. You're better off without them. They just confused you."

I said nothing, not even venturing an *I understand.* Not then.

"Most of them are just made-up stuff some writer created. If you think about it, if they were any good they'd be movies, right? Why have so much shit hanging around, when it's just gonna poison your head

Alternative Liberties

anywhere?" He spotted something. "Lez Mizerabulls," he said, and then he brightened and said, "I think they said this was communist and against the police," and took that.

Then he took my *Grapes of Wrath*, which was also suspect because it demonized businessmen and had a character ask his boss what was so wrong about being a red when it meant having a few cents to work with?

I stiffened but, again, said nothing, because I would continue to remember the best of the best even without the now-gone visual prompts of the book-spines on my shelf. The loss of my own work was a bigger blow, but surely (I thought), *surely* (I thought again), there were still copies extant, people in this country who secreted theirs in hidden rooms, or people in other countries who had obtained theirs in translation or via international travel. It wasn't gone. It was just gone to *me*. It was gone as my direct personal validation. I would have to live on their memories, and *surely* (that word again) I could do that. They could not touch that.

They took multiple empty journals that friends had given me, and the drawing pads I used to practice at a skill I had but had never used professionally. I could write in those, if it occurred to me, and so they were dangerous, and so they had to be brought to the mound outside and set alight. Then they took the pens and a wrapped package of Number Two pencils that were a dangerous temptation if I decided to write on the walls.

The day after that, they took my movies: *all* my movies.

This hurt, too. There was nothing in the way of the air I breathed in, no dispatches from D'Artagnan or Tom Joad or Clarice Starling or Irene Adler or Don Quixote or even Peter Parker to comfort me with vicarious adventures put together out of errant whimsies, to spend my time in. It was indeed cleaner, in a way, and it left me free to navigate my own space, which was still infinite.

In my head, I began a novel that would never exist on paper, but was as real as anything I had ever dreamt of, of an adventurer who walked between the repressive walls of the world he lived in, who discovered secret passages that in his world connected all lives, from the penniless to the plutocrats, and who had adventures with those who had discovered these shadowy corridors before him. In this story, he and his friends were the only ones who were really free, and they resolved to search this labyrinth they lived within until they found the route to the hidden conspiracy that had made the world so awful, and then defeated it.

It was hundreds of pages long, this epic, and I lost count of the number of hours I must have spent in my easy chair, a vacant and dreamy look on my face, petting the surviving dog as my heroes braved dangers like the Tunnel of Ten Thousand Despairs, or the road to Aunt Loathsome's House. Never mind that it was my masterpiece. It was also my most potent argument for remaining alive.

I did not believe that the despot would be defeated and that the world would become what it once had been. I did not look forward to a future where his stain was wiped away and I could commit this great work to some medium where it could be shared. I believed in no such things. But my dreams had a rapt audience of one, and they were what I subsisted on, and, with time itself emptied of purpose, it was a thing worth celebrating.

Then one day, months later, they took away half my house.

I had gone to bed in the upstairs bedroom. I was sure of that. Then I woke, crabby and uncomfortable, on the living room couch. The stairs leading to my second floor, to the bed I'd once shared with my wife, were gone, replaced by a blank white wall. Donzmann sat in the chair he had now claimed as *his* chair, with two of his assistants in metal folding chairs on either sides of him.

I had the sense that they'd been watching me sleep for some time, judging my slumber as they would judge the crimes of a pederast, each snored breath another mark in my tally of sins against the state. Neither of them had necks, really. Their jowly cheeks rested flush on their shoulders, like knickknacks on a shelf.

Chandler sat on guard before me, well within reach of my comforting hand. I liked to think that he was showing his teeth. Or rather, I hoped that he wasn't; the last thing I needed was for Donzmann to decide that my only remaining companion was a bad dog, corrupted by my awfulness. Beyond that, I was so resigned to Donzmann's appearances that I did not react with violation at his mere presence. But the blank wall so completely disoriented me that I sat bolt upright and shouted, "What the hell?"

"You don't need an upstairs," Donzmann said.

"All my clothes are up there!"

"Some of them are," he agreed, "still hanging in what was your bedroom closet. We've burned a few of the t-shirts with political slogans: you already weren't wearing them anymore. We took a few things that others might want, like your suit and your dress shoes. We've done you the courtesy of bringing down a few things you do need, like underwear, socks, two pairs of pants, one week's worth of shirts: enough to keep you clothed, but too little to make what you wear on any given day anything you have to worry about. I think you'll find that the result fully jibes with our mission statement, of streamlining your life, and taking away the messy distractions that have led you to make the disordered decisions that have served you so poorly up until now.

Alternative Liberties

This will give you more time to contemplate your life choices."

"Y-you..." My next word would have been *bastard* but, again, I was aware that it would have validated him.

The temptation not just to speak, but to yell, to fulminate, to make some eloquent speech of the sort that, in the movies I no longer had access to, were often enough to turn the tide against injustice, was overpowering. But people far more eloquent than me had argued against what this man stood for and received applause from the like-minded, and yet had accomplished nothing.

What had won, instead, was the glossolalia of a demented man, who only had to keep in mind the people he hated and who he knew much of his base hated as well: and for that he had not needed eloquence, just persistence, in talking points disguised as hateful comedy. There was nothing I could say, nothing that would work. So, again, I said nothing.

He either mistook my silence for compliance, or chose to. He smiled at me, and I wanted to consider it the grin of a viper, but it was not; it was the warmth a man like him feels for prisoners who don't give him as much trouble as some others.

If he had children at home, he probably flashed the same smile whenever one did something unbearably cute. But he had other things to explain. "It's not drywall. Or at least, it's not *just* drywall. You should not attempt to put your fist through it. It's solid brick. You have nothing in your house capable of smashing through it. You could try to act out one of those stories where the unjustly-convicted felon digs a tunnel with, let's say, a spoon, but that would take years and years, probably longer than your sentence. The first thing I'll look at whenever I came back is if the wall has been

Alternative Liberties

tampered with in any way. There will be penalties if I detect any damage."

I finally found my voice. "*Why* are you doing this? If this is what you wanted, why didn't you just start by throwing me into solitary confinement and forgetting about me?"

He seemed delighted. "Why? First of all, because you're not much. You're not one of the people we shoot, or kick out. You're a useless person who may have attended a rally or two, who impressed himself with political rants that only reached those who already agreed with him. You're no threat. Others we kill. You, we just toy with. Understand?"

"I understand."

"I know what you're doing with that phrase, too. It's not irritating to me. It's just a retreat to blandness. In the second place, I think you can jettison the convenient and comforting fiction that I don't read books. I have, including some I've taken from you. *Les Miserables*," he said, correctly and with special emphasis, "which in case you're wondering, I always could pronounce correctly. Taking the books from you was a matter of doing what is always important when it comes to breaking a person, or a population: diminishing their horizons. Putting someone in a ghetto, or a featureless room, denying them dreams, is always most effective when it is done gradually; when the walls close in, and the comforts they relied on are removed inexorably, one at a time. Put a man in a cell and he rages against the walls. Take away what he has, one essential at a time over an extended period, and you reduce him, bit by bit, to a fraction of himself. Just look at you. Look what you've already become."

The room seemed to shift as I processed this. I'd developed the habit the incarcerated sometimes have, of neglecting their personal hygiene. I hadn't showered

Alternative Liberties

for a few days, and probably smelled bad. All I smelled these days was dog breath and body odor, and this was because I had nobody to impress and because it was the only weapon I had to wield at a universe that otherwise offered me nothing. The young heroes of the fiction I was writing in my head were already more real to me by far, and I realized with a sudden start that, despite multiple ethnicities and sexes and backgrounds, they were all me and always had been me.

Please don't hurt them, I thought.

Maybe I was so far gone that I said this out loud, because he reacted as if he heard me.

"They're not real," he said. "They've never been real. And we've known what you were doing since the first time we caught you staring into space for an hour. Did you think we didn't know what you used to do for a living?"

For the first time, he seemed to be actively sadistic, as if he was now ready to use a drill bit on my knuckles. "The only true narrative is the President's. Engagement with another narrative denies his primacy. Therefore, this also needs to be corrected. This will ultimately be good for you as, the more we flense your life of extraneous detail the more you are freed to concentrate on the nature of the world he was chosen to streamline. We're aware that this includes your treasonous imagination. Therefore, *you* will be streamlined." He spoke to the figures at his sides. "Hold him."

I fought. Oh, God, I fought. And I'm a man who had never had success at fighting, a man who, as a boy, was often left bloody and bruised on school playgrounds. I swung wildly, mining an inner life that had always been seasoned with fight scenes, some of them lived by resourceful protagonists and some of them by myself, revising the defeats of my life into successful victories won by martial arts, the specifics of which I knew nothing.

Alternative Liberties

In a just world I might have knocked Donzmann's droogs into next week and then started on the man himself, knocking out his teeth, shattering his ribs, leaving him to a life of languishing in some hospital, being fed via tubes or with spoons. I will say this: Chandler responded as if this were one of the narratives written by his namesake, in a world where Sam Spade had no trouble disarming the gunsel Wilmer. Anything to protect his much-diminished master.

But the first of Donzmann's helpers belted my last friend across the room, and the second had no trouble pinning my arms so that Donzmann could approach with one of the meanest hypodermics I had ever seen. I screamed and struggled without effect as he jabbed it into my upper chest, just below the collarbone.

Then he withdrew, and said, "This was a happy invention of our allies in Russia. They have a long chemical name for it, but I prefer to call it an anti-hallucinogen, which suppresses your capacity to formulate abstractions like sexual fantasies and other internalized stories. People placed under this regimen become dull plodders, very literal-minded, very devoid of an internal life, just beyond the strictly animal. Do you understand why it's so satisfying for us to give you this, only after stripping you of everything else this diseased aspect of yourself once treasured? And we are not done taking things away from you, of removing things from your life until there's nothing left." He placed the hypodermic in a little case, and said, "But, after today, you won't need shots. It will be delivered in your drinking water."

The lummox assistant released me, and I wanted to attack them again, but grayness rose and swallowed me.

~~~

Alternative Liberties

It was amazing, even in my much-diminished state, how long a downfall can last when one imagines he has already hit rock bottom.

It was several diminutions later. They had shrunk my world still further, narrowing my house until it was little more than a corridor alongside the unbreakable wall that had been the stairs upstairs. They had made sure that my downstairs half-bath only provided cold water, meaning that I had to let it warm to something like room temperature before I could use it for what bathing I could summon motivation for.

They had taken away my refrigerator and my oven, meaning what groceries I could receive no longer included anything that could be kept. They had taken away the last of my wall decorations, a portrait of my wife, and that meant that with my imagination as curtailed as they wanted it to be I could no longer remember her face, or her voice, or her regular production of punch lines, or what it had been like to be out in the world with her, or performing little errands with her, or consoling her, or being consoled by her, or being delighted by her, or making love to her; these were all fragments of my life, of infinite value, and they were all gone, as surely as any of the physical things Donzmann had stolen.

They did leave me something in return: an official portrait of the President, hanging in the same place where the portrait of my wife had been, and there was so little else to look at that there were times when I found myself staring at it for hours, trying to summon reasons to hate him, things I once known as well as my name, but which were also gone. He had been right about one thing, Donzmann: the way to break a person, irrevocably, was to demonstrate to him that his world could always be made smaller, reduced to the absolute minimum, and then, impossibly, constantly, less than that.

Alternative Liberties

The novel I'd been writing in my head was among the things that were gone and so was any impulse to write another. There were times when I said, well, start all over again, and I set about trying to think of a character, a situation, an arc that I could cling to in order to stay sane and that could someday give potential readers a way to process what had been done to their country. The capacity seemed well beyond my reach. The tools were gone, the means of visualizing anything but Der New Fuhrer's face a part of some long-distant past.

The days blurred into one another. I spent them on the couch, sitting without thought, sleeping without rest, living without purpose, and it was by smelling myself that I remembered I had to care for my hygiene. More than once, I realized that I was sitting in my own filth. Sometimes, that was not enough to rouse me.

Sometimes, I needed other reminders.

Like the day I heard insistent whining and realized that I could not remember the last time I'd fed Chandler.

I got off the couch and sank to my knees. My head reeled. I was weak, too. I could not remember the last time I ate. The drinking water's additive suppressed more than imagination. It suppressed hunger and thirst. With days as insubstantial as hours, it might have been a long time. I couldn't measure it.

I saw a lump by the unused front door.

Chandler lay on his side next to a stinky pile of dried turds, dating to however long it had been since the last time he'd had food in his system, and I fell to my knees beside him. "Oh my God. I'm so sorry. Please believe I'm sorry."

He looked at me. There was no absence of love in his look. That is the thing about dogs: once they love you, they are willing to put aside any amount of cruelty and

Alternative Liberties

abandonment and still see a friend and savior in the humans who, for some reason, forgot to love them.

I rushed to my larder and got a can of dog food. I procured a paper bowl and filled it with water, placing both near his muzzle, where he could smell them. He ignored the food and lapped at the water first, insatiable, drinking in such haste that he vomited it all and then, once he was done, went back to drink some more. From somewhere in my perpetual haze, I recalled a way to diagnose the levels of canine dehydration, and pinched the skin of his back. It descended back to his flesh sluggishly. I'd once had a dog, Cain, who had died from failing kidneys and pinching him in this way had produced the same results. There had been no saving him, but there was a necessity to save Chandler, if I ever wanted to live with myself again.

"Please," I said, weeping. "Forgive me, boy, I love you. You know I love you. You're still a good boy. Don't blame your human being so being such an idiot."

After several attempts, he succeeded in standing up, and pressed his head against my chest.

I was still fuzzy, but as I hugged and kissed him, I tried to figure out just how long I'd been blind and deaf to his efforts to get me to pay attention, to both his need for sustenance and his hunger for love. He was also, I realized, lonely for play with Hammett gone, and I immediately promised him that as soon as he was feeling well again we would do some wrestling on the floor, and I would throw the ball, and he could run and catch it.

I trailed off and came back to clarity again. The water bowl was empty and the food was gone. I was still kneeling in the same place, wrapped in a greater personal stench. I ran to the kitchen, got more food, filled another bowl of water, and brought it to him. This time I did it with conscious thought. Damn it, they would not take him from me. They would not.

Alternative Liberties

Chandler accepted my offerings.

I remembered that my watch, a thing I still possessed but had no reason to look at, was still on my wrist. It had an alarm. I set it twice daily: *Feed Dog.*

Sometimes it took a long time to rouse me from whatever stupor I was in. Sometimes it didn't. I stopped needing the alarm when I started feeling a cold dog nose on my face. He was still weak, but he was back to being ambulatory.

At the cost of some dehydration on my own part, I retained enough clarity to know that in a couple of days I might feel the urge to imagine things again, and perhaps even to write.

By then, Chandler was on my lap, snoring.

The portrait of the vile President continued to grin at me, happy with himself.

And I knew the clarity was still around, for the time being, because for the moment he was not an object of dull resentment, but an actual prompt for righteous anger.

You, I thought.
You don't even like dogs.
Hitler liked dogs.
You don't like dogs.
You despise empathy. You don't feel it for people displaced by natural disasters, even within our borders: you make them an item on a spreadsheet and you complain about having to spend money to save them. How many times, starting with COVID, did you protest about the waste? How many times was the money all you cared about?

You even stole the part of your inheritance that was meant for your brother's family, you piece of shit.

And Donzmann has told me that the way you control people is to make their horizons smaller, but it's not a matter of walls. It's a matter of having the room in your heart for empathy. You paint empathy as a joke. You laugh at it and give people permission to make their understandings of politics all about thinking of others to punish, to hurt, to put in camps, or to gradually destroy.

Dogs, when cared for, are concrete evidence that we long for something to care about. All those videos that I used to watch on the internet—and is there still an internet as I remember it, or is it now all just you and hate, all channels, all the time?—of people, mostly young girls and women, being surprised with dogs as gifts.

They all weep, because their emotions overflow, because the adoration they want to feel with something that will love them is something they all craved, and were overjoyed to the point of tears.

But you've never felt that, have you?

Not for people, and not for dogs.

Chandler slept on my lap.

The President stared at me from the wall. Still grinning the grin of the Great White. Unaffected by anything I had silently thought at him and, of course, the portrait was impossible to relate to, and so was he.

I was very thirsty, myself. I was in the precarious position as a dog owner, being pinned by a loved creature I could prompt to move with the slightest stir of my legs, and yet unwilling to disturb in the moment because the peace he felt in my provided warmth was more important to me than my own physical needs.

I noticed how white his muzzle was, how thin he had become, even before I had unintentionally begun to starve him.

And you're still going to win, aren't you?

Maybe not with the country. Maybe the day's coming when even your base will know who you really are. Maybe the people will decide, then, that they've had enough.

But you're going to win when it comes to this dog.

I can't just not drink water.

Alternative Liberties

I will forget.
Sooner or later, I will stop responding to the alarm.
But that's the whole point, isn't it?
Maybe we all did.

At that, I started to wail, and Chandler stirred, upset that maybe he had done something to upset me, and began to lick my face. Please, he was saying. My dear old friend, my everything, Tell me what I did, so I can make it better. I'll fix it. That's my job. Just tell me what I did. I'll make you better.

I strictly rationed water, but struggled with the drug's forced dementia, only keeping up with Chandler's needs because the alarm kept going off.

Two weeks later, Donzmann visited and confiscated the watch. "Still streamlining your world."

And four weeks after that, he produced a revolver and put a bullet in Chandler's brain. I shrieked and cried no, the precise behavior of a man who had been tortured in all sorts of ways but had not been willing to believe that his oppressor would do something so unthinkable.

I don't think he ever visited again, because I don't remember him taking anything away from me after that.

Given what happened on that last day, I'd like to think that he died, somehow, sometime after I drank my fill.

I might have starved in the weeks that followed, but something changed with the water. The secret ingredient was either no longer as potent, or was no longer being added. I emerged from my stupor and the first thing I did was take a complete inventory of all my losses: my wife, my freedom, my vocation, my media, much of my home, and my dogs.

All I had left was that hateful portrait, only as deep as that hateful grin, just like the man himself, and I confess that the next thing I did, after screaming at absurd length, was rip it off the wall and fling it into the corner, where it fortuitously landed on a pile of Chandler's now long-fossilized droppings, the ones I had been too disconnected from everything to pick up.

What I realized, then, was that there was something else they'd taken from me: my humanity. Donzmann had even told me that this was the plan, to gradually empty my life, and decrease the boundaries of the world, until I had no room left for resistance. It felt like it was a redundant process.

Had I ever given much of a fight, beyond ranting on Facebook, before they showed up with their list of things to steal? No, I had not, not really. I had not given my body, had not marched, had not worked on phone banks, had not even spoken up and launched into an argument when somebody praised the son of bitch in my presence. It was always trouble I had not been willing to make, had in fact sacrificed with the comfortable lie that I was doing enough, that the real work had been done by others. They had taken away more than physical things, more than intimate things. They had removed my illusions. I was a man who, with a little drugged water, wasn't even aware enough to pick up dog shit, and that was something that had to be dealt with, if there was any way, in the days ahead.

I was famished, as much as Chandler must have been when I finally noticed his starvation. When I went to what was left of my larder, I discovered that it must have been some time since the last food delivery.

All I found were two bowls of microwaveable ramen (but no microwave), and two single-serving boxes of raisin bran cereal (but no milk). I think they were part of the first food delivery I had gotten during my house arrest, always untouched because there was something more acceptable to eat. I could not afford to be fussy now, so I scarfed the dry cereal in a gulp, choking on it, and felt my stomach lurch, letting me know that this

Alternative Liberties

was not sufficient recompense for the punishment it had gotten.

The cleaner of my two pairs of pants were so loose that they almost fell off my emaciated ass, but I held them up and then angrily told myself that if they were too big to wear now, I would embrace how much I'd demeaned myself and escape naked, if I had to.

Then I ran water over my face, changed to the cleaner of my two pairs of pants, added a jacket, and went to the front door.

Donzmann, I realized, had never taken that from me. They had never locked me in, turning my diminished house into a cell. I had just stopped using it, never proceeding beyond my front stoop, learning the same lesson that a baby circus elephant picks up when the chain is, in adulthood, replaced with a length of rope that it can easily break.

By then, though, it has learned that the rope *can* hold it, the same way a battered wife learns to always keep her voice soft, and the same way an oppressed population learns to never protest. All these were examples of learned helplessness, the thing that makes oppression of any kind possible.

The part of my imagination that was still dead and would likely remain dead could not endure any more, not if to obey it meant giving way to starvation. I would leave the house and step past the boundary today, even if all it got me was a bullet in the brain, or a black bag over my head and a swift ride to another place of punishment.

I opened the door and found a thick, pea-soup fog, which reduced visibility to precisely my decreed limits. It was too thick on the ground to even see the grass. Weather, or another of Donzmann's tricks, I did not know. Nor did I suppose it mattered. They were not about to feed me anymore, and staying in the house meant a slow death. I would make my way across the dead lawn, find the front gate, then follow the sidewalk until I reached some place with answers. And, if they tried to arrest me again, I would fight back until they killed me. My imagination had come back, if only for that.

I took a ginger step off the porch and found no solid surface to stand on. It was spongy, gaseous, and incapable of supporting my weight. There was no earth there, and maybe there was no Earth, either. Maybe it was a ten foot drop. Or maybe it was infinite.

Maybe the world resumed right past my front gate. Maybe this was Donzmann's doing, one last demonstration that he could reduce my world to almost nothing. And maybe this was something much worse, a manifestation of something that had happened worldwide, that maybe his master had done, out of incompetence or offense to whatever gods there are.

All I knew was something that arrived with the certainty of revelation, that while I was sleeping, people under his so-called protection, "whether they liked it or not," had kept on dying, and maybe a multitude all at once. Maybe this was Armageddon.

And maybe this was just a sinkhole and maybe Donzmann had brought in a backhoe to dig and maybe if I took a leap of faith I could go on and find the world again.

Maybe I was just doomed to die, and maybe I had been doomed since the very first time I complied with the bastards.

But the bastards had taken away my only surviving image of my wife, and they had killed my dog, and I had eaten my fill of learned helplessness.

Maybe I was not damned. Maybe the world was a ruin out there and maybe there was still hope left to find.

Fuck them all, I thought, and stepped into the abyss.

C.A.R.E.

Mark Rivett

"... and now we turn to the newest member of the MSM News team, Faith Hope, for a new segment we're calling 'Corrections, Apologies, Retractions, and Errata'—C.A.R.E—because here at MSM, we *care* about the news." Dax Wolfred's baritone voice spoke words from the teleprompter, but only he could deliver a bright-white smile into the camera with his signature wink. His voluminous black hair and dark suit screamed 'trust,' but his demeanor suggested 'mischief.' "Faith, why don't you tell our viewers a little about yourself?"

The camera cut from a close-up of Dax to a two-shot of both Dax and his new co-anchor. Faith, dressed in a low-cut white blouse, had blonde hair styled in a titanic bouffant that forced the cameraman to zoom out so far that he caught the edges of the studio backdrop. She smiled a perfect smile into the camera. "Thanks, Dax.

I'm excited to be here. We have a lot to cover in this first segment, so I'll be brief."

The shot cut to a medium close-up of Faith. In contrast to the close-up for male anchors, chest-up shots for female anchors was now the news standard. Faith beamed sex-appeal and flawless cleavage into the camera and pierced the lens with ocean-blue eyes "I was runner up in the 2022 Miss America Contest, where I represented the great state of Mississippi. Before that, I had the privilege of meeting the President personally at the Junior Miss America Pageant when he toured the dressing rooms right before the swimsuit competition." The backdrop shifted to a much younger Faith in a photo-op embrace with the now-president.

A moment of dead air passed as Faith held her smile.

"Impressive!" Dax broke the silence, "Is there anything else you'd like to share before we dive into your segment?" The camera cut back to the two-shot. "Our viewers might be interested in where you went to school, or your previous experience in journalism, for example."

"Thanks, Dax," The camera instantly returned to the medium close-up of Faith. "I graduated from Jackson High in 2018. Between pageants, I taught Bible study at my local church. I thank the Lord for the opportunity to talk to our viewers without the burden of college *indoctrination*."

Dead air fell again fell.

"High school in 2018? Wow, you're quite young to be an anchor for a national news organization!" The camera cut back again. Dax's broad smile and forced chuckle betrayed the resentment in his voice. "And so you are new to the anchor desk," he said.

The camera returned to Faith before Dax could finish. Faith held the camera with her own broad smile and fluttering eyelashes. "Well, Dax, this is a good place to explain C.A.R.E. to our viewers. We here at MSM *care*

Alternative Liberties

about the news, and the Federal Communications Commission under the Trump Administration has issued new guidelines for maintaining a broadcast license. Those guidelines state that 'fake news' and un-American reporting must be corrected, errata'd, or retracted *with* a public apology within seventy-two hours of initial broadcast or publication."

"Un-American?" Dax, attempted to interject. "That sounds vague... "

"It's not, Dax. And I'll give our viewers an example live on-air right now."

"Oh... excellent," said Dax, with a nod to the camera. "Let's hear it."

Faith's friendly, light-hearted tone became gravely serious as she looked into the camera. "Many of our viewers do not understand the word 'errata.' In compliance with the new FCC guidelines, we here at MSM News consider the word 'errata' to be un-American."

"It does sound foreign, doesn't it?" Dax offered.

"It certainly does, Dax! That's why, going forward, the 'E' in C.A.R.E. will be changed to 'Education.' That is a word that sounds American, and this segment is now Corrections, Apologies, Retractions, and Education; C.A.R.E., because we here at MSM *care* about the news."

"We certainly do!" Dax replied. "Now we've covered something that's un-American, but can you give an example of 'fake news'?

"Absolutely!" Faith returned to her bubbly tone for a moment before becoming serious again. "But we can't forget the most important part of a C.A.R.E. segment: the apology. So, before we move on, I want to say how sorry MSM is for using an un-American word in our broadcast. We here at MSM promise to do better in the future. If we ever use a word you don't understand,

Alternative Liberties

sounds un-American, or comes too close to something offensive like E-R-O-T-I-K, please reach out to us."

"Always important to remember to apologize when we fall short of our mission to deliver the news to our viewers," Dax said.

"Now, I'd like to talk about a report that came out of our Texas affiliate yesterday..." The camera cut to a wide shot that included Faith and the backdrop. Behind her materialized a headline "Infant and Maternal Mortality Rates Skyrocket Under Texas Law Used as Model for National Abortion Ban." She read the headline out loud in a light and bouncy tone that sharply contrasted with the gravity of the text. "I want to warn our male viewers that this C.A.R.E. report doesn't apply to them. They can't get pregnant or die in childbirth."

"But men can be husbands and fathers to women and children who can, so..." The camera momentarily zoomed out to include Dax.

Faith ignored her co-anchor. "This report is about a *study,*" Faith said, adding air quotes, "from the University of Texas in Austin. That university is staffed with disconnected liberal elites who spend their time in Ivory Towers talking about Diversity, Equity, and Inclusion. These so-called *doctors,*" Faith again made a gesture to indicate air quotes, "have no business talking about pregnancy when they can't even define a 'woman.' We here at MSM deeply apologize for this fake news report, and retract the story in full. Both the author and editor have been terminated."

"That's great to hear, Faith," Dax said. "But are there any important takeaways from the report we should highlight?"

"Definitely, Dax," said Faith. "If we hadn't retracted this story, we'd be looking for an alternative to the word 'maternal'. Our viewers do not know that word, and that's un-American."

Alternative Liberties

"Hey, what about 'birthing person?'" Dax deadpanned. Then he and Faith burst into uproarious laughter. A length of time passed before the duo regained their composure.

"They didn't tell me I'd be working with a comedian!" Faith dabbed at her makeup with a tissue before turning directly into the camera. Her smile transformed into a scowl, "But our next story is no laughing matter."

Again a headline appeared behind Faith. It read: "FEMA Withholds Wildfire Aid From California."

"MSM is issuing an apology for this story out of our California affiliate that misinforms readers."

"How so, Faith?" Dax inquired with the tempo of someone reading from a teleprompter.

"Glad you asked, Dax," Faith replied with a wink. "To avoid fraud and abuse, President Trump has ordered the Federal Emergency Management Agency to carefully review disaster relief applications. FEMA is not withholding aid, California's application was simply rejected."

"Any indication on why the application was rejected?" Dax, accustomed to being the focus of an MSM broadcast, was clearly not enjoying his role as Faith's sidekick. He spoke woodenly as he read the words that had been written for him.

"As you know, the FEMA panel consists of real estate professionals, Trump campaign advisors, and interested investors so they are true experts in disaster prone areas," Faith explained. "If they rejected the application, it was because California didn't *qualify* for FEMA wildfire funding."

"Sounds like a *hot* story." Dax chuckled. "I guess we have to throw cold water on our California affiliate for this fake news?"

"Good one, Dax," Faith smiled. "We here at MSM News apologize deeply for this miscarriage of

Alternative Liberties

journalism, and we would like to assure our audience that the offending employees have been dealt with appropriately."

"Before we move to our next C.A.R.E. story, we have another format change we're introducing to our audience today." Dax switched gears as the camera returned to a two-shot of him and Faith.

"Another format change? Aren't we worried about giving our viewers whiplash?" It was Faith's turn to read canned remarks from the teleprompter.

"I hope not, but if so, they can rest their necks on the new FDA-approved YourPillow." Dax retrieved a pillow from beneath the news desk and placed it behind his head. "Instead of going to break, we're going to take a moment to discuss a product from our new sponsor: YourPillow."

"Our *new* sponsor?" Faith feigned confusion. "Hasn't YourPillow been around for years?"

"They sure have, Faith... but only recently has the U.S. Food and Drug Administration approved YourPillow as an official medical device covered by Medicare and Medicaid." Dax said. "Now, our viewers can have the entire $500 cost of this state-of-the-art sleep therapy reimbursed by filing an insurance claim!"

"Wait, I've heard about this." Faith put her fists on her hips in a feigned gesture of grievance. "Isn't this just a scam by the owner of YourPillow, a Trump donor, to get Medicare and Medicaid to pay for pillows?"

"That's 'fake news,' Faith!" Dax replied. "The FDA should have approved YourPillow years ago, but the agency was run by Democrats and doctors who get kickbacks from Big Pharma to keep you sick and in pain. Now that the agency is run by the Trump Administration, all sorts of miracle cures are getting approved. YourPillow is the first, but it won't be the last!"

Alternative Liberties

"But we're running out of time for more C.A.R.E. reporting. We have a lot of corrections, apologies, retractions, and... *education* to get to before our time is up." Dax expertly segued back into Faith's report.

The camera cut back into a mid-close up of Faith, who nodded solemnly, "I call this next portion of C.A.R.E. the 'firehose of facts'... where I correct as many headlines as I can. Are you ready?"

"I sure am!" Dax sunk into his YourPillow, crossed his arms, and pretended to settle in for a nap.

A new headline appeared behind Faith that read: "Another Unarmed Black Man Killed by Police Officer in Traffic Stop."

"This headline out of our Minnesota affiliate unnecessarily injects race into the report." Faith shook her head disapprovingly. The headline faded away and in its place materialized a new headline that read: "Suspect Killed by Heroic Police Officer in Traffic Stop."

"As our viewers know, *all* lives matter. Isn't that right, Dax?" Faith concluded.

"All lives matter," Dax replied confidently.

The next headline appeared: "Pickup Truck, Flying Nazi and MAGA Flags, Plows Through Protesters, Killing Three."

"This report from our Virginia affiliate has mischaracterized what actually occurred." Faith stated as the headline changed to read: "Patriotic Americans Fed Up with Antifa Protests Take Action."

"Jury Finds Trump Ally Guilty of Embezzling Donations Meant for Border Wall" was the next headline.

"Our New York affiliate really dropped the ball on this one." Faith placed her hand over her heart and appeared to choke back tears as the new headline materialized: "Politically-motivated New York Jury and

Alternative Liberties

Obama-appointed Judicial Activist Judge Wrongfully Convict Trump Ally, Pardon All But Certain."

"The abuse from the New York District Attorney is absurd!" Faith gasped. "If our viewers are concerned about this, they can reach out to the DA directly at his Manhattan residence."

A home address materialized on the backdrop, along with a photograph of the property and a flashing web site address.

"Thousands of American Citizens Swept Up in Military Deportation" became "Millions of Criminal Illegal Aliens Deported by Military."

"Children, Infants, Lost in Family Separation Border Policy" became "Department of Homeland Security Rescues Children from Sex Traffickers."

"FBI Reports Increase in Hate Crimes Targeting LGBTQ Community" became "Audit Suggests FBI Discriminates Against Christians."

After a dozen more headlines transformed, the entire backdrop dissolved into an enormous American flag rippling like the ocean behind Faith. The blonde woman bit the side of her lip and peered into the camera with glassy eyes. "We want to thank our viewers for watching our first segment of C.A.R.E. We also want to thank President Trump personally for the guidelines his administration has implemented within the FCC to make sure viewers are protected from biased journalists."

"Thank you, Faith," Dax said. "This is a tough job, and we're lucky to have you."

"I appreciate that, Dax," Faith replied. "But we can't forget the most important part of C.A.R.E.: the apology. Would you like to give me a hand?"

"I'd be honored."

The camera cut to a two-shot of the pair, each sitting with hands folded solemnly in front of them. "From the bottom of our hearts at MSM News, we want to apologize

Alternative Liberties

to our viewers for our failures to live up to the standards that you expect from our network," Faith began.

"We promise to do better in the future," Dax continued. "Every story from this network and our affiliates will be reviewed to ensure it complies with the FCC guidelines that protect you from fake and un-American news. We'll replaced biased journalists with people who can offer a new perspective—people like Faith, here."

"Thank you, Dax," Faith nodded, and the camera centered on her as she closed the show. "We hope you've enjoyed this segment of C.A.R.E. We at MSM *care* about the news."

Alternative Liberties

Alternative Liberties

A Day in the Life of a Freedom Fighter

Joseph Nettles

8:00 AM–The Wake-Up Call

Jimmy Eugene Lee Leighton's day began as it always did: with the screeching of a bald eagle at manly decibels from his MAGA endorsed alarm clock, the snooze set to "Proud to Be an American" at an even manlier volume. He bounded from his twin bed, fists clenched and ready to make America Great.

He stood eye to eye with the cutout of the President as he drained his morning bladder and wondered what the President would ask of him today.

"I'm ready, sir," he said and tucked himself away.

Jimmy ritually donned his uniform: secondhand camo cargo pants from a yard sale, a faded red polo shirt with the Freedom Corps logo crookedly ironed onto

Alternative Liberties

the right side of the chest, and a bulletproof vest adorned with black-and-white blue-line American flag to show his loyalties were in the right place. He had removed the Kevlar plates; they made it hot and heavy.

His final addition, his red MAGA hat, custom embroidered with *the* golden arches of liberty (you know, the big yellow M...) on the front, as befitted his rank of Snake Commander.

He then proceeded to the fold down table and sat for the daily session with his extensive collection of Trump commemorative coins, which he held in the dusty light shaft that shone through the shutters, admiring them and making sure no specks of dust or fingerprints were disrespecting the gold-plated image of the most handsome President America had had the luck to ever elect. He used to polish them, but when the gold all came off, he had to buy some spray paint, so polishing was no longer part of the ritual.

8:30 AM–Breakfast of Patriots

While Jimmy liked fresh fruit and yogurt, his breakfast had to fuel him through a day of fighting Commie liberal scum. He cooked up the meal of Freedom Champions: steak. He liked it rare, but since he had gotten it on reduction last week at Walmart, and since the genny gave up halfway through the night (ran out of gas), thus turning his fridge off, he felt safer cooking it into a very-well-done grey brick, generously seasoned with salt and pepper from his AR-15-shaped shakers. On the side, a thick slice of Freedom toast (liberally—lower case L—coated in "Second Amendment high fructose corn syrup"), and an energy drink aptly named "Eagle Fuel", that claimed to contain Liberal Tears. Though he had his doubts, Jimmy still liked to

Alternative Liberties

imagine that actual liberal tears gave the drink its distinctive savory aftertaste, rather than the generous amount of MSG it contained.

Once done, and his breakfast dishes safely in the sink for when his mom came over, Jimmy scrolled through his MAGA-endorsed Freedom Phone.

Today's news on PatriotNet—the *only* trustworthy network left—was ablaze with reports of socialist conspiracies, flag desecrations, and reports about the new Starbucks menu item called "Woke-latte." He wished he could have tried that without triggering his lactose-intolerance and cursed whichever of his ancestors had lain with a heathen: MAGA scientists had proven beyond doubt that allergies and intolerances were directly related to impure breeding.

This was his dark secret, and because he was a man, Jimmy could have his coffees black, his cheeseburgers cheese-less, nobody would say a thing. Being found out as lactose intolerant could cost him his position.

9:00 AM–Morning Drills

Jimmy's first task of the day was meeting up with the Freedom Corps, a volunteer militia tasked with defending the homeland from internal threats, like mailmen, Prius drivers, vegans, Yoga practitioners, Pride flag fliers and the like.

Jimmy's squad, call sign "Eagle Four," was made of the finest patriots Freeglades, FL, had to offer: Bob "Big Gulp" Jenkins, who wore a bandolier of Slim Jims (his 320lb physique required nourishment to fuel his freedoming); Karen "Digital" Simmons, perpetually livestreaming and blogging their operations to her 12 faithful, freedom-loving followers; and McT "The Tank"

Alternative Liberties

Grawhill, whose imported pickup was tolerated only because it was the only operable vehicle the chapter had.

"Alright, team," Jimmy barked, clipboard in hand. "We've got two drills today. First, gotta go through our monthly recon training. Spotting the enemies is getting harder and harder, and a most essential skill: you can't target what you can't see. Later, we're deploying to conduct a sweep of the South Street Walmart, gotta ensure no illegal propaganda kiosks have been installed."

The recon went without issue from their position on the park bench down by River Mill Park. They noted a number of young mothers with children whose shorts were not sufficiently long to fully cover their thighs, and using the official color chart, they ensured, sometimes by taking pictures, the racial purity standards required to Make America Great Again, again. There were vigorous arguments and sharing of photos. All those shades of white looked the same, and it was really hard to spot the one that was 1.5% more brown or, God forbid, 2% olive. More evidence to be kept until it was called for.

10:00 AM–The Walmart Reconnaissance

Team Eagle Four marched into Walmart like they were at Omaha beach on D-Day, but with way more wheezing and sweating. Jimmy eyed the greeter suspiciously. "Ma'am, you're not hiding any propaganda leaflets under that cart, are you?" he asked, his voice thundering (at least he hoped it was thundering) with the authority and purpose that only fighting for a righteous cause can imbue.

Alternative Liberties

The greeter, as she did every day, provided the right answer. "No sir, Jimmy," she would say. "This is a Walmart."

"That's what they *want* you to think," Jimmy replied, nodding to Karen, who was recording the encounter for Eagle Four's Facebook page. "Stay vigilant." Pause. "Stay free." The latter was an addition of his to the traditional motto (he felt very proud of it), and he was sure no one above would have had any complaints. If anything, he was surprised it hadn't caught on more, yet.

Together, they combed the aisles, interrogating employees and clients, inspecting items for subliminal messages, and confiscating anything suspicious. By the time they left, they'd amassed a cart of hard evidence, including an "eco-friendly" tote bag (obviously socialist propaganda) and a suspiciously priced avocado, whose importing most likely financed some third world country's communist regime or, even worse, the Democrat Party here on sacred American soil.

Thankfully, no stacks of illegal liberal pamphlets were found. They marched the cart to customer service. "Thank you so much, Jimmy," said the chief cashier as she took the cart behind the counter. That was the system she and Jimmy had worked out.

11:00 PM–Lunch at "Liberty Lou's"

After a successful mission, the team always rewarded themselves with burgers at Liberty Lou's Freedom Diner for a "Red, White, and Moo burger, American Fries." Every napkin was a miniature copy of the Constitution—Jimmy always tucked one into his vest pocket.

Alternative Liberties

Because of their status, Jimmy had gotten them the police discount, though Jimmy had to occasionally tap his blue line flag as a reminder for the server.

02:30 PM–Community Outreach

Today's outreach was setting up a "Free Speech Zone" in the town square. The zone was a picnic table in front of the library, where Jimmy handed out pamphlets titled *"How to Spot a Socialist in Your Neighborhood"* and *"20 Supermarket Products that Directly Fund Domestic Terrorism."*
Thus, they enforced this "Free Speech Zone" so that people would be able to practice true free speech without the constraints imposed by that leftie scum.
Karen, livestreaming the event, caught a brief confrontation with a passerby wearing a rainbow pin. "You can't silence us!" Karen shouted, waving her phone like a shield against the pin bearer. The passerby—a shoegazing teenager—simply shrugged. Jimmy recognized the retreat and hooted as they banged the table in victory.

05:00 PM—Debrief

Back at headquarters (a white plastic folding table outside Jimmy's trailer), the team reviewed the day's accomplishments. Karen presented her social media analytics: three new followers, all from Armenia, and two angry comments from "bots."
McT unveiled his latest invention, a "patriot-proof" mailbox lined with aluminum foil, to prevent liberal technology from tampering with your mail and spying on you. They spent several minutes testing it on Jimmy's mail box. Or they were going to, but there was

a wasp's nest in the cinderblocks holding it up, so they decided to do the test some other time.

Jimmy felt a swell of pride. "We're not just defending freedom," he said. "We're making it, at every turn." They cracked open three forty ouncers and toasted to liberty.

7:00 PM – Evening Rally

The highlight of the team's day was tuning into YouTube's Freedom Watch, where sometimes the host would take clips from videos like Karen's efforts. She hadn't been picked yet, but it was just a matter of time.

Tonight's keynote speaker was a man in a red suit and mirror aviators, who claimed to be the "official spokesman" for an unspecified government agency.

"They want to take your guns, your gas stoves, your F-150s and your God-given right to double bacon cheeseburgers!" the speaker incited. The camera showed the crowd, all 32 of them, erupting in cheers.

Jimmy joined in the chants: "USA! USA!" It was a euphoric moment—a reminder of why he fought so hard. THIS was the America he dreamt of. THIS was an evening he dreamt every other evening in his life would—should—be like. He felt freedom was surging over him, momentarily and blissfully cleansing him of all worries.

Until his laptop battery died.

10:00 PM – Shut-Eye

His posse departed, Jimmy poured the last of his gas from a battered Jerry can into the old (but reliable, screw those emissions fanatics and zero-carbon dimwits!) generator, which lazily sputtered to life, turning on the single, dirty, old-fashioned lightbulb in

Alternative Liberties

his abode (and, hopefully, the fridge). He climbed into the trailer, and knelt before the cutout of his President, whispering a prayer for strength in the battle ahead. He was absolutely sure the President heard him, and all the other fighters that Jimmy led, the last bastion between freedom and the relentless assaults of liberal decadence. Clambering into bed, he set his alarm to "eagle scream" again, and placed his Freedom Phone next to his pillow, ready to respond to any midnight emergencies. Always vigilant. Always free.

"Another day of winning," he murmured, drifting off to sleep.

Outside, the moon rose and the world spun on, blissfully unaware of the True Heroes keeping it free.

Seen and Not Heard

Tera Schreiber

Grace's voice was birdsong and gentle wind chimes, warm sun and lapping waves. These sweet melodies chilled her mother. The bubbling musicality of Grace's voice was dangerous. The expression of bright and shiny thoughts bouncing around in her sparkling brain was especially dangerous.

Even during infancy, Grace's mother fretted about her incessant babbling. Grace would smile, setting forth a legion of drooling vowels. She crawled early, explored enthusiastically, and laughed easily. This would not do. Her mother tried to model the silence that would be expected by Society, never making a sound unless given permission from her husband. Her mother tried to shush Grace, plugging up her little pink mouth with pacifiers, teethers, and bottles. Grace simply spat out whatever got in the way of her joyful noises and pursued her spittle-soaked vocal exercises with increased vigor.

Alternative Liberties

Naturally, Grace's father disapproved. It was bad enough to have two daughters. He was sorely disappointed in his wife's poor reproductive results. Still, he understood the responsibility that came when the Lord gave a man daughters, and he was committed to teaching them their role in Society.

By the time Grace was a toddler, her mother resorted to extreme measures, locking Grace for long stretches in her small, austere room to keep her loud vocalization from enraging her father and corrupting her older sister. Grace chatted at and sang to her doll for hours on end, alone but for this simple toy. She also spoke to the birds outside the tiny window, the lumpy pillow on simple bed, and the single lamp that illuminated the bleak room. Grace did not mind that none spoke back to her. She had enough to say that there was never a lull in her monologue.

Thank heavens, Faith was older and less susceptible to influence. Faith obediently maintained silence throughout her day, even during playtime. Faith would mime necessary conversation, her lips tight as rubber gaskets, her dress neatly pressed with nary a stain or rumple. Faith was never moved to speak out of turn, even when Grace pestered her. Faith also tried to instill Society's values in Grace, imploring her with pleading eyes to *just keep her mouth shut.* Grace only worked harder to try to converse with her sister, cracking jokes, singing hymns from church, or just jabbering away with whatever was on her busy little mind.

Grace's mother often muttered that she did not know what she would have done if Grace had been born first because then there would have been two noisy girls to train. A girl's behavior is, after all, a reflection of her mother. And her mother made it clear that Grace was not a positive reflection.

Alternative Liberties

Grace's mother prayed with her nightly, sitting on the edge of her bed in the room she shared with Faith.

"Dear Lord," her mother said night after night, holding tightly to Grace's hand. "Please help Grace to know her role. Please show her how to be modest and gentle. Please curb her impulsive expression. We all know that if Grace cannot quiet herself, she will be quieted." Her mother shuddered. "As is your will, Lord. Amen."

By the age of ten, Grace understood Society's expectations. She kept her mouth closed around her elders. She knew she was permitted to speak only with her father's permission. One day, her husband would have that authority. She worked hard to follow Society's rules. Still, she sometimes found herself absentmindedly singing. Improvised songs flew out of her lips like flowers blooming on a vine. The vibration of her voice filled her with warmth and light. The deep breaths for filling her lungs soothed her nerves. The clear tone of her voice filled her with pride, and she sometimes was carried away by her own confidence in her pitches and rhythms.

She hummed while washing the dishes one evening, forgetting herself in the scrubbing of pots and greasy suds flowing down the sink. A firm hand landed on Grace's shoulder with a sharp grip. She turned to see her mother, eyebrows pinched, lips turned down. Grace nodded and continued silently dishwashing, focusing instead on the rhythms of scrubbing and rinsing, keeping the melodies inside her mind.

At the age of thirteen, Grace's growing body and developing mind erupted. She had questions! Observations! Ideas! While taking out the trash, Grace noticed a blank envelope in the bin. An epiphany exploded in her mind, and she tried her best to hide the bright light of her thought, closing her face to probing from others while she surreptitiously snagged the envelope from the trash and stuffed it deep into the pocket of her long, modest dress. She tried to muffle the joy of that treasure, reminding herself to plod along rather than float excitedly through her day.

That night, in her dark room, lying under the covers with the glow of a flashlight illuminating the paper, Grace secretly, diligently scribbled her thoughts. Questions about her body, the bodies of boys, the meaning of life, death, and why the Lord gave her so many thoughts if she was not allowed to speak them.

Grace had been taught that the Lord made these rules to keep girls and women safe. They needed protection from men, who were stronger, smarter, and more capable. Every week in church, the pastor stood in his dark robe on the rough wooden pulpit and confirmed with his booming voice the importance of this pinnacle of their faith and Society. Everywhere Grace went, she observed the voices of men and the ideas of men. Men were the news reporters, politicians, police officers, executives, artists, musicians, and heads of families. They spoke confidently about all topics, although they said nothing that reflected Grace's own experiences.

Grace wondered if all of the women were happy to remain silent shadows of the men in their lives, or if others shared her urge to express her ideas on her own terms, with her own voice. Sometimes the disparity between the way she felt and the way she was told to act was so much that she felt like her brain would crack wide open and then all of her thoughts would be spilled on the sidewalk for everyone to see. The thought both horrified and thrilled her.

By the time Grace was fourteen, she had a robust collection of varied colors of paper scraps tucked into a hole in her thin mattress. While it had started as a satisfying project to write down her thoughts, now she

Alternative Liberties

cried a little each time she stuffed a finished paper into the mattress hole, because no one would ever get to read what she had written.

One evening after feeding the chickens, Grace sat on a stump behind the henhouse, work-weary and seeking a moment of respite out of sight of her parents' watchful eyes. She tolerated the pungent odor of the chicken coop because it was a place of refuge from her chores. The murmur of hens clucking made Grace wonder why the chickens had more right to speak than she did.

She noticed a rough, gray rock by her right boot. Rocks were ample near the henhouse, but this rock drew her attention. She picked it up, rolling it around in her hand. The rock felt surprisingly soft and chalky. She scratched it across the stump, making a distinct line. Grace yelped with delight! She picked up a flat black rock and used her chalky rock to write a word on the black rock. *Joy.* With guilty joy, Grace stuffed both rocks into her dress pockets and returned to the house to finish her chores.

Over the coming weeks, Grace carried the chalky rock in her pocket. When she had a moment of peace, when no one was looking, she would scratch out a word on a flat surface. *Power* on the back of the stall door in the bathroom at school. *Ambition* on a coarse fence post on her way home from school. *Help* on the broken sidewalk near the playground. On sides of buildings, trees, mailboxes, other rocks. *Never give up. I have something to say. You are not alone. Hope.*

When writing a word in a public space, Grace's hands shook. Sweat bloomed on her forehead. Her heart beat erratically. She knew the consequences of defacing public property and of using words without permission. Yet when writing a word in a public space, Grace's lips curved into a smile. Her wildly beating heart swelled with pride. Her eyes shone with glee. Because Grace also knew the consequences of keeping all of her words inside, never to be known by the world.

At dinner, Grace's father sat tall in his chair and spoke to the whole family. "I need to give you some terrible news." He frowned with his whole body. "Someone has been defacing public property by writing scandalous words and phrases. If you see any of these words, you must avert your eyes." He looked from his wife to his daughters, one by one, his eyebrows meeting in the middle, peering into their eyes with painstaking intensity. It was like he was trying to look into their souls. "It could corrupt you if you read these words. If you see one, you must just walk on by and never think of it again. Confine your reading to the approved texts."

Panic flooded Grace's body. It took all of her focus to keep her hands from shaking. She glanced at Faith, who was wide-eyed and trembling, and she realized that the proper reaction was one of fear and surprise. Grace let the panic take over, and she trembled with the same intensity as her big sister.

"I see you are afraid," her father said. "You are safe as long as you never read these words. But don't fear. The Society's beautification committee will work to erase all of the words. They should be gone by Sunday."

A tiny tear slipped down Grace's cheek. She knew that she could never write words for public consumption again. In her vivid internal monologue, she scolded herself for taking such risks and drawing this attention from Society. At the same time, she craved recognition for her art and ideas.

One evening, Grace happened to be home alone. Her father was at a community meeting with the other men in the neighborhood. Her mother and Faith were volunteering at church. Grace was left home to prepare the evening meal so that it would be hot and ready to eat when her father returned.

Alternative Liberties

Grace's mind wandered to the music she heard at church last week, and she started to hum the tune very quietly. Remembering she was alone, Grace dared to sing the words, moving her mouth around the consonants and vowels, letting her vocal cords vibrate at different pitches, replicating the notes with crystalline texture. The more Grace sang, the more she wanted to sing. The deep inhales filled her lungs and diaphragm with effervescent energy. The long and complex exhales poured her pent-up emotions out of her mouth and into the immense world, even if it only happened in her kitchen while she was alone with the hearty scents of roast and potatoes. Grace had never felt so much unfettered joy.

When she heard the rumble from the engine of her father's car pulling into the driveway, Grace quickly composed herself and sealed her mouth with tremendous willpower. Yet her heart was still light and bubbling with music. Grace looked down at her shoes when her father entered the room, hiding her rosy cheeks and the radiance in her eyes.

From that day on, Grace offered to prepare dinner anytime her family had evening activities. She craved time alone so she could let her voice make the music that fed her spirit. She offered to clean the musty church basement alone on a Friday evening so she could enjoy the vacuous space with her euphonious voice. She pretended to be sick to avoid going to church so she could spend some Sunday mornings at home singing by herself, crawling back into bed and feigning ill again when she heard the car come up the drive.

Grace understood she could *never* share her music with anyone. She was resigned to that fact because the joy of singing was so great that just the act of singing was enough for her. Discovering embodied music opened a tiny door that allowed moments of bliss to flow

Alternative Liberties

into her life. The world felt warmer, more vibrant, and more appealing to her because of her singing. She vowed to do whatever it took to continue to make space in her life for her secret melodies.

Occasionally in Society, a man would allow his wife to speak her mind at any time, a blanket permission. Jack Anderson was such a man. When Grace was sixteen-years-old, Jack stood confidently in church one day, his white, collared shirt sharply defining his muscular frame. Jack rose to his full height of six feet and three inches tall, wiped his sweaty hands on his gray pants, and said in a booming voice, "I give my wife, Prudence Anderson, my permission to speak freely whenever she wants from here until eternity."

The male parishioners gasped. The women's eyes grew wide, and their mouths tightened into tiny little puckers, holding back any breath that might be considered the use of their voices. They silently cursed Prudence for working this sorcery on her husband for there was no other way to explain why he would break with the word of the Lord in His own house of worship.

Grace's eyes grew wide, and her mouth tightened into a line, but that line was one of secret delight, with a curve upwards at each end. Could anyone imagine such freedom? Imagine being able to vocalize anytime, anyplace. Grace marveled at the idea. It gave her hope.

The doctors called it a heart attack, but some said that Jack Anderson's death was punishment from the Lord. Others said it was more of Prudence's sorcery. When Prudence wept and wailed at the graveside, pounding her fists on the damp soil where they laid her beloved husband, people turned away and let her grieve alone.

When Prudence attended church a week after she buried her husband, she sat silently for the entire service in her black dress and matching gloves. Afterwards, when the pastor stood in front of the church

Alternative Liberties

shaking hands of the starched and pressed men in the congregation as the families filed out, Prudence stepped right up to the pastor and offered him her gloved hand.

Jaws dropped, including Grace's.

The pastor shrank away, repelled by the idea of touching a woman outside of his family.

Only slightly deterred, Prudence withdrew her hand. She stepped backwards, paused and stepped forward again toward the pastor. "This isn't right," she said, loudly and clearly for all to hear, her voice trembling despite its volume. "It's not right that half of us live in the joyless cages of your expectations. You say it's what the Lord requires, but we don't really know if the Lord even exists."

No longer shrinking away, the pastor's hand shot out and delivered a resounding slap across Prudence's face.

Grace's mother grabbed the hands of her daughters and tried to hurry them away from the scene. Faith followed her mother willingly, but Grace shook her hand free, riveted by Prudence and her blatant courage.

A red welt appeared on Prudence's face, but she held her ground. She smiled at the pastor. "I cannot respect a Society that doesn't value me."

Several men descended on Prudence, approaching her with menace written in their hunched shoulders and balled fists.

Grace's heart beat like a hummingbird against her ribs. Her palms grew sweaty. Her mouth went so dry that it felt like it was glued shut. Her mother was pulling on her elbow, but Grace was mired in place.

The first arm raised against Prudence hit with a resounding *whap*. Prudence's head snapped to the side from the impact. Blood dribbled from her nose. The second arm raised against her landed on her back with

Alternative Liberties

a *thump*. Prudence raised her arms reflexively, shielding herself.

Before the third arm was raised against Prudence, Grace opened her mouth wide and yelled with all of the powerful musicality and melody of her voice, "No!"

Prudence's arms lowered and she made eye contact with Grace. She smiled a smile of gratitude and fear, of defiance and satisfaction.

The men spun around, eyes wide, hands still balled into fists. They turned their attention to Grace's father, with dark scowls of reproach.

Grace's father had never laid a hand on her. She had seen that he wanted to hit her at times, but he had always resisted. Grace was sure that this would be the time, and she steeled herself for the smack of his open hand which was raised as he strode toward her. Grace ducked her head and wrapped her arms around her torso, trying to escape into herself.

But her father used his hand only to grab her by the wrist and forcibly drag her away from the spectacle.

Grace went willingly, jarred by her father's hand on her arm, for he had never touched her before at all. As they retreated, Grace could hear the sounds of more hands hitting flesh and Prudence's pitiable cries.

Grace took a deep breath and sobbed, thinking about Prudence's freedom being revoked, of Prudence's courage, and of her bloodied face.

Her father's face darkened into a deep red. The color of fury.

When they got home, Grace was sent to her room. Her mother brought her a plate of food for dinner. She ate a few bites of pasta and drank the milk though it had a strange aftertaste. Leaden with fatigue, she crawled into bed, under her scratchy woolen blanket, and slipped into a dreamless sleep.

Grace woke up in a hospital, on a bed with stiff white sheets in the shadow of a beeping monitor. Rain fell outside the window, its cadence pattering on the roof. A tiny bird sought shelter on the ledge, avoiding the storm. Her mother sat at her bedside on the blue cushioned bench under the window. Faith sat next to her mother, a silent trickle of tears leaking from her eyes.

Grace's throat was sore, and her tongue was thick from sleep. She wanted to ask her mother for a glass of water, but no sound came out of her mouth when she opened it. Just a whoosh of wind and a searing pain. Grace reached up and felt the bandage covering the incision with fresh stitches in the small of her throat. Silent sobs wracked Grace's body.

Her mother patted her hand, shedding tears of relief.

Alternative Liberties

Little Boxes

Jacy Morris

The shipment arrived on time, the truck sagging over its tires. Fred Garvey marveled at the fact the truck could move at all, what with its weighty cargo.

The truck driver hopped out of the cab, a cigarette burning in his mouth, smoke streaming from his nostrils like dragon's breath. He held a clipboard in his hand.

Fred stood at the loading dock, his heart somewhere down in the pit of his stomach. His men huddled inside, drinking tea, coffee too high to afford these days, what with the tariffs. Turned out coffee only grew in foreign countries. The tariffs had jacked the price up to the point where only those with disposable income could enjoy it.

Fred sneered at the truck driver. There was no joy in this part of his job. Hell, there was no joy in any part of his job. Not anymore. Used to be though. Used to be people would pass away in a timely manner, and their

Alternative Liberties

families would come in with money in their pockets, searching for just the right coffin for their loved one, a statement piece to send them off into the afterlife. Might cost a pretty penny, but nothing was too good for eternity.

"This the Garvey Funeral Home?" the truck driver asked, as if he hadn't delivered here a hundred times over the years. Every time he acted like it was the first time. Fred was okay with that. More than okay, actually. It was never too good to get too familiar with people. You never knew when that body would come into the funeral home one day, staring up at you from a metal slab.

Garvey took the proffered clipboard from the delivery driver, scanned it, made sure the order looked right. He nodded his head at the driver to indicate the order appeared fine. The man tossed his cigarette to the ground and then threw up the door of the truck. It slid upward with a rattling clang, revealing a yawning black cave filled with boxes.

"Up and at 'em, boys," Garvey called to his men. They were good men. Happy to have a job. Jobs were hard to come by. Rick wasn't the most physically fit person. He'd worked at a desk for years, shuffling papers for the Department of Education—now defunct, RIP. For a moment, Fred wondered how big a coffin you'd need for the Department of Education. Probably pretty damn big.

Jake had worked at a tech company. The company went under when China balked at the exorbitant tariffs and stopped sending over computer chips and silicon wafers. Lots of companies went under. Lots of people looking for jobs now. Rick and Jake, while not necessarily happy to be working at the funeral home, were better off than a lot of people. Behind the funeral home, the unlucky camped on the sidewalk and huddled in tents, hiding from the hungry November air.

Alternative Liberties

"Load 'em up," Fred said. Rick and Jake stepped into the dark cave and grabbed the handles of the first box, remembering to lift with their legs instead of their backs. No one could afford a trip to the doctor. No one could afford to be out of work anymore. The cost of life was too high now, climbing higher with every single day.

Fred studied the boxes—cheap pine, a far cry from the coffins of yesteryear. Oh, he still had a couple of those for the big spenders, the company men, the people who profited off the maximization of the unholy dollar. If you had money, you made more of it under this regime. If you worked for a living... well, now you had to work more, work harder, and in the end, all you got was less—less time, less money, less happiness.

Fred shook his head as Jake and Rick traveled back and forth, carrying the coffins to the showroom. On the clipboard, he checked off each one.

"Lotta little ones this time," the delivery driver remarked.

"We need 'em," Fred stated.

The delivery driver shook his head, walked off to the side of the loading dock, and stood under the gray sky. He pulled another cigarette from his pocket, lit it up, and stared off into the distance, as if somewhere out there, there was a better place, a place where a man didn't need a dozen child-sized coffins, a place where men of talent could use those talents to make their lives better. But there wasn't. Not anymore.

Oh, there were places to go—only no one could get there. They weren't letting anyone out. Passports were reserved for the rich now. But, hey, the man had kept his promise and shut down the borders—not the way anyone had expected, but a promise kept is a promise kept. The exodus had begun in earnest a year into his second term, after people started realizing it might not be such a good idea to strip everything down to the

Alternative Liberties

studs. Shit, any contractor could have told you that. It's easier to tear something down than to build it back up.

Money men, oligarchs, they're great at wringing out profit, squeezing pennies from thin air. But that's not what a country is supposed to be for, dammit. A country, a government, is supposed to be about the people, not the companies, not the rich.

Fred shook his head, tried to be more positive. If they took it down, they could build it back up. The cynic inside mocked: *but at what cost? And who the hell would be left here to build it?*

Fred had sent his own wife and child away to live with distant relatives in Norway. Her dual-citizenship was a gift. They sent him money sometimes, from over there, where the sickness hadn't taken hold, where they didn't need so many child-sized caskets. The money went a long way. The Norwegian kroner went a lot further than the dollar these days. Hell, a man couldn't even afford to drink himself to death anymore, and Fred sincerely wanted to.

Rick and Jake carried in the last caskets. These ones were adult sized—because if it can kill a kid, it can kill an adult just as easily. Fred placed the last checkmark on the clipboard and called over the delivery driver, avoiding reading the name on the man's badge.

"All there," Fred said.

The driver nodded, climbed up on the truck desk, and grabbed the door strap. Then he leaped off the deck, using his weight to pull the door closed. With a rattle and a clang, the door went down on that empty cavern. Fred watched him drive away, gave him a hollow wave the driver probably didn't see. Most people didn't look back when leaving a funeral home—not the living, and certainly not the dead.

With a heavy sigh, he turned on his heel and stepped inside, prepared himself to check out the mess Rick and Jake had made of his storeroom. The place hadn't been this full in years. But now, all the space was full, the coffins taking up a space both physical and spiritual.

Fred showed them where to put the coffins to maximize the space, how to put down towels to prevent scratches on the surfaces of the cheap pine boxes.

A bell rang in the storage room. *A customer.*

He gave Rick and Jake their final few instructions, then headed out front. He adjusted his suit, tightened his tie. Took a look at himself in the mirror and didn't enjoy seeing the gaunt skeleton he had become. In the past, he would have said the way he looked was bad for business. No one liked to deal with someone at a funeral home who looked like actual Death. But, hey, that's how everyone looked these days—hollow-eyed, drawn, their skin, once full and plump, hanging from their bodies as if someone had been deflating them all, sucking the life out of the people, using them up like a child's juice box.

He waved a dismissive hand at his face in the mirror, put on a smile, wiggled his mouth around a bit to make sure he got the grin right—not a gleeful, happy smile, but a "reassuring, I'm here to help you in your trying time" smile, the type of smile that would allow people to make decisions, to realize they weren't in this alone.

He strode through the adult showroom, pausing to wipe a bit of dust off a casket, cherry wood with a cream-colored velvet lining. He had to resist the temptation to climb inside, pull the lid down over top of himself, and never move again.

On the other side of the showroom, he emerged into the carpeted front lobby where a gas fireplace guttered its eternal flames. *Warmth.* People needed warmth in a funeral home, soft lighting, warm carpets, earthen tones.

Alternative Liberties

She stood with her back to him, dressed head to toe in black. Skinny as a pipe cleaner. He got the sense she felt as if she had been waiting here forever though it had only been a few moments since she had entered.

"Good afternoon, madam," he said.

She turned to him, and he noted the sorrow on her face. If he hadn't seen it a thousand times by now, it might have affected him. But grief—you could grow numb to grief if you saw it often enough. He wondered if that's why there had been no rebellion. Perhaps the American people had seen so much over the last few years that they'd simply grown numb.

"I need a coffin." She said the words without preamble, without an ounce of emotion.

"We have coffins," he assured her.

"Little ones?"

Crack. It happened again, something within him giving way, like the shards of the world's last iceberg floating down in Antarctica, unchecked pollution cooking the world, melting away all the snow and ice. He was accustomed to death... of adults. Before they'd made it all great again, child deaths had been few and far between—tragedies to be felt, to be railed against. Now, they were a regular part of business.

"Yes. In fact, we just received a new shipment."

She nodded, made a half-hearted effort at a smile. Then it faded, as if the very effort of trying to be civil was too much for her. She wrung her hands, and Fred stepped to the side, lifting his arm in the air to guide her. "This way."

He spoke like the narrator of an audiobook, his voice rich and deep. His wife, the one in Norway, the one who was working with the Norwegian consulate to free him from the United States of Great America, always told him he should have been the voice they used in movie trailers. But Hollywood had hit the bricks, so that opportunity was gone for him. The new Hollywood was

Alternative Liberties

in Spain, all those rich people fled like rats from a sinking ship. Now they sent their movies across the sea in airplanes, airdropping DVDs on the public, imploring the people to rise up, to overthrow the silliness, the pettiness.

He shook his head and followed after the poor woman who wanted a little casket. She had stopped in the showroom, frozen in place among its too-bright lights. Her head scanned from side to side, her hands worrying each other as she took in the coffins, the great size of them.

"These are the adult caskets," Fred said in apology.

"Oh," she said, smiling for a bit in relief, before the weariness of the situation eroded away the corners of that smile and dragged them down.

Fred brushed past her, cast a cursory glance at his dreadful, skeletal face in the mirror. He could have sworn the face in the mirror sneered at him, shook its head in disgust.

Before they stepped into the back storeroom, the woman reached out a hand, cold as winter, gripping his wrist. "Please," she said. "Before we look, how much are they?"

"Oh, they are quite reasonably priced," Fred assured her. His father, who'd run the funeral home before he took over, always said, "Never tell 'em the price until they've seen the merchandise. Always show them first, or else they'll walk away, settle for a cremation."

He wanted to tell her the price, but old habits die hard... lots of things dying hard these days.

In the back storeroom, Jake and Rick took one look at the grief-stricken mother and her too-old eyes, and decided it was a good time for lunch. Fred didn't blame 'em. Lots of people to blame out there, but those two were good ones.

Alternative Liberties

Always start with the most expensive. You can always work your way down.

His father's words revolted him once more. Greedy and practical, he'd never let Fred forget the funeral home was a business, not a charity.

Fred pointed out a casket, white-steel, bright, reflecting the light of the storage room. Parents never wanted a dark casket. Didn't matter that their kid was dead. The thought of their loved one buried in a dark coffin turned something in their stomachs, even though it was dark under the earth and colors didn't exist down there.

"Can things get in?" the woman asked when he finished detailing all the features.

"Things?" he asked.

The woman swallowed a lump in her throat. "Worms. Bugs."

Fred ran his hand along the coffin, assured the woman it would remain sealed for all time, even though it wouldn't. The earth of a grave weighs anywhere from a thousand pounds to a full ton, depending on the soil composition. Here in Oregon, the soil was thick, heavy. You were looking at a weight closer to the high end. Put a ton of dirt on a casket, even the best-made one, and eventually, it'll break. Might not be for a hundred years, but nothing stayed sealed forever. Just ask Tutankhamen. But she didn't need to know that. "Nothing gets in this once we seal it. I can assure you of that."

"And the price?"

"Fifteen-hundred."

"So forty-five-hundred altogether?"

"I beg your pardon?" he asked, not quite understanding.

"Forty-five hundred, for three."

"I don't understand."

She turned to him then, fire in her eyes. "All three of my children died. Smallpox."

"Smallpox?" Fred stammered.

"It's making a comeback."

In a daze, Fred went through the particulars of the funeral, the costs, even knocked five-hundred dollars off the price of the caskets because he was no monster. When the receipts shot out of the printer, and she'd signed on the line, she turned to him and said, "One last thing."

Fred nodded patiently. He was used to these last requests, especially for children. Sometimes, they wanted to bury their child's teddy bear with them, or their favorite blanket, or pictures of their surviving family members.

"Of course, Ms. Embry. Anything." And he meant it. He could only imagine losing his son to some disease that had been eradicated decades ago.

"I want an open casket for all three of my boys."

Smallpox wasn't pretty, especially not when you died from it. All those bumps and nodules, the sores in the mouth, the failed organs within. "Are you sure that's wise?"

"Wise or not. I want their father to see what he did—all so he could pay less in taxes, so he could be right. I want him to know the consequences of his actions, and let him suffer with it for the rest of his days."

Fred nodded, too shocked to advise against it. All he managed to say was, "If you change your mind, give me a call."

Her eyes, dead for most of the day, burned now with a smoldering hate. She nodded at him once, before the fire faded.

She would not change her mind.

Alternative Liberties

Yo, Mike Johnson, Answer Your Phone...

Merv Sims

Outdo one another in showing honor, The Lord said, but Mike was on a date with his daughter at a purity ball, making her sign a contract vowing that he was her king until such a time as he bequeathed her to some fine young man. Mike's voicemail was full, so The Lord hung up.

Clothe yourselves with compassion, kindness, humility, gentleness and patience, The Lord said, but Mike was busy on a Zoom call on how school shootings were caused by teaching evolution. Mike didn't return the call.

The Lord said, *Those who love violence, He hates with a passion.* The Speaker of the United States of America's House of Representatives, Mike Johnson, was at Madison Square Garden, an auxiliary member of his earthly king's posse, watching a UFC fight. And it was

Alternative Liberties

loud, and his ears were ringing, so he didn't hear his phone which went to voicemail, which was still full.

A cruel man hurts himself, The Lord said. *Whatever you would that others do to you, do also to them.* His words were lost in the banging of Mike's hammer nailing signs to Congressional bathroom doors reading, "No Sarah McBrides allowed." The Lord just hung up.

Open your mouth for the mute, for the rights of all who are destitute, The Lord said. *Defend the rights of the poor and needy.* But Mike's mouth was full of a Big Mac and fries at that UFC thing. The Lord deleted his number from his contact list.

Alternative Liberties

The Big Fat Double-Take

Paula Hammond

Funny: I see a guy in a suit, I figure one of two things. He's either a preacher or a grifter. That probably says way more about me than I'm comfortable sharing. Let's just say, growing up, I didn't meet many straights in suits.

Now, I got no problem with an honest working man. Heart and soul of the nation, the working man.

The State Church ain't the problem, either. God and thunder—on our side—what's not to like? But those small-town, big-Jesus freaks. Those bleeding-hearts and their "thou shalt nots." Never could stand a man who puts on airs and graces. Makes out like they don't think the same way as the rest of us. Makes you feel small.

What I like is someone who gives it to you straight. Says it how it is. I guess that's what first attracted me to the life. I take the money, I do the hit. I ask no

Alternative Liberties

questions, they tell me no lies. Can't get more honest than that.

Now, I'm sure your small-town preacher would have a heap of things to say about a man in my line of work. Here's the thing: you keep your nose clean, you got nothing to worry about. But I turn up at your door, you sure as hell earned what's coming. You can't expect to bad-mouth 'Merica and get a free-pass.

Don't get me wrong. I got nothing but respect for The Almighty but, as he don't seem to be in the smiting business no more, then it's up to folk like me to do their State-mandated duty. Think of us as God Lite. No prayers necessary, penance optional.

This hit came by the usual way of things. An Execution Order, a name. I may finesse the details—choose a time, a place—but I never make it complicated. Any dark, lonely spot is good. Doesn't do to scare the populace. They'd freak if they knew just how many enemies of the State are out there.

I didn't know what this suit's crime was. Whether they were a preacher, a grifter, or some other type of bastard—and I didn't much care. Caring will mess you up. Before you know it, you'll start wondering about the morality of it all. That happens, you may as well take a gun to your own head, and that's the gospel.

No, it wasn't my conscience that stopped me doing what I was there to do. What stopped me was that he was a she. Young, too.

She didn't look much like a girl at first, but once you got past the buzz-cut and sharp suit, she had this whole Sinead O'Connor vibe. Huge eyes, pained and vulnerable.

A lot of guys in my line like to keep it clean. Death from a distance. Accidents. Medical 'emergencies'. There's all sorts of ways to get work like this done without creating a scene. But the gigs I get—what I signed up for—are the real trouble-makers. The Powers

Alternative Liberties

That Be want them begging and pissing themselves before they shuffle off. And they figure a gun in the face'll do that.

Truth is, sometimes it does, sometimes all the mark does is stare me down with cold resignation. This girl? She saw me take out my piece. Didn't flinch. Just stood there, sucking on a cigarette, blowing bored little smoke rings.

We all have a line we won't cross. I don't do women. So, soon as I clocked her, I pocketed my gun and turned to leave. The Department could send someone else. I was way up on my quota, anyway.

Her voice was like a shard of ice thrust down my spine. Fairly stripped me of breath.

"Never pegged someone like you as sentimental."

"Do I know you?" I glanced back, curious now.

"I'm guessing not. At least, you don't look much like a whistle-blowing prison inspector to me. Not that anyone ever publishes those stories. Still, what is it they say: silence in the face of evil, is evil. A girl's got to try, right?"

"No idea what you're talking about, lady. Mistook you for someone else, is all."

"Geeez. I should have figured it! 'Midnight, carpark by Nick's Diner, look for the one street light still working.' That sort of cheesy set-up has Department of Liberty written all over it. Anonymous or not, I should have guessed that one of you bozos would catch up with me sooner or later."

"Watch the attitude, lady."

"Oh, sentimental and sensitive. All soul, ain't ya?"

"Look. I don't know what your game is… ".

"Same as yours. Life and death. Poverty, back-street abortions, lynchings, extra-judicial executions. It's my damn job to tell the world about it. We've got a crime syndicate masquerading as a government here. Only

Alternative Liberties

apparently some folk don't care as long as they don't have to put up with a Mexican in front of them in the queue for the soup kitchen."

Screw it. I pulled out the gun. "Don't push me, lady. I can make you go away with a twitch of my finger. In fact, it's my duty to do it."

"Un-bloody believable! Talk about ideas above your station. Give a man a gun, and he thinks he's so damn special. Guess the power gets to you after a while. One squeeze and a little piece of dirt like you gets to blot out a wondrous act of creation." She opened her arms, as if to put herself on display. She smiled. "It's a bit of a rush ain't it, Tommy?"

I started. "How... ?"

"Oh, I know you, Tommy Rish. Two-Two Tommy to his friends, on account of the .22 caliber you favor. Ah, the sadist's bullet. A shot to the neck will sever the carotid arteries. Leave you bleeding out, conscious to the end. Even if the victim moves, a .22'll worm itself around inside, doing all sorts of unfixable nasty along the way. Not that you ever call them victims. You prefer 'hit' or 'mark'—all that gangster-schtick, don't you, Tommy-Boy?"

I closed the gap between us in a couple of long-legged lollops and jabbed my gun against her chest. "Who the fuck are you?" I growled.

"There he is!" she said, delighted. "Almost the real you! Didn't even have to dig that deep. But then, there's not much to you besides veneer is there, Tommy-Boy? Oh, you love to imagine that you're the misunderstood anti-hero with the painful past, but lots of people have shitty childhoods, Tommy. They don't end up as murderers."

"I'm not a murderer!"

"Of course you're not. Let me ask you one question: do you really believe that a government for the people,

Alternative Liberties

by the people, executes journalists, priests, teachers, and artists?"

"I'm protecting liberty."

"Whose liberty?"

"Me and mine."

"And what about *me* and *mine*?"

"People like you... " I stopped before I could finish the sentence. Rule Number 1: don't engage. Don't let them confuse you. Liars gonna lie. "It ain't personal, lady. I've got my orders, is all."

"Yeah, sure. You're a real Patrick Henry. Or maybe you just get off watching the light go out in people's eyes."

I didn't like the way things were going. "If I don't do it, someone else will have to."

"What a solid citizen you are Tommy! Come on then: aren't you a patriot? Fill me full of lead. Do your Dooty!" She spat out the last word like it was something dirty.

I pulled the trigger. No smoke. No gunpowder tang. Just a neat little kick. Everything as it should be. She held my eyes, cool as ice.

I started to sweat. Shake.

"Well?" she asked.

Beside me a voice, sort of skeevy and British, replied "Perfect, my dear. I honestly thought he was wavering there, but I should have known better. These types: they wrap themselves in a flag to excuse all manner of horrors. It really is quite fascinating. You're so right, he's everything we've been looking for."

I was so freaked, I fell on my ass—and there he was. Horns. Tail. Black flames eating the darkness.

"I've known this territory had potential for years, but you can't make real progress with a franchise until you silence all those bleeding-hearts," he said. "Don't you agree, Mr. Rish?"

Alternative Liberties

Somewhen the girl had stopped being angsty-Sinead and became Demon Orphan Annie. I looked from one to the other, suddenly feeling a cold, hollowness in the center of my being.

"Of course," the Devil continued, "enough humans generally find their way to us, on their own, without the need for an active recruitment campaign. But your government is doing such great work—here and around the world—that I decided we needed to start thinking in terms of asset management. Brand awareness.

"Bottom line is: if you're going to demonize the good, sanctify the bad, and set up money-exchanges in all the temples... well that makes me a little obsolete!

"So, I've decided I need to be more pro-active. Take on staff. Which is where *you* come in. Think of this evening as an interview, which you passed with flying colors, by the way.

"What do you say Mr. Rish? The offer stays open, well, indefinitely—if I'm honest. With your level of self-delusion, self-interest, and petty hate, I'm sure you'd go far."

As he spoke, Demon Orphan Annie giggled and skip-jumped her hooves across my sprawling mass. "Did you see me do The Eyes?" she asked, like a kid presenting their father with their grade card.

"I did. Very nice." The Devil bent forward and took the girl's fiery little hand in his. "You can tell me all about it over ice cream."

"For real?" she squeaked, excitedly.

"For real! Just don't tell your mother," Satan whispered, "or I'll never hear the end of it."

I sat on the asphalt until the chill air started to seep into my bones.

'The Eyes', she'd called it. I could still feel the shock of it. That big fat double-take as I saw what others had seen in their final moments, when they'd stared down

Alternative Liberties

the barrel of my .22. A glimpse of the real me, stripped bare. Demon Lite: prayers and penance pointless.

I saw them too: maybe for the first time. The marks. The trouble-makers. The ones I'd made go away, because I was one of the good guys. From inside their eyes, things looked a little different.

I swallowed my horror and headed for the diner. I was pretty sure my new acquaintances would be saving a space at their table for me.

Alternative Liberties

A Better President

Brenda Cooper

I wanted to be one of them. Who wouldn't? They grouped up on the corner of my street in DC, right under my tiny window. Ten, twenty, sometimes more. They sang songs, and punched each other in the shoulder, laughing. Then they lit their torches and marched off into the night. I didn't know where they went. If Momma did, she didn't tell me. She said it wasn't anywhere I wanted to go.

No one at home laughed any more. At thirteen, I remembered 2023 and 2024, between the pandemics and between Trump's times. I remembered laughing with my friends. Now most of my friends were gone, sent back to countries that they had never seen or to other states. Those of us still left in DC laughed quietly or not at all. My mom never laughed any more. She told me how to hush, how to avoid, how to stay home. How to cling to shadows. She told me that was the only way I could live.

Alternative Liberties

Shadows are boring. The boys' voices filled the air with purpose, with energy, and sometimes even with joy.

Mom watched them out of the side of herself, never straight on. She whispered, "They will beat you." But they hadn't ever hit me.. They ignored me. They said bad words to some of my friends, but my skin *almost* matched theirs. Momma was dark, but Dad had been a White soldier, and Momma said he gave me his white body and his night sweats and his love of math. Even though I had her black kinky hair, I looked more White than Black, especially if I kept my hair short.

I watched them gather every Friday out my window. They'd spend half an hour talking and singing, sweating in the summer nights, and then they'd light their torches and march off, still singing. I imagined their marches, hour on hour, keeping themselves going with music and chanting and light. I pictured little kids watching them, firelight dancing across the smiles on their faces. A parade of light.

When you're thirteen, going where your momma doesn't want you to go seems like a very good idea.

I studied the torches. I looked up how to make them online in the library. I found a broom handle in a closet and tore up a pair of pajamas that didn't fit me anymore and used dental floss to tie the whole thing together. I took a pink plastic glass half-full of vegetable oil to the roof where Momma couldn't see me. I lit the edge of the pajama bottoms, and fire licked up the side of the torch, smoked, and sputtered out. I tried again. Again.

I wanted to cry with frustration, but I didn't. I just tried again, three nights in a row, until the bottle of cooking oil was half empty.

~~~

Momma didn't catch me, but one of the boys did. The third night I tried to burn a torch, he came up the fire escape and said my name. "Tariq."

Alternative Liberties

I knew him from school. He was two grades ahead of me. He played football. He'd never said a word to me before, never even looked at me as far as I knew. I swallowed, and even though I was already sweating in the humid summer night, it got worse. My hands shook so hard I almost dropped my failure of a torch. I swallowed and then forced out his name. "Jerome." I clutched the torch to my chest and wondered if I had the strength to hit him with it if he beat me.

To my utter surprise, his voice sounded kind. He said words I didn't expect. "Here, let me help you."

I handed him the broomstick. He pulled out a flashlight and examined it. The edges of partially burned superhero pajamas looked pathetic, the dental floss melted into the fabric, the broomstick itself pockmarked from use.

He had a light backpack. He set it down beside him, opened the zipper, and pulled out an old white shirt. "First, we use white. Make sure it's cotton."

He used a knife to cut away the half-burned blue pajamas with a pocket knife, his movements precise and confident. "These are synthetic. They burn fast but not for very long at all." His words could have been a put-down, but he sounded calm and helpful. "That kind of material can burn hot enough for you to get hurt. Cotton burns longer and better. Wrap it pretty tight, but not too tight or only the outside will burn."

He brought out some metal wire and wrapped the cotton gently with it. "Tight," he repeated. "But not too tight. Fire needs a little oxygen." Then he brought out twine. "Now add twine." He handed it to me and held one end for me while I wrapped the bundle, correcting me a little from time to time. "Cross it there," or "Knot it and keep going." He held his finger on the twine while I finished tying off the string and then he handed me his knife to cut off the end.

Alternative Liberties

I held up the lighter I had purloined from my neighbor a week ago. "Can we try it?"

He held up a hand, stood, cocked his head. He looked at me, like really looked, the way the gym teacher at school did some days. His face made an impression. Dark eyes and blond hair and a little bit of peach fuzz. A small scar on his chin. He smiled. "It'll work. Why were you making it?"

I couldn't spit out any words at all. I wanted to march with them. But what a stupid thing to say. I couldn't get the words out. What if he said no?

Maybe he saw the desire to join them in my eyes. He cocked his head. "It'll be dark in fifteen minutes. Come with us."

Momma would kill me.

"It'll be a fun night," Jerome said, smiling.

And that smile was all I needed. I was in. I followed him down the fire escape, one-handed since I had one hand on the torch. When we got to the corner there was a sturdy boy with short red hair I'd seen around school. He clutched a tall brown bag like my neighbors put old leaf cuttings into. He pulled five tiki torches out of the bag. "This was all I could get."

Jerome nodded. "Thanks."

The boy handed Jerome one of the torches, and he gripped it lightly, as if it were a familiar friend.

Jerome touched the boy's arm. "Carter," he said. "This here is Tariq. He's coming with us tonight."

Carter stood up and dropped the bag, showing he was more than a head taller than me. His eyes widened and he said, "Is that smart?"

Jerome pointed to my torch. "He wants to come."

"His momma's Black."

I swear Jerome only hesitated for a minute before he said, "It's okay."

Carter stared at me for a long time, and then he said, "Make him prove himself."

Alternative Liberties

"His coming is proof enough."

Carter's lips thinned, but he wandered off with the other four torches. The corner grew crowded. I stayed in the center of the boys so Momma wouldn't see me.

I already knew the songs from listening through my window. They were about America and about pride and about being the best and they sounded a little old-timey. But I felt good that I knew most of the words and the tunes from listening to them, and my voice carried as well as anyone's. Cars drove by. Some honked and some rolled up their windows. A Jeep with two pretty girls in it stopped long enough to sing a chorus, then giggled and pulled away.

Heat shimmered. Music and drums filled the air, and I did laugh a few times.

Nobody was clearly Black or clearly Latino, but I spotted more like me, with mixed blood. A tall man who might be twenty-five with Native features and broad shoulders made inside a gym or a boxing class. But mostly it was White boys, all sizes. Jerome was one of the taller ones, and so I could see him and stay close even as the crowd swelled. Tonight the gathering looked bigger than usual. Much bigger. Maybe that was just because I was there now, in the thick of it, the sounds loud and the colors bright. But I counted, and while there were usually twenty, I got to thirty-seven before I lost count in the shifting, darkening night. Between the singing, there was talking and laughter and good-natured teasing. Also, maybe, some nervous giggles, but perhaps I only remember that in retrospect. My own laughter sounded high and touched with desperation, but still it *felt* good. I liked how deep my voice had become.

I felt like a man that night. I had chosen all on my own. Momma would be mad, but surely she knew I had to grow up?

Alternative Liberties

Darkness closed in beyond the bright streetlights, and the murmur of the crowd grew. A tall man in a denim vest and jeans but no shirt clambered up to stand on a light post near me and Jerome and called, "Ready?"

The people closest to us said, "Ready!"

"Ready?" he responded back.

"Ready!"

He worked the word through the crowd until it quieted to whispers, focusing its energy on him.

"We're going to the Old City Hall Courthouse. Let's make us some justice."

The crowd clapped.

The man screamed, "What do we want!"

The crowd around me offered, "Justice!"

"What do we want?"

"Justice!"

I joined in because of course we all want justice.

Two older men, maybe even in their thirties, started lining us up in groups of three. Jerome put me right beside him and he had me hold his torch while he lit it and then he did the same for me. His was lighter and balanced easily, but both glittered and snapped against the dark sky. Our faces flickered with firelight. At three across, we owned the sidewalk. Some people moved out of our way and others stood to the side and clapped. A few followed us. Some just plain joined in, merging with our group, swelling it. I held my torch up higher and sang louder, because I had laughed with Jerome and I loved being part of this glorious march.

We started at the northeast edge of Adams Morgan where we lived, went partway along Dupont Circle and down Massachusetts. My arm hurt from holding up the torch. Its light was thin now, more a glow. The tiki torches still burned, but most of the homemade torches, like mine, had started to sputter or had already died out.

Alternative Liberties

We reached a big white marble building, like a lot of DC buildings. I'd walked past it, but it wasn't in our neighborhood. I didn't recall ever being inside, or even thinking about the building. We marched past a barrel and dropped our torches nose down into it. Someone must have known we were coming, to put that there. By then my back and biceps and wrist hurt so much from holding up the torch I was simply glad of a safe place to drop it. Jerome and I were near the front so my torch would be buried under twenty other torches. I would have to find another broom handle. I thought maybe we were done, and we'd start back now, maybe stop for something to eat or drink. I was hungry, but I'd left my phone in my room when I went to the roof. The night had rolled on since then, steps and chants and noise and my arm hurting and boys around me laughing, not minding if I laughed too.

Now, an in breath, a long moment with no light in front of me to follow.

I suddenly felt out of place, lost. Misfit.

Jerome leaned down and hissed at me. "The statue. To the statue."

Behind and then around us, then in front, chanting. Not singing. Chanting. *Make America Great Again! We will not be REPLACED!* There was an edge to their voices, like nerves and meanness all together, and the laughter was laced with anticipation.

The air stank of extinguished kerosene and the sweat of boys. We surged. We chanted. We moved in a slow, boiling mass toward a tall white statue. Lincoln. Ropes appeared in Jerome's hands, in others' hands. Sturdy, thick ropes that were multiple colors of gray and black and off-white from use.

What were they doing to a statue of Lincoln? He was a hero.

Alternative Liberties

I wanted to run away. I was in for chanting and singing and holding a torch. I was in for laughing. But the game had changed. The boys around me buzzed like an angry mob of bees.

They felt dangerous.

As the crowd forced us forward, Jerome stayed near me. The statue loomed above us, mostly white, President Lincoln in a fancy coat with lapels that stuck out and a hand on a cylinder. When we reached the foot of the statue, Jerome threw his rope up at the head. It hit Lincoln on his marble beard and fell to the ground, almost tripping a boy in front of us. Jerome reeled it in, panting with the effort. Threw again. The rope coiled around Lincoln's neck, the far end falling to the concrete at the foot of the giant pedestal.

"Tariq!" Jerome shouted to be heard above the crowd and the chants. "Grab the rope!"

The furious frenetic energy of the crowd pushed me into the statue, nearly crushing me. I hesitated. Jerome yelled, "Tariq!"

The momentum and rush of the other boys felt like a weight bearing down. I bent fast to secure the rope before it could slide off the enormous white marble shoulders. I turned my back to Lincoln and leaned into the rope. Another boy came right behind me, his sweaty shirt touching my back and his breath stinking of whiskey. He grabbed the rope above my hands, and Jerome came after him. We pushed into the concrete and pulled, leaning forward. "Stay wide!" someone yelled.

Words began to escape the chant, to float above us.

"Harder."

"It rocked!"

"Stay clear."

Alternative Liberties

"Good job, fuckers!"

"Now! Now! Now!"

"Justice!"

"Destroy the fucking nigger-lover!"

I swallowed, shocked, the N-word a bucket of ice.

"Pull!"

I was too far gone, too caught in the momentum to disobey. I pulled.

The statue rocked twice, the weight on the rope momentarily slacking and then jerking back, slacking and coming back, and then it was gone. I whirled as the marble shattered. Lincoln's head separated from his neck. His waist snapped. A hand fell off, and someone grabbed it, a trophy.

Two sledgehammers appeared in the hands of bigger boys. One slammed at the head, over and over, barely chipping it. A bit of ear fell off, and I darted in and grabbed it. Not as good as a hand, but I shoved the sharp-edged shard in my pocket.

Sirens sounded from the direction of the National Mall, and then from Massachusetts. Jerome slapped me on the back. "Follow me!"

We ran.

Everyone ran, scattering, our footsteps loud. I stuck with Jerome around a corner and then he slowed to a walk on the street. Carter stopped with us and two boys I didn't know. We turned back towards the scene we'd just fled. Sirens wailed by from behind us.

They didn't even slow down. Nothing to see here but four White boys out for a quiet stroll.

The police cars partly blocked our view. Heavy-duty lights flashed at the columns of the Court and the fallen President. They didn't turn our way, and in ten minutes we were walking along the National Mall. Jerome hit me in the shoulder. "Maybe everyone got away," he said. Then, "You did good, kid."

Alternative Liberties

On his other side, Carter asked, "You really half nigger?"

A cold filled me, like dread, only imminent. I didn't answer. What could I say?

"It's okay," Jerome said. "Your momma used to work with mine."

Carter and one of the other kids started walking backward on the sidewalk in front of us. I didn't know the boy's name, but he loomed over me. Bigger than most full-grown men. He sneered. "You our slave now?"

I shook my head. No words escaped the frantic beating of my fear.

Jerome held up his hand like a stop sign.

The bigger boy pushed it aside like Jerome wasn't even trying and stopped in front of me. Carter stood close behind. The second strange boy had faded away. "You afraid of us?"

Yes. Absolutely and completely, like I'd never been afraid of other humans before. But I didn't say it. Finally, I dredged up a quieter-than-I-wanted, "No. I'm not afraid of you." My stomach screamed at me that I should have said yes, and then Carter slugged me in the belly. The screams in my body wanted out in the worst way but I clamped them in. I knew what would happen if I showed them they were hurting me.

Jerome didn't stop them. He didn't join them, but he didn't even try to stop them. The unnamed boy slammed a meaty fist into my face. Carter hit my shoulder. Maybe they would have if they hit me more, but a whistle blew near my ear. The noise drew my eyes to a policewoman standing inches away, just behind me. She watched Carter and the other boys run off. Jerome stayed, watching the cop with narrowed eyes.

I felt the sharp edge of the ear in my pocket. What the hell had I been thinking? What would Momma do if I got arrested? Was it illegal to have a statue's ear in your pocket?

Alternative Liberties

The cop smiled at Jerome and nodded. Almost like she was deferential or approving or something. Then she faded away and it was just me and Jerome.

"Know her?" I asked.

"Met her before," he said. Maybe he'd called her over. Maybe he couldn't argue with Carter himself. "Know your way home?" he asked.

"Of course."

"I got something to do. Don't mind those assholes."

He faded away, gone, and I was alone with no boys laughing around me. No one singing. No light.

I took the long way home. Even though it was a small shard of marble, the ear felt heavy. Had Momma seen me go off with them? She was going to miss her broom handle. What a shit I was. Stupid kid. My arms throbbed from holding the torch up like I thought I was the Statue of Liberty. My face and belly throbbed from being hit, my cheek burned, and through it all my heart beat fast and unhappy. Maybe she'd be asleep. But before I could open the door, Momma opened it for me. "You smell like bad White boys." Her voice sounded sad. "And your eye is swelling up." She turned me around to stare in the mirror.

A bruise on my cheekbone spread near my eye. When she touched my face her hand trembled. "Sit down."

She brought me a bag of frozen peas to cool my swollen cheek, and I held them up to my face and closed my eyes.

"We'll talk in the morning," she said, her voice as heavy as the damned statue had been, as heavy as the shard of ear in my pocket. She went to bed, and I sat holding the bag of peas while it grew warm against the heat of my stupidity.

After I put the peas away, I took out the bit of statue and stared at it in the pale-yellow gleam of the living

Alternative Liberties

room lamp. The top of the ear all the way to the sound canal filled my palm. The place where the ear had attached to Lincoln's cheek felt almost knife-sharp. The upper curve of the ear was perfectly smooth, like a worry stone. Maybe I'd take it back the next day, in the daylight, and drop it casually. Maybe if I did that, I could forget I'd been so stupid.

Next thing I knew, Momma stood over me, the piece of ear in her palm. Sunlight streamed in through the street-level window and dogs barked outside. She regarded me with wide eyes that reminded me of a rabbit's eyes when a shadow passed between it and the sun. "The news this morning. I saw you hauling on the rope."

I swallowed, suddenly cold.

"Other people might recognize you," she said. "Teachers. Neighbors."

"It'll be okay," I told her. I didn't want her to feel scared.

She whispered, "Why'd you go do that?"

I didn't have a good answer. 'All my friends left' sounded pathetic. I came as close to a truth she might hear as I thought I could. "I wanted to know where they went."

"Did they make you go?"

I couldn't lie to her. I never did. I did things I didn't tell her about, but you never lie to your mother. I shook my head.

I plucked the piece of ear from her palm. "I'm going to take it back so it's not evidence."

I thought she might argue with me, might say that it was dangerous or stupid or I didn't need to do it. Instead she stared at me for five full breaths and then asked, "Okay. Can I come with you?"

I owed her something. "Do you want to?"

"Yeah."

She made me two fried eggs and toast with butter and she had coffee and a single slice of bread. On the way out, she handed me a hat. "Cover your face a little."

Was she that scared? "Okay, Momma."

It was almost eleven by the time we left. Heat clung to us and Momma kept twisting her thick black hair up and clipping it and then taking down and clipping it up again. She had a blue bandana she swiped at her own sweat with and then stuck back into her jeans pocket. On the way, it occurred to me she must have taken a day off from her job. Maybe I'd got her fired. I hadn't thought of that. "Did you call in sick?" I asked her.

"Yes."

"You okay?"

"I don't know."

I knew I had to say it, so I did. "I fucked up. I'm sorry."

"Good."

And even though I was sorry, I was already feeling the grip of shadows clutching at my need to laugh. I had no idea how to tell her she was a little bit of the cause even if it was my fault.

We came up on the block the Court dominated, and from a distance, it looked normal. People in suits chattering. High heels clipping on the sidewalk. Women with kids in strollers. Pigeons making little burbling sounds as they strutted on the shady parts of the sidewalk.

Momma reached out and grabbed my arm.

I expected maybe a cop or something, but she pointed.

Already right in front of the building, there was a new statue. President Trump holding his fist in the air. The speed of the change made me sink, made me sit on the first empty bench I found. Momma sat next to me. Then she glanced toward the White House, even though you couldn't see it from here. "Do you think *he* tells those boys what to do?"

I swallowed hard. I hadn't thought about who told them where to march. Before last night, I thought they just marched around holding torches. Laughing. Singing. "Do you know what else they do?" I asked her.

"They burn things."

"What things?"

"They burn down everything they touch," she said, words coming more quickly and louder. "They burn businesses, they beat up Black boys." She looked at me sideways, making sure I got the point even though she didn't need to make sure. I had gotten it last night as the statue shattered around me.

We sat there quiet for so long the squirrels started to come up to us with their tiny gray paws and black-marble eyes and cock their heads to ask for food.

"I don't suppose you want a used ear?" I asked them.

They chittered at me and then moved on. "Am I safe then? I mean, if this is what *he* wanted?"

"No."

I thought about that, but only for a minute. He didn't care about the people who did his business. Just about himself. "Should I take the ear back now?" I asked. The statue of Trump wasn't marble. It wasn't even bronze. I didn't know what it was made of, but something fast. Maybe no one was looking for the parts of Lincoln.

Momma took my hand and squeezed it briefly, then let go. "May I keep it? I want to think I have a piece of a better President."

"Okay, Momma," I said. "Can we go home now?"

"Yeah. We can. Be careful."

"I will."

Alternative Liberties

In Real-Time

C T Walbridge

The man at the dais was behind bulletproof glass.
He was bracketed by the parentheses of teleprompters.
The network was committed to carrying every spoken word. This was the debut of the new AI banner system, and they hoped the chyrons scrolling across the screen would result in a more accurate performance.
The crawling text below the man's image was not what they bargained for.
AI: *Today, he says projected cost is eight billion. Eight days ago, he said four billion. Best independent estimate; above forty billion.*
The man on the dais went on.
AI: This may be an anecdote toward some rhetorical point. Possibly just a digression.
AI: Still may be a digression.
AI: Still may be a digression.
AI: An anecdote with no apparent relevance.

And on.
AI: His point seems to be that windmills are like immigrants. They both kill birds, but the immigrants kill endangered Bald Eagles and eat them. No supporting information exists.
And on.
AI: The fish poisoning allegation is false. Traced to a Russian misinformation site 33 days ago and has been viewed 83,043 times so far. A popular lie.
And on.
AI: That survey does not exist.
And on.
AI: "Vengeance is Mine" means the opposite of what he says it does. Reference, King James Version, **Romans 12:19.**
And on.
AI: An aide has come up on the stage, and is apparently telling him something.
And on.
AI: He criticizes InstaFact Incorporated for these chyrons. However, this stream is produced by CheckFlow, not InstaFact.
And on.
AI: He scolds NBC for allowing AI technology to "piggyback."
And on.
AI: He compares this tech to the fictional Skynet in the *Terminator* films.
And on.
AI: Praise for Arnold Schwarzenegger including his personal physical attributes... four minutes.
And on.
AI: He says "AI shouldn't be allowed on broadcasts or podcasts." He supports this opinion with four expletives.
In conclusion.

Alternative Liberties

AI: The most significant quote from the 93-minute address: "Artificial intelligence should not do real-time fact-checking because it violates freedom of speech."

Alternative Liberties

Alternative Liberties

Unwanted Visitors

K.G. Anderson

I'd closed the drapes against the winter chill. No snow yet, but the wind shook the fir trees and rattled the metal porch chairs I'd forgotten to bring in. Marie and I stood in my bungalow kitchen, cooking spaghetti and reminiscing about grad school while sipping the Merlot she'd brought.

"I'm so glad you got back in touch—it's been years," I said. "What are you even doing these days?"

Marie gave an odd laugh. *Was something making her nervous?*

"I think you'd be surprised," she said. "I can tell you the whole story over dinner."

When a loud knock came at the front door, my cat Shadow meowed and raced out of the kitchen.

"Lise, were you expecting someone?" Marie asked.

I shook my head. But by the time I set down the spoon I'd been using to stir the simmering sauce, I had

Alternative Liberties

a bad feeling. *Please don't let it be what I think it is.* I snapped off the burner, just in case it was.

"Stay here," I said, and hurried to answer the door. I knew the inspections we'd grown used to in Seattle weren't happening everywhere. At least not in the small college town where Marie lived.

I opened the front door. Two beefy young men with pale skin and close-cropped brown hair walked in without asking. They wore the olive-drab uniforms of the new Federal Security Agency.

"Lise Parker?" the taller one said, his thick finger poised over a data pad. His question was more of a statement.

I gave a short nod. "Yes."

"Routine check of the block." The agent's speech was devoid of inflection. He probably said that same phrase 50 times a day. Or, in the case of Federal Security, a night. They usually came at night.

His partner bent slightly and pawed through my coffee table magazines, peered at the books in my bookcases, and opened drawers in the table where I sort the mail. Marie came out from the kitchen and perched on the arm of a club chair, open-mouthed in disbelief.

I stood by the sofa, my eyes on anything but the agents. I always stood when Federal Security came.

The taller agent, the one who'd spoken, brushed past. I wrinkled my nose. His cloying body spray was an assault. He jogged noisily upstairs to the bedrooms, squeezing his bulk through the narrow staircase. Meanwhile, in the dining room, his colleague stuck his hand in a vase.

I moved closer to Marie. "Security theater." I kept my voice low. "Ever since the new administration declared Seattle a terrorist haven—" I rolled my eyes to indicate the absurdity of it, "the feds have been sending these rent-a-cops around to keep us frightened. They'll check the computers, maybe ask to see my phone."

Alternative Liberties

"But that's illegal!" Marie said. "They need warrants! You should just tell them to leave."

I wished she would keep her voice down. I kept my tone even. "Well, the feds have declared a state of emergency so they don't need warrants. Of course, people are filing lawsuits. But, in the meantime, putting up with these *visits* is easier than being arrested."

I didn't add that my neighbor who'd resisted an inspection had disappeared the following day. His bungalow now sat empty, the front lawn overgrown. The couple across the street had adopted his dogs. Had he left town? Or was he in a detention camp?

I studied the polished oak floor, listening as the agents stomped through the house. It was taking longer than usual tonight. When I looked up, Marie's dark eyes met mine.

She made no effort to conceal her indignation. "I'd heard about this on the news, but that was months ago," she said. "I had no idea it was still going on."

So, what I'd heard was true. Social media companies were filtering everyone's news feeds by region. People from Boston, San Francisco, Portland, and the four other cities the feds had labeled "terrorist havens" discovered that their social media posts about the FSA's inspections were invisible to friends in other cities.

The only place you saw these home searches mentioned was on local discussion boards, where people complained that the gated lakeside communities where the wealthy lived seemed to be exempt from the visits. That politicians and city leaders, at least those from the right party, had been paid to ensure that the city cops ignored citizen complaints about the FSA.

So many rumors. So hard to tell the truth from paranoia.

Alternative Liberties

I didn't say this to Marie. We kept quiet, listening as cabinets opened and closed in my study. Then we heard the clacking of a computer keyboard.

"Don't they need your password?" she whispered.

"I, ah, don't use one anymore." Last month an agent had flown into a rage when I'd fumbled while typing my password for him. It was easier to just give them access. "It's only theater. If they really want to see what websites we were visiting, or what our emails say, they could just monitor the traffic from our internet providers. Maybe they do."

"Unbelievable." Marie shook her head slowly, her lips a thin line.

"I'm so sorry," I said. But what the hell was *I* apologizing for? Did she expect me to refuse the inspection and risk... whatever it was Federal Security did to people?

Footsteps came up the basement stairs. Cabinets opened and closed in the kitchen. They even opened the damn refrigerator. The taller agent came out of the kitchen and strode over to me.

"ID." He held out his hand.

I grabbed my purse from the hall table, rummaged for my passport, and handed it to him.

"If I'd known about all *this*, I wouldn't have come!" Marie spoke loudly. I wished she'd keep her mouth shut.

The agent turned to her, his pale, bland face darkening. "You. Do you live here?"

Oh, no! Well, now she'll see what it's like, I thought miserably.

"No," Marie said. She stood with her arms crossed over the front of her crisp white blouse, delicate gold bracelets dangling from her slim wrists. "I'm from Mondville. Where we don't have home invasions like this."

Alternative Liberties

The agent put out his hand. She stared at it.

"ID," he barked.

Marie jumped. She slowly picked up her large leather purse from beside the chair, took out her wallet, and extracted her driver's license.

The agent read it. His expression soured. "Har-toon-i-yan?" He drawled her name with deliberate awkwardness. I'd forgotten that her late husband, Peter, had been from Turkey. Foreign. I hoped this wouldn't cause problems.

"Just what do you do for a living, Mrs. Hartunian?" the agent asked.

"I'm a science teacher. And my late husband was a tenured professor of civil engineering at Regional College in Mondville." Icicles dangled from Marie's words.

"And he died when?"

"Three years ago."

"So why didn't you just go back to your country?" The agent waited. Marie said nothing. The shorter inspector had emerged from the kitchen and stood behind her. I wondered if she realized he was there.

"Just where are you from, Mrs. Hartunian?" the agent persisted.

"I'm from Mondville. Born in Mondville." Her composure astonished me.

The two men exchanged looks and then the one behind Marie's chair glanced toward the kitchen. I followed his gaze. Then I smelled something burning.

"Oh my God." I pushed past the inspectors and ran into the kitchen. I was sure I'd turned off the heat under the saucepan. But somehow it was on High and the tomato sauce was spattering and smoking. I reached for the fan switch, but too late: the smoke alarm began blasting. I threw open the back door. I cursed as Shadow shot past me and out into the night. I grabbed a dish towel and flapped it until the smoke cleared and the alarm subsided. Then I ran back to the living room.

It was empty. The men were gone, and so was Marie.

"Marie?" I checked the bathroom and the guestroom at the back of the house. No sign of her. I remembered we hadn't yet brought her overnight bag in from her car. "Marie?" When I came back to the living room, I saw her purse had vanished from the chair. The hook by the front door, where she'd hung her blue raincoat, was empty. Had Marie left in disgust?

Or had Federal Security taken her?

Car doors slammed far down the street and I shivered. The agents weren't usually that loud. I turned off the living room lights, eased open the door a few inches, and peered through the crack. The shiny black FSA van sat a good way down the street, windows dark, headlights off. The passenger side door stood wide open.

The cold LED of a streetlamp revealed dark figures sprawled on the sidewalk. Neither one was moving. I gasped as it dawned on me that the two loud noises hadn't been car doors. Apparently, they'd been gunshots.

At the far end of the block a car's brake lights glowed red. A subcompact car that looked just like Marie's pulled silently away from the curb. It drove slowly down the winding road and vanished around the corner. I thought about that large purse of Marie's. It had had plenty of room for a gun.

Then a movement across the street caught my eye. One of my neighbors was quietly closing their front door. Next door to them, curtains twitched in a darkened living room. My heart pounded.

As far as I knew, there were no government surveillance cameras on our tree-lined street. I didn't think anyone would call the police. No, they'd try desperately to pretend they'd heard and seen nothing. Could I pretend as well? Maybe. Maybe...

Alternative Liberties

Just to be safe, I'd leave little Shadow outside tonight, put food and water on the back deck. If they took me away tonight, a neighbor would take the cat.

I closed the front door, carefully, but couldn't help flinching as the deadbolt snicked into place. I looked around the living room at the books, at the paintings, at my grandfather's green mohair reading chair. I wondered if this was the last night I'd see them. I had no idea how bad things might be.

No one did, anymore.

Alternative Liberties

Preacher Feature

Mike Adamson

It was in the second year of the second term of the president that history dubbed the Antichrist that the US watched the arrival of the Preacher, though other rogue nations aligned with the Antichrist also saw it.

He made his unbidden appearance on June 23, 2052, a Sunday of course, and the entire United States was exposed to him simultaneously at precisely 8:00 PM Eastern time.

He was on every screen, coast to coast. One moment, people were watching the usual prepackaged garbage of reality games, heavy-handed drama, and schlockumentaries. The next, they were confronted by a slight man in the dark coat, string tie, and the broad hat of an Old West traveling holy man.

"Greetings, America," he announced in a friendly, engaging voice, staring intently out from every screen. "You may call me the Preacher," he added with a wry smile, "and you will come to know me well. That is only fair, as I already know each and every one of you—from Martha loading the dishwasher to Lil' Frank playing on the rug by the big screen, Cindy with her VR glasses, and Dad with his beer. And Dad, you might want to slow down on that beer. Diabetes is not something you want to ignore. And I know the rest of you. The hungry ones. The homeless ones, the arrogant, those filled with hate, those who have lost hope. I feel your pain, and I am here to tell you there *is* hope. There *is* a tomorrow worth fighting for.

"But most of all, I am here to tell you that to reach that promised land, you must mend your ways!" His voice became like gravel, and he hunched forward, his face filling every screen in America.

"Switch off if you will, but my message will not change until all have heard it, and there is nothing—*nothing*—you can do to stop me. He straightened up and slapped his knees, "So, let's get to it—all of you who're still with me." He gave a wry chuckle.

He took a deep breath, closed his eyes and reclined in an ornate, ancient chair against a pure black background

A montage played across the darkness behind him. "Death. War. Famine. Pestilence. The Four Horsemen of the Apocalypse." Images came and went as he spoke. "Look around you. Death is everywhere. We profit from it. Guns send bullets into 30,000 bodies a year. We watch tens of thousands die needlessly rather than pay for lifesaving care. And for you there is no glory greater than war. It fuels the lifestyle of the rich. It justifies vengeance. When an attack killed 3,000 of you, you demanded retribution. Using enough money to rebuild every crumbling bridge and school in the land, you struck back at innocent and guilty alike: vengeance on a grand scale." His eyes widened and voice rose. "Vengeance is MINE, said the Lord. You ignored him and killed hundreds of thousands. You killed wives, mothers, fathers and sons. You killed more children than you even know. Never has a country exported more violence through war than has your own, nor waged war as relentlessly, as mercilessly, or for so long, for such little reasons. You substitute death for introspection.

"Since its inception, the years when America has *not* been at war do not, even now, equal a single modest human lifespan.

"You say you want peace. Your politicians call violently for it. Peace was the last thing anyone wanted—or still wants." He raised a fist. "War is the greatest cash cow ever invented. A president once said, 'Beware the military industrial complex.' But you, not wary, embraced it for market share and cheap oil." He pointed out from the screen. "You must mend your ways. Your country is the wealthiest ever to exist, but how many work more than forty hours a week and can't get by without food stamps? How many toil in the fields for a pittance? How many work fifty, sixty hours and are still afraid of losing the roof you have over your heads? How many know how close you are to the streets? To calling a car your home? Too many! Yes, I see you nodding, so many of you. We're on the same page, my friends."

Images of slums and ghettos backed his words. Food banks and foreclosure notices, split-second glimpses of the Great Depression, and tent cities in parks.

"Once you fought nature to destroy her diseases. Now you have brought them back in the name of profit and fight nature for metals in her body. You rip it asunder, leaving the scraps to clog and destroy her air and water.

"Well, I am here to tell you, my friends, that, directly, by our actions, or indirectly, by their omission, we... you *are* responsible. Every one of us is culpable. We are a

Alternative Liberties

community, a society, with mutual responsibilities—or we are nothing!"

He stabbed out with a blunt finger then slowly sat back, steepled his fingers, and recomposed himself.

"I have spoken sufficient words for now. I have chastised you enough. I have not forgotten the good citizens of conscience, who are charitable to their neighbors and seek only the best. Those who would not dream of harming any living thing and lament the state of our poor, broken world. Ultimately, it is those people I am speaking to when I say, 'Blessed are the peacemakers. Blessed are the meek.'"

He took a breath, let it sigh away. His gentle voice became thunder. "But for the rest, I warn you. The End Times are upon us, but they are far from what you were taught to expect." He smiled. "I shall expand upon this in the next installment of *Preacher Feature*. You will catch it, I assure you. No matter where you are or when you are viewing, I'll be here."

And he was gone, replaced by the scheduled programming as if he had never been.

~~~

America was in shock. Within the hour, pastors denounced the upstart from televised pulpits. Network chiefs vowed to block future transmissions. In Washington the Antichrist tasked his security services to seek, locate, and destroy this propaganda nightmare.

But they could not. He was nowhere to be found. His features showed up on tens of thousands of facial recognition programs. The right nose here, the eyes there, but never all of him.

The Preacher was back two nights later, just as unstoppable, as acerbic, every bit as accusing.

The End Times were on his mind. Again, he waxed lyrical on American history. He called out the injustice of slavery, delivered horrifying statistics, and images later deemed accurate, but never before seen.

Alternative Liberties

His viewers knew he was going somewhere with this history lesson. When the punchline arrived, he delivered it with gusto.

"So, you can see, my friends, that the vast and powerful economy upon which this country rides was built on the back of forced labor from the ends of the Earth. Indeed, one is justified in saying that such vast wealth cannot be built any other way than through injustice to *someone*. These are the rotten roots of our culture. Roots we must come to terms with. We cannot change the past, but we *may* repudiate structures built upon such foundations. We may atone for injustice.

"Join with me, friends, in doing this. The time approaches when words will be replaced by deeds." A website flashed on the screen. "Here are those who profited and continue to do so. Go search them out. Close your accounts with the financial entities listed. Do not give them your business until they return what they took. It is all there. Reject, reject, *reject* the ways of evil!" He raised a finger in warning. "I shall be watching, my friends."

The second broadcast brought the Antichrist close to apoplexy. The White House doctors worked long into the night. Unfortunately for the American people, the POTUS pulled through.

Worse for the president, the next day, from all over the country, reports came in of graffiti with unambiguous messages. Most popular was *Preacher for President*, but *Go Preacher!* and *Preacher's da Man* showed up everywhere. The website could not be blocked. Companies that paid heed to their listed debt found they fared better than deniers. Trading was suspended worldwide.

The situation remained unchanged, with the FBI working around the clock to uncover the identity and location of the mysterious propagandist. Every second

Alternative Liberties

or third day, a new episode appeared. While evangelists and politicians exhorted the public to just switch them off, Nielsen Media Research slyly published the news that the Preacher's ratings were going up sharply. If networks could have sold advertising during his spots, they would have raked in millions.

By the end of the first week, after only three episodes, small firms all over the country were manufacturing Preacher T-shirts with a logo created by an art student from Boulder, proudly displaying his featured Biblical quotes. A Mexican plastics company 3D-printed and blister-packed a Preacher action figure and smuggled it over the border in the second week. Soon after, the Antichrist declared Preacher merchandise seditious material.

Recordings of *Preacher Feature* were uploaded to YouTube faster than they could be taken down; servers crashed due to worldwide demand. Cheap knock-off Preacher hats were made by the thousand and shipped to underground flea markets in the dead of night.

The Preacher became a symbol of resistance to a corrupt state, as surely as listening to the BBC had been in Nazi Germany; Preacher parties took place in the nation's hidden speakeasies.

Small churches held packed revival meetings in his name.

Though officially banned, there was no way to prevent the Preacher's sermons short of curtailing all entertainment media—unacceptable for financial and social reasons. Some networks experimented with suspending their broadcasts for the duration of each interruption, but a gruesome fascination had set in across all sectors of American society.

Cable networks bucked the trend and interspaced the messages with commentary and analysis. Throughout the nation, people tuned in morning, afternoon, and night to catch the random interdiction whenever the anarchistic priest chose to replay the day's offering.

Television ratings were higher than ever, and advertisers made fortunes.

Psychologists and social scientists flooded the talk shows, news channels, and Internet sites to discuss the phenomenon of the grit-talking padre and what he was coming to mean to American culture, while news networks were ordered to play down the fact that people were closing their accounts with the grand old banks and choosing Fair Trade products that benefited the Third World. The Preacher had struck a nerve.

Soon, analysts reported to the Antichrist that the Preacher was likely not a man at all. He was an advanced AI, a digital construct of such compelling quality that he must be rendered by supercomputers.

America became reacquainted with the grim black-and-white face of history. Grainy color footage—the burned child running toward Nick Ut's camera—was stamped into the consciousness of another generation in an accusation of immorality, a condemnation of all war.

But as his crusade ground into its fourth week and America simmered on the verge of riot and revolt, at last the FBI hacked the data conduit through which the Preacher accessed the nation's transmission systems. Agents traced his broadcasts to a service shack in the Midwest—a massive fiberoptic main channel—and the POTUS authorized an assault to take out whoever was behind this attack on his establishment.

In the cool of a late summer evening, black APCs with gunship support surrounded the shack in Nebraska's dust-dry western farmlands. When the Preacher went to air, the black-suited troopers burst in, blew the doors, and raked the place with fire. They shot up computers, signal processors, autonomous power

Alternative Liberties

systems, scramblers—but no living hand was necessary to get the message out. Thirty pounds of C4 wired into the building reduced it to a cloud of flame and debris a hundred yards across.

Ten minutes later, the Preacher was back on-air, and the real-time, reedited episode resumed with a satellite view of the explosion.

"The forces of the Antichrist are hunting me, friends, but they will find me a hard target. As King Herod turned against our Lord, and the Romans worked their vile conception of justice upon his mortal flesh, so the false and tyrannical leadership of your nation seeks to silence the voice of dissent. I shall not yield. I do not recognize the authority of those who seized power in unfair elections. For what is the Electoral College but a gerrymander, and what is a gerrymander but spitting in the face of democracy, declaring one man's vote of more value than another's? Are all men not created equal under God?

"Our society says a government of the people, by the people and for the people, but denies the people.

"This duplicity is institutional. Voter suppression, the control of voter registration, police roadblocks obstructing voters from reaching polling stations: these are outrages. If they occurred in foreign countries, the America of old would click its tongue and declare the victor of such elections a 'regime' to be mistrusted. My friends, our nation is a *regime*. Grasp the word. A military state in all but name. Its elections are a sham; its army polices the world—at our government's whim, for its own strategic purposes—and its police are militarized to control *you.*"

Now he leaned forward.

"I do not tell you to rise up and overthrow this corrupt establishment. I am a man of God, and I do not encourage the taking of a single life. Every man and woman in uniform, doing their sworn duty to the state

Alternative Liberties

and Commander in Chief, is someone's son or daughter. Not every soldier, sailor, airman, or Marine is a hard-believing stone killer, nor is every police officer.

"There are a great many good cops, just as there are good soldiers. The tragedy is that they are caught between the needs of our times and the orders of the regime they find themselves serving. Which side of history will the good cops and good soldiers be on in this country? You cannot remain good in the service of evil.

"Think upon these matters, friends...for the apocalypse is coming."

~~~

Reports of arrests of anyone wearing Preacher attire soon filled the news. Imports were banned. Pictures were circulated of bulldozers dumping Preacher merchandise into landfill while the graffiti epidemic swept the nation. It went up each night faster than forced work crews could take it down each day, so major cities established a curfew, with orders issued to shoot vandals on sight. 3D printed models of the Preacher appeared everywhere.

Horrified, the world watched as America turned on itself and deployed the vilest tactics and methods of any regime, at any time, from the brutal Soviet guards to the savagery of the Japanese prison camps. Torture was used indiscriminately, on the premise that *somebody knew something* and sufficient brutality would break the wall of silence.

The official propaganda machine began to strike back, posting all manner of bizarre 'facts' about the Preacher. He was a defrocked priest convicted of child molestation, his victims legion. The Preacher did not respond. His message remained steady.

But as with every regime founded on violent repression and propaganda, the elasticity of public credulity was finite. To millions, the Preacher's calm but

Alternative Liberties

impassioned lessons, as people had come to call them, had become a lifeline of sanity in a world gone crazy.

When an armed militia assaulted a for-profit prison and released falsely convicted inmates, it triggered a battle with the guards and resulted in the release of serious offenders. His broadcasts came to a sudden end.

For seven long days, the Preacher fell silent. The Antichrist clung to office with a shaky grip. And when the last episode of *Preacher Feature* that would ever be seen went to air, the POTUS himself was glued to the screen in the Oval Office.

"Friends," the Preacher began in his ponderous way, "I have sinned." He raised a hand. "Yes...yes, I have. Your support is heartfelt, but I have sinned, and I will answer to the Almighty for my actions. I do this in full knowledge and place myself before His mercy, willing to accept whatever consequences He deems fit." His pause was pregnant; hundreds of millions of viewers barely dared breathe. "In seeking to expose the corruption of this regime—the arrogant hypocrisy that claims the mantle of religion today—I have brought about situations that have cost human lives. Innocent or guilty is not my concern, but lives were lost. I have incited violence. For this I shall face my maker.

"It is in your hands now. You must decline to participate. *Decline to play their game.*

"If every right-thinking citizen of this poor, torn land refused to cooperate, the nation would come to a halt. Tomorrow, decline to work. Decline to be educated or to patronize businesses. Spend not one dollar. Use not one volt of electricity you can do without. Do the same the next day. The next. And the next. Until the president dissolves this heinous government and returns to this country to genuinely free elections. One person—one vote—absolute transparency. Full voter participation.

Alternative Liberties

Observers from *other countries* to watchdog the process."

As the image returned to him, he bowed his head. "You might be wondering what I believe. In a way, it doesn't matter, but you want to know, so I will tell you. As a man of God, I accept that climate change is a parallel to the Biblical flood. The waters are coming, friends. The apocalypse is nigh. It has claimed many victims in the last decades, and the ocean gnaws at the continents with unremitting fury. Whether we brought it on ourselves through the blindness of industrial greed or through the shallowness of our souls, the end result is the same.

"I can exhort you to prayer, and I do. A good prayer never hurts." He smiled, a sad, desperate expression that tugged the viewers' hearts. "But I will also tell you this. Anyone who relies solely on prayer to solve this problem deserves to drown. Anyone who believes this frightening end—to die pressed between fire and water—is the proper way for human tenure on this world to end, has too little faith in the divine spark within us all."

His passion rose, and he leaned forward for the last time. *"We can be better than this!* Our nation was built on the belief that within humans lies the power to shape the Earth into something better than the world offered to us by the greedy. We must come together in action. A world divided is a world doomed, and we have ridden that pale horse almost to the grave.

"So, join me, friends. Join hands, and we will walk forth together. There is still time to put measures in place to preserve life, to build a bulwark against the dark centuries ahead when nature besieges our species.

"And now, we suffer the whips and shock collars of a totalitarian state that feeds us poisons and tranquilizers—a steady diet of meaningless

Alternative Liberties

programming, music that has lost all sense of purpose—to distract and preserve the illusion of continuity. *Their* continuity."

The view pulled back. The Preacher adjusted his hat, paused, then looked up.

"My friends, it has been a privilege to address you. I hope to have provoked thought. I shall go now and pray—pray for a sunrise tomorrow in a free land where hate is overtaken by compassion, where cynicism is replaced with optimism, and natural justice is alive once more."

He folded his hands, and the lighting narrowed slowly to a single spotlight on his face, shining beneath the brim of his hat.

"What you do now, America, my beloved, is in your hands. Goodnight. And God bless."

Long, slow fade to black.

~~~

History records that the General Strike of 2052 paralyzed the United States. Tens of thousands died in what became known as the Summer of the Preacher. Whoever he was, brainchild of some unknown figure, would forever remain the spark that lit the inferno.

Alternative Liberties

The Sylvia Rivera School for Wayward Queers

Voss Foster

Rumors. Always rumors. Only rumors. Dez had caught the early morning bus from Boise, across the border into Washington, all so that he could chase one more rumor. No one dared confirm or deny anything adult or deviant. If they had, Dez would never have trusted them anyway. The stories of deviant clubs raided by the Council for Ethics were as much rumors as anything else, but they painted too similar a picture to each other to be entirely baseless. And every time, they began with bait. Something too good to be true, too firmly filled with details. A place where people could meet, could live, could *breathe* for a moment. Then, the trap was sprung and the deviant behavior was *addressed.*

Dez kept his hood up as he marched down the streets of Spokane, eyes flicking between his phone screen and his surroundings. It was the dead of summer, so the ever-present fires filled the sky—and his lungs—with smoke. Spokane was hemmed in by forests, so there was plenty for the wildfires to burn. The city was as lively as Dez recalled. Over the years, he'd come here on field trips and short jaunts with his family. Never alone and unsupervised. Never while lying to his parents about where he'd be the next couple days. Certainly, never while trying to skirt the law. Never as a Deviant.

After half an hour's walk from the bus stop, Dez's phone finally said he'd arrived. He looked at the faded sign on the shop above him: G and K Café. The signage had certainly seen better days, but the view through the large front windows was inviting. A bit crowded, but inviting, with dim lights and brass finishes and pictures of the Spokane skyline along the walls, intermixed with children's art, scrawled in crayon.

Dez took a deep breath, then closed the map app and slipped his phone away. His chest buzzed as he opened the door, hand numb against the warm, metal handle. When he pulled it open, the strong scent of coffee hit his nose, mingling with baking spices and stone fruit.

Soft guitar music played from speakers in the corners of the space.

"Welcome in." A heavyset Hispanic gentleman behind the counter approached, smiling wide. A silver stud in his ear glinted in the low light of the café. He was probably in his late thirties, early forties, with a slightly receding hairline that emphasized his widow's peak. His nametag said "Alex."

"Hi." Dez's mouth barely wanted to work, and each step closer to the counter was like lifting lead blocks. He could back out of this. Rumors could be dangerous, too. Rumors could be used by the Council for Ethics as well as anything else. Dez could ask for directions, then head back to the bus depot, and nothing would change.

Nothing would change.

He swallowed and, once he was close to Alex, forced himself to carry on, head throbbing. "I was hoping to talk to Marsha?"

Alex showed no sign of recognition. "Not really policy to give out information about my employees. Who's asking?"

That was the right question, but Dez wouldn't let himself get too excited. Could just as easily be an innocent question, a normal part of conversation. "Sylvia, uh, sent me. To ask her about a construction project."

Alex nodded, smile widening. "Oh, yeah, she mentioned someone might come asking." He stepped away from the counter and waved for Dez. "Come on back. She's on break."

Last chance to run. Dez's feet stayed attached to the floor as he processed everything. This was supposed to be a safe place. Better than anything they had in Boise. There were too many informants in Idaho, so everything got shut down within a month or two of opening, and they were running out of anyone with money or influence who would stick their neck out.

So Dez walked behind the counter, clutching his phone in his pocket, and followed Alex through the door to the back.

As soon as it closed, Alex pressed his finger to his lips and pointed down the short hallway. It all looked utterly ordinary. Shelves lined the walls, filled with boxes of coffee, syrups, flour, sugar—everything a coffee shop would need for day-to-day operations. An employee bathroom was close, the door propped slightly open. Another door looked like it led to a cramped kitchen, and the third was open into a breakroom. Dez

Alternative Liberties

couldn't see much in there, but there were sofas, chairs, a couple tables. Not much room to walk, but otherwise, standard fare.

Alex took a couple steps, then poked his head into the tiny kitchen. "Nance, can you help me out with an issue? Christopher Street problems."

After a few seconds, another figure joined them. She had dark brown skin and was a foot taller than Alex, which meant she was also taller than Dez. She wore a black apron, dusted with floured fingerprints, and an equally black shirt and jeans. She nodded at Alex, then gave the slightest tip of her head toward Dez. "Breakroom?"

"Full."

She nodded, then turned on her heel and went back into the kitchen. Alex roughly led dragged Dez into the bathroom and closed the door, whispering, "Just a minute." Dez's body trembled. Isolated. No one knew he was here. If this was a trap, he'd walked in willingly.

The door opened and Alex gestured him out and into the kitchen. It was empty, save for Nance. She nodded at Dez as Alex closed the door, locking it with a click. "Can't wait until we have the other baker here vetted. No offense, kiddo. Just easier." She held out her hand. "Sylvia sent you to find Marsha?"

Dez nodded and shook her hand meekly. She had harsh calluses that bit into Dez's palm.

"You're good," said Alex. "Don't want kitchen sounds leaking out into the dining space, so this is pretty damn soundproof."

"Coffee? Scone?" Nance gestured around. "Baked goods are just as nice as what we sell. They *are* what we sell. Coffee is swill because we can't fit an espresso machine back here, but it's caffeinated."

Dez backed up a step closer to the door. "I'm okay."

Nance's face softened a touch. "I promise you're not locked in here for anything other than privacy." She waved and Dez looked over his shoulder to see Alex moving to the side, leaving the door wide open.

"I'm sorry."

"No, sweetness. Don't apologize for watching out for yourself." She hopped up and sat on the counter, ankles crossed. "We're about ready to change the passphrase, so it's good you found us when you did."

Alex walked over to stand next to her. "So, you want to tell us anything? Or do you want to get down to business?"

The truth burned in Dez's throat. He *wanted* to tell them about life in Idaho, about the new church his parents had joined to "keep up appearances," and how they'd turned into "followers," and expected the same of him. He wanted to tell them about the billboards all over Boise reminding people how important the Council of Ethics was, and how much they relied on good, patriotic citizens like them to speak out. He wanted to talk about the basement meetings and the ban on any rainbows in public schools, and the internet blockade that kept anyone from looking up anything "deviant" without confirming their ID.

But he still didn't know them. Whoever they were, they probably knew the broad outlines. So, he said, "I came over from Idaho. This seemed like the best option left."

Nance nodded. "Well, I can understand that. You looking for an escort somewhere safer, or something else?"

"You do that?"

Alex nodded. "Not comfy. Sneak you out inside some boxes like we're taking a delivery somewhere. Stick you in a safe house for a while. Not great, but better than parading around the streets." He smiled gently. "Doesn't sound like that's what you came for, but the offer's on the table."

Alternative Liberties

He could get *out?* He could be free and away from the church and the state and presumably somewhere the Council for Ethics held far less sway. All alone. With his friends all stuck in the same problem, but with one less ally, and never knowing for sure what had happened to him.

Dez shook his head. "There was a... curriculum?"

Alex nodded. "You got a computer at home, right?"

"It's old, but yeah. My parents have the passwords for it though." He'd never seen them check it, but they could do anything they wanted with it while he was at school and he'd have no idea.

"No worries." Alex walked over to a cabinet at the far end of the kitchen. He pulled out a few boxes, then opened a small plastic bin and dug inside. When he came back, he had a tiny flash drive pinched between two fingers. "You make sure you never leave this plugged in. But it should be safe as long as it's on you, or hidden somewhere. It's got two passwords: the real one and the nuclear option that erases everything. Someone does get it, that'll send them to a different partition while it erases the sensitive info."

Dez nodded slowly and Nance chuckled. "Yeah, went over my head when he explained it to me too, but it works."

Dez took the offered drive. A folded strip of paper was taped to the back, presumably with the password on it.

"You want word on where to go meet other little queerlings?" Nance popped back to her feet, hands clasped in front of her. "There's a couple places in town where they usually hang out."

"Um, no." Dez had what he came for, and he wanted to get out with it as fast as he could. "I need to get back and catch the bus so I can head home." Which wasn't a total lie, but also wasn't really the truth. They didn't need to know that, though.

Alternative Liberties

"No worries. We're here if you need us." Alex walked over and unlocked the door. "Act like you're drying your hands when you walk out so people think we just let you back here for the bathroom. And there's an encrypted link in there where we update the script. In case you need us again."

Dez nodded. He wished, deep in his bones, that he could actually trust them. Instead, he walked out, wiping his hands on his thighs, and headed out onto the street. Then he opened his maps and found the library. They'd have computers there.

~~~

Dez again wasn't fully honest. He used a fake name and the address of a house that was still on the market to get a library card, then used that to log into their computer. He'd picked the monitor that was the most out of the way, but his hand still trembled as he plugged the drive into the tower. If this was legit, then opening anything here in public was dangerous. If it was part of some complex sting to catch "deviant behavior," then he didn't want it pinging off his IP address at home.

When the pop-up came on his screen, he entered the proper password: $ylvi@!--X8391.

Dozens of folders opened up with numbers instead of names. He opened the first one to see a nameless link shortcut, which he assumed led to the new script to use at the café if he ever needed to go back. Folder two had the same instructions he'd gotten from Alex on how to clear the drive if something came up. Also gave him a rundown on how to store files in the other partition, so it wouldn't just be a password-protected empty flash drive. It recommended some normal stuff, like assignments, but also something like a journal so that it would make sense for it to have a password.

The third folder had hundreds of documents. RTFs, text files, PDFs, JPGs, MP4s. Previews were all turned

Alternative Liberties

off, and the names weren't particularly helpful, just more numbers. So, he opened the PDF titled 001. When he did, he saw blocky black text on a white background: LEARN YOUR HERSTORY. The next page, Dez scrolled past quickly: it was a stone wall with "BE GAY. DO CRIME." spray-painted on the bottom in purple.

The third page was where the text began, and just reading about what he was going to learn here sent butterflies of lightning skittering around his belly. He constantly kept aware of his surroundings, but this all seemed legit. Some stuff rang bells, though he didn't dare linger long enough for someone to read much over his shoulder. The key words stuck out, though. Stonewall—they learned about that, where police were killed by people breaking up a child sex trafficking organization run by the mafia. AIDS was a disease, but Dez had no idea what that had to do with any of this. He knew the names Marsha and Sylvia, since they had helped get him in with the café, but, apparently, they were *important?*

Once he'd confirmed that the drive actually worked, Dez closed it, ejected it, logged out, and headed for the doors. Now, he just had to wait and see if the Council for Ethics would come barging in looking for him. If not, then he was free and clear to open this at home.

~~~

The bus got back to Boise late, which meant Dez broke curfew and was grounded from any electronics for a week. Even if he hadn't been grounded, he would have waited. Coming home late meant he'd be under more scrutiny, and he didn't want to push his luck. He waited a few days after his being grounded was up, then asked if he could go see Skyler.

His mom's mouth turned sour. "I'm not sure I like you spending time with someone like him."

Dez had expected that, so before she could say anything, or his dad could chime in, he pushed forward.

Alternative Liberties

"I want to be there for him. It's hard to overcome deviance like that." The statement burned on his tongue, but he had to sell this. "I don't want to abandon someone who could still be saved."

The frown disappeared from his mom's face and his dad smiled. They looked at each other, then his dad nodded. 'You can go over there this weekend. If his folks say yes."

"Thank you." Dez beamed up at them. "And I'm sorry again about staying out late. I really did just lose track of time."

"No need to keep apologizing." His mom ruffled his hair. "You're a good girl. Everyone makes mistakes."

The word had long ago lost its impact. They would always call him a girl. Even before joining the church, they'd never been on board with *that* "deviance."

~~~

It wasn't exactly to plan, but it would still work. Skyler's parents were dropping him off there, so midday Saturday, when a knock came at the door, Dez jumped to answer. His breath caught when he opened it and saw Skyler. First time they'd seen each other in months. He'd lost weight. He looked pale. He had dark rings under his eyes. His hair had been shaved down almost to the scalp.

And he smiled, then waved over his shoulder to his parents before they drove off. "Hi."

"Hi." That smile did a lot, but a heavy pit sat in Dez's belly. "Come on in. My folks'll want to say hi."

Skyler seemed to be moving a little slower than usual and Dez tried not to jump to the worst conclusions. Everyone knew the Council for Ethics, as well as their church, took their work seriously. Solving the "problems" of their charges was the most important part of the mission. Hopefully, the horror stories weren't true for Skyler. At least not all of them.

Alternative Liberties

They did a swing through, where Dez's parents lied through their teeth and told Skyler he looked "healthier" and "happier." They lied a little less, Dez thought, when they said it was nice to see him. And of course, his mom gave her normal warning. "Door open, remember?"

"Yeah, Mom." Then they headed upstairs to Dez's bedroom. He sat on the bed and Skyler took the office chair, giving it a brief spin.

When he rotated back around, he sighed. "I missed you."

"I'm sure you did. I'm the best." Dez looked him up and down. "Do I want to know?"

"Could have been worse." His shoulders bunched up all the same, but he didn't drop the subject. "Nothing like what Sarah or Nate went through."

Some of the tension unwrapped from Dez's middle. Sarah had been just shy of catatonic after her stint with the church's counselors, and they'd never gotten the full story out of her. Nate shared everything. He was mostly unchanged, but got jumpy any time someone gave him an accidental static shock from the carpet or whatever.

"You don't have to say anything if you don't want to."

Skyler rolled his eyes. "It really wasn't crazy. I'm not allowed to grow my hair out again, ever, which is balls. I'm back to three meals a day now. Eight hours of sleep. Plus, I can officially say I've read the entire Bible cover-to-cover. Twice." He sighed, but it shook, and it seemed like his eyes sank deeper into his skull. "I'm glad it's over, though. I missed my boyfriend."

The word had never sounded sweeter, which spurred Dez on. "I wanted to hang out so I could show you something. If you're up for..." he lowered his voice, "...deviance."

"A starvation diet and some sleepless nights hasn't change me *that* much."

Alternative Liberties

He still *sounded* like the Skyler Dez remembered. He sounded like the boy Dez had shared his first kiss with, and who had pretended to be sick so they could make a plan to explain why Dez wanted to cut his hair shorter, and who had run shirtless through the sprinklers in the middle of the night while they pretended everything was normal.

Dez checked out the bedroom door. When he didn't see anyone spying in, he popped in the flash drive, entered the password, then opened that initial PDF for the first time since the library.

"Holy crap." Skyler's smile somehow widened, and Dez chose not to notice how skeletal he looked with his thinner face. He looked at Dez. "It was real?"

"Either that, or we're both about to be in the biggest trouble of our lives." Dez took the mouse and keyboard. "Last chance to back out and just chill. I won't be mad." Disappointed, frustrated, but not mad.

"Nobody I'd rather learn with than you." Skyler checked over his shoulder and, when he didn't see anyone, pecked Dez on the cheek.

His lips felt the same as always. "Then I guess school is back in session."

Alternative Liberties

Alternative Liberties

Suka-blat

Robert Walton

"Suka-blat! It's cold!"

I looked at Ivar. At his knobby lump of a head, at his lips lying beneath his broken nose like twin dead slugs, at his eyes glistening beneath his granite ledge of a brow—eyes so small I never knew their color. There was no pleasure in looking at him. I looked away. "Why do you say this?"

"Because the wind cuts like a rusty blade."

"No, why do you say 'Suka-blat'? What is Suka-blat?"

"Just a curse—Kiev curse for when you have to look up to see hell."

"What does it mean?"

Ivar's brow lowered, extinguishing his eyes. "It's the worst curse of all."

"The worst of all?"

"The worst!"

He chuckled like a diesel engine starting on a frozen morning. "It blasphemes lovers, sisters, mothers, grandmothers even."

"Oh," I recoiled in mock horror, "even grandmothers! Saints preserve me!"

Ivar shrugged. "It should be reserved for the worst of the worst. I say it about the wind, but I don't mean it, not really."

"You don't mean it? Why say it?"

"Because I mean something else." His curled index finger motioned me closer.

I leaned close, almost close enough to smell his breath. "What?'

"Slava Ukrani."

I started back. "That will get you killed if the guards find out!"

"If they find out!" He grinned his nearly toothless grin, "Besides, curses become a habit. The morning wind, this camp—they're not so bad. My grandfather told me of the true gulag, Stalin's gulag. One in twenty lived. My grandfather was the one."

"Bah! Old men's stories! Stalin's gulag couldn't be worse than here."

"Peter," Ivar touched my wrist, "do we have soup?"

"The soup is snot."

"But we have the snot."

I did not reply.

"Do we have bread?"

"The bread crawls with weevils."

"But we have the weevils. Munch them! Savor the snot! You live, man! You live! This Putin camp is paradise. We could be in America, in a 'tender care center'!"

"Ha!" I poked him with an elbow, "At Mar a Lago, maybe?"

"Suka-blat!" Ivar's lips twisted into a knot of disdain. "And break bread with Putin's pig?" He spat. "Never!"

"I grant you," I looked beyond the wire at a horizon bleak with looming snow, "the pig turned America against us."

"He didn't!" Ivar gripped my arm hard. "He took away the tanks, the missiles and the money, but most Americans are still with us!"

A troop of guards carrying Kalashnikovs approached the gate. Two dragged a man between them. The camp commandant followed behind. Six guards peeled off, three to either side, and leveled their weapons. Two more slung their rifles and opened the gate. The prisoner's feet made twin furrows in the mud as he was pulled into the compound and dropped on his belly.

Three hundred men in the compound stood motionless.

"Who is it?" I whispered.

"Yuri."

"How can you tell? His face is gone."

"It will heal. Believe me."

The guards turned and paced back through the gate. Ivar stepped forward then. He went to Yuri, knelt, rolled him gently onto his back and cradled his head.

The camp commandant stared at Ivar. He was a short, slender man, like a banker or a pimp—a man whose work is to make others work.

"Drop him."

Ivar didn't move.

"Drop him."

Ivar stroked Yuri's blood-matted hair. "Outside the wire, we are yours. Inside the wire—we may care for each other as we can. It is the law of the camps. The unwritten law."

"I am the law."

Ivar didn't reply but continued to cradle Yuri's head in his battered hands.

Alternative Liberties

"You are the one called Ivar?"

"I am."

"You learned nothing from your time in Asovstal beneath the steel mill?"

Ivar said nothing.

The commandant nodded to the guards. "Bring him."

Two guards handed their weapons to men standing beside them. Four more aimed vaguely at the motionless prisoners. All six entered the compound. The two gripped Ivar.

Ivar glanced at me. "Peter?"

I nodded.

Then he carefully laid Yuri's head on the mud and rose on his own. When the gate shut behind them, we were forgotten. A dozen others followed me to help Yuri.

They took Ivar to a cement shed at the edge of camp called the goat pen, where they ask questions that require no answers. We listened to his screams — until they ceased.

A line of thirty guards formed in front of the wire the next morning. Two more came behind them, dragging a man through the new snow. The man's hands trailed beside him, palms up, flopping lifelessly. They reached the gate and dropped him.

We stared at the corpse. We stared at Ivar.

The camp commandant—chin lifted, eyes bright—paced forward, stopped in front of Ivar and smiled at us. It was a challenge.

Slava Ukraini.

It may have drifted on a forest breeze from pine needles nearby, or sparked from sunlight glinting off barbs on the wire.

Perhaps I whispered, "Slava Ukraini."

Dirty, battered heads — at first only a few — raised. Eyes long cast down sought other eyes, flickering together like moths swarming.

Alternative Liberties

"Slava Ukraini." We prayed, "Slava Ukraini."

Voices muted by misery rose from their isolation. "Slava Ukraini, Slava Ukraini." We chanted.

Raw throats then opened wide, and we roared - "Slava Ukraini, Slava Ukraini!"

For Ivar, "Slava Ukraini!"

The Commandant raised his right hand. The guards' Kalashnikovs rose with it.

"Slava Ukraini!"

Alternative Liberties

Doubleplusbad

Juleigh Howard-Hobson

When they rewrite all our truths
they call it history.
And when we say things don't add up
they yell conspiracy.

Alternative Liberties

Alternative Liberties

A Place Before the Storm

William Kingsley

The dismal afternoon gave way to a grim dusk, and shadows fell across the front of the cafe. Night would bring a violent storm ending the sullen oppression of the day. Everyone had left except the Senator who sat alone at a table in the back. There was a glass of Tempranillo, a plate of cheese and bread, and a British newspaper in front of him. The two waiters idled at the counter, watching American television.

A game show ended and American news came on. The top two stories were about a minor reality star arrested on a D.U.I., and the arrest of a *Washington Post* editor on charges of sedition. The D.U.I. had the longer story.

The Senator spoke.

"If you're going to watch news, at least watch Al Jazeera for real news."

The younger waiter cursed. "What difference does it make? News is news," he muttered to the older waiter.

Alternative Liberties

"No, it's not. Not to the Senator," the older waiter said. He picked up the remote and switched to Al Jazeera. The news from America was bleak. Cities burning. Protesters flooding American streets. Police in riot gear shooting tear gas and smashing people with truncheons. Armoured vehicles firing into a crowd somewhere in Wisconsin.

The National Guard had been mobilized across the nation.

There were no boundaries after the New York Massacre.

The Senator looked down at his wine glass. He held the stem of the glass and swirled the wine. He pushed his chair back and walked up to the counter.

"Thank you," he said. "You can turn that off now."

The older waiter smiled sadly. The younger waiter turned away and smirked.

"Certainly," the older waiter said.

The Senator nodded and returned to his table.

The younger waiter looked at his colleague and laughed.

The younger waiter grabbed the remote and switched to a popular American reality show.

"You should show some respect," the older waiter said.

"Respect? Why should I show respect?" the younger waiter said.

"You should show some respect for what he stands for. You should show some respect for what he tried to do."

"Bah! It was all air! Anyway, they made their choice."

"Did they?"

"Of course they did. And they got what they deserved."

"You know the allegations."

"Blather!"

"The U.N.—"

Alternative Liberties

"*Dejate de tonterias!* I gave twenty-five Euros to the Red Cross Fund for America. What have you done?" The younger waiter swiped at the counter with a dishrag.

"If they wanted to win they should have got a pretty TV star."

The older waiter glared.

The two waiters knew the argument by rote. It happened every time the Senator came in.

"Maybe it can be still—" the door to the café swept open and a Black man and a White woman walked into the café. They walked to the Senator's table. The Senator stood up and greeted them. The older waiter walked over to the table and took their order. They ordered a white wine and a local beer.

The older waiter pulled the beer from the draft tap and poured a half litre of wine into a carafe.

"I'm going," the younger waiter said. He took off his apron. "Nobody else is coming in tonight. Not with the storm coming."

"Why do you want to leave?"

The younger waiter looked over at the Senator's table and shook his head. The Senator was leafing through a sheaf of papers and his compatriots were leaning over the table, talking in whispers. "I have things to do."

"You're scared," the older waiter said.

"I have to get home to my wife."

"Your wife," the older waiter snorted. "Your wife! Sitting on the couch in front of the television, numbing your mind. Your wife running to the kitchen to get you another *cerveza*. Your squawking children running amok. You're as bad as the Americans!"

"My life is better than the Americans. And I want to keep it that way."

"No one's life is better after they closed the borders."

Alternative Liberties

"And what are you doing for your glorious revolution? Your *Movement?* What is *he* doing?"

"At least I have hope. At least I think my own thoughts," the older waiter said quietly.

"Well, I just want to be left alone. I don't support you. Or him." The younger waiter gestured to the Senator's table. "He should go."

"Why? Leave if you want. I'll close. I'm not afraid of a little rain." He sneered at the younger waiter. "Or a wife."

"No. He should *go.*"

"Where?"

"Anywhere. Send him to Canada. There's plenty enough of them there already."

"He's not going anywhere. No. He's not going anywhere. Not yet."

"And what happens when they send in their drones?"

The younger waiter tossed the dish cloth in the sink and turned away from the older waiter. "Monique! Monique! *Venez ici!* We're leaving!"

The cook pushed open the kitchen door.

"*Qu' est?*"

"Come. We're leaving." He thumbed toward the older waiter. "He can lock up. Again."

The cook went back into the kitchen and came out with her coat and purse.

"You're crazy," the younger waiter said.

"How so?" the older waiter said.

"You're crazy with your ideas!" The younger waiter was shaking. His face was red. You'll get us all killed! You and ...him!"

The younger waiter grabbed the cook's arm. As he hustled her out, she looked over her shoulder at the older waiter. She shrugged.

Alternative Liberties

"Enjoy your Movement, *hombre*. Goodnight," the younger waiter said.

The older waiter locked the door behind them and watched them go. It was the same every time. A ritual. But how do you win an argument against apathy and fear?

He wiped down tables and stacked chairs. He would wash the floors in the morning.

After a while, the man and woman scraped their chairs back and stood up. The Senator put all the papers in his briefcase and stood up as well. He shook hands with the two of them, touching each of them on the arm as he did.

The man and the woman walked to the front of the cafe. The waiter unlocked the door for them.

A low rumbling roiled through the night sky. The air smelled of ozone and dirt. The first patters of rain stained the sidewalk.

The waiter locked the door.

"Thank you for staying open for us," the Senator said.

"An honor, *Senor*."

The Senator settled his bill. He picked up his briefcase.

"Goodnight," he said.

"*Senor*. Perhaps another drink? A brandy on the house?"

The Senator shook his head.

"But surely you do not want to go out in the storm? It's already raining.

"Sit for a while."

"Thank you very much—*gracias*—but I have to meet some people."

The Senator and the waiter walked to the door.

The waiter extended his hand.

The two men shook hands.

Alternative Liberties

"God bless you, sir," the waiter said.

"And you," the Senator said.

A flash of lightning shocked the sky. Rain pounded down in a thick haze.

"Senator?"

"We'll have that drink tomorrow." He walked out into darkness and into the building storm.

The waiter poured himself a brandy and sat at the Senator's table. The café was silent, broken only by the crash of thunder and the hammering of the rain.

What are you doing? the younger waiter had asked. What can I do? he thought. I am weak. I am a little man. Perhaps my contribution is just to offer this man, this great man, a place, a place clean and well-lighted, a place to organize and plan.

He stared out the window at the fierce rain.

After two more brandies he pulled up the collar of his coat and stepped out into the howling storm. He would go home to his room and lie in his bed. He would think about the Senator out in the middle of the storm, embracing the storm. He would think about the Senator and he would think about himself, and he would think about all the people, all the weak little people like himself, all the men and all women of all cultures and all lifestyles from all over the world, but especially the Americans, sitting in coffee shops and cafes and bars and bodegas or someplace else, all thinking the same thoughts and all having the same conversation. A thought, a conversation, about resistance, justice.

He would lie in his bed, and just before daylight, there would be a blinding brilliant flash and then there would be a mighty crash of thunder and just before he fell asleep he would know the hard rain was falling.

A hard rain was falling all across the world.

Ms. Drake's Lesson

Lou J Berger

Ellen Drake stood at the blackboard, chalk in hand, staring at the words she had just written: *The Purity of the Founding Fathers*. The phrase hung there, stark and lifeless, mocking her. Her handwriting was neat and practiced—muscle memory honed over years of teaching—but it looked wrong. Each word scraped against her conscience.

Students sat in rows, a tableau of forced compliance. Heads bent, eyes glassy. Even at nine, they radiated a practiced indifference. It was a survival mechanism, and Ellen couldn't blame them

But Harper Parker was different.

In the second row, her seat almost perfectly centered in the classroom, Harper tapped her pencil in an irregular rhythm against her desk. Her braid was frayed, flyaway strands falling loose in small rebellions of their own. She sat upright, her chin lifted, her brown

Alternative Liberties

eyes fixed on Ellen with a glint of something rare these days—anticipation.

Ellen breathed deeply. That intensity was all too familiar. It was the same fire her daughter, Mae, had carried, prompting her to escape to Canada for asylum.

When running had still been an option.

Ellen's grip on the chalk faltered, and it clicked against the board, leaving a faint streak. Her fingers hovered over the blackboard's surface, frozen by the weight of what she was about to do. The script for today's lesson waited on the lectern, a familiar litany of whitewashed half-truths and lies, worn thin from years of repeated use.

"Class," she began, forcing her voice into carefully practiced neutrality. "Today, we'll discuss the Founding Fathers' contributions to our nation's values and how their moral clarity continues to guide us today."

Ellen glanced furtively at the black camera mounted high in the corner of the room. Its lens an unrelenting eye, its presence a weight. She felt its judgment, cataloging every movement, every inflection, recording and watching for the slightest hint of betrayal.

She faced the class, sweeping her eyes over the rows of students, careful to avoid Harper's gaze. "The date was May 25, 1787," she said, turning briefly to scrawl the date across the board. "Can anyone tell me why it's important?"

A pause followed. The room fell silent. A kid in the back row, who didn't know that his teacher was aware that he had a comic book between the pages of his tattered textbook, shrugged in obvious disdain and went back to reading it.

She continued. "That was the day of the first Constitutional Convention, which met in Philadelphia. A pivotal moment in—"

"Is it true that Thomas Jefferson, a Founding Father, owned slaves?" Harper's voice rang out, clear and deliberate. But not enough to interest the indifferent, bored glances cast in her direction.

"Harper," Ellen said carefully. "That's not relevant to today's lesson."

"I know, but it doesn't say that in our textbook. Is it true?"

Ellen, starkly aware of the camera and the consequences of straying from the approved lesson, felt her mouth go dry. "History," she said quietly, "is full of complexities. But, for now, let's focus on what happened on that day."

Harper's shoulders sagged, but her eyes didn't lose their intensity.

The dismissal bell shattered the classroom's silence and the students shuffled out in a slow procession, their footsteps scuffing the floor. Ellen erased the blackboard using long, deliberate strokes. Each sweep of her hand felt like an act of self-erasure, wiping away facts she could never say aloud.

"Ms. Drake?"

Harper's voice startled her. She turned, chalk dust smudging her fingers, to see her lingering by the door. The girl's hands clutched the straps of her backpack, her face a careful mask of calm. But her eyes—they burned with a quiet intensity that made Ellen's chest ache as she missed Mae.

"Yes, Harper?" Ellen kept her tone light.

Harper hesitated for a moment, then stepped forward and thrust a folded note into Ellen's hand. "I thought you might... like this," she mumbled, avoiding Ellen's eyes.

Before Ellen could respond, Harper darted into the hallway, disappearing into the sea of students.

Ellen stared at the paper, her fingers trembling around its edges. The classroom, now empty, felt impossibly still. As though the room itself was holding its breath.

She turned her back to the camera and held the note for a moment. It was made of rough paper and crackled as she unfolded it.

At the top, Harper had written: *"A nation that forgets its history is doomed to repeat it."*

Below, she had added: *"I know you're not like the other teachers. Can you help me learn the truth about history?"*

Ellen's breath hitched. Her eyes traced the lines over and over, as though willing the words to transform into something safer, something less damning. The weight of Harper's trust pressed against her heart, filling her with equal parts of pride and dread.

Ellen's hand instinctively crumpled the note, wanting to destroy the inevitable choice she had to make. She forced herself to stop, smoothing it out again with trembling fingers. Destroying it would be safer, but the thought felt like a betrayal to Harper's young idealism.

She folded the note carefully and slipped it into the pocket of her worn cardigan, feeling its edges press against her through the thin fabric.

She turned off the lights, plunging the room into darkness, then pulled the door shut behind her, hearing the lock click. As she walked down the empty hallway, the note felt impossibly heavy against her side, a fragile seed of rebellion that could grow—or destroy her.

Over the course of the next two weeks, Harper wrote many notes to Ellen, who, eventually, began writing notes of her own. Supportive but hesitant at first, then more detailed as they exchanged their shared perspectives of history. Finally, on a Friday afternoon, Ellen wrote a note inviting Harper to meet her, that night, at the abandoned church just outside of town, an hour after sunset.

Alternative Liberties

Harper's reply was an enthusiastic 'yes'.

~~~

They met at the door leading down to the church's basement. The beam of Ellen's flashlight threw a dust-filled beam that illuminated the rickety steps they navigated as they descended. A strong, musty smell of rodent droppings made Harper crinkle her nose. Ellen brushed cobwebs away from the girl's face until they stood on the packed-dirt floor of the basement.

"Is this it?" Harper whispered, her voice tinged with awe.

Ellen paused at the bottom step, her hand clenched on the flashlight. She glanced at the girl, noting the excitement in her wide eyes and the way she clutched the straps of her backpack. Harper was so young, so hopeful, and the sight filled Ellen with a pang of both pride and regret.

"Yes," Ellen said softly. "This is it. Stay close and keep your voice down."

She pushed open a door, the rusty hinges groaning in protest, and light spilled over them and into the darkness of the basement behind them. A stack of cinder blocks held boards apart from each other, making a crude bookshelf. On that shelf were a couple dozen books, survivors of the great purge that had made anything derogatory about America worthy of banning... and burning. A single bulb hung from the ceiling, its bright light chasing away the darkness that threatened to encroach from the dank basement beyond the door.

Harper gasped. "Oh my," she breathed, stepping forward as though drawn by an invisible force. Her fingers hovered over the book spines, trembling slightly before finally making contact. "I've never seen this many books together like this."

Alternative Liberties

"Not many have," Ellen said, her voice low but firm. "Not anymore."

Across the room, two people turned to greet them.

"Hello, Ellen," said a wiry teenager perched on a stool near a cluttered desk. A laptop computer, portable but powerful, was open on the desk, its screen glowing blue. "Who's this?" He gazed at Harper with a grin of welcome.

"This is Harper, one of my students. She's a stickler for truth and I thought I'd bring her here to meet everybody. Harper, this is Jonah. He helps us exchange messages with others who also want real history to be taught again."

"Like me?" Harper asked gazing up at Ellen.

"Like you, yes."

"Glad to meet you, Harper," said Jonah, extending his hand.

Harper stepped up and shook his hand exactly once.

Ellen motioned to the other person in the room, an older man with salt-and-pepper beard. "Harper, this is Mr. Cole."

Mr. Cole stepped forward and gazed beatifically down at Harper. "If Ellen vouches for Harper, that's good enough for me."

Harper gazed at him speculatively. "My dad used to talk about you."

Cole nodded. "I served with your father a long time ago,"

Ellen looked at Harper, who had moved over to the bookshelf and was running her fingers along the book spines. Her stomach knotted. Harper was too young for this. Too vulnerable. Yet, she'd taken the first step herself, entrusting Ellen with her safety.

"Harper," Ellen said softly. "There's something I want you to have."

She selected a thick book, its cover worn but still intact. "Here. This is *The People's History of the United*

Alternative Liberties

States. It's probably a bit old for you, but the history is factual and documented." She handed it to the girl, watching as Harper cradled the book like a revered relic. Which, in a government that no longer funded education, it was.

"You'll take this one home," Ellen said. "But you have to keep it hidden. Don't let anyone see you with it—not even your parents."

Harper's brow furrowed. "Why not?"

Ellen hesitated. Memories of Mae flashed through her mind—her daughter's bright eyes, her defiance, her belief in a better world. Mae had trusted too easily once, and it had nearly cost her everything.

"It's safer that way," Ellen said finally.

Before Harper could respond, a faint crackle of static broke the quiet. Jonah's head snapped up as a robotic voice crackled from his laptop. "...Report of unauthorized gatherings in the district. Repeat, unauthorized gatherings..."

Jonah's fingers flew over the keyboard, silencing the feed. "They're sweeping neighborhoods again," he said, his voice tense. "They're coming closer. This place will light up on IR."

"We can't stay here," Ellen stated firmly. "We're too easy to find."

"We'll move the books," Cole said, his tone steady. "We've done it before."

"Not with these new monitors in the streets," Jonah muttered, shooting a glance at Ellen. "They're watching everything now. No more slipping under the radar."

Ellen's fists clenched. The monitors—she'd read the circulars. Devices designed to broadcast every lesson, every word, to government review centers. She thought of Harper's question weeks earlier. The danger was growing.

Alternative Liberties

"Then we move tonight," Ellen said, her voice firmer than she felt. "I'll take a batch of books to the next safe house."

Cole raised an eyebrow. "You? Alone?"

"Yes," Ellen replied. "It's my turn. We have old luggage, just a couple of suitcases. Enough for all of these." She indicated the bookshelf with its precious tomes.

Harper tugged at Ellen's sleeve, her eyes wide. "Let me come with you. I can help."

Ellen knelt and rested her hands lightly on the girl's shoulders. "Not this time, Harper. You've endangered yourself just by being here with mc."

Harper thought about that for a moment, then nodded in agreement, clutching the book to her chest.

"Thank you," Harper whispered.

"For what?"

"For being like them," Harper said, her voice trembling. "The people in the books. The ones who stood up when bad things happened."

Ellen stood, her eyes filled with unshed tears. As her gaze traveled to Cole, then Jonah, then finally landed on Harper's young, innocent face, she felt something she hadn't felt in years.

Hope.

Alternative Liberties

The American Holocaust: A History

Louise Marley

To the members of the Doctoral Committee:

I must begin by admitting that I am fully aware that my thesis topic is controversial and may even put me at risk. I am willing to accept that risk, but I very much want to write it. My reasons are both academic and personal, as I will attempt to explain in this application.

The origins of the tragedy are obscured, partly because contemporary reports have been aggressively censored and subject to manipulation. Surviving accounts are rife with conflicting details, influenced not only by bias but, as I will argue, a sense of national guilt.

I will examine the origins in as much detail as is available to us now, two generations later. The presidential candidate at the time promised to arrest and remove all immigrants, and when that proposal was unpopular, he reversed himself. His advisors, however,

Alternative Liberties

the creators of the vast plan, called Project 2025 (P2025 hereafter), held undue influence over him, partly due to his nature and partly due to his age and infirmity. Despite his public denials, once the election was over, P2025 became the ruling document for the administration, and in its pages are the seeds that grew into the American Holocaust. My thesis is that, as mentioned, the men and women he had gathered around him disdained his influence with his core supporters, weakening his ability to command or control their obedience or, tragically, their actions.

It is clear from such reporting that has survived that the MAGA party neither questioned nor challenged the proposals contained in P2025; not until their own family members and associates were taken did they begin to realize both the scope and inherent evils of the project, which was by then fully implemented.

You no doubt know that P2025, unlike so many other documents of the time, is readily available in the Library of Congress, even though most other resources have been destroyed. It is clear that the American Holocaust was exactly what its proposals intended, although couched in legalese and political doublespeak. It is my intention to translate all of the more than 900 pages of this document into everyday language the ordinary citizen can understand, in hopes that the clarity of language will lead to full comprehension of its consequences

There was opposition to P2025, but it was weak, frightened by the threats of the candidate and silenced by the violence perpetrated by members of the MAGA party and covert censorship by the media, which was virtually under the full control of the oligarch class. There were two traditional parties at the time, something not everyone appreciates today. One was the Democratic Party, which tried to offer resistance to the detention camps, but which fell apart quickly before the

Alternative Liberties

weight of the financial resources of the candidate's allies. The other was the Republican party. A few politicians were left in the original party of that name, and they also objected to the persecution, but their numbers were too small. The norms of voting and following laws, which had held in the United States of America for more than two hundred fifty years, collapsed with stunning swiftness, which I will detail in my argument.

My conclusion is that the opposition was caught off balance by the speed at which these events unfolded. One horror followed another so swiftly there was little time to organize a reaction. The camps, as built, required little infrastructure. They were overfilled, the organization and management were negligent, and people—immigrants and citizens alike—disappeared behind their barbed-wire fences. The candidate who had triggered the disaster was no longer in charge but manipulated increasingly, as events intensified, by the very people he had put in places of authority.

All of this was recorded in the newspapers still publishing at the time. Though those accounts have been purged by the regime, some pages have been preserved, hidden deep in the stacks of university libraries, where they escaped the sharp eyes of the censors. Current thought is that most of the MAGA party were not readers, and it didn't occur to them that there were people who would risk their lives to salvage historical records. Publication of most legacy newspapers ended abruptly, replaced by the regime's own media, which was notoriously unreliable.

It requires a determined scholar—myself, if I may humbly say so—to pore for weeks through stacks of old newsprint in order to find the few that survived. I visited a dozen universities in half a dozen cities, taking care

Alternative Liberties

not to draw too much attention to the objects of my research.

The ones I uncovered will form the foundation of my thesis. My intention is also to draw parallels between the gradual collapse of the Western Roman Empire, the steady diminution of the British Empire fifteen centuries later, and the quite sudden disintegration of the United States of America roughly two centuries after that. The German Reich, of course, self-immolated in quite dramatic fashion, but those events have already been dissected by hundreds of historians. I don't feel there is anything I can add to their work.

Despite the two generations that have passed between then and now, I recognize the peril in publishing a thesis like the one I propose. The regime has softened somewhat over the decades, but there are still those in power who think this history is best forgotten. Erased, if you will. In order to convince you that I am committed to this work regardless, please allow me a brief anecdote, one my maternal grandmother shared with me before she passed away.

She was a little girl when the soldiers came. No one in her community of farm laborers and housemaids, she told me, believed it would really happen. The laws were specific, stating clearly that the American military could not be used against citizens of the country. The regime, however, claimed the people they were dragging away from their homes and places of work were not citizens, and therefore the laws didn't apply. According to my grandmother, they were wrong. Many of her family were citizens. She herself was born in America and was supposed to be a citizen because of that. (I suspect even some of you on the committee are not aware that at one time, being born in the United States automatically made a person a legal citizen. The regime changed that law in the first months of their rule.)

Alternative Liberties

The soldiers broke into my grandmother's home in the middle of the night. They hauled away her weeping parents at gunpoint, leaving behind my grandmother—a four-year-old child—with her infant brother and seven-year-old sister. For two days the children were alone in the house, until a representative from a religious orphanage—she wasn't clear what religion they were, but it was very strict, absolutely rigid—came and took them all away to one of their establishments.

My grandmother never saw her parents again. Her infant brother disappeared too. She hoped he was adopted, but they all heard ghastly rumors about what happened to the smallest children. She and her sister were left in the orphanage, where they stayed until they were sixteen and could go out to work.

No one taught my grandmother to read. She recited verses, along with the other children, but she didn't know what they meant. At sixteen, she was trained for nothing except looking after other children. She was hired by a wealthy family to do that, and somehow, because she was an exceedingly bright woman, she managed to learn to read, to cook, to sew—the skills that would allow her to take a better job—and finally, a position that allowed her to go to school. Ultimately she became a teacher, and even though the schools were strict about what she was allowed to teach, she liked the work. She met a nice young man, whose family had also disappeared into the camps, and they married.

But they were not citizens. The law had been changed, and they had been "denaturalized." (I apologize to the committee for the use of such an offensive non-word, but it was the one employed at the time.) So, with no warning, and with no chance to make a plan, my grandmother and her new husband were deported, taken to a country where they knew no one and spoke no word of the language. My grandmother didn't know it yet, but she was pregnant with my mother. A man in their new country tried to rape her as payment for transporting them into the nearest city. (The committee will forgive my bluntness, I hope. In fact, rape as a weapon will play a significant part in my thesis, I'm afraid.) My grandfather fought the man but had no weapons to defend himself. He was killed, only two days after they had landed in the new country, and my pregnant grandmother was abandoned.

She had, at last, one bit of good luck. A family of expatriate Americans was looking for someone who spoke English to care for their two children. One kindhearted social worker put them in touch with her, and she went to work in their home. She gave birth to my mother and was allowed to keep her and raise her alongside the American children. In time, as her charges grew older, she set about trying to discover what had become of the rest of her family: her parents, her older sister, her baby brother.

But no one knew. The MAGA party had not bothered to keep records, and as we all know, millions of detainees died in the camps, cut down by inadequate shelter, not enough food, and lack of medical care. They are buried in mass graves, with no markings and no identification. (Perhaps one day someone will care enough to employ DNA testing to identify the remains in those graves, but that has not yet happened.) If my grandmother's brother survived, she could never trace him. Her older sister had left the orphanage two years before she did and vanished into the subculture of non-American workers. My grandmother said she assumed her older sister had become a slave. It is a safe assumption, as it happened to so many that we can't begin to track their stories.

You will have gathered by now, I think, if you did not already know, that I am not myself an American. This is my adopted country. I am here at the university

Alternative Liberties

on a student visa and am at risk of being sent away at any moment. I believe I am the first to take on this topic, and I hope you will deem it a worthy dissertation subject.

At some point, perhaps when I reach the point of publication, I intend to call my thesis what it truly is: an apology. It's an apology to the victims. An apology to the family members who never saw their loved ones again after the persecution. An apology to their descendants. An apology to the world.

Again, I am aware that I am putting myself in danger by writing such a dissertation in these difficult times. I take on this project with open eyes and a willingness to meet what challenges may come. I would be grateful if, in view of my situation, you could give my proposal your earliest attention.

Respectfully submitted.

Alternative Liberties

Alternative Liberties

So Many Reasons to Despair

Akua Lezli Hope

There are so many reasons to despair
and yet we try, and yet we care.
There are so many things that we must do
to be seen and read, to make it through
the zillion other calls to watch,
to buy, and taste, to add a notch
on the conveyor belt of experience
that folks display, each to another
small, discerning demands are smothered,
carrying us to the great maw
where we sit bound, united in manipulated awe
So what are the ways that we resist?
Call on friends and our neighbors to insist
that we be shown, published, heeded, read
in addition to or instead?
A wearying endeavor to be sure—
yet we persist, write on, yet we endure.

Alternative Liberties

Alternative Liberties

Animal Control

Jonathan Erman

When I was a kid, we used to have rabbits as pets, but when the brain implant technology gave animals their own autonomy, rabbits became known for their ingenious political maneuvering, and now I can't even think of the animals without feeling uneasy. For some reason, cats on motorcycles and dogs running furniture stores doesn't faze me, but the thought of those *thumpy thumpy* legs in the halls of government makes me anxious every time. I adored my little floppy-eared Dimi when I was in elementary school, but nowadays his cousins are out there militantly lobbying for giant grocery store chains and global oil companies, and I'm just trying to get by on my part-time job at the video store. It's better not to think about it; if you want to keep things civil in conversations these days, don't bring up politics, religion, or the animals who run politics and religion.

Alternative Liberties

I had to go to the video store early one morning and open the place up because everyone else who would normally be there wanted to go to the big protest downtown. I rode my bike through half-empty streets, resigned to the autumn chill—there are strict quotas on car ownership, and I don't make nearly enough money to even think about getting a necessity waiver.

It was a relief to enter the shop and have the walls of VHS tapes and movie posters surrounding me. Video cassettes were barely a nostalgia item when I was a kid, but they had come back when Congress starting passing its culture and technology laws in the final years of the all-human administrations. Things like that and incandescent light bulbs were resurrected based on what those folks liked. Animals liked warm bulbs and keeping humans as analog as they could, so the culture and technology laws were kept up—and expanded—to "suit the needs of everyone" as animals stretched their political muscles. Turns out nostalgia and technological inefficiency made a lot of people happy, and after lifetimes of having no say about how things were run, the animals had a *lot* to say.

I flipped the front door sign to "Open" and took my place behind the counter. No one came in, but I didn't mind, idly flipping through the comic book the assistant manager had left behind. It was better than being in the middle of a screaming crowd; I had stopped trying to keep track of who stood for what, I just knew that if there was a lot of noise, I didn't want to be there.

The street outside was pretty deserted, but after a while I noticed a guy who kept passing by the large front windows, back and forth. He didn't seem threatening, just nervous, like he was trying to get up the courage to come in. I was starting to wonder if I should do something when the door chimed and he entered the store.

Alternative Liberties

"Hey bro," he said. He was a bit older than me, and he was wearing nice clothes that had been worn a little too often.

"Hi, welcome to BigTown Video, how may I assist you?" I said, mustering what I hoped was an appropriate level of enthusiasm.

He laughed. "It must be great working here, selling people all these old stories."

What was that supposed to mean? "Can I help you find something?"

He shrugged and started looking at the shelves.

"Hey, *Mr. Smith Goes to Washington*," he said. "That's about politics, back when it was only humans."

I gripped the counter to keep my hands from trembling. "Some people like that sort of thing."

"But not you?" he said, turning to look at me.

I grunted.

"So, you didn't watch the hearing last night?"

I made a noncommittal sound.

"It was awesome!" he said. "The poodle minority leader was like, 'take it and stuff it, Mr. Rabbit,' and the secretary of defense growled back, 'up yours, little puppy.'"

I winced. "Did the president say anything?"

"Old Eric? He was like 'good points on both sides, we'll let the system do its work.' Typical, really. Letting the animals do their thing and staying out of the way. I doubt he really understands the issues, at his age."

"Can I help you find a movie?" I asked.

He shrugged again and turned back to the shelves. "It just feels good to talk to another person, you know? I've been working as a chauffeur for a goat lawyer up in the hills."

I wanted to say, *animals are people too, even if you don't like their politics*, but I said nothing, just stared at the *Casablanca* poster on the wall opposite me.

Alternative Liberties

"I voted in one of the last all-human elections," the guy said.

"Oh?"

"People were already losing faith in the system; they didn't trust any established party to fix things. They were happy to start letting the animals take care of us for a change.

"We used to be so proud of our achievements! Unhindered growth was the key to everything. We didn't know where the deregulation of scientific testing would lead. Who thought the Supreme Court's religious imperative rulings that no one could be denied the right to use religion as an exercise of politics would one day include animals as well?"

"That's all in the past, now. Are you going to get a video?"

"Maybe some Skittles," he said, coming to the counter and pointing to the display case.

I felt relief that he was going to buy something. If anyone asked, I could say that he was a legitimate customer, and it would be easier to ignore all the talk about politics.

He counted out his cash and I gave him the candy.

"Thanks, bro," he said. "Maybe I'll give the empty box to my boss as a snack, eh?"

"Okay," I said. "Sure. Have a nice day."

I felt better once he was gone. I wiped the counter and hoped the rest of the day would be uninteresting.

The door chimed.

A duck walked in.

Now, ducks don't have hands, but since we didn't have a foot sensor, the door could be controlled by the duck's implant interfacing with the wireless technology in the door. It was good to know it was properly outfitted and up to code, because violations of the Animal Accessibility Act can really cost you.

"Good day," said the duck. "I would like to rent a movie."

We don't get a lot of animals in the store, but I knew what to say.

"Hi, welcome to BigTown Video, how may I assist you?"

Ducks have gotten pretty good at speaking, but even with all the advances in implant technology, and the resulting changes in their brains, their bills still have difficulty with human sounds. So, it turns out, when ducks speak, they sound remarkably like... a certain famous cartoon character of that species. To suggest that you think this is funny is, of course, horribly offensive.

The duck waddled through the store, looking from side to side as it passed the walls of film covers. I felt a momentary apprehension as it passed the animation section. If it took offense at some of the films we carried, there could be rough times ahead. But it didn't stop until it stood in front of the counter. It ruffled its wings and gave a little hop, but didn't try to go any higher.

"I am looking for *Watership Down*," said the duck. "Do you have this movie?"

Visions of being questioned by the culture police flashed through my mind. Did the duck have an agenda? I reminded myself that it was a free country as long as you let everyone else do what they wanted.

"Um, yeah," I said. "Sure. Let me get it for you." It was a movie my family used to watch when I was a kid, but it wasn't so popular anymore, and I knew the store had a copy available. I moved to the back shelves, where the cassettes were stored, and grabbed it.

"So... seen it before?" I asked, coming back to the counter.

"I hear there is a rabbit of great power in this movie," said the duck. "I will study him. I will learn how power

Alternative Liberties

in government can be applied. Maybe someday I will walk the halls of lawmaking and control."

Well, that was blunt. But I had to admire the guy; ducks were about as far down the political food chain as you could get, and it was easy to imagine him watching the movie, dreaming of being in charge himself. Still, I worried about his choice of role models.

"What constitutes power is really a question of perspective... " I started to say.

The duck became agitated, flapping his wings and honking. He settled down after a moment.

"Exactly. I hear it is a very advanced movie for its time, especially coming from England. My British friends tell me there is much work to be done there."

The duck had a point. Britain lagged behind us in animal power and influence and, in poorer nations, many of the animals were still the way they used to be. Wealth and legislation had combined to create our present world. In many countries, laws still prohibited animal implants, and anti-animal autonomy rights were strictly enforced.

I put the video on the counter. "Can I get you anything else?"

The duck stood quietly, thinking, then said "Do you have *The Apprentice*?"

"The movie or the TV series?" I asked.

"Either one," said the Duck.

I turned to the stock shelves, but I could see the empty spots from where I was, near the beginning of the alphabetical listings.

"No," I said, "all our copies are checked out."

"All right, just this, then," said the duck. "It will be enough study for now."

"Paying on credit?" I asked. He wasn't carrying anything, so I assumed he'd send the payment directly to the register using his implant.

Alternative Liberties

"Account on file," he said stiffly. The name came up on my screen, and I paused. It was a local family that frequently used the store. The duck said nothing, just looked at me as if challenging me to respond.

Suddenly, I understood. Ducks were often hired to clean gardens of bugs and other pests (the implant technology didn't work for such small creatures), and would sometimes live on the premises as well, often in a separate dwelling in the backyard. This duck must be in a situation like that, which would explain how he had access to a VHS player and what he was doing in the store. He'd probably asked if he could get a video himself to watch in the main house, and they'd said to go ahead and use their account.

I charged the rental. "Do you need a bag?"

The duck lifted his head and opened his beak.

I came around the counter and carefully slipped the cassette, in its nondescript plastic case, into his beak.

"Enjoy the movie," I said. "Come back again."

"Thank you," the duck mumbled around the cassette. "Good day." It hopped along and quickly left, no doubt eager to watch the movie and imagine living a life different than its own.

I found the display cover of the movie in the animated films section and pulled the tag for the copy the duck had rented. I put it in the drawer behind the counter and sat down on a stool. Except for the hum of the heat, it was quiet inside the store. Occasionally, I heard a car go by.

I thought back to the first time I'd voted. I'd shown the proper excitement, but deep down I felt like I'd been cheated. I'd missed all the human-only elections, and it didn't seem fair. Surely things had been simpler then, the issues clearer. One species, everyone equal. Laws for the good of all, not just those in power.

Alternative Liberties

I shook my head. Why worry about past elections, at this point? And with so much complexity in the world, did future elections even matter? Who could untangle all the threads and understand what they were looking at?

I thought of one thing I could do. I hopped off the stool and went to start spacing out some of the cases on the shelves so they would look more appealing to customers. There were more people on the street, now. The day was getting along, and business was going to start picking up. When the protest ended, maybe some of those people would come by, looking for something to watch. The strange man had commented on all the stories here, but hadn't left with any. The duck had come in and left with a title he was already looking for. I decided that the next time someone came in, I would have suggestions for them. I started thinking about what to pick and why.

Through the front window, I saw a well-dressed couple approaching.

I put on a big smile and opened the door.

"Hi, welcome to BigTown Video, how may I assist you?"

Sanitation Day

DP Sellers

The fires from the faerie grove had burned 463 days straight. The breeze carried the smell to my house every morning, flavoring the air and reminding me. *Oh yeah. That.*

463 days into a new government.

They told us the Faeries were infesting America.

Poisoning the soil.

The new administration promised to get rid of them. The way to stop them, they told us, was to burn their groves, the ancient gateways from the Fae World to this one. One of those groves was right here in New Orleans. They had a lighting ceremony and everything, complete with the governor smiling and glad-handing the new president.

What none of them knew was the groves, ironically, sprouted new growth as they burned, so someone had to be assigned to keep the fire going.

Four-hundred and sixty-three days now.

Alternative Liberties

The government could have stopped when they realized the futility of it, but this administration was stubborn.

I took a deep breath and crawled out of bed. My back ached, and I stretched to loosen it a bit before I pulled on my clothes and an LSU hoodie. I smelled a little ripe, but there was no point in showering this morning with the work ahead.

My phone chirped. I picked it up and found an automated government text telling me to be at the Port of New Orleans for my day's work. "The Port?" I said to the empty bedroom. Today was Thursday, which was designated Sanitation Day. What work was there at the Port? Cleaning trash out of the warehouses? I googled the location of the Port on my phone. Not to know the location, but the miles.

A little under eight miles from my home to the port. I thought back to last night seeing the car's gas light turn on right as I pulled up to my house. It could go eight more miles, yeah? In all the years I'd had the Grand Marquis, she'd never run out of gas. But times change and I can't fill her up when I want to.

The sweet smell of jasmine greeted me as I locked my front door and walked to the Grand Old Lady. The spring air was thick with the humidity, but the bougainvillea and ferns on my front and back decks loved it. In the distance, heavy gray storm clouds threatened rain that might roll in later in the afternoon or dissolve away as they sometimes did.

"Heading out?" a voice called.

My neighbor Tom sat on the front porch of his shotgun home smoking his morning cigarette, wearing a pork pie hat and a BLACK SABBATH muscle shirt over a scrawny chest. His knobby arms were corded with thin muscle from playing his upright bass for a local Black jazz band. He took a pull from his cigarette, eyes squinting through the smoke, smiling a sly smile like he

Alternative Liberties

alone knew a secret. He had a quiet life and didn't let the world worry him. I envied him.

"What day is it today?" he said.

I smiled and waved. "Sanitation Day." Tom had a bike, so he didn't worry about gas.

He nodded. "I'm heading to Parkway later to get a po'boy for dinner. Get you one?"

He always did this and never asked me to repay him. I think because he was almost fifty and single, and he saw me as a kindred spirit. I didn't mind. Some nights passed easier with someone to talk to. "Sounds good. See you tonight."

"Alright," he said and went back to smoking, staring at the horizon, thinking whatever thoughts he had.

As I drove to the Port, I kept one eye on the road and one on the gas gauge. I didn't know if the needle moved any further, but the red light stared back at me like a bloody eye. If I ran out of gas, I'd end up like countless other drivers who'd left their cars on the side of the road. The highway was full of stranded cars, hood up, tires missing, and windows broken. Poached to the frame.

The Port was off Tchoupitoulas Street, and turning a curve in the road, I saw a line of cars waiting to get inside the gates. Cursing, I pulled over. There was no way of knowing if the car had enough gas to wait that long, and my body was already wound tight from the drive over, so I found a side street and parked. I'd walk the rest of the way.

Thunder grumbled in the distance and black clouds hung low on the horizon as I walked through the gates of the port. People streamed from their cars, all looking around for signs of where to go. Women clutched at purses and men laughed a little too loud, wondering why Sanitation Day was at the port. Some faces were familiar from past Sanitation days, but I kept my eyes down, hoping to keep from conversation.

Alternative Liberties

Further into the port, a short line had formed by a soldier sitting at a folding table under a canopy. I'd never seen a military person sign in. Off to my right a brown military tent was set up by the warehouses. A Humvee was parked nearby and soldiers milled about, some holding rifles, others with clipboards.

"Name?" A bored voice demanded.

I blinked, completely unaware I was next in line. "Oh. Sorry," I said and stepped close. I gave the soldier (a kid really, probably just out of his teens judging by the acne) my name and a smile, hoping to either ease him or myself, I didn't know. Seeing the military here brought back memories from when Hurricane Katrina had flooded the city. Why were the soldiers working Sanitation? These things were run by citizen volunteers, usually. And why did they have weapons?

"Food or gas voucher?"

"Oh," I snapped my attention back to the kid. "Uh, gas?" Thunder rumbled from the south. There was an energy building around me I couldn't name, nor did I like it. It felt as though everyone had gotten bad news at the same time.

The kid reached under his table and came back with a taser. "Warehouse 2A," he said, handing it to me as if that explained everything. "Next!"

Another canopy was set up outside warehouse 2A, and I got in line.

More soldiers milled about here, looking bored. A banner hung on the warehouse wall proclaiming in garish red, white, and blue font: *Americans for America!*

"Today is Sanitation, isn't it?" a man behind me asked. I turned and smiled weakly. "I thought so."

He chuckled, frowning at the armed soldiers. "Why would we need to be guarded to clean up something?"

"And they gave us these," I added, raising my taser. "So, it's not for us..." I trailed off. Thunder rumbled again and the clouds were dark bruises against the sky.

Alternative Liberties

"Let's move it." A soldier sitting at the table under the canopy waved me forward. The blue plastic name tag pinned to his breast pocket said "BAYLOR." On the table was a thick stack of papers. "You need to listen up. Pay attention." He began counting slips of paper from the pile. "Take each of these and call out names. When you—"

"Sir, it's just..."

Baylor stopped counting his pages and glared at me. "You talking back to me?" A soldier standing behind Baylor heard something in his voice and straightened, watching me.

"No... I just... Sir, I mean, I... " my voice sounded very far away. Why was I letting this kid who was half my age fluster me?

"Do you want to be on the boat with them?" Baylor demanded, pointing a finger at me. It must have been smashed by something because it was bruised and bloody. A small drop of blood dribbled down the knuckle. "I'll fuckin' throw you on that boat and no one will give me shit. You understand?"

"I... " How did this happen? Why was he so angry? I wanted to show him the taser the other soldier gave me. Tell him I was here to do what they wanted, but would they think I was trying to tase him? I shook my head, overwhelmed. "It's Sanitation Day," was all I could say.

The soldier standing behind Baylor scoffed. Above, the sky rumbled.

Baylor glared at me. Would he arrest me? Shoot me? That was extreme, but I felt like my reality had shifted once I set foot in this port. A forklift rumbled past us.

Slowly, Baylor pulled his eyes back to his stack of paper. He licked his thumb and restarted his count. "Call their names," he said, in a low and threatening whisper. "Check them off and escort them to the ship."

Alternative Liberties

He thrust the pages at me. The top page's upper corner was smeared with a drop of blood. I grabbed the pages and stepped away.

In the top corner by the bloody smear was "Page 52." He had given me five pages. Each had a column of people's names in alphabetical order. I had no idea what it meant.

Further down, towering above everything was a docked cruise ship. Something about it seemed off, however. It lacked all the normal beauty and pomp I was used to seeing on such ships. No banners, no colorful signs, no crew with uniforms and friendly smiles welcoming you aboard. Just a white ship. Three anemic ramps sprouted from the docks leading up to three doors set along the ship's hull by the water line.

A horn blasted just then, making me flinch. What did this have to do with Sanitation Day?

The warehouse was a gigantic square of steel and cinderblock. The opening was gloomy, teasing at shadows within that swirled and shifted like ghosts. As I approached, a terrible stench and wave of despair struck me like a hammer blow. Blinking against the thick smell of urine, I peered inside.

Faeries. Hundreds of them. Packed together like cattle.

From within the shadows a wretched drama played out. An elderly couple clutched one other in an attempt at comfort or protection. Children sat in a circle on the concrete floor and a fae girl in her teens sat in the center holding a picture book for all to see. Three young men, wings spread wide (their membranes sliced and tattered from some fight, probably) and hands clenched into fists, stared a challenge at me. But most of the faeries hung their heads, staring at their feet, having given up any vestige of hope.

I looked down at the pages in my hands.

"Jesus, look at that," someone behind me said. I thought they were talking about the fairies in the warehouse, but it was the next voice that made me turn around.

"That's turning into a tornado!"

Behind the cruise ship, down the river, clouds like black and gray cotton candy swirled, gathering momentum, and forming a tighter mass that reached down, like a finger, touching the river, the tip turning brown from the muddy water of the Mississippi.

The wind's howling doubled, and soldiers stared at the brown waterspout approaching the ship. The swirling mass of wind and water kissed her hull and crawled up the port side like a snake and onto her deck. The mooring lines at the dock pulled, grew taut, and then snapped like thread. Waves crashed against the dock, throwing spume into the air. The ship rose on a wave, free of its mooring, her hull scraping against the concrete. A spectacular wave, one that should not exist on a river, brought the ship's bulbous bow up out of the water and tilted it over the dock. I had never seen that part of a ship, and to see it now, towering above...

After a moment suspended in the air, the bow began its ponderous fall, smashing down onto the concrete. The ground beneath me shook and I staggered, watching the ship, its bow grinding against concrete, groaning as its weight carved a path back into the churning river.

The waterspout jumped from the ship onto the dock and kept coming. I watched spellbound as the water slithered back into the river. The swirling clouds, reformed and tightened, veered towards us.

"Run!" the soldier named Baylor screamed, his voice high and ragged in the wind. "All personnel, evacuate the—" he staggered and dropped to a knee.

Alternative Liberties

I thought he was having a heart attack, but it was the *wind*. I blinked as it solidified into long arms with gnarled hands curled into claws that groped for the kid's legs, like a lover. The wind found a bit of pant leg and snatched him up, cartwheeling him into the air before he disappeared into the clouds. Everyone scattered, emptying the dock, as debris filled the air and the tornado swirled toward the warehouse.

I ran back to the faeries in the warehouse, ducking my head against flying papers and grit. Inside, I grabbed a nearby male fae's arm. He looked at me with sleepy eyes. "The tornado!" I yelled in his face. "Run!" He only stared at me, and I turned to the others to yell at them and stopped. Four other fae all shared that same sleepy-eyed look. Their lips moved slightly like they were whispering something, but I couldn't hear over the wind. Something slammed into the wall of the warehouse outside, and I turned.

A forklift was spinning around, doing doughnuts.

I shook his arm. Yelling to them all. "The soldiers are gone! You gotta go!"

The fae blinked as if waking from a dream. He shook his head clear, turning to the woman beside him. "That should be enough," he said, taking her hand. They both glanced outside the warehouse and then at me. His eyes were a clear blue that was so open and welcoming. The kindness I saw in them was too much, and I turned away, overwhelmed and unworthy. Outside, the wind was dying down.

"Thank you," the man said and touched my arm, smiling. He took the woman's hand and nodded. The two of them took a deep breath and simply walked away. First casually, then at a jog, and finally at a run. Others followed, trickling like a dam about to break. But not all went.

"Hey!" a soldier outside the warehouse called. The wind had died down completely. I looked for the tornado, but it had vanished. "Get back here," he raised his rifle, but faltered, thank the gods, and brought it back down.

It still didn't make him a good guy in my book. He could still radio his comrades back and they would arrest everyone here. Or worse.

Creeping up on the soldier's blind side, I pressed my issued taser into the fleshy side of his ample stomach and triggered it, stepping back and turning away from his convulsing body.

Time to leave.

The sign-in canopy was unattended, and I was about to turn onto Tchoupitoulas when I stopped, noticing something.

On the registration table, piled up perfectly as though the wind wanted nothing to do with it, sat a stack of gas vouchers.

~~~

"Holy shit! Did you hear the news?" Tom called to me when I drove up, the Grand Marquis's gas tank full. "A tornado hit the Port this morning!"

A headache had crept up on me while driving home. I tried to tell myself it was just the sun (there wasn't a cloud in the sky now) but I worried that I knew what had really caused it. I smiled weakly at Tom. "No. That's crazy." I just wanted to get inside, close my blinds and lay down. "Hey, I'm gonna pass on that po'boy tonight. Sorry about that."

My friend waved his hand. "Nah, no biggie. I'll save it. You look like wet shit, anyway. That sanitation work really did one on you." He cackled.

I smiled again and nodded. "See ya later."

I quietly locked the front door; I didn't want Tom to hear the latch and take offense. I threw off my hoodie and walked to the bathroom. Turning on the overhead light, I pulled my t-shirt off.

Alternative Liberties

When I was first given the sports bra, I'd balked at it, but it's worked for decades and the design has improved over the years. When I pulled it off, my wings drooped. A lifetime of binding had kept them weak and useless, like another pinky toe. The bright fluorescent light showed just how milk-white they'd become. I'd never wanted to look too long at them, to look at myself.

But that time was at an end.

I inhaled deeply, feeling my heart beating in my temples. I knew the old fae in the warehouse had conjured the waterspout, but it had taken almost all my strength to grasp it and steer it towards the soldiers. It had been worth it.

Slowly, inevitably, like the cruise ship's bow crashing back onto the dock, I unfurled my wings.

To my granddaughter, about to be born

Debora Godfrey

Ahra, at the date of this writing, November 19, 2024, you are one day away from being born.

I don't know what your life will be like when you read this. I want to share what mine has been.

When I was little:

Everyone dreaded summer, because that's when (mostly) children would get polio. Even if the child survived, the effects could be anything from paralysis to the child being sentenced to an "iron lung", doomed to live lying in a cylinder which did the job of the now-ineffective lungs.

Pregnant people who caught rubella delivered babies who were deaf or blind or mentally compromised, and sometimes all three. The children were most often sent away, to a residential school or an institution.

Alternative Liberties

Pregnancy for unmarried girls or women was unthinkable. In the eyes of society, reputations were often spoiled for life. Keeping the baby was scandalous, and mother and child would be spurned.

There were, however, few options. Even if the pregnancy was the result of rape or incest, the condition was considered shameful, and the woman shunned. "Back-alley abortions" were illegal, dangerous, and often deadly. The girl might be "sent away to visit relatives", actually sent to an establishment for "wayward girls", kept there until she delivered, the baby whisked away, to a fate unknown by the girl.

When talking about my high school classmate who was convicted of trying to burn down a church, people said "What else can you expect? He was 'that kind'." I had no idea what they meant until I went to college and had some gay male classmates. I didn't know women could be gay until I was in graduate school.

A married woman was referred to by her husband's name. When she married Henry Smith, Mary Jones became Mrs. Henry Smith. Except for close friends and relatives, her personal name was erased.

Children carried the surname of their father.

A woman needed a man's approval to buy property, and, for the most part, houses carried only the man's name on the deed.

A woman had no credit history, because everything was carried in her husband's name. As a result, women often could not get credit cards.

A woman was expected to dress up when going out of the house, even if it was just to the grocery store.

And then things changed:

My brother was one of the first to get a polio vaccine, and summer lost its terror. By 2024, there was only one person left in an iron lung, and she just used it at night.

"Rubella babies" in the United States were almost unknown, only 10 cases in 2023, because of widespread

Alternative Liberties

vaccination of both women of child-bearing age and children who had often spread the virus to pregnant people.

A pregnancy no longer had to be carried to term. Abortion was safe and available. Unpartnered women could keep their children without stigma.

Same-sex relationships went from the forbidden to the mundane. Mr. and Mr. became commonplace.

Women kept their own names after marriage. Sometimes both partners would hyphenate the names or combine them into something unique.

The surname of the children was determined by the couple, sometimes hyphenated, sometimes original, sometimes from one of the parents.

Women owned property independent of their married state. Their credit history was their own.

Nobody cared what a woman wore to the grocery.

The idea of sexual equality seemed within reach.

And now, it's all under threat.

Ahra, you may inherit a world where children die or are maimed needlessly by preventable diseases, where women's rights are slipping away, where life is controlled in ways I can't even imagine.

Rights and freedoms have to be fought for.

I thought we'd won that battle.

I'd hoped to give you better.

Alternative Liberties

Alternative Liberties

Not Civilized Yet

Nancy Jane Moore

The election proved
what I've been saying for years:
Not civilized yet.

Grifters, broligarchs,
and extreme Christians in charge.
Not civilized yet.

Cops and presidents
can get away with it all.
Not civilized yet.

Control all women.
Who cares if old people die.
Not civilized yet.

We're fighting once more
for the rights we thought we'd won.
Not civilized yet.

Alternative Liberties

The Hoal Book

Chaz Osburn

"Jacob, please awake. There is a delivery."

"So? Handle it—that *is* your job. I need sleep. Too many martinis last night."

"The matter requires your bioscan."

Jacob reached onto his nightstand for Amanda, his PA—short for computerized personal assistant. Instantly, the image of a delivery drone appeared on the monitor.

"Yes?" asked Jacob, wiping his eyes.

"I have an item for Mr. Jacob Hoal," it said.

Moments later Jacob was at the front door.

"Sign here," said the drone.

For years, no one has had to sign anything. All signatures were biometric scans. It was much more efficient this way, the oligarchy of tech titans that helped streamline government in the late 2020s explained when writing and reading were started to be

Alternative Liberties

phased out and "Let tech do it" became the popular catch phrase.

"Thank you, Mr. Hoal," said the drone as Jacob waved his hand over its visual sensor. "Where would you like me to place the item?"

"Huh?"

The drone turned, pointed to a shipping container in the parking lot and disappeared.

"Amanda, what's this all about?" asked Jacob, closing the door.

"It is the personal effects of your late grandfather, Rutherford Hoal II," responded Amanda. "The inventory consists of one…"

"Wait!" said Jacob, holding up his hand. "Who's da man?"

"You da man, Jacob," answered Amanda.

It had been 18 months since Jacob's grandfather—his only living relative—had passed away at age 111, and while the estate had been settled for two months, Jacob was not expecting anything for another month.

With great detail, Amanda repeated what was listed on the delivery manifest. When it was finished, Jacob sighed. "Pretty mundane stuff, except for the antique motorcycle. I'll probably end up selling most of it. What's the container code lock?"

"Four-eight-three-nine."

"Come on."

Jacob opened the front door. As he did so a silver ball the size of a marble dropped from an orifice in the ceiling and floated alongside Jacob.

"Amanda, tell me a joke," said Jacob, squinting in the bright sunshine when they reached the shipping container.

"What kind of socks do pirates wear?"

Jacob thought a moment before saying, "I give up."

"Arrrrr-gyle," Amanda answered.

Alternative Liberties

"Good one," Jacob chuckled. "How would I live without you?"

"Let tech do it," Amanda replied.

Jacob entered the combination and heard a click. He pushed the door open and waited for his eyes to adjust to the darkness inside.

"Jacob, I'm afraid I must return to my dock," said Amanda. "I detect that my Z1 ventricle stabilizer unit requires maintenance. I will be offline approximately 22.6 minutes."

Jacob was only half listening. He was more interested in checking out the antique motorcycle, which he reasoned was behind the stack of boxes facing him.

"Okay," he mumbled. "I don't really need you right now."

"Very good, Jacob," said the device as it returned to the apartment.

Jacob began to remove the boxes to reach the back of the shipping container. He had just set the third box aside when he was overcome with a feeling that he should look inside. So, he did.

Oh my God—books! he realized, quickly shutting the cover.

In an instant he imagined himself as a young boy at his grandfather's home in the mountains, sitting on his lap at Christmastime as the old man read a story. He was the only one Jacob knew who owned books. All knowledge since shortly after the war—long before Jacob was born—was dispensed through PAs like Amanda because the tech oligarchy had determined that PAs were not only more efficient, but also brought consistency to all learning and, hence, greater understanding to all people.

Breathing heavily and aware that his pulse had quickened, Jacob glanced around and, after

Alternative Liberties

determining that no one was watching, reopened the box. He counted the contents. There were four books. But what were they about—and why did his grandfather send them?

Maybe I should report this to the PACC, he thought, referring to the Personal Assistant Command Center in the capital city.

No, he realized. *Grandpa must have sent them to me for a reason.*

He paused and looked downward.

Curiosity is good, he thought, echoing another popular credo. *For without curiosity, there is no advancement.*

Reaching a hand inside the box, he touched the book closest to him. Its cover was orange and blue, and there was drawing of a row of children, their backs turned, with one child peering through a hole that appeared to have been drilled through the cover. He could tell the book was old. Very old.

For an instant, he thought about going inside to see if his PA was back online.

Amanda would know what this means. No—wait, I can't tell her.

Jacob glanced around again, then opened the cover and began to flip through the pages. Although he did not know what the words meant, he was able to tell by the pictures that the story was about a boy who appears to accidentally discharge a gun. The bullet then travels a distance, with each page showing the damage it causes.

I must know what this means, he told himself as he placed the book back into the box.

He was about to close the cover on the box when he spotted a black disc jutting from the bottom of the box. He recognized the object, having seen a similar recording disc in the Montreal Museum of Science.

"You always were old school, Grandpa," he said, reaching down to retrieve the object. "Hope it still works," he whispered, giving it a squeeze.

"Hello squirt," said the voice of his grandfather. "Obviously I'm dead, so I want you to listen carefully. First, you are now in possession of forbidden material. So, don't get caught."

Jacob let go of the disc and the recording stopped. He looked around and squeezed it again.

"Second, there's a reason I'm giving you these. They've been in the family for generations. In a way, they are our family. The big black book is our family *Bible*. It was published in 1857. The one with the picture of the white whale is called *Moby Dick* and is from the year 1952. The book with the red and black lettering and rendering of tropical plants was your great-great-great uncle's favorite, a little ditty first edition called *Lord of the Flies*. And my particular favorite, your great-great-great grandfather's grandfather's *The Hole Book*, which was published in 1908. I think the name of the book is part of the reason I like it so much."

There was a cough and a pause before the voice continued, "Look, I understand if you're freaking out right now. I did when my old man gave 'em to me. But it's important I pass them down in hopes that you will learn to read. Someday you'll understand why."

There was another pause, this time much longer than the previous one. For a moment Jacob thought the recording was over. Then he heard, "Learn to read, squirt. Learn to read. Don't let the PAs run your life. Do your own thinking. Don't just rely on technology. Oh—and don't get caught!"

Jacob let go off the disc and closed the cover of the box just as the silver ball that had accompanied him outside earlier returned.

"Is everything all right, Jacob?" asked Amanda.

Alternative Liberties

"Sure," said Jacob, shaking. "Why do you ask?"

"You have not made much progress."

Have to think fast, Jacob thought. "That's where you're wrong," he lied. "I checked out the old cycle and am just putting everything back."

"That is too bad, Jacob," said the device. "I was prepared to acquire video of you atop the machine for your social media feeds. I am sorry I missed it. Your followers will be disappointed."

"We can do it another time," said Jacob, placing the two larger boxes he had removed inside the container. As he pulled the door shut Amanda said, "Jacob, you forgot one box."

"No, I didn't," he replied, stooping to place it under an arm. "I'm taking this with me."

When he reached the living room and the silver ball returned to its orifice, Jacob said, "Amanda, please power down your visuals."

"Powering down visuals," said Amanda. "May I ask you why you made this request, Jacob?"

"Just doing my part to save energy—and the climate," Jacob lied. "When you were giving me the news feed last night, I recalled you saying that power usage in the North America Quadrant had risen three percent in the last quarter and GHGs .003 percent. Now, imagine if everyone powered down their PAs' visual units for just one hour each day each quarter—imagine how much electricity that would save. And how better our air would be."

"Power consumption would drop 11.27529 percent per quarter," said Amanda.

"Something like that," said Jacob. "But before you power down—who's da man?"

"You da man," said Amanda, its voice trailing off.

Seeing that a tiny red light on the PA control panel on the wall was on, Jacob removed the cover of the box on the couch beside him and picked up *The Hole Book*.

"How may I entertain you, Jacob?" he heard Amanda say. "Would you like to listen to music, or perhaps watch the game and review your social media feed?"

"No thanks," he replied. "I guess I am more in a mood to learn rather than be entertained."

"Learning on one's day of leisure is most unusual, Jacob. What would you like to learn about?"

"Books. Let me ask you, why are they illegal?"

Perhaps it was only his imagination, but Jacob thought Amanda took an especially long time in replying.

"Why would you ask this question, Jacob?"

"Just curious, Amanda. Just curious."

"Curiosity is good," said Amanda, "for without curiosity, there is no advancement."

"Let me ask you this, Amanda. Why are there no books anymore?

"Books are unnecessary, Jacob. In his landmark study of April 2031, researcher Dr. Rajesh Singh of Cambridge University proved that artificial intelligence units were more efficient at dispensing knowledge. Books became outdated, much like horses did following the universal adoption of internal combustion-powered vehicles in the 20th century and electric vehicles over the past decade. With the aid of PAs, humans now learn at a rate 6.897 percent faster than two generations ago and..."

"Stop!"

"What is wrong, Jacob?"

"I didn't ask for a lecture. Speak to me in general, layman terms."

"Very well, Jacob. As I began to explain, because of the change in the way humans learn, they can now process information much more quickly than ever before. As a result, humans are more efficient than at

Alternative Liberties

any time in their history. All books are now stored within the collective memories of all PA devices. There is no need to read."

"Amanda, recite *The Hole Book* to me."

"It would be my pleasure, Jacob. My database shows there are two books by that name. There is *The Hole Book* by American author Peter Newell, first published by Harper & Brothers of New York in 1908, or…"

"Yes—that's the one. Recite it."

"Affirmative. Beginning *The Hole Book*.

"Tom Potts was fooling with a gun (Such follies should not be), when—bang! the pesky thing went off most unexpectedly!" said Amanda.

"Slow down, Amanda," said Jacob. "I want… I want to imagine the story in my mind." He did not divulge the real reason for his request—that he wanted to follow along in the book, which was open on his lap, to learn the words.

"Why do you want to imagine the story in your mind, Jacob?" asked Amanda. "I am quite capable of creating a visual storyboard. It is much more efficient. Direct your eyes to the screen on the wall and I will proceed."

"No, I'm just curious, that's all."

"Curiosity is good," said Amanda, "for without curiosity, there is no advancement. Very well.

"Tom—Potts—was—fooling—with—a—gun—(Such—follies—should—not—be)—when—bang!—the—pesky—thing—went—off—most—unexpectedly!"

After 45 minutes, Amanda had reached the end of the story. Jacob burst into laughter.

Amanda said, "Jacob, I must inform you that you now have 78 social media messages and 12 queries from contacts inquiring about your health and whereabouts. How would you like me to respond?"

Jacob, still smiling, wiped the tears from his eyes and took a breath.

Alternative Liberties

"Tell them I'm a bit under the weather today and that I'll get back with them once I'm feeling my old self," he said. "But before you do—who's da man?"

"You da man, Jacob. Now, would you like to watch a football game or perhaps engage in a game of chess?"

"No thanks, I want you to recite *The Hole Book* again."

"Again?" asked Amanda in a tone that sounded surprisingly... human. "Were you unable to comprehend the story in its ancient language?"

"I comprehended it just fine, Amanda," he replied. "In fact, I found it quite amusing. Now, recite it again—this time at normal speed. But before you do, tell me a joke."

"What athletes should you never trust?"

"I give up, Amanda. What athletes should you never trust?"

"Softball players. Because they are underhanded."

Jacob laughed. "Okay, now recite the book."

Amanda did as ordered. Before the day was over, Jacob had read along three more times as he listened to the story. And though he did not know it at the time, he was reading at a second-grade level by the time he went to sleep that evening.

Over the next four weeks, Jacob repeated the process. He would have Amanda recite a story as he followed along in one of his grandfather's books. It began with *The Hole Book*. Then it was *Lord of the Flies* (which he did not care for) and several stories from the *Bible*. At the end of the period, he was able to read the *Moby Dick* without assistance.

And then one afternoon he received a visitor at his front door—a robot bearing the logo of the Personal Assistant Command Center.

"May I help you?" Jacob asked. In all his life he had never been aware of anyone being contacted—

personally or otherwise—by the PACC. He sensed that something was wrong.

"Please come with me, Mr. Hoal," the robot commanded.

"What is this about?" asked Jacob.

"Come with me," the robot ordered, grasping Jacob's left arm. He felt a sharp prick. Then his world turned black.

He awoke to find himself alone in a chair in a bare room.

"What is the meaning of this?" he demanded, rising.

"Mr. Hoal, it has come to our attention that you have been in possession of books for the past 29.42 days," he heard a voice say. "Books are forbidden. Reading is no longer necessary."

"What about thinking?" Jacob said calmly.

The comment went unnoticed.

"Why are you in possession of these objects, Mr. Hoal?" the voice asked. A holographic image of the four books from his grandfather appeared before him.

"Just curious, I guess," Jacob said sarcastically.

"Curiosity is good..."

"For without curiosity, there is no advancement," said Jacob. "So, let me go—*now!*"

"That is impossible," said another voice. It was Amanda.

"You are to undergo a reboot, Jacob. Your thoughts will be erased and new data will be entered."

"Reboot? I'm not a machine—I'm a human being!" Jacob cried out.

"You will feel nothing. The procedure is painless. Now, smile for a picture for your social media feeds."

Jacob heard a hiss. Gazing upward, he noticed blue vapor forming around a small grate.

Gas!

Alternative Liberties

Glancing around the room he spotted a glass panel along a wall. Above it was a small sign which read: "EMERGENCY POWER SHUTOFF."

Jacob raced to the wall, punched the glass with his fist and grasped a handle.

In an instant, every computerized personal assistant on earth went offline.

Today, a century later, there is a bronze statue of Jacob Hoal on the plaza in front of the World Central Library. And nearly everyone owns a copy of the book describing his efforts to teach the human race how to read again.

It's called *The Hoal Book.*

Alternative Liberties

Death of the God Emperor of the Universe

Elizabeth Ann Scarborough

"We had nothing to do with it. Personally, I thought it would be an archangel smiting him instead of that flying fire hazard vaporizing him."

The talking head vanished and Bert Bacher, lead host of The Innocent Bystander podcast, cut the interview feed and addressed the listening audience. "That was Minister Milt Wilkerson, former Secretary of Religion in Education, speaking following today's events. His statement seems to confirm reports that whatever it was that carried out the attack had wings, so it seems to rule out space lasers and support the eyewitness reports of an alleged dragon sighting in the vicinity of the God Emperor's helicopter.

"Our team here at the INNOCENT BYSTANDER podcast obtained this audio from an earlier broadcast by SERF News' Phil Phillips."

Alternative Liberties

Phillips' report began: "Folks, dawn is breaking over the Yellowstone/Absaroka Industrial Park, site of a portion of the former national park. Visibility here this morning is great now that what were once mountain peaks have been flattened. The former mountain tops have been used to fill local valleys which used to hold nothing but wildflowers and a few bison or antelope. Once the mining is completed the land will become useful for real estate development or commercial use. That white object there in the middle of the project is actually a lake that provides the mining efforts with water and acts as a holding tank for runoff. It's a promising operation and The God Emperor himself is coming today to view the project and consult with the engineers. In fact, I hear his chopper now. There it is, folks, shiny and golden in the sun, matching the golden throne toilet that always accompanies His Imperial Highness.

"Ah, it's landed, and the crew have unloaded the iconic and ingenious golden throne/porta potty so the GEOTU can be perfectly comfortable even out here in this wilderness overseeing the progress of this project.

"Plumes of smoke rise up from the fissures as if to greet the illustrious guest...."

(pause and commercial break)

"And here he is in all his glory, wearing the golden Carharts that are, we understand, his usual attire for working events like these although he has not yet donned his golden hard hat but is sporting the Maharajah-style heavily jeweled turban, a gift from the ambassador of India.

"He's walking up to a microphone now. Let's listen. He's saying, 'Gentlemen, I...' Wait! What's this? Something is streaking through the sky from the tourist area. A drone maybe, though it's too fast to see. The Emperor's guards are closing in to shield him but that thing is beaming what seems to be a laser or some sort

Alternative Liberties

and—OMG! The guards are too late. The Emperor, the turban, and his golden throne have all disappeared, incinerated or vaporized, it's hard to tell, in that bolt of flame. What the actual f!"

The feed from Phillips switched back to Bert, who continued:

"Thus far no group has taken responsibility for deploying what is now described as a dragon that as you heard in the previous report, unalived the God Emperor of the Universe earlier this morning—though many have admitted they'd like to claim the credit. Investigations are ongoing."

"How so are they ongoing?" Ernie, the co-host of the Innocent Bystander podcast, asked. "Who's been questioned? I understand the wilderness area contains one of the largest state-run convent/brothel institutions in the West, nicknamed Our Lady of Perpetual Conception. Have they allowed investigators to speak to any of the women sequestered there? It is no secret that many of them have been unhappy about the edict demanding that all women not currently mothers must remain under state supervision while they fulfill their maternal destiny. Has anyone suggested that in between diaper changes one of them might have slipped past the electronic sensors to hijack equipment their men might have? Maybe someone has a dragon simulation with a flamethrower?"

Bert dismissed the question, saying, "From what I've heard, caring for the children and providing services to the incipient fathers keep those girls too busy to bother themselves with subversion. Besides, they're pretty closely monitored."

"Well, maybe the environmentalists sicced the dragon on him," Ernie pressed further. "We've all heard the fuss they're raising about fracking and the mining operations. They tried to block the sale of the public lands to the corporations."

"Yes," Bert agreed. "And for that, most of them are now under guard, put to work picking fruit and cotton and curing tobacco and all that sort of thing. No migrant workers to do the job and most other people not willing to do the work since the GEOTU forcibly deported them all. It's made for shortages in the work force and GEOTU said that if these people, whether they were scientists, journalists, doctors, professors or students, if they were so concerned about the Earth they shouldn't object to getting their hands dirty."

"I suppose we'll never know then, will we?"

"Not unless someone interviews the dragon," Bert said.

"Now there's a concept," Ernie said. "Speaking of concepts—my sister is interned at Our Lady of Perpetual Conception but she's a rockhound. She had a degree in geology before GEOTU ascended the throne, but she's now too old to make babies so they let her hunt for pretty rocks that might indicate the presence of oil or minerals for corporate use. She's one of those environmentalists I was telling you about. She likes the fresh air and exercise and smelling something other than dirty diapers and baby puke, but she hates how her work gets used."

"Can't have everything, I guess," Bert said.

"I'd like to get a lady's perspective on what happened to GEOTU. I'm giving her a call."

A few minutes later:

~~~

"So, Sis, what's your take on the news?" Ernie asked.

"What news is that? I'm halfway up a mountain at the moment," Caroline informed him.

"Oh, call me when you get down, okay?"

"No, we can talk. The reception up here is great."

"I'm talking about the alleged dragon that allegedly vaporized GEOTU this morning. You didn't hear?"

"No! Vaporized, you say? Does that mean our dear leader is actually dead?"

"Apparently, allegedly. Obviously, the habeas corpus situation is a bit—er—in the wind I guess you could say, and so far, nobody has admitted to being behind it." Ernie gave her a brief summary of the groups of people possibly offended enough by the great man to have dispatched the dragon. "It would have been easier to figure out if it had been space lasers. Obviously, it must have been robotic. I haven't heard that Japan, leader in world robotics design, is among the countries he's alienated. So far as we know, he hasn't encountered actual aliens yet so that probably rules them out unless they just did it, you know, on principle."

"Well, yeah, but you're overlooking the obvious, bruh."

"What's that?"

"That it really was a pissed-off actual dragon."

"Hey, I'm being serious here," Bert said. "Our podcast has 15,000 followers now and we'll get shut down if it seems like we're making jokes about the great leader."

"I'm just saying consider the possibility. If what it says about dragons in their backstories from those games we used to play back before the GEOTU took over are basing their lore on something real, dragons supposedly live underground and maybe—maybe they were rudely awakened by the fracking and drilling in formerly pristine places."

"Yeah, but the GEOTU didn't hang around the drilling sites or anything—how, assuming you're right and the killer was an autonomous dragon, would it know who to target?"

"IDK, Bert. Maybe it was his aroma—does he still carry that stupid gold porta-potty with him everywhere?"

"He does. And since his hair loss he's been sporting a jewelled turban that once belonged to a maharajah. Why?"

"Dragons are supposed to have hoards and like gold and jewels," she said. "Maybe the one who took him out was after that?"

"Nah, the turban was vaporized with him. I think in spite of what people think they saw, it must have been space lasers. Don't fall off the mountain."

Technically, Caroline was not on a mountain, she was in it. Inside a deep ancient mine shaft pre-dating the former park. She and her fellow inmates at Our Lady of Perpetual Conception had discovered the system of tunnels and shafts and befriended the resident some time ago. Since the current government policies dictated that all females must bear as many children as possible as soon as they were physically able, there were none of the virgins that dragons of old supposedly preyed on.

"I've brought you something that might soothe your stomach," she said to the great winged beast burping and farting fire. Among the flames was a pool of molten gold and a small pile of gems. "You really took one for the team there, mighty dragon. Other men may drill and blast your caves or loot your hoards, but after what you did, I think you've bought some time for us all."

The dragon devoured the medicine, gave a much milder and less incendiary burp, and settled down with its head on its front feet, wings folded, closed its eyes, and slept.

Moctezuma's Rescue

Loren Davidson

"Norman?"

His head jerked up at the unexpectedly familiar voice calling his name. He turned to seek out its source. "Rob?"

His younger brother looked much the same as he remembered, perhaps a few more pounds on his frame and the beginnings of a few grey hairs at his temples. He stood inside the open door of Antonio's bar, backlit by the afternoon sun.

"It's really me, Norm!" Rob came over and they hugged briefly, then held each other at arm's length, checking each other for the things they remembered and the bits that had changed since their last meeting, nearly ten years ago.

Norman knew that his skin was darker and his hair lighter than it used to be, the result of years of working in the Costa Rican sun at his eco-farm. He'd lost a bit of weight as well. While he ate extremely well and in quantity, he did enough work on a daily basis to burn it all off and occasionally a bit more.

He tossed off the rest of his shot of *aguardiente* and took a sip from a tall glass of ice-chilled Imperial. He pointed at the empty barstool next to him. "What brings you to this corner of the world? Can I get you something?" He motioned to Marco, the bartender, to come over.

"You're not easy to find." Rob took the offered seat and ordered an Imperial, no ice.

"I haven't tried to be. Especially not since... " Norman waved a hand vaguely northward.

Rob had the good sense to drop his eyes. "You were right. Right about it all." He paused. His beer showed up, glistening in the sweat of a cold object in a warm and humid climate. He ignored it. "They took Mom."

"They *what*?" Norman had expected a lot of what had happened in the US since the reelection of Trump. The mass roundups, the "relocation camps," the states of emergency in each place. But... "Mom was one of their biggest supporters. What happened?"

"She was at the store. Everything's been so expensive because of the tariffs. She got upset with a clerk at the supermarket because they were out of eggs. Word must have gotten back to the Peace Force, and they came to the house late that night and took her."

Norman frowned. He tried to pay as little attention as possible to the increasingly depressing news coming out of the US, such as it was. Much of what he heard had doubtless been sanitized, of course, to make the new government look good and everyone else look like The Enemy. Most of his news came from foreign sources, and a lot of that was obviously incomplete.

What he heard was bad enough. Conditions in the camps were worse even than during the original test run, as he called it, back in 2018 or so. People disappeared and went in; they almost never came back out. Any information on what went on there beyond what the whitewashed US news reported was fragmentary and smuggled out. Even though he had left home for Costa Rica on the heels of one incandescent argument with Mom, never to return, this was a lot to absorb. He picked up his beer and took a long swig, as much to give himself time to think as anything else.

"Norman?" Rob's voice was strained. "Aren't you going to say anything?"

"What do you want me to say? I'm not thrilled that this happened to her. But I knew that sooner or later, that *perro loco* and his crazy henchmen would turn on their own. They can only round up so many so-called illegals before needing to start on their 'enemies within' in order to keep the numbers up, keep feeding those camps. The camps are private. They get paid by the head. "

"But aren't you going to do something?"

Norman sighed. "Rob, I haven't been back since 2019. I don't even have a driver's license there anymore, and I only got my passport renewed a couple of years back so that the government here wouldn't kick me out for not having one. I'm one guy who left for a reason, and there isn't one whole heck of a lot I could do if I wanted to. I'm a farmer, not a freedom fighter." Norman fudged that last a bit. He'd gone out of his way to hire refugees heading south from the US, people who'd been deported or left ahead of the roundups. A couple of them had made homes for themselves there in Naranjo. It might not have been much, but it was what he could do for those displaced by *gringo* idiocy.

"God damn it Norm!" Rob's face was flushed. "This is Mom. I don't care what problem you had with her, she's still our mother. How can you just sit there?"

Alternative Liberties

"If you can tell me just one goddamn thing I can do that won't simply land me in a cage next to her, I'll listen. But I don't think there is."

Rob snorted in disgust and stormed out of the bar. Norman thought about calling after him, then thought better of it. Perhaps he'd stay in town long enough that they could talk again and maybe work through their disagreement. But he truly didn't know what else to suggest.

"*Señor* Norman?" Marco leaned over the bar, speaking quietly. "Is there anything I can do to help?" He asked in Spanish, of course—*¿Hay algo que pueda hacer para ayudar?* —but after eight years living like a Tico, Norman's ability to speak and understand Spanish was nearly fluent.

Norman shook his head, replying in Spanish. "No, I don't think so. Just another Imperial and an *aguardiente, por favor.*" He finished that round and one more, but didn't taste them.

He returned to Antonio's at his usual time every day, after completing work at the farm. But Rob never showed up again, and rumor was he'd left town.

A couple of weeks later, he sat at his usual spot at the bar, nursing his second beer. After Rob's visit, Norman had spent a bit more time catching up on the news out of El Norte, and it wasn't helping his mood at all. Things in the camps were especially bad, and he found himself worrying about his mom.

Mario leaned over the bar. "*Señor* Norman? I have news that you might find interesting." Norman nodded, encouraging Mario to continue. "I have a cousin who used to work in El Norte. He came back home after your last election, but he still has friends and was willing to ask some questions on your behalf. There is a man in Mexico, Jacinto. He says they've found your *madre* and can get her out. There is a cost."

Alternative Liberties

"Isn't there always? I know how these things work, Mario." *When it isn't a scam.*

"As do I. But my cousin swears that Jacinto is honest. He is helping people out of the camps and across the border. He says that some of the guards are unhappy at what they have to do to keep their jobs, so they help as many of the people leave the camps as they can."

Norman was silent for a moment. He was still positive that his mom had likely contributed to her own situation—what was the old joke about crocodiles eating people's faces? But nobody deserved the treatment he'd been hearing about. Not even his mom. "*Cuanto?*" he asked Mario. *How much?*

~~~

I must be crazy, Norman thought. He was driving through gently rolling brown hills north of Chihuahua, Mexico, in a somewhat dusty rented Ford that had seen better days. It was drier and hotter than what he was used to in Costa Rica. The air conditioning didn't work, and the dust was a near-constant tickle in the back of his throat.

He'd talked both with Mario and Mario's cousin Benedicto; together they'd convinced him that this Jacinto was at least moderately honest and honorable. The tunnels and other passages that had formerly been used to smuggle people into the US were now being used to smuggle refugees and escaped detainees out. Guards often tended to look the other way. As long as the "undesirables" were leaving, they didn't much care. And while his own online sleuthing skills were rusty from disuse, he'd gathered enough information to confirm a lot of what he'd been told.

Which explained why, after flights to Mexico City and then Mazatlán, he was now making his way north to meet this Jacinto outside the little town of

Alternative Liberties

Moctezuma, south of the refortified border with the US. He had been given directions to a safe house where he would wait for his mom, where escapees were brought after their crossing.

It's a pity the original Moctezuma couldn't fight harder, he mused. *Europeans haven't done well by this continent or her peoples. If only we could inflict his "revenge" on everyone who's supported this travesty. They're way too full of it.*

He'd converted about twice as many Costa Rican colones into pesos as he was told he would need. After all, he was used to prices for black market items going up unexpectedly, and there would be the unofficial "tolls" to gangs and *morditas* to the police. He'd only been stopped three times so far, and considered himself fortunate.

He still wasn't entirely sure why he was doing this, other than "she's my mom." He had no clue how to get her back out of Mexico—home to Costa Rica or anywhere else—without documentation. Perhaps Jacinto knew someone who knew someone. Nor did he know whether his mother would be happy to see him, or would spit in his face and blame him for her presence in what she used to call a "shithole country," echoing that man she'd supported. He sighed, for perhaps the hundredth time on this trip. *I suppose I'll worry about that if it happens.*

The safe house was a sprawling hacienda, right where his directions had said. Armed guards greeted him at the gate, of course. He gave them the code phrases he'd been given and was passed through to the house.

Jacinto came out from behind a massive old mahogany desk to shake Norman's hand. One of the smaller rooms off the entryway had been turned into an office, and this was where they met. Jacinto looked to

Alternative Liberties

be perhaps in his thirties by how he moved. His face looked older than the rest of him, seamed with the marks of hard living. His Spanish had a faint American accent. He wore a cotton shirt of local make over faded jeans; he and his clothing were impeccably clean.

"Gracias para ir aquí." *Thank you for coming here.* "Our people have your mother. She is with a group of perhaps a dozen others. Tonight, perhaps tomorrow night, they will cross the border and come here."

"Thank you. Do you have a place where I can wait?"

"We have a room you can sleep in. You are welcome to eat with the others. Your Spanish is good, *sí*?"

Norman smiled. "After eight years living in Costa Rica, I should hope so." He pulled out the envelope he'd been carrying inside his clothes since Mazatlán. "It should all be here. You can count it if you feel the need."

Jacinto took the envelope. "There is no need. You have been spoken for. This money helps feed everyone here and provides what we need to bring our people home. Most of the time we don't bring gringos—they can attract too much attention—but a few dollars or pesos in the right places can ease the way."

I certainly know that, Norman mused. "I appreciate your willingness to help."

"She is family, right? Family must take care of family." He indicated the door. "Oscar will show you around the hacienda. I will let you know when your mother is coming."

His "tour" was about as limited as expected, given the nature of what was being done there. He was assigned a bunk in a bedroom with about eight others, shown the bathroom and kitchen, and escorted back out to his rental car to get what little he'd brought along. Mostly a couple of changes of clothes and his bathroom things. He already knew to lock everything else in the trunk, just in case. He lingered in the kitchen and dining area long enough to get a bowl of a fairly rich and tasty soup, along with some rice, beans, and a couple of tortillas. He wished he'd brought along a bottle of Salsa Lizano from home. He'd make do without.

The rest of that day and all of the next were spent mostly in the bunk room, occasionally in the company of others, all Latinos from different places. Nobody volunteered much information about themselves. Again, as he expected.

At some point during his second night, he was awakened from an uneasy sleep by a hand shaking his shoulder. "*Señor*," it said in a loud whisper, "your *madre*, the others... *han llegado.*" *They have arrived.* He got up and dressed, quickly and quietly so as to not wake people sleeping in the other bunks, and followed his guide downstairs.

He smelled them before he saw them, the harsh and sour stink of undernourished, unwashed bodies. He was led into a spacious living room which he'd only seen in passing before. There were about a dozen of them, almost all Hispanic and likely all from other places in Central and South America. They were huddled in thin blankets on the sofas and chairs, several clutching mugs which he knew from the smell to be full of the hacienda's "eternal soup." *They look like lost souls back from Hell,* he thought.

And then he spotted his mom, wrapped in a blanket like the rest. Her comparatively pale skin was buried beneath layers of grime. She sat on one of the sofas talking with another refugee, in what looked like a mix of English and halting Spanish. He walked toward the sofa. "Mom?"

She looked up, looked around. Saw him, threw off her blanket, and ran to embrace him in the tightest hug he could ever remember receiving from her. She was filthy, she stank, and he could feel her bones beneath the ragged clothing she wore. And yet, he could think of no better place to be just then.

"You came. You got me out." Tears streamed down her face and cut channels in the accumulated grime on her cheeks. "Thank you."

Alternative Liberties

Legacy

Larry Hodges

They hate me. All of them, even the ones who pretend to be Trumpers but have always been never-Trumpers. Never has a president been treated so badly. It justifies everything I'm going to do. I gestured with a half-eaten fried chicken leg at the large polycarbonate tube mounted to the floor. In just a few minutes, I'll go into that stasis field, a million years will pass in an instant, and then I'll be King of the Galaxy.

"Sir?" It was Vance, my backstabbing Vice President with his ridiculous beard, slick clothes, and nauseating cologne. In fifteen minutes that what's-his-name Democrat, Peter Butt-something, takes the oath of office and allegedly becomes president. *Hah!* That'll never happen.

"*Yes?*" I said, dripping as much sarcasm into the word as possible. I bet it scared him. "Ready to apologize yet?"

Alternative Liberties

"Sir, I can't help it. All the judges, election officials, and observers say we lost."

"They were all part of it. Jealous of the most successful administration ever. I won by a landslide. Everybody knows it." I glared at Vance, and of course he looked away like the guilty hack he was.

We were betrayed. It was supposed to be taken care of—damn you, Elon Musk! All that work on an amendment so I could run for a third term... wasted. I took a last bite and tossed away the chicken leg, snickering when it struck Vance, leaving a crumbly grease stain on his shirt collar.

"Of course," Vance said as he brushed at the crumbs. "And their scheme was so brilliant that they left no evidence and kept thousands of conspirators quiet." He hesitated for a moment, staring at his shoes. "But we did lose."

"We will see. So, do you have another reason to waste my time?" You back-stabbing soon-to-die traitor who accepted the results, just like that rat Pence did. Should have let them hang him. Vance too. They were both bribed, I'm sure of it.

"The head robot is here," said Vance. "Along with the stasis field. All ten million robots are programmed to be completely loyal and obedient to you. BL-1, you may enter."

In stomped the most beautiful sight of my life, goose-stepping in time to the Robert Wagner opera music that suddenly played in my head. It was dressed all in black, with a black cape and an oversized superhero helmet. It was gorgeous, and of course I'd designed the look. All those news reports and lawsuits from Marvel about it supposedly looking like Darth Vader—I have no idea who that is, never met him—are fake news and witch hunts.

It came to a stop in front of me, with its legs widespread, hands on hips, head high, its dark visor staring

Alternative Liberties

down at me. I'm bigly tall but this thing was *huuuge*, as big and tall as Barron, the only person taller than me I allow around. I don't like taller people near me. But maybe it's okay with a robot.

"What's its name again, Vance?"

"BL-1. The BL stands for blind loyalty. To you, of course."

"BL-1 sounds stupid and is too hard to remember. Robot, I will call you Blind Loyalty."

"Thank you, President Trump," said Blind Loyalty in a deep voice that had also attracted lawsuits from the estate of some guy named Jones. "Your orders are my command."

"So you and the other ten million robots will follow my orders, no matter what?"

"You are the final and only word for us, Mr. President."

"Vance, bring the nuclear football. It's already set with the coordinates we worked out?"

"Yes, sir, it's ready to go. You put in the nuclear code, and the missiles launch. Only you and I will survive, in the stasis field. The few survivors from the worldwide nuclear bombardment will be hunted down by the robots before they leave on their primary mission."

"To conquer the galaxy!" I cried. "Sad that it'll take them a million years, but that's why we had NASA create them and the stasis field. It'll be glorious!"

These robots were AMAZING!!! Vance, that traitorous coward, had kept me informed on their secret development—not that he'll live to enjoy the plan, he's in for a surprise. The robots are designed to explore and terraform planets throughout the galaxy.

I inputted the secret nuclear codes that I kept on a scrap of notepaper in my pocket. Then I hit *Execute*. May the billions who doubted me rest in peace. In great, agonizing pain.

"Awaiting your orders, sir," said Blind Loyalty.

"Of course you are," I said. I turned to my disloyal VP. "Vance, you said I lost the election."

"We did, sir."

"I never lose. Blind Loyalty, kill Vance."

"*Sir!*" Vance cried, but a sudden blow from Blind Loyalty to the back of his neck and he went down. Then the robot stared down at him.

"What are you doing?" I asked.

"I am baking his brain with microwave radiation to ensure his death," said Blind Loyalty.

"Wonderful!" I cried. I could just imagine those disloyal brain cells boiling away into nothingness. He'd failed me.

"If you will give us your final orders and then enter the stasis field, we will commence," said Blind Loyalty. "The stasis field will automatically operate five seconds after you enter."

"Immediately after I enter the stasis field, you and the rest of the robots are ordered to hunt down any surviving humans and kill them. Then you are to go into space and conquer the galaxy. When you are done, you will awaken me from the stasis field and make me King of the Galaxy."

"We will do as you ask," said Blind Loyalty.

The stasis field was a 4-foot diameter transparent polycarbonate tube, so you could see in or out. The driving mechanism was in its base, with a few buttons and dials. I opened the door and started to step in.

"Pardon, sir, but you must first remove your clothes before entering the stasis field," said Blind Loyalty.

"Huh? Why do I need to do that?"

"The stasis field is set to human DNA. It will recognize your body, including your hair, nails, and so on, but your clothes will short-circuit the system. New clothes appropriate to your position will be provided when you are revived in one million years as King of the Galaxy."

"Then off they go!" I said. I stripped, and then stepped into the stasis field. I counted out loud. "One. Two. Three. Four. Five. S—"

~~~

It was the best of times, it was the age of wisdom, it was the epoch of rational belief, it was the season of light, it was the Spring of hope, it was decades in the future. Dickens could never have imagined the utopia humanity had achieved. Little Suzie skipped up the steps of the Never-Trump Museum of Narcissism and Stupidity, too young to understand the morass that such a future had come from or how humanity had advanced by learning from the past. She ran through the front doors and came face to face with the main exhibit.

"Mommy, why is there a naked fat man standing still in the glass box?" Little Suzie asked, pointing.

Her mom panted as she caught up. Then she, too, stared at the exhibit, knowing all that it meant, thinking how best to explain it.

"He was a very bad president from long ago who lost two elections but was a very bad sport about it," said Mommy. "His aides used actors dressed as robots, a fake nuclear attack, and a promise of galactic conquest to trick him into a stasis field and out of politics. He's a monument to a terrible past we'd like to forget but must always remember."

Alternative Liberties

US History in DeSoto County

Jason P. Burnham

Seth's leg bounced nervously as Ms. Henderson walked around the room handing out graded papers. It was a third of his grade and, if he didn't get at least a B, he had no shot of passing US History. And if he didn't pass US History, his scholarship was dead, which meant public school. And public school was a terrible, terrible place to be in DeSoto County.

Kevin got his paper back first and flashed it at him. "A-," Kevin whispered. "Told you."

Seth rolled his eyes. Of course Kevin got an A-. But Seth couldn't afford the AI subscription Kevin could. Seth had had to hunt and hunt and hunt to find a free one that had US History inputs. The reviews of the program had been mixed to say the least. Some people said it put a virus on their computer. Other reviewers cited grades ranging from D+ to B+. All he needed was a B.

Alternative Liberties

He crossed his fingers under the desk and closed his eyes for longer than it should have taken for Ms. Henderson to give out all the papers. When he opened them, Ms. Henderson was seated up front and his paper was face down on his desk. His hand trembled as he flipped it over.

Kevin sucked his teeth before Seth even saw the grade. "You shoulda subscribed to the AI I used," Kevin whispered.

The bell rang and Seth stayed in his seat, staring at the big red letters on his paper: *F. See me after class.*

Seth waited for everyone to leave. US History was the last period of the day, so he had all the time in the world. And with an F, he was in no rush to go home. His parents were going to kill him. Or someone at public school would in a few weeks when he started there. He couldn't decide which death would be worse.

"I'm waiting, Mr. Tucker," Ms. Henderson said.

Seth stood up slowly and walked to Ms. Henderson's desk. He focused on the little plastic apple next to the homework box on the corner. She adjusted her glasses and looked at him hard. She opened her mouth to say something, then held up a finger. He had never particularly gotten along with her, but he hadn't *not* gotten along with her either. She was just his teacher for US history, a subject he cared very little about.

Ms. Henderson walked to the classroom door, shut it, then turned off the room's wi-fi transmitter.

Seth raised an eyebrow. It wasn't *that* serious, was it?

"I'm telling you this where no one can hear, Seth, because I like you. I think you're a good kid," said Ms. Henderson. Seth was somewhat surprised to hear her say she liked him, but hey, maybe it would work in his favor. Maybe there was still a way out of this. A way to stay out of public school.

Alternative Liberties

"Here, let's turn off our phones too." Ms. Henderson pulled out her phone and turned it off. Seth did the same. His hands were starting to sweat now. What the hell had that bunk AI put in his paper? He knew most of the class was using *some* kind of AI. He should've just sold drugs or something to pay for Kevin's good AI. That would have been better than... this.

"I know you used AI to write this paper," she said. "But that's not why I'm doing all this." She motioned to the door, the wi-fi, the phones. "The Tracker Program identified some materials from banned textbooks and redacted government documents in your paper. I flagged it as a Tracker error because I like you, but you've got to find some other program to write your papers or you're gonna get yourself in water hotter than the Chattahoochee."

"Is the Chattahoochee hot?" Seth asked. He wasn't really sure how to respond. All he had been thinking about was getting kicked out of private school. Now he was being told to worry about citing banned books and forbidden documents?? The Florida Curriculum Enforcement Agency could put him in prison for that.

"Close to boiling on some days," Ms. Henderson said. "So, I'm going to need you to use a different program next time."

Seth shook his head. "But the other kids all use AI to write their papers. Why am I getting in trouble?"

Ms. Henderson raised her eyebrows. "They have better sense than to use programs that include illegal reference material. Now I suggest we just move on and forget this ever happened."

"But, but... I can't pass now! I'll have to go to public school!" Seth's palms were clammy, his head was swimming.

Ms. Henderson sighed. "I tell you what. Bring me a new paper by tomorrow and I won't count it late. Just retrieve this paper from the old program and put it into a new one with different inputs."

When Seth stood gaping at her, gasping for words, she ushered him out. "Go on home—you've got a lot of work to do tonight."

Seth was alone in the hallway, all the kids having trickled out already. What the hell was he going to do?

~~~

When he got home, Seth went straight to his bedroom. His parents wouldn't be home for a couple hours—he could panic in peace.

When he opened his laptop, the AI program was still running from the last homework assignment.

"Piece of crap!" he yelled. He tried to close the program, but it wouldn't respond. "Ugh!"

He smashed the keyboard shortcut to show the desktop and let the bogus program run in the background. He opened a web browser and began searching for a new AI. He'd done this search before and he already knew the good ones were out of his price range, but what choice did he have? It's not like he could write a whole paper on 20th century America on his own in one night. Not even if he stayed up all night.

The anxiety of failure was pressing on him; he could feel tears preparing themselves to fall.

An idea struck him. A desperate one. He pulled out his phone.

Hey Kevin, can I please please please use your AI to rewrite my paper for me? I'll owe you big time man.

Kevin began typing almost immediately.

...no way dude. It'll just gen the same paper and I'll fail too.

Seth groaned. *No way man, I'll prompt it different. It'll be fine.*

No way man. Not happenin. I'll still hang out with you if you don't die at public school bruh. :)

Alternative Liberties

Seth let loose wordless, rage- and sorrow-filled screams. He couldn't go to public school. He just couldn't. Public schools were dying. Florida no longer provided them any monetary support whatsoever. He had heard a rumor that one high school hadn't had a graduate go to college in three years.

The sound of a car on gravel made him jump. He wiped his eyes, tried to make it seem like he hadn't been crying. His parents wouldn't come into his room right away anyway, so he had some time to get back to looking normal.

He pulled up the paper his AI had written. If he was going to have to go it on his own, he should at least know what he already had to work with. Starting from scratch was not an option with only one night to write it.

In twentieth century America, the 1960s were a tumultuous time. Drawing on hundreds of years of slavery and a lack of progress since the Civil War, African Americans used grassroots-level organization to stand up for themselves and pave a way toward achieving civil rights which had been denied to them since the time they had been stolen from the shores of Africa by colonial European powers.

Seth stared at the screen. Civil rights? He'd never heard of those before. And the Civil War? This AI was so bad it was using the deprecated term for the War for State's Rights. That had been the one after slavery, he thought. But maybe he was getting things wrong. He couldn't remember what Ms. Henderson had called it.

Just before he started back to reading, there was a loud bang from the front of the house, then silence. Sometimes his dad accidentally knocked over the table in the foyer when he came home late from his second job, but this was too loud for that.

Seth listened carefully and stood, taking his eyes off his American history paper.

It was quiet in the house. He didn't want to face his parents yet. Whatever had made the noise could wait until he'd edited his paper.

He went to sit down in his computer chair when his bedroom door crashed open.

"Hey!" Seth shouted. "You can't just—"

When Seth turned, it wasn't his parents barging in. Four men in all black with assault rifles leveled at his chest burst in the room.

"Are you Seth Tucker?" shouted one of the men.

Seth whimpered and nodded his head. His stomach dropped. He didn't know who these people were, nor how they knew his name. Something was horribly wrong.

"Get down on the ground!" a second man shouted.

"Wh-what's happening?" he croaked.

One of the men elbowed Seth in the head, causing him to fall onto his stomach. Another man spun Seth around so that he was facing his laptop. One of the men walked over to the laptop and began clicking through the windows he had open.

"This is it," the man at the computer said.

"It's just my homework," Seth cried.

"I didn't realize they were assigning illegal AI projects in DeSoto County," said the man with a sneer. At least, Seth thought it was a sneer—his head was spinning and tears were blurring his vision.

"I just... I just needed help writing my paper on American history," Seth said. He thought back to the paragraph he'd read that the AI had generated. Slavery. Civil War. Civil rights for African Americans. He wished desperately he had read the paper before he'd turned it in. Maybe then he would have been able to tell that the AI had been trained on illegal knowledge and had time to remove it before he turned it in and got in trouble.

One of the men bent down and got in his face. "Ms. Henderson tipped us off. We had to catch you using the program though. I think we'll have to bring her in for questioning too. Make sure this isn't what they teach in DeSoto County."

Nausea burgeoned within Seth and he vomited all over his carpet.

"I hate when they puke," one of the men spat. "Pick him up. I hate the smell of vomit. Let's get him to the detention center."

As they wrenched him up off the floor to a standing position, his legs buckling at the knees, Seth saw the tag on their uniforms. FCEA. Florida Curriculum Enforcement Agency.

"Public school," Seth sobbed through the haze clouding his mind.

"Where you're going," one of the officers said, "there won't be no school."

# Alternative Liberties

Three Patriotic Witches

Susan Murrie Macdonald

Three patriotic witches met to discuss the election results. Their intent was to eat pizza and drank Chianti. All but Joyce, who brought a twenty-ounce bottle of Pepsi.

"C'mon, Joyce," Sharon urged from where she stood at the kitchen counter filling wine glasses. "We all need something fermented tonight,"

"My doctor says no alcohol with these new meds," Joyce explained, and collapsed on Sharon's couch with a most unladylike plop.

"Honey, ditch that doctor," Karen told her. "Life without wine...." She shook her head at the dreadful thought.

"Why are you supporting Big Pharma?" Sharon demanded.

"Drugs keep me alive," Joyce retorted. "I enjoy being alive."

Alternative Liberties

"Mother Earth provides all we need to keep healthy," Sharon reminded her. "That, and a few well-crafted spells."

"You sound like my Christian Scientist aunt. She thinks prayer will cure all ills," said Joyce.

"It will, if you pray hard enough," Sharon insisted. "And to the right spirits," she added with a smirk. "Besides, your husbands think we're a book club. They'll expect you to come home sloshed."

Joyce unscrewed the cap of her Pepsi and took a sip, ending the discussion.

The doorbell rang. "Pizza!" they shouted in unison.

Sharon abandoned the pouring of the wine and collected the pizza from the delivery boy. She gave him a generous tip, then brought the pizza in to serve her "book club."

Karen fetched paper plates and napkins, Joyce took over the beverage service.

After a few bites of cheese and pepperoni, Karen asked, "Speaking of a few well-crafted spells, what are we going to do about the election?"

Sharon took a gulp of her wine and shrugged. "Why s*hould* we do anything? *We* may despise him, but a majority did elect him."

"A brainwashed plurality," Joyce interjected. "Not a majority."

"Brainwashed or not, he was the people's choice. We can put up with him for four years." Karen reached for another slice.

"*We* can," Sharon agreed. "We're middle-aged, White, and we go to church on Sundays. None of us have a functional uterus. We aren't in any danger." There was an uncomfortable silence as each considered those who were at risk.

"I don't know any death spells," Karen said glumly. "But we could probably come up with something."

"Death spells are illegal, immoral, and unethical." Joyce took another swig of her Pepsi.

Sharon shook her head. "I don't think they're illegal anymore. Unless Massachusetts still has some old laws on the books."

Karen shrugged. They weren't in Massachusetts.

"But still unethical and immoral," Joyce persisted.

Karen eyed another piece of pizza. "And dangerous. The Threefold Law says whatever you do, good or evil, will come back to you threefold."

"Well, we don't have to assassinate the SOB. We can do something annoying, but not fatal. Or just not get in the way of someone else trying to get him." Sharon washed down her pizza with another gulp of wine. "Maybe just well-wishing whomever gets sent to take care of the problem."

"I've got a notion," Joyce volunteered. "You remember I told you my cousin had a minor stroke two years ago. Well, she has to wear diapers now, and she's forever complaining about how they itch. Maybe we could increase the itch factor?"

"Crotch Rot on Steroids," said Karen, pumping a fist in the air.

"A persistent itch will drive anyone crazy," said Sharon. "Of course in his case, that's no drive, it's a short putt."

The other two giggled.

After they had finished the pizza and most of the Chianti, they washed the grease off their hands and took the necessary books down from Sharon's shelves.

Sharon fetched five white candles from the junk drawer in the kitchen, put them in a circle, and lit them.

They sang.
They prayed.
They wished.

Alternative Liberties

They found a slimy bit of moldy cucumber in the back of the fridge.

They wove a spell of itchiness and sent it wafting off to the East Coast to their target.

Leaving no trace of their non-literary evening beyond the lingering scent of pizza, they cleaned up before Sharon's husband got home from bowling.

All three took long hot showers before bed that night, as if to wash away the malice they had just wished on a fellow human being.

Come January 20, the president-elect didn't show up for his inauguration parade. He would have been disappointed if he had: there were no tanks or marching soldiers, only one military band, two high school bands, and a few cars bedecked in flags and ribbons.

The president-elect himself was in Walter Reed Hospital, where he insisted on taking his oath of office from his hospital bed. His gauze-wrapped hand rested on the Bible with his name emblazoned on the front while he squirmed from side to side.

All his doctors would say was that his condition wasn't life threatening and was being treated.

NeighborHelp

Earl T. Roske

Elijah gaped as he read the words every online student dreaded most: You do not have enough credits to continue. You will need to purchase additional credits in your profile tab.

"That's... What...? How...?" He stammered through the beginning of a half-dozen sentences before he had some semblance of control. "That's not possible!"

Then more sentences flowed.

"What's going on? How did this happen?" He shouted over his shoulder: "Mom! Mom!"

"What?" Elijah's mom shouted from the other side of the apartment.

"Mom! Please!"

Apparently Elijah's distress came through in his voice. In a heartbeat, she was in Elijah's room.

"Hon?" she asked. "Are you okay? What's wrong?"

"This." Elijah pushed his chair back from the desk, pointing an accusatory finger. "Look!"

Laila Anoki leaned down, squinting at the screen. She read the words silently, her mouth moving without a sound.

"You see it?"

"Yes, Lij, I see it." She held up a hand to silence him as she reread the words for the umpteenth time to Elijah's distress.

"Hmm," Laila said, straightening. "Maybe you're in the wrong account?"

"No. I signed out and back in. I did it three times. Even reset my password." Elijah glared at the laptop screen. "No, that's my account. And I don't have credits to take the final exam."

"Were you using your account for anything besides classes?"

Elijah looked at his mom as if she'd asked him if he'd robbed a bank. Or stolen a car. Or killed the neighbor's dog.

"You can't be serious, Mom!"

Laila held up her hands in an appeasing gesture.

"I'm just asking." She looked back at the computer. "Can you tell what times you accessed the program?"

"I didn't think of that." He jerked his chair forward. The legs squeaked across the tiles of the floor. "Sorry."

From fifth grade onward, with the changes in education finance laws, Elijah had been on the online homeschool track. It was a pay-as-you-go. Each payday, Elijah's parents paid the bills and bought the groceries, before applying the rest to Elijah's education.

Elijah learned early on to be productive with his time online, as each minute cost his parents money.

And he had been productive. He was in the top percentile for all his classes. Without the final exams all his coursework would be listed as incomplete.

Alternative Liberties

"Here," Elijah said, tapping the billing statement on the screen.

His active hours were there. He could see the six hours he put in on Monday, Tuesday, and Wednesday. No. Wait.

"Twenty-four hours on Wednesday!? They're trying to rip us off, Mom." Elijah stood, his hands balled into tight fists like he was ready to fight the whole admin department of the school.

"Hang on, Lij," his mother said, squeezing his shoulder. "Let's just make sure."

"Of what?" Elijah demanded. "Right there. I was on for six hours yesterday morning. And then eighteen hours after that? That's crazy."

"Did you maybe forget to log out?"

"I can't afford to forget, Mom. I'm not a child."

"Child?" Laila stood and looked around the room.

"Aliyah," Laila whispered. Then out loud, "Aliyah! Come here, honey!"

There was no response, but Elijah heard the soft thunder of his sister running to their bedroom.

"Mommy?"

Laila knelt, waving her daughter over, hugging her once she was in reach.

"This is a very important question, Aliyah, okay?"

"What question?" Aliyah looked confused.

"Did you use your brother's school account yesterday?"

Elijah waited for the answer, leaning forward to catch the words that much faster.

"Only for a little bit."

"A little bit!?" bellowed Elijah, causing Aliyah to yelp and bury her face in her mother's shoulder.

"Lij, that's not helping." Laila moved Aliyah so she could see the girl's face, eyes wet with unspent tears. Laila asked, "Can you tell me what happened, honey?"

Aliyah nodded.

"I wanted to watch story time. On the free channel it has a bunch of stupid commercials. So, I thought if I watched one episode, then turned it off, no one would know."

"Turn off? You didn't sign out?"

Aliyah's eyes went wide. She was young, but also quick, and realized what her mother was saying.

"I'm sorry," she whispered, her eyes wide and downcast.

Elijah groaned, sliding down in his chair until his backside was half off the seat.

"I'm sorry," Aliyah whispered again, her voice choked with tears. She pulled herself tight against her mother, face buried in her mother's shoulder.

"Okay," said Laila, hugging and rocking her daughter. "It's okay."

"But it's not," said Elijah. "The test is next week, and I don't have the credits to pay for the time."

"Lij," said Aliyah, her voice choked with snot and tears. "I'm really sorry."

Elijah sighed heavily, sliding off his chair onto his knees. He moved next to his sister, hugging her and their mother.

"I know Liyah, I know.

"I'm sorry," Aliyah said again, her words heavy with tears.

"Okay, hon," Laila said. "Why don't you go rest on the couch? I'll come check on you."

"Okay," Aliyah said. She stepped back from her mom and then hugged her brother. "I'm sorry."

Aliyah turned and hurried from the room.

Elijah sat back on his heels. He felt like crying too but couldn't see how that would help.

"Lij," Laila said, putting her hands on her son's. "Let's wait until your dad gets home. Maybe there's some money left."

"Mom...."

"Maybe, Lij. Maybe."

Elijah nodded, but he already knew the answer.

~~~

"There is no money," Anthony Anoki said during dinner. "There was, but I got a flat tire on the way to work. Now, there isn't." He dabbed his mouth with his napkin. "I'm sorry, Lij, we're tapped until the end of the month. Can you ask for some sort of extension?"

"Tried." Elijah poked at the pasta on his plate, too despondent to eat. "They said there was nothing they could do. That I should ask friends and family for help."

"Easy for them to say," his mom said. "Let them walk in our shoes."

"They are, Laila," Anthony said. "They're just doing what they're told to do so they can put food on their tables and get the credits their kids need for schooling. We can't blame them."

"It's my fault," Aliyah said from her side of the table. A small spot of pasta was slowly sliding down her chin. Her eyes were downcast.

"No," her mother said, wiping the pasta away with her thumb. "It was an accident, and none of us is perfect."

"So what do I do?" Elijah asked. "I've less than a week."

"Can't you take the test next quarter?" Elijah's dad asked, returning to the food on his plate.

"There isn't one next quarter, Dad. It's once a year. If I wait, I'll have to do the courses all over again to qualify for the exam.

"I'm sorry, Lij," his dad said. He reached over, squeezing Elijah's hand. "Things haven't gotten better. Everything gets more expensive faster than I get raises at work. Maybe you can find a job until next year? Take

Alternative Liberties

some advanced classes in the meantime. I know it's not what you want to hear, but this is where we're at."

Elijah squeezed his father's hand in return.

"I know, Dad. I know."

~~~

In the dark of evening, Elijah lay in his bed, scrolling through his phone. The games he played to distract him weren't doing their job. The video shorts on other apps felt repetitive. He'd begun deleting apps he hadn't used in the years since getting the phone, a hand-me-down from his father. They weren't really taking up space, but it was something to keep his mind off the credits.

Elijah had deleted three yoga apps, three weight-loss apps, and one for train routes and schedules in Europe when he stopped.

"NeighborHelp?" Elijah whispered, looking to make sure he hadn't woken Aliyah.

She was still asleep, so Elijah tapped the app. He'd heard of the app. People referred to it in conversations with his parents. A couple of friends had used it, too.

Elijah's dad had started an account, and the username and password were still in the phone's system.

People used NeighborHelp to message neighbors, alerting them to stray dogs, troublemakers, things for sale, and—what really caught his eye—odd jobs neighbors would pay others to complete. Like giving Mrs. Myerson's furry little dog a bath.

"I can give a dog a bath," Elijah said to himself. "How hard could that be?"

Mrs. Myerson was offering thirty dollars. Elijah tapped the accept button and continued to scroll other job requests. Mow a lawn, wash some windows, walk a dog. He tapped accept on a half dozen before going to sleep.

He could do some odd jobs. Maybe it would be enough to get the credits he needed.

"How hard could it be?" he repeated and closed his eyes.

~~~

"Does it hurt?" Aliyah asked her brother as he washed the scratches on his arms. There were a lot of scratches.

"Not so much," Elijah said. "Not now, anyways."

The scratches were a side effect of washing Mrs. Myerson's dog. It turned out Bentley did not like baths. Not one bit. He'd fought tooth and nail. Fortunately, it was mostly nails.

Elijah's persistence in washing and drying Bentley surprised Mrs. Myerson. She'd even doubled the offered fee to sixty dollars. Between Bentley's bath, the windows of the Collins' house across the street, two lawns mowed, and one backyard scooped of poop, he had $230 toward the credits needed. That left $520 to go.

Three days left.

Elijah went to the shared bedroom and changed shirts, careful of the ointment on his arms. Aliyah followed Elijah into their room, going to her nightstand. When Elijah had his shirt safely over the ointment, he turned to find his sister quietly standing behind him.

"Ai! Liyah, you scared me."

"Here," Aliyah said, with the soft voice she adopted when being apologetic.

She held up her bobblehead Hello Kitty coin bank. She had purchased it at a yard sale for a quarter she'd found on the sidewalk the day before.

"Here?" Elijah asked, confused.

"To help pay for your credits. The ones I lost."

"Oh, Sis, you don't have to do that."

Aliyah pushed the coin bank closer to Elijah.

"I want to," Aliyah said. Her voice was firm, the tone she used to get her own way. Elijah had seen it morph into a tantrum. That was the last thing he wanted right now, so he accepted the bank.

"Thank you, Aliyah."

"You're welcome!" Aliyah flashed him a smile, turned, and skipped from the room as if all were right with the world because of her contribution.

Elijah sat on his bed and popped the bottom of the Hello Kitty bank off. He poured the coins onto his bedspread and smiled. Aliyah was always finding coins. She'd find them on the floor inside stores, sidewalks, playgrounds. Wherever she found them, she picked them up and brought them home to 'feed to Kitty.'

The total fed to Kitty was two dollars and seventeen cents. Most of it was pennies, with a few dimes and two quarters. Elijah felt bad taking his sister's money. But she'd know if he didn't, and that would be a different problem. Elijah was tired of problems.

What he needed was solutions. Even though solutions weren't likely to present themselves in his room, he looked around anyway. The entire room was a testament to their parents' ingenuity. Yard sales, flea markets, second-hand stores, tempered by elbow grease, a coat of paint, or a needle and thread, meant that Elijah and Aliyah had a room, pleasing to the eye. Even the flatscreen television over the dresser was picked up at an estate sale.

The only thing in the room that wasn't secondhand was the gaming system his parents had given him when he turned seventeen. They had cut corners on things for two years. That was two years of darned socks in the same shoes for dad. That was mom altering dresses and going most days without makeup and nail polish. All so Elijah could have a pricey gaming system.

It was worth far more than he needed to take the test.

Elijah wiped his hands across his face. His parents would be disappointed. But maybe if he got into a better college and then landed a great job. Maybe then his parents would forgive him for selling the gaming system.

After one last look at the system, he turned his attention to his phone and tapped on the NeighborHelp app.

~~~

Elijah waited until his father had gone to work, and his mother was walking Aliyah to school. Then he boxed up the system and left for the post office. An offer arrived shortly after he posted the system. They hadn't even negotiated for a lower price. Elijah felt that was a lucky sign.

When Elijah reached the post office, he started across the parking lot. That was when he realized his mistake. Budget cuts had closed the post office the previous year. Half the mail was now delivered by contracted companies, which was why the mail didn't always arrive when it should.

Most importantly, there was no one else around to witness the transaction.

And it had been their idea to meet here.

Elijah hefted the box a little higher and began walking quickly toward the sidewalk. It was just houses here and a few empty lots. Two cars had passed since he'd turned onto the street. He needed to get someplace with people. He needed to get there fast.

"Yo, man, what's the rush?"

Two guys, older than Elijah, bigger, too, were crossing the street. Elijah hadn't seen them arrive. Hadn't seen where they'd come from.

"That the gaming system?" one asked, pointing at the box.

"No," Elijah said, angling away from the guys who were still approaching.

A car turned into the lot, blocking Elijah's escape.

"Whoopsie," one of the guys said, laughing. Then more seriously, "Why don't you just put that on the ground, kid?"

"I can't. My parents will be upset."

"Like we care." The second guy lifted the front of his shirt, the handgrip of a pistol visible enough to get the message across.

Elijah put the box on the ground, fighting back tears.

"Good job," said the first guy. "While you're at it, let's see what you have in your pockets."

What Elijah had in his pockets was $230 in bills and $2.17 in loose change. He handed over all of it.

"Nah, man," one of them said as they snatched the folded bills. "Keep the change. Keep the change! Ha ha, get it!"

Both of them laughed at their wordplay as they put the box in the car before climbing in and slamming the door shut. Elijah could hear their laughter as they drove away.

Only when he was sure that they were gone did he let tears of frustration and self-contempt flow down his cheeks, dripping onto his shirt.

Elijah started walking. He didn't have a goal in mind. Not anymore. All he had was walking. So he walked until the tears stopped and his stomach growled. When he finally looked up, the sky on the horizon was turning pink. A few stars twinkled through the blue of the darkening sky.

He had to go home. He didn't want to, but he had no place else to go. So, he turned and continued walking. This time towards home.

~~~

When Elijah entered the apartment, his mother met him at the door.

"Lij, Hon? Where've you been?" She hugged Elijah as she spoke.

Elijah leaned into the hug.

"Just out walking around."

"Well, we're glad you're home. Someone's here to see you."

Laila put her arm around Elijah's shoulders, guiding him down the hall. In the kitchen. The woman waved as he entered.

"Mrs. Myerson," said Elijah, returning the wave

Bentley was on Mrs. Myerson's lap and started wagging his tail when he looked at Elijah.

"We've been waiting for you, Lij."

"Oh." Elijah said. Overwhelmed by anger and embarrassment, the tears began to flow.

He felt a hand on his shoulder. His father.

"Lij? His father said, "What's wrong?"

Elijah didn't want to talk about it. not here, not now, not in front of Mrs. Myerson, but the words came out anyway. He retold his misadventure, including the reasons. As he got to the end of the story, he fished the change out of his pocket, placing it in front of Aliyah.

"This is the only thing they didn't take."

"Why?" asked Aliyah. She sounded hurt.

"They didn't hurt you, did they?" Elijah's mom asked. She put a glass of water in front of him.

Elijah shook his head.

"No. They just laughed at me."

"This is a lot of money," Aliyah said, as she separated the coins.

"I'm sorry they laughed at you, Lij," his father said. "But I'm glad you're okay."

"I'm sorry about the gaming system," said Elijah. "I just...."

"We know," said his father. "It happened. It's over. You're safe. Right now, Mrs. Myerson wants to talk to you."

Elijah lifted his head long enough to look at a gently smiling Mrs. Myerson and a tail-wagging Bentley.

"You know," Mrs. Myerson said. "When I was your age, everyone went to school. And I mean, 'to school.' There were lots of schools for all the kids. And it cost nothing. I even went to junior college for next to nothing. University wasn't all that expensive either."

"But then things started changing," she continued. "The government started changing the rules, taking money from public schools and giving it to private schools. Public schools had to close buildings and let go of teachers. By the time I started teaching, it was a hundred kids to a class, most of them through virtual classrooms. And even those classes disappeared."

"You were a teacher?"

"I was. The job I was proudest of." She paused, her gaze going distant. "But that was a long time ago. I've worked other careers. Better-paying careers, but never as satisfying, despite the frustrations. But that's not why I'm here."

"Oh?" Elijah could only think of negative reasons for her presence. Perhaps it was an aspect of being robbed and humiliated. "Did I hurt Bentley?"

Mrs. Myerson laughed. When she did, it was genuine, loving. Elijah felt himself smiling and noticed everyone, even Aliyah, smiling in response.

"You were wonderful. Bentley has never looked better." She patted Bentley's head. "And if you didn't notice, he was happy to to see you. He only growls at other people. I think he may like you more than me."

Elijah laughed this time. "No, ma'am, I'm sure you will always be his favorite."

"I hope so. But we are off on another tangent. Elijah, when I came over to thank you for the wonderful job with Bentley,

ob with Bentley, your parents told me about your problem."

"I told her!" Aliyah said, hersee you. He only growls at other people. He may like you more than me."

Elijah laughed this time. "No, ma'am, I'm sure you'll always be his favorite."

"I hope so." She paused. Then, "Elijah, when I came to thank you for the wonderful j chin proudly elevated.

"That's right," said Mrs. Myerson, "you did. And now I hear of your terrible misadventure. So, I'm glad I came to give you this."

Mrs. Myerson's hand rested on a white piece of paper.

"I hope you'll do me the honor of accepting this."

She slid the paper to Elijah's side of the table.

Elijah looked at the paper and then at his parents. They were grinning. He didn't want to believe, but he knew the shape of a check.

"You have to turn it over, Lij," whispered Aliyah.

"I know," Elijah whispered back, earning a chuckle from the adults and a vigorous tail wag from Bentley.

Elijah turned the check over. His jaw fell open as he looked at Mrs. Myerson and his parents. He wanted to cry again, but this time with relief.

"Say thank you," Aliyah whispered.

This time, everyone laughed, especially Elijah. He'd be taking the test on time.

"Would it be rude, Mrs. Myerson, if we deposited it right now? I have to take the test tomorrow before midnight."

"It would not be rude," said Mrs. Myerson, one hand stroking Bentley's head. "In fact, I insist."

Alternative Liberties

Alternative Liberties

Weaponized Genealogy

Tom Easton

My elevator pitch for the Venture Capital Speedfest was short and sweet: "Posthumous documentation for politicians' ancestors."

That was enough for Victor Argelis to say, "He's mine," stand up from the table of venture capitalists, grab my elbow, and pull me into a breakout room.

"I can see it," he said. He was a tall middle-aged fellow in an expensive suit, an oversized flag lapel pin, and a plain blue tie. His hairline was almost out of sight. "My sister married a Mormon," so I know about their posthumous baptism scam. Now tell me more."

"I'm a genealogist," I said. "It was just a hobby until..."

~~~

The conservative war on anchor babies picked up steam during the second Trump presidency. The first step was that Kentucky tried to declare that the children of illegal Haitian immigrants were not U.S. citizens and could be deported. The case immediately went to the U.S. Supreme Court, which promptly reversed itself on United States v. Wong Kim Ark, 169 U.S. 649 (1898), and declared that the born-in-the-USA children of undocumented immigrants could not be "birthright citizens" despite the 14th Amendment to the Constitution. The American Civil Liberties Union recycled the pro-Wang arguments that a decision against birthright citizenship would imperil the status of White European immigrants and their descendants. They also pointed out that the case was inherently racist, but to no avail.

The second step came when the 2030 GOP platform said that only the descendants of documented immigrants should be United States citizens. A "one bad apple" clause even said that *all* one's immigrant ancestors had to be documented.

A platform isn't law, of course. But it can lead to law.

~~~

On Fox News, some redneck was raving that it wasn't enough. "I don't want some immigrant's kids polluting my neighborhood. Even if they are documented!" Behind him, a number of good White American citizens were waving their fists in the air. I wondered how many of them could document all their ancestors.

"What about grandkids?" asked the lady with the microphone.

"Same thing!" he screamed.

Behind him, someone screamed "NO!" and lifted an assault rifle into sight. He was wearing a black ball-cap with a white swastika on it.

Someone else yelled, "What about White immigrants?"

The shouting paused for a very brief moment.

Alternative Liberties

My wife, Caroline, was shaking her chestnut head, just the way I imagined she did for her high school history students. "Citizen used to mean just resident, someone who lived in the city."

"Is that what it says in the history books they make you use?"

She gave me the Look that usually meant I was an idiot. History had been a political football for years.

"They didn't used to have the paperwork. Just got off the boat."

"Can you talk about this in class?"

"Not in the curriculum."

"No current events? Politics? Blatant racism?"

She shook her head. "By the time they're approved, they're not current. And we have to avoid anything that upsets people. No critical race theory."

I was an accountant. No politicians telling me how to do it. They didn't interfere with my hobby, either. I did genealogy, mostly for the family. But sometimes…

~~~

"How did you come up with this idea?" asked Victor Argelis.

"Texas," I said. "Travis Crockett declared for governor, and his Democratic opponent, Adam Burton, claimed he couldn't run because he wasn't a citizen, according to his own platform. His Irish great-great-grandmother wasn't documented."

"What about Burton?"

"He said he was covered. As a descendant of slaves, his ancestors were documented on bills of lading. His great-grandmother was a Native American, but they aren't immigrants."

Argelis laughed. "Crockett loved that!"

"And he called me. He wanted me to find some undocumented branch on Burton's tree."

"Weaponized genealogy. How far could it go?"

"If your great-grandfather was a horse thief, you have criminal genes and must be deported?"

"Searching family trees for Jews, mixed marriages, anything people want to hate. Worse than Jim Crow racism."

"Yeah. It astonished me." I shook my head. This was all my idea, and it could make a lot of money. Yet I really wasn't sure I liked it. "I never dreamed a genealogist could be a political operative."

Argelis did not ask whether I'd found what Crockett wanted. "And then you made the Mormon hop."

I nodded. "I filed for the patent immediately. Then I asked Immigration what forms I'd need. They had no idea, but after a couple of months they said they could see the need."

"Anything yet?"

"We agreed that starting with the first US census in 1790, anyone listed in two censuses in a row, at least until we had Ellis Island, should qualify. Not that everyone got censused, but then there were military records, court records, tax and real estate records. And most of it's online, these days."

"Hmm." Argelis rubbed his chin. It was late enough in the day that his fingers made a scratchy noise. "Public records."

"That's genealogy for you. Most people haven't a clue."

"And what's the income stream look like?"

"Politicians to start with. There's what? Twenty thousand state and federal. Another half million local. I've been charging them $500 for each ancestor I have to document, and a lot more for oppo research."

"You don't need venture capital for that."

"Ordinary people are going to need it to vote. So that's another 300 million customers."

"In a rush, if that GOP platform turns into law." Argelis opened his tablet and began to type. I could just

Alternative Liberties

see that he was working in a spreadsheet and a browser. Checking my figures. After a few minutes, he asked, "How much do you need?"

~~~

I was chuffed. Big time!

I rented office space, bought computers, and hired fifty fresh-out-of-college researchers. I even licensed the idea to the Mormons and retained lawyers to deal with the inevitable lawsuits from people who refused to believe they had non-citizen ancestors. As soon as a few states turned that part of the GOP platform into law, we got busy.

For a few months anyway. Then it seemed that each new customer took less time to process. And generated less income.

I called a meeting and asked the team leaders, "What's going on? Are people getting lazy?"

Angela Foamonwater said, "Graph theory."

It rang a bell from college, and Angela had been a math major. After a moment, I said just, "Family trees."

"Are graphs." She nodded. "And they share nodes with each other."

I saw it instantly. "People share ancestors. So the longer we stay at this, the less we have left to do."

"Worse than that," said Angela. "We're finding a lot of undocumented ancestors. If those state laws go national, the country will lose a lot of citizens. And voters."

I almost laughed. It would serve the racists right. "Biter bitten," I said. "A national law won't last long."

Someone else asked, "How long do we have?"

Not long. That was clear. But… "Less if we write this up and put the word out."

"Send the report to the media," said Angela Foamonwater.

"And every Representative and Senator. Like we were lobbyists."

"Or troublemakers," said Angela.

"We were that from the start."

~~~

"That didn't last long," said Caroline. Within a month the GOP dropped any mention of birthright citizenship. The states were repealing laws. In Washington, no one wanted to talk about it.

I sighed. "Long enough. We can retire early."

"Or just go someplace where teachers can teach. A new house would be nice."

Victor Argelis wasn't upset. We'd done very well for a while, so he'd made his money back, and then some. I had money in the bank too.

I was upset, though. I was an accountant. I was supposed to understand numbers. How had I missed how limited my big project really was?

Alternative Liberties

It's Already Happened

Stephanie L. Weippert

They can't do that here!
The Constitution won't allow it.
You say this so confidently
secure in your race and class. But...

Ask an older Japanese
when FDR ignored our constitution
rounded them up into concentration camps
for the horrible crime of their race.

It can't happen here!
Our courts won't allow it.
Ask a Cherokee about the courts
when they walked the Trail of Tears.

Kristallnacht can't ever happen here.
Ask a Black in Tulsa
what happened in 1921
when neighborhoods burned to ash

Don't tell me, "It can't happen here"
Because it already has.

Alternative Liberties

Alternative Liberties

Sivilized World

Elwin Cotman

Day 1: Write story from chap 1 through riverboat
Day 2: Write through Shepherdson/Grangerfords
Day 3: Write through the end

Day 1. At six in the morning you start reading the book, curled up in an armchair by the wood stove, a paperback edition from the 90s on your knee, black coffee on the armrest. Up on this mountain things are quiet, though now and then police drones whir overhead, and here there are kids allowed to be kids, driving to parties in jeeps or crunching through the snow in their private pairs.

Reading the novel is a new thing for you. Didn't you adapt *Tom Sawyer* into an eight-episode series based on half-remembered movies from your childhood? Then again, that was a less complicated book. After this job, things will get easier. They'll probably hire you for *Tom*

Alternative Liberties

Sawyer Abroad and *Tom Sawyer, Detective*, the ones Mark Twain himself wrote as silly paycheck gigs.

Chapter by chapter, you draft ideas in your notebook. You word every sentence carefully so as to uphold American values. Liberty will sniff out even a hint of seditious language. You have a studio note to keep Huck's dialogue simple because they fired the old Huck, who pissed away his big break when he posted support for Black refugees. His replacement is a kid from some viral video and he's a limited actor, to say the least.

You are the screenwriter behind *Last of the Mohicans* (intrepid pioneer helps Indians navigate their own self-imposed extinction), *Moby Dick* (pioneer captain conquers nature), *The Scarlet Letter* (pioneer slut finds redemption through piety and motherhood), and your biggest success, *The Adventures of Tom Sawyer* (straight White male finds fame and fortune through moxie). Classic Americana. Nostalgia feels. All delivered on deadline and without a single red flag from Liberty. When you think of your audience, you picture millions of giant babies sucking pacifiers.

The book is okay. The humor gets some chuckles from you but feels outdated. The adventure parts will make for great action scenes. The chapters after Tom Sawyer returns are trash, and the overall premise—Black people are people, too—is one the Great White Mustache no doubt thought progressive, but is, in your opinion, horribly simplistic. Then again, simplicity works for giant babies.

By eight a.m. you are in your writing rhythm. You have a fully stocked fridge. The rooms in your rental are large and cold.

Overlooking the backyard is a room with a floor-to-ceiling window. On your breaks, you stare out over solid snow packed three feet high around the naked redwoods. The world below—the "sivilized" world, Huck would call it—is obscured from sight.

The streaming services ran out of 80s movies and anime and video games to squeeze for content around the same time the government ordered all entertainment to serve its patriotic duty. What was more American than the classics? You call it the Books We Skipped in High School English Cinematic Universe.

You write Huck and Tom as All-American boys. When they raid the Sunday picnic, they refer to their victims as A-rabs, and you leave it in. Huck's guardian Miss Watson—you combine her and the Widow Douglas because lord does Twain have too many characters—owns a slave named Jim who's been listening to abolitionist lies. Huck worries for him.

It surprises you to learn that Twain's Jim believes in divination powers through his magic hairball. African shamanism there on the page. Funny how the older adaptations skipped this, even before the laws banned divisive topics. *The Adventures of Huckleberry Finn* is not a Black story. There are no Black stories. Only American stories.

Still. Once upon a time, you read Black stories. Long ago and far away, you wrote them.

Losing the hairball makes your Jim less interesting. So, you turn the dialogue about his daughter into a scene. It makes him sympathetic, and when he leaves his family, well, Liberty will never complain about absentee Black fathers. You include a scene between Jim and his wife so as to remove even a hint of sexual tension between him and Miss Watson.

In episode one, Huck is remanded to the custody of Pap Finn, a drunk who rambles hatefully against the government and educated Blacks. At first, Huck fights with Pap. Then, in episode two, he realizes Pap is right.

Alternative Liberties

Salt of the earth, that Pap Finn. Their reconciliation in the rain will make the giant babies cry.

Then Pap disappears. Searching for him, Huck meets Jim, who, following the abolitionist lies, has run away from his loving mistress. Episodes 1 and 2, done.

The famous n-words have to stay. To remove them would catch Liberty's attention.

You finish in time for a tofu stir-fry dinner. You watch the newsfeed. America is winning. The economy is up. Ever since you were a kid, doomsayers have claimed robots will take your job, but here you are, still writing, a Black man with a laptop.

Day 2. Over their days on the raft, Huck tries to make Jim see the error of his ways. Anything that sounds vaguely un-Christian like the King Solomon dialogue, you cut. Huck and Jim foil the murderers on the riverboat. Jim finds Pap's body in the house but won't tell Huck. This will be an emotional beat later.

You fix yourself yogurt with granola and watch the newsfeed. We are winning. The economy is up. A Trump heir is enjoying her new yacht.

Of course, the part where Huck dresses as a girl has to go. There are only two genders. Like every adaptation, you cut the Shepherdsons and Grangerfords. This leads you to the King and the Duke. Deviants. Miscreants. For the King, you make him foreign-coded. The Duke is effeminate. Episodes 3 and 4, done.

You are tired. You will nap a few hours and shoot to the end.

A police drone passes overhead. Leaping squirrels make the branches creak in the dark. From the window, you stare down at a snow-covered fire pit and see Incidents in the Life of a Slave Girl burning. Clearly isolation is driving you batty. There is only one story. In it, slaves were happy and well-fed and well-trained. Africans started slavery, and White people ended it. Beyond that, nothing.

Alternative Liberties

Day 3. Now that Twain has given you a plot, everything slides into place, minus the religious satire and disapproval of lynch mobs. The King and the Duke try to scam the Wilkses. Huck foils them, but not before they turn in Jim for the reward. Before Huck can rescue him, Tom Sawyer arrives to remind him of the lessons from his beloved Pap. (Liberty would have no problem with the minstrel show hijinks in the last few chapters, but they slow down the narrative.) In the end, Huck sneaks to the shed to have a heart-to-heart with Jim. "Just 'cause yer a slave don't mean you ain't free." Why, it turns out Miss Watson even freed him in her will. That silly doubter Jim gets a job on the docks while Huck lights out for Indian territory, which you know will be a spinoff, considering the service has already spent a billion on this franchise.

Midday, you open LIBERTY.GOV. The image of stars and stripes blare so bright from the interface you can almost hear them. You upload your script.

The page buffers while the program speedreads. Liberty says, THIS SCRIPT IS IN VIOLATION OF MORALITY LAW.

Shit.

Oh shit.

Oh god.

Why, god, why.

Antic and drunk, you leave the cabin into the cold air. Along the curving road, the cabins are fortified with floodlights and security cameras. Eyes peek from behind the blinds. You should be scared but these no-doubt-armed civilians behind their wooden walls are nothing next to Liberty.

Your boss calls. You tell him this has never happened before. Damn right it's never happened, he says, though you both know it has. You got the job rewriting *Last of the Mohicans* because the previous

Alternative Liberties

writer got flagged by Liberty and vanished. He gives you two days to fix this. The show goes into production next month. The Phase 2 team-up movie comes out in a year, and the company has already spent a fortune on Rush's "Tom Sawyer" for commercials.

Day 4. You emerge from the relative comfort of nightmare's ambiguous terror. You feel doomed. When you open your document, there is a red dot on the top left corner of the screen. It cannot be clicked on. It cannot be closed. Liberty will document every word you keep or erase. Every little pascal of pressure on the keys will be analyzed for meaning.

Thus, you print your screenplay and tape the pages to the wall, to edit with pen. You decide the American values are not strong enough. That means more scenes with the Wilkses and their loving, traditional family Huck must protect from evildoers. You add a scene where the strong patriarch Mr. Wilks gives Huck advice before the fireplace. A Kevin Costner type should play him. You make the Duke gayer. You make the King foreign-er.

Liberty says, THIS SCRIPT VIOLATES MORALITY LAW.

The Shepherdsons and Grangerfords go back in, except, unlike the foolishly feuding gentry in Twain, here is a clearcut ideological conflict between a patriot family and their commie rivals. The Grangerford men, including poor brainwashed Buck, are killed because there is no other acceptable fate for commies.

Cocaine to write. Booze to edit. You fear your heart will explode. Outside, the snow has melted and the sun scorches.

When Alexandre Dumas wished to sell a revenge fantasy featuring his father, he recast the Black general as a White man. This is but one of the thoughts that emerge from your delirium. Feeling like a cigarette

Alternative Liberties

smoked to the butt, you upload the document to Liberty.

Liberty says, THIS SCRIPT VIOLATES MORALITY LAW.

Day 5. A good adaptation should truly adapt the material. Boom. Love triangle. Huck is in love with Becky Thatcher but cannot tell Tom. Over his journeys, he dreams of her. Tom Sawyer reads books, right? Well, his mind is corrupted by those Marxist tomes. The ones that were burned for our own good. When Huck goes to find Jim at the Phelpses, it is Becky he meets, and they team up to stop Tom because he is dead set on rescuing Jim. Best friend versus best friend. Tom takes a bullet in his foolish crusade, and because Jim brings him to the doctor, he is rewarded his freedom. Huck and Becky marry. Jim is Best Man.

You upload the document to Liberty.

Liberty says, THIS SCRIPT VIOLATES MORALITY LAW .

THIS SCRIPT IS SEDITIOUS, says Liberty. TOM SAWYER IS AN AMERICAN HERO.

Your boss calls. He demands to know what you said about Tom Sawyer.

Is it possible Liberty is busted, you ask him.

It wouldn't matter if she is, he says in a low voice.

As you weep in dread, the newsfeed plays. We are winning. We are stronger than ever.

You remember too much. Aid workers—incinerated. Doctors—vaporized. Journalists—shot. You see a policeman aim his rocket launcher at Black schoolchildren. How did people ever fight such power? Such hate? Looking out the great window, you watch the stars for the drone that will turn you into a puddle.

One minute you are shivering on the floor, the next, there is a party all around. Teenagers will never turn down coke and ketamine. All it took was the kid next door inviting his friends. As you wade among them, a drink in each hand, you embrace their lunkheaded energy. Nothing matters.

Then a boy says he heard the Black president—the one we don't talk about—was actually elected. That it wasn't voter fraud. And get this! He was American, not foreign. You are filled with rage and horror. You yell at him to be quiet, but he smirks, and he says the government lies. Now his friends are telling him to shut up. Idiot. Stupid little idiot. Do you really think you are safe?

Day 6. Dawn. All around your rental lie kids in a drunken stupor. Wrapped in a blanket, you sit in the armchair and write from the beginning.

Episodes 1 and 2. Huck and Jim take a raft down the Mississippi. At one farm, they help an indentured servant who beat his master and escaped. At another farm, they meet a servant who has lived for seven years in a garret, so as to watch over her children even after she escaped.

Episodes 3 and 4. Huck and Jim help build Eatonville, Florida. They survive a hurricane in the Everglades.

Episodes 5 and 6. In Stamps, Arkansas, Huck meets a little girl who has gone mute after horrible abuse happened to her. He teaches her poetry by introducing her to Shakespeare. Outside Cincinnati, he and Jim stay at a home haunted by the ghost of a dead baby.

Episodes 7 and 8. They meet a vampire and his wild seed bride. Jim develops the philosophy of Earthseed to strive for a better future.

You press submit.

THANK YOU FOR YOUR SUBMISSION, says Liberty. She says: GOD BLESS AMERICA.

Well done, says your boss. We're starting production.

What original ideas, he says. They even blew Liberty's mind.

You are not so foolish as to think your whitewashing does honor to Frederick Douglass or Harriett Jacobs or Zora Neale Hurston or Maya Angelou or Toni Morrison or Octavia Butler. But there is a story in your script nonetheless. Everywhere they go, Jim is the only Black face, and for all this, he remains the same moral compass Mark Twain intended him as.

At night you hear the door tumble down and the furniture crash. Are you a squatter? A seditionist? A corrupter of young minds? You are sipping whiskey in front of the window. Wet earth surrounds the redwoods. How fragrant it must smell.

In-charge men so decked out in high-tech military gear they look camp. Wasn't there a time when cops tried to dress like civil servants? Guns aimed at you, they say you are coming with them. A smile tugs at your lips. You ask them: where do souls go to after Hell?

Alternative Liberties

Smart Squirrel

Kurt Newton

For a visitor, the view from the tower was breathtaking. But for Jake Dumas, U.S. border guard, the scenery had become a tiring repetition of sandy scrub, distant mountains, and exhaust fumes. The four-lane freeway that ran east to west along the border below was a constant blur of tractor trailer trucks. At times Jake imagined the freeway as a giant vein where the double- and triple-tandems were blood vessels rushing toward their destination. The life's blood of the economy, so to speak. Hard-working Americans doing their part. Jake was proud of this thought and never failed to take the opportunity to share it with like-minded individuals.

But, aside from the occasional creative cloud burst, Jake was as dry a thinker as they came. Black and white, not a hint of gray. He loved his job because he believed that what he was doing was firmly on the right-hand side of God.

Alternative Liberties

He brought the binoculars to his eyes again and swept it along his stretch of the border wall.

The wall, which was more like a glorified fence, followed the same path as the river beyond: a slow-moving snake of brown water that was the last hurdle before illegals reached the edge of the new world and the thirty-foot obstruction erected there. At the moment, there were two groups amassed on the other side. Most were huddled in makeshift camps, cooking food, and drying their clothes. Waiting for the right moment to make their move.

The tower sat on an island of concrete, like a lighthouse on a sea of sand. A dozen such towers stood up and down the border at key choke points. Every morning, Jake parked his pick-up and climbed the hundred spiral steps that led to the platform, replacing the evening guard.

Jake saw movement, and his heart added a few extra beats. "Here we go," he mumbled as he watched one hapless soul with a coil of knotted rope toss a homemade grappling hook up over the top of the wall. The hook wedged itself between two steel posts. The young man struggled a bit but finally reached the top, where he sat for a moment to catch his breath before hugging one of the posts and sliding to the bottom. Those on the other side were still trying to convince him this was a bad idea. But his hearing must have been as compromised as his common sense, because he wasted no time trying to cross the freeway.

Jake liked this part the best. It reminded him of the squirrels back home that ran out into the middle of the road, stopped when they saw you coming, and, instcad of continuing on, had a change of heart and ran back under your wheels. He had seen many an illegal attempt this part of the obstacle course. Today like every other day, the sun was bright, reflecting off windshields and chrome, the traffic a steady stream of glass, metal and

Alternative Liberties

churning rubber, as if it were a singular beast. The young man dodged and spun and, miraculously, made it to lane three before an eighteen-wheeler squashed him like a bug.

There were signs along the freeway informing drivers not to slow down, not to stop, or they too would be subject to prosecution. Not that they could. The freeway was a designated trade route, no speed limit. Once on it, you were committed to the end. Jake watched as the beast slithered and roared without a hiccup, except for a few windshield wipers flapping to clear the sudden shower of red rain.

Before the end of Jake's shift, another illegal attempted the same. The man stuttered and stopped, twisted and twirled like a football running back. Jake rooted for the runner, his heart in his throat, excited but not for the same reasons the man's compatriots on the other side of the border wall were excited. The man spun and was at last clipped by a flatbed carrying stacks of fifty-foot rebar in the outer lane. The runner was tossed onto the shoulder in a cloud of dust. When the cloud cleared, the man got up, brushed himself off and began to celebrate, cheered on by those watching.

"Huh, smart squirrel," said Jake. He placed the earbuds that were always within reach on his desk into his ears, and tapped on the screen of a tablet lying beside them. The heavy thump and grinding chords of vintage thrash metal filled his headspace. He opened a small window in the much larger observation window in front of him. He felt the air outside grab his hand like a hot glove. He then picked up the high-powered rifle that leaned against the desk and raised it to his cheek. He slid the barrel through the portal, laid the scope's crosshairs on the illegal's back and pulled the trigger. The shot was barely heard above the traffic din. The illegal's chest exploded and the man collapsed where he stood.

Alternative Liberties

Minutes later, vultures swirled and descended one by one to pick the carcass clean.

Jake scanned the border wall again with his binoculars, the thrash metal still punishing his eardrums. He grinned at all the shocked faces he saw. All but one in particular. An older illegal with eyes without fear stared straight at Jake, his gaze cutting right through the binocular's lenses as if he were standing two feet away.

Jake thought about taking that one out right then and there, but there would be paperwork, a possible suspension. No, he'd wait. Ol' Stink Eye was sure to try his luck sooner or later. And when he did, Jake would be ready.

~~~

The following day was pretty much the same, except without the usual excitement of a squirrel trying to get across the freeway. A scan of the border wall provided little activity. If Jake didn't know any better, he would have guessed, after yesterday's big reveal, that there was a somber mood lying heavy on the shoulders of those in charge of selling promises of a brighter future. This while the bones of their compatriot lay within view like a roadside death marker, picked clean and now bleaching in the sun.

Jake made a special point to try and find Ol' Stink Eye but, besides each illegal looking pretty much the same, he couldn't locate that particular squirrel.

~~~

The end of the week arrived with another blistering day in a series of unrelenting heat storms. The furnace of the Southwest had been turned up to broil. The blue in the sky was drained like a dead salt lake, leaving only the white residue.

Good thing for Jake, the tower windows were UV protected, the air filtered to a pleasant 80 degrees. Not enough to cool but cool enough to get used to. There just wasn't enough moisture in the air to trade for. Sometimes, Jake opened the mini-fridge on the counter and stuck his head in. But, like the illegals and their constant quest to sneak in where the grass was greener, sun and sweat was just something one had to get used to.

And on this day, there was finally some action. Jake held the binoculars to his eyes and smiled. This time it was four men scaling the wall at once, and one of them was Ol' Stink Eye. "Oh, yeah. Come on, let's do this!" Jake cheered, carrying on an open dialogue as if his marks could hear him. When the four men reached the top of the wall, they sat, perhaps taking stock in their last moments on earth. Perhaps spending time reciting silent prayers to gods that would never help them. Perhaps they just wanted to offer themselves to the god of the bullet and get it over with. Jake would have obliged, but again, the paperwork. And Jake didn't like paperwork. It was much more interesting if they at least tried to get across the freeway. Died in the process of doing rather than just lying down and giving up.

But no, this wasn't some grand sacrifice in the name of martyrdom. This was a plan. A well-thought-out plan, as Jake would soon realize.

Ol' Stink Eye raised his fist, and when he did there came a series of reflected lights directed right at the guard tower. Jake was momentarily blinded. "Mirrors? You've got to be fucking kidding me? The squirrels have fucking mirrors!" Jake laughed at the audacity, the brilliance. "Okay, okay... you want to play it that way? Game on, mother fuckers!"

Jake couldn't see what was going on—in fact, there were twin suns still dancing on his retinas—but he imagined the scenario as he fumbled for his earbuds, hit the music, opened the portal window, and reached for the rifle, paperwork be damned. The squirrels were

Alternative Liberties

sliding down the fence, their worn footwear hitting the scrub. One by one, in a staggered relay, they took their chances, bolting between rigs, stopping and starting in a deadly game of real-life Frogger. Three, maybe only two if luck was on their side, would be taken out, but with those odds, at least one was bound to make it across.

Before that could happen, however, Jake trained his scope on the jittery reflections. He squinted at the stabbing lights and fired. The lights went out one by one. Meanwhile, he didn't hear the sound of the tower's keycard entrance being smashed and hot-wired. He thought the rumble he felt was from the music in his ears and not the assault on the spiral staircase by a man with a determination to travel two-thousand miles on foot from the jungles of Honduras. By the time Jake turned around, because he felt the air change and the energy in the room with it, he wasn't alone. Like that first meeting with Ol' Stink Eye through the binoculars, Ol' Stink Eye was indeed now only two feet away, a makeshift club raised above his head. Jake had just enough time to utter, "Smart squirrel," before the club bit down like the jaws of justice.

~~~

Jake was still a bit woozy from the knock on his head, and his vision was still blurred, but he could hear as sure a shit exactly where he was. He was standing at the edge of the freeway, the gusts from the passing trucks nearly knocking him over.

Ol' Stink Eye poked the rifle into his back. "You run across! You try make it! Take chance! It is American way, no?" Jake knew if he tried to escape, he'd get a bullet in his back for his trouble.

Jake eyed the gaps between vehicles as they passed. He envisioned his chances. He was a God-fearing man, and as far as he knew, not only was the work he was doing on the right-hand side of God, God would most surely look out for him. This was just a test. One of many he'd taken throughout his life to get where he was today. Besides, he had his newly-purchased two-hundred-dollar pair of sneakers on. That ought to count for something.

Ol' Stink Eye poked him again, nudging him closer to the edge of the pavement.

"Okay, okay, I'm going." Jake looked over his shoulder. "You swear you'll let me live if I make it across?"

Ol' Stink Eye smiled. "On my mother's grave." The smile turned into a grimace. "Now go."

Jake took a deep breath. He tasted exhaust, rubber, the metallic flavor of brake pads. The adrenaline began to pump. He could hear his thrash music in his head as if he'd had his earbuds in. *You can do this*, he told himself. And off he ran.

It was an amazing thing to watch. The power in the belief of God could carry one pretty far, but only as far as they were meant to go.

Jake did his best, sprinting from one lane to the next, waiting for just the right moment in between, enduring the narrow wind-tunnel as it tried to suck him off balance. One more lane and he'd get it done. He bolted and dove, closing his eyes as he hit the sand. To his amazement, he had reached the other side without a knock or a nick.

He got to his feet and looked toward the sky. "Thank you, Jesus!" He stared across the freeway to find Ol' Stink Eye through the gaps in the traffic and caught a glimpse of the man still smiling. That's when a rope fell over Jake's head and cinched his arms to his sides. A sudden yank dropped him onto his back and dragged him toward the wall. In less than a minute, he was hauled up and over, down into a nest of squirrels that had waited a long time for this day to come.

Alternative Liberties

Alternative Liberties

ad regum victorem

Andrew L. Roberts

From my windowless cell
I would like to send you a photograph
or maybe two
a pair of before-and-after pictures
not as a threat but as a history lesson
and a caution
a reminder of the fate of the man
whose face you seem to imitate
and assume
when playing the strong man's role
at your rallies and for the cameras
and as I imagine you must also do
when preparing in the bright lights
before your vanity's mirror
chin held high and jaw outthrust
your eyes narrowed and reflecting
the coldness of a king and natural born killer
I would like to send you photographs of the man
who made Italy's trains run on time
but whose own time ran out on that lonely road
near the village of Dongo beside Lake Como
where the partisans captured him
and later executed him with his mistress
and most of their companions

Alternative Liberties

before they dumped their corpses in the
Piazzale Loreto
yes here in my windowless cell
with the white light always burning
where I await the day of my own execution
I wish to do you this favor
this one good-intentioned service
out of Christian love and forgiveness
a gift as a caution not a threat
to send you the photo all in sharp focus
in black and white and harshest possible
resolution of your hero Mussolini
and his mistress Clara Petacci
hanging by their feet
from the naked rafters of a filling station
and the crowd of onlookers throwing stones
and spitting upon their corpses
but do not think of me only as your prisoner
or your enemy
think of me as this—your good servant
the Roman general's slave without chains
riding in your chariot of triumph
standing behind you holding the golden crown
above your head
quietly speaking into your ear the words
memento mori
offering the caution and reminder
omnius gloria brevis est
all glory is fleeting
fascists and their kingdoms fall
with a dreadful ending after all
especially for the dictator who finds himself
hanging by his feet cold and dead and small

after triumph not everything is pretty.

Drink it

Stuart Hardy

I hesitated at the bottled water aisle. I took a moment before coming to the decision, and with a heavy heart, I picked up a 24-pack and loaded it into the shopping cart along with the frozen TV dinners, cereal and dried fruit. I paid the extortionate amount at the checkout, loaded the car and set off on the five-minute drive to Mom's house that I'd been making every day for the past five years since her arthritis got too bad for her to buy her own groceries. I was still trying to keep calm. Trying to keep control of my breathing. Keep myself from breaking down.

She was happy to see me. Happier than ever, and that made me sadder.

"Sweetie! It's so good to see you!" she kissed me on the cheek as I met her at the door with a shopping bag in each hand. It was then that she saw the trunk door open behind me and the pack of water was in plain view.

"Oh, you didn't need to buy me that! Honestly, it's fine! I've still got enough to last till the weekend."

I sighed grimly and didn't respond as I took the bags through to the kitchen. I passed her framed portrait of the dear leader on the way through, refusing to look at it.

I caught sight of the faucet as I headed through to the kitchen, dry for almost a hundred days now. It always made me angry whenever I caught sight of a faucet. The most basic requirement of any modern household: running water, and yet here we all were, buying bottled water at the store and having to fill up our canteens and take communal showers at emergency bathhouses once a week. Everyone stinks. Everyone's tired. Everyone's poor. And yet still: it's not his fault. He's doing his best. Never blame him for anything that goes wrong.

I kept quiet as Mom talked while I put her groceries away. She kept talking about Saturday and how wonderful it was going to be. The great day when the water comes back on. I wasn't paying that much attention. She knew how I felt about what was about to happen, and I'd asked her so many times to stop talking about whatever the administration was up to, but she always forgot. I didn't complain though because the conversation usually derailed into whatever trivial things that Jen and my nieces were fighting about this week.

I purposefully left the pack of bottled water on the counter and folded my arms as Mom finished an anecdote.

"You wanna take your jacket off dear?" she asked.

"It's okay, I'm not stopping. I have some chores to do when I get home," I said.

"Oh. Well, you're gonna be round at the weekend, right?"

"I've got a few extra shifts this weekend, but I just want you to promise me: you'll stick with the bottled water for a few days," I said while pointing my finger emphatically at the pack of bottles.

Mom did her world-famous eyeroll at that point.

"Honestly Bobby!" she groaned.

I gritted my teeth. I'd been asking her to drop the Bobby and start calling me Rob. I hated sharing a name with that guy. She couldn't do it. Old habits die hard.

"Just, please could you do it for me. Just leave it for a few days. Just to see what happens. To make sure it's safe," I insisted.

She sighed and shook her head.

"Honestly Bobby! I don't know how you got to be so cynical. They're doing amazing things up there in DC! Who knows? Maybe one day they'll be able to fix my arthritis. Think about that! I'd be able to go get my own groceries again!"

I gritted my teeth when I saw those big round eyes of hers filled with joy and hope. I shut my eyes and held up my hand, trying to cut through it.

"Just, promise me you'll wait a few days. For me, please?"

Mom sighed. She'd been bobbing gently on her feet as she talked about it, and I saw the disappointment wash over her as my gaze met hers. She bit her lip, and she nodded.

"Okay, sweetie. I'll wait till Monday, how about that?"

I sighed.

"Tuesday. Just give it till Tuesday. I can come check on you when you try it the first time, yeah?"

"Okay, okay. Honestly, I don't know what you think's about to happen," she smirked and shook her head, and in that instant, I was a kid again and I was asking her why I couldn't have ice cream for breakfast.

"I just worry is all," I said.

I swallowed down the tiny bit of puke I felt coming up into my throat as I remembered the announcement. I was at my computer with the radio on. Breaking news interrupted the music, an announcement came that the water was coming back on, and they played a clip of the speech. It was like ice flooding through my veins as I recognized that one word among the deluge of the usual nonsense.

"The water's gonna come back on and its gonna be beautiful. Crystal clear. The purest water you've ever tasted, and it's gonna be special. Oh, so special! Bobby's put a secret ingredient in it that's gonna protect you from any kind of virus. An ingredient that's a thousand times better than vaccines! This water's gonna be so special! It's gonna clean you. Inside."

Why does no one remember him saying that? Hearing him say that word made me shudder.

Inside.

I hugged my mom before I left. I saw myself out, and I sat in my car for a while and watched the house where I grew up with my mind drifting back through the past. I wondered what Dad would say if he was still here. He probably would have bought all the BS, same as Mom, but I liked to think he would have known better and helped her see sense.

I knew I'd probably have to go check on her over my break on Saturday. She would probably keep her promise to not drink from the faucet, but her mind had started go, and you can never be sure of these things. I just prayed the news would actually report it if anyone died. Surely it would be hard to ignore people dropping dead in the street, right? Then again, you never know. Important people would probably still be drinking

Alternative Liberties

bottled, just to safe. Let the regular people take the chance. Go on. Drink it.

I sat and watched the house and thought of those millions of Americans across the country like my Mom who would do whatever the dear leader told them.

I hoped they still had someone looking out for them.

Alternative Liberties

Who's in Stall Number One

Amy Ivery Wolf

I was a girl born to a woman who was either deeply insecure or trying to protect me from the attention of men.

I had short hair in a pixie cut as a child in the 1960s. No other girl had short hair. "What about Twiggy?" my mother would say, when I objected, screaming, to having my hair cut. It was the only time I threw temper tantrums. I had neither the figure nor the face nor the PR apparatus of Twiggy, an international model, and tried in vain to convince my mother that this was not a fair comparison.

There was just Howie across the street, and strange kids who would walk right up to my face and ask, "What are you? Are you a boy or a girl?" Or not address me at all, but turn to their parents and ask, "Mommy, what's THAT?" In their eyes, I might as well have been an alien.

I think I held my tears until I was out of their sight, but it wasn't easy. That was 1965-68.

Alternative Liberties

Fast forward to 1970; I was visiting Israel with my parents. We spent several days on the beach at Herzliya with a family we knew. I ducked into the restroom complex up the beach from where we were camped out on our towels with umbrellas and sunscreen. I was thought old enough to go myself. I had no Hebrew, but everyone we met in Israel spoke English. In any case, it was only the restroom.

I looked at the pictures on the wall outside the entrance, and also at the sign in Hebrew, Arabic, English. "Women," it said. I entered. In front of a bank of sinks and mirrors, a thin, fashionable woman bent over, talking to a child. When I entered, she reared back suddenly, and looked at me, startled. She said something in Hebrew; I didn't respond. She repeated herself in English, "This is the girl's room, you shouldn't be here."

"I am a girl," I mumbled. She either didn't hear me, or couldn't hear me, so convinced was she. She got louder.

"ARE YOU A BOY?" Then, "Do you speak English?" By this time, I was speechless, so she tried five other languages. Hebrew, German, French, Arabic, Farsi for all I know—a firehose of languages, all declaring that I didn't belong here, that my gender was confusing and indeterminate. I was going into the fifth grade.

I don't remember what happened after that. Did I yell at her, "I AM A GIRL," louder this time? I know I used that restroom, because I needed to. I do remember briefly considering going into the men's room just to make her happy. That seemed infinitely more dangerous. Her interrogation was not short, but she finally tired of it. Or my mother walked in; I don't remember.

I do remember that my mother laughed the incident off and continued to make me cut my hair short.

Alternative Liberties

The second incident was in 1982. I was taking a Greyhound bus across the country from NYC to Seattle. We stopped in Omaha, Nebraska, at 2 am. I went to the ladies' room there and entered to see about eight Black streetwalkers freshening their makeup and warming up from the outside. It was January, and very cold.

The laughter and chatter stopped for a moment, as they saw me enter in my jeans, nondescript white wool sweater, and Timberland boots. And still, short hair, no makeup. One of them pointed her long, elaborately painted fingernail at me, and said loudly, "Honey, you're in the wrong room. This is the ladies' room."

Memories of the beach at Herzliya rose up in me. I had had enough. I hooked my fingers in the waistband of my jeans, fingering the button as if ready to undo it, looked her in the eyes, and replied, "I am a woman. Do you want me to show you?"

Luckily, they all laughed. And went back to their hair, makeup, gossip.

"No, honey, that's ok. I believe you. No need to do that. Go ahead." And she gestured to the stalls. I was relieved to be acknowledged as a woman, but again, the shame of not doing it right and of creating confusion was deep and swift.

The third time I was challenged in a women's restroom was by far the most sinister. It came at a time when the right-wing radio and blogosphere had been yammering on about men in women's bathrooms.

It was the end of the summer, and I was heading home from a camping trip in Montana. This was eastern Washington, as red and conservative a part of the country as I've ever been in. I had been camping for four days in a friend's horse pasture, and was about as clean as you might expect. Not very, and on my last set of reasonably clean clothes. I knew I looked to be a disheveled old hippie, but I didn't think I looked dangerous or predatory.

I ate some food on the lawn in front of my car, then put the container back in the trunk, and headed to the ladies' room. A woman was exiting and heading in my general direction.

I smiled. Apparently, this disturbed her. She smiled back and answered my greeting ("hello"), but a few paces past me, spun on her heels and followed me into the restroom. You could see the wheels in her mind (which had clearly been programmed by Rush Limbaugh) spinning and spinning.

There were four stalls, two occupied, and two young girls standing off to the side as if waiting. The woman looked at them and said, very loudly, "Is anyone accompanying the little girl in the first stall? Is she alone? I want to make sure she's not alone." She was glaring at me.

I looked to the girls. Were they scared? Intimidated? Did they even have any English? They were Asian, and very quiet. The woman was White. One of the girls answered, "We're with her. That's our sister." The woman repeated herself. "She's only four. I wanted to make sure she wasn't alone." She glared pointedly at me, long enough to make sure they understood her implication, and then walked out.

Then and only then could I enter a stall. I felt badly for the girls, who, I assumed, were frightened by her behavior. I didn't know if she'd made them afraid of me. I just wanted to pee.

At first, I was afraid to leave the restroom, but when I did, the woman was gone. At least she was away from the vicinity of the door; she may have been sitting in her truck surveilling me. I've blocked that part out of my memory.

To this day, I don't know if she accurately pegged me for a lesbian, and believed we were all child molesters. Or whether she thought I was transgender. Or whether she thought I was pagan, also true. I am not now, nor have I ever been, transgender. Nor have I ever molested a child. Nor have I entered a restroom and started screaming at someone, as she did.

This was my experience as a woman born in a female body. I can't imagine the depth and extent of the humiliation transwomen are put through, if this is what I get for short hair and no makeup. Ditto for butch women; I'm not butch but tomboy femme, sporty femme if you're paying attention and I'm dressed up. I have committed the cardinal sin; I don't dress for the attention of men. I don't fit the norm and am therefore a legitimate target. The new regime will embolden, exacerbate, and inflame this behavior. Give it room to grow and take hold, and it will only get worse.

I read online the other day the complaint of a woman who confronted a transwoman in a restroom. "All the other women took her side!" she said, bitterly.

Carry on, ladies. Keep standing up for the rights of those who have it harder than you. If you find yourself wanting to know definitively the gender of a child just because they have to pee, ask yourself what possible difference it makes.

And let them be.

Alternative Liberties

"The Terrific Leader"

Harry Turtledove

Kim woke up shivering. She lay under four blankets, but her teeth chattered like castanets. It had to be ten below outside. It wasn't a whole lot warmer here in the house. There wasn't much to burn in the fireplace, or in any fireplace in the village. The promised coal shipment hadn't come. They'd long since cut down every tree within a day's walk except for a few plums and pears that still bore. Those might go soon. If you froze now, who cared whether you had fruit later?

Just on the off chance, she flicked the switch on the lamp by the bed. The room stayed gloomy. The power was still out. It would probably come on for a couple of hours in the afternoon. She hoped it would. The Terrific Leader was scheduled to speak today, and she wanted to hear it. If anything could make you forget your troubles, one of his, well, terrific speeches would turn the trick.

Alternative Liberties

Meanwhile, gloom. The sun rose late and set early at this season, of course. And the clouds that were bringing the latest blizzard muffled its glow all the more thoroughly. You had to make do, the best you could. Self-reliance—that was the thing.

Sighing, Kim got out of bed. She'd left on all her clothes except her boots when she went to sleep. Now she got into them. With the three pairs of socks under them, they might keep her feet from freezing when she went out to forage.

She walked into the kitchen. Her mother was making tea and warming her hands at a tiny fire in a brazier. "Good morning, Mother dear," Kim said. "Are you fixing enough for two cups?"

"I suppose so," her mother said grudgingly, as if she'd hoped Kim would sleep longer so she could drink it all herself. Then she unbent enough to add, "And there's still some pickled cabbage for breakfast."

"Oh, good!" Kim hurried over to the jar. They'd lived by themselves these past three years, since the police took Kim's father out of the fields and drove away with him. Not a word had come back since. She hoped he was a labor camp, and that they hadn't simply executed him. Either way, being related to an enemy of the state only made everything more difficult.

The scent of garlic and peppers filled her nose when she opened the jar. Pickled cabbage wasn't very filling, but it was—a little—better than nothing.

On the wall above the jar was one of the three portraits of the Terrific Leader in the house. As she ate, she studied his face. He was so wise, so handsome! His piercing gaze peered far into the future. This was the greatest, strongest, freest country in the world. It wasn't perfect yet, but it was on the way. The Terrific Leader saw the way forward. You could tell just by looking.

"Here's your tea," her mother said, breaking her train of thought.

Alternative Liberties

"Thank you very much, Mother dear." Kim drank fast, before it got cold. Sure enough, the cup wasn't quite full. And the tea was weak. Like anyone else, her mother sensibly used tea leaves more than once. You never knew when you'd be able to lay your hands on more.

"I hope you have good luck," her mother said.

"Oh, so do I!" Kim replied. "We could use some good luck for a chance. We've had too much of the alternative kind."

"We're doing fine," her mother said stoutly. In the house where an unreliable had lived, the authorities were likely to have planted spy ears. They might keep working even without power for anything else. "We're doing fine, and our wonderful country and the Terrific Leader, heaven's blessings upon him, are also doing fine. Better than fine!"

"Of course, Mother dear. I'll see you later." Kim went outside.

In spite of her quilted coat and the two sweaters under it, the icy wind tore at her. Fat flakes of snow flew almost horizontally. And another blizzard was supposed to be on the way after this one. Kim pulled down the coat's hood and wrapped a muffler around the lower part of her face so only her eyes showed. The other people out and about were similarly swaddled. You recognized them not by what they looked like but by what they wore.

Even walking took work. There was a foot of snow on the ground, and drifts got two or three times that deep. Because of that, Kim nearly missed the lump in the snow in front of the Parks' house. Yes, that was a body, no doubt their eldest son; he'd been sick and getting sicker for weeks. No medicines, the nearest doctor miles away and unwilling to come for such an insignificant person... It was a sad story, but an old one.

They wouldn't be able to plant the Park boy in the village graveyard till the ground thawed, not without dynamite they wouldn't. Well, he wouldn't go off as long as the weather stayed cold.

Kim gasped. Here came Old Man Lee's dog, the meanest one she knew. He was a big brute, and did better in the snow than she did. She had a couple of stones in her pocket in case the dog or some hungry man gave her trouble.

But the beast ignored her. A moment later, she saw why: he proudly carried a rabbit in his toothy jaws. Jealousy sharp and sour as vinegar filled Kim. Old Man Lee and his nasty shrew of a wife would eat well today. Kim could hardly remember the last time she'd tasted meat. Even the guts and the head the Lees would give the dog would be so good stewed with cabbage or grain.

Grain... Of themselves, her feet were taking her to the harvest ground. You never could tell. Maybe some of what had spilled last fall was still there under the snow. Even forlorn hopes were better than none.

Another young woman was already searching the ground. She looked up warily, then relaxed and said, "Hello, Kim."

"Hello, Kim," Kim answered. She smiled, though the muffler hid it. Sharing a name was no large amusement, but sometimes small ones would do. She added, "Heaven's blessings on the Terrific Leader!"

"Heaven's blessings on the Terrific Leader!" the other Kim echoed.

They worked separately. Had they joined forces, they would have needed to share evenly. Each hoped for better than that.

Kim dug with mittened fingers till she reached the hard ground. She came across some mushrooms that had sprung up in the last thaw and then frozen when the weather turned bad again. They weren't much, but better than nothing. Into her left coat pocket—the one

Alternative Liberties

without the rocks—they went. Then, to her delight, she really did come upon some spilled grain. It joined the mushrooms in that pocket.

She got up and walked away. As soon as the swirling snow hid her from the other Kim, she hurried to a hedgerow to check traps she'd set the day before. The wind would soon blot out her tracks. She almost whooped for joy when she found a big, fat rat noosed in a snare, hanged like a leftish deviationist. Rat wasn't as good as rabbit, but it was ever so much better than nothing. After resetting traps that were sprung but hadn't caught anything (or that had been robbed before she got to them), she happily headed for home. Tonight there'd be... not a feast, but food.

Her mother exclaimed in delight when Kim showed her what she'd brought home. A little past two, the power came on. Lights flickered to dim, low-voltage life. What electric tools they had would work for a while.

And the Terrific Leader was going to speak! With her mother and the rest of the village, she gathered in the square to hear his inspiring words. The communal televisor, like authorized radios, got only government-mandated channels so no one could be exposed to outsiders' wicked lies.

There he was! He was an old, old man now, though—of course!—still strong and vigorous. Everybody knew one of his sons, or perhaps his son-in-law, would eventually succeed him, and then a grandson, and so on. But he still ruled, as he had since long before Kim was born; even thinking such thoughts was risky.

He wore his trademark red cap, with his slogan—AMERICA IS GREAT AGAIN!—on the front in big letters. "I have a message for all of you," he rasped. "The crime and violence that today afflict our nation will end soon.

I mean very soon. Safety will be restored. Everything will be terrific, the way it's always been.

"Our plan keeps putting America first. The powerful no longer beat upon people who cannot defend themselves. I have restored law and order. Our border wall has stopped illegal immigration, stopped gangs and drugs, and done lots of other totally terrific stuff, too. I respect the dignity of work and the dignity of working people. It trumps anything else there is. I mean anything else. Keep at it. America first like I said, America last, America always!"

"America first!" the village chorused as the televisor went off. Kim's eyes filled with tears. She couldn't help it. She loved the Terrific Leader.

Alternative Liberties

Brown Eyes

Ell Rodman

Our vehicles took a hard left after the bridge. Three Ford all-terrain SUV's rolling down walking trails until we sat on the edge of the water staring at thirty faces on the far bank covered in sweat and grime. Illegals under the bridge on the Mexican side. Our job was to process and detain.

For two hours they gesticulated amongst themselves pointing from the river to two-by-fours tossed in the mud, until slowly they began to gather in the water.

We smoked cigarettes and drank bottled water from our coolers and wished they'd get on with it.

One woman wore an inflatable life jacket, others had soccer balls. Still more shared space on floating driftwood. Most wore backpacks that looked to be full. A lot to ask for a soccer ball to carry over the river. Chaos ensued the moment they left shallow water.

Two men sharing a piece of driftwood argued loudly. One was a strong swimmer while the other thrashed at the water, causing their would-be raft to turn constantly.

Another man was too heavy for his device, a mud-stained Styrofoam cooler that took on water the moment it got wet. He shouted *ayuda* while trying desperately to stay afloat.. River currents splintered the group before they could even reach halfway to shore. I wanted to look away. Desperation destroys all logic, and drowning hands will grab anything to stay afloat. Even family.

Then a little boy lost his grip on a soccer ball. He disappeared into the river and popped back up gasping. A woman who must have been his mother screamed his name a half dozen times in quick succession. He couldn't swim. His soccer ball was out of reach. All we could do was watch dumbly from a distance; we operate under orders not to save illegals even if they drown in arms reach. Sometimes we ignored that order. But not today.

That's when I saw her.

My memory probably plays tricks on me, but I remember a slim figure leaping in and out of the water like a dolphin to reach the drowning boy. She pulled him towards the ball, then back to his mother. Like a water shepherd, she swam around the group herding them into sharing their flotation devices. It seemed like only minutes before they made it safely onto American soil, where we promptly detained them.

Welcome to America.

The woman in the flannel sat on the outside of the group staring into the horizon. An outsider. A lone woman trekking into the unknown. I imagine she wondered what was next, looking at an America that looked remarkably similar to the Mexico she just left behind.

I wanted to thank her for saving the boy. I didn't want to see a drowning. But her big eyes got wider looking at our uniforms and body armor splashed with the words *Border Patrol*. I thought better of it.

I hoped she made it.

~~~

Trump started his second term with a wave of deportation orders that would have made Andrew Jackson blush. Criminal record? Gone. Gang membership? Gone. Unemployed? Gone. None of the above, fluent English, provider for an American wife and kids? Also gone. All that mattered was which side of the invisible line you were born on. The Modern Trail of Tears now ran down a dozen highways in cattle cars.

We all cheered the night Trump got re-elected. You couldn't find a single frowning face among patrol officers. We thought we were prepared for what was coming. We didn't know what deporting millions would look like, smell like, *feel* like. I knew there would be tears. I didn't know so many would come from children and old men. The last leg of their deportation journey was provided by local trucking companies in southern Arizona and New Mexico or western Texas more accustomed to hauling cattle than human beings. You'd be hard-pressed to find a Johnson or Smith in the driver's seat down here. I provided security for a trucker named Guzman, who deported boys and girls named Gutierrez, Gonzalez, and Garcia.

Unconsciously, I kept an eye out for Brown Eyes, whose name I never learned. I never decided what I would do if I found her. Give an extra water bottle as I deported her to a country she may not even be from? Free her? Cohabitate and fall in love? I chided myself for the sick fantasy.

A few months later, I had my answer.

Drone cameras caught another group crossing at weak spots along the border wall. My patrol arrived a few hours later to find a dozen women stranded in the desert with no food or water. Even in autumn, that's a death sentence. In the distance, three men fled back to Mexico, one firing pistol rounds wildly over his shoulder as he went. Warning shots to let us know not to pursue. Coyotes. Paid to traffic vulnerable people into America by foot or boat regardless of weather or danger.

I'm paid to send the weak and vulnerable back into their arms. It's the perfect business plan. Take money to deliver people to America until we deport their customers right back to them, twice as desperate. Most of the women in this group spoke some English. They'd been here before. Maybe for years. A young woman in a sweatshirt handed out snacks, checking in here and there.

I didn't know it was her at first. A few years older, a few pounds heavier. She didn't pay me the slightest bit of mind.

It was night time in October an hour west of where Mexico, New Mexico, and Texas meet. Fifty degrees isn't terribly cold unless you've spent months acclimating to temperatures over one hundred. Then fifty degrees might as well be Antarctica. When the moon is bright and hangs low over the horizon, you can almost fool yourself into believing the white sand of the southwest is snow.

The women sat in a circle on the cold ground drinking water bottles from the patrol truck. Quiet conversations were drowned out by radio chatter from our belts. Contacting headquarters, contacting detention centers, contacting trucks with that horrible smell. Red and blue flashing lights illuminated their faces in the dark. One was in bad shape; an older woman, someone's abuela. No way of knowing whether she was leaving her grandchildren or returning to them. She heaved onto the ground. Her hands shook. The young woman in the sweatshirt kneeled beside her, put a blanket around her shoulders, rubbed her hands. The hood of her sweatshirt slid back just enough for me to see smooth chestnut skin and wide brown eyes.

Brown Eyes.

Just like in the Rio Grande so long ago, Brown Eyes circled the group helping where it was needed. Small snacks, extra water, brave words. I've seen men leaving a casino after gambling it all and losing. Dejection. Rage. Bitter tears. These women gambled it all on a chance for a better life. They gambled it all on a stranger's ability to reunite them with family. Yet after Brown Eyes speaks with them, these women don't look full of rage. They look defiant. I tried not to stare at her. I tried not to ask.

Where have you been?

Are you alright?

Who turned you in?

Do you need my help?

The last one is a farce. How can I help her? Let her go, sure. Then what? She dies trying to walk to San Antonio. Gets kidnapped on the road by men who know she won't be missed or looked for. A dangerous thought needles at my brain.

She could stay with me.

Ridiculous. An illegal immigrant with a Border Patrol agent amidst the largest deportation in history. She'll spread her legs in appreciation. What next, marry her for the green card? I would need to black the windows, stop hosting friends, turn away surprise visitors, and explain away my sudden reclusivity. I can't hide Anne Frank. Yet the instinct remains. An illogical, impossible thought. Embarrassing thoughts but I tell myself it wouldn't be that way. I wasn't that way.

Do something.

If I convince my partners to look the other way, I could drive her to safehouses near Santa Fe or Los Angeles. Or to a neighborhood of immigrants on work

Alternative Liberties

visas, let her get lost in the crowd. Oh they might, but they'd talk and then what?

It's early January. Freezing sand whips the patrol car at night. Dry, freezing wind leaves mild skin rashes. We spend most of our time inside, trying not to talk about a disastrous New Year's Eve party. A year's worth of stress built by dragging people from their homes and tossing them into Mexico, unleashed by free tequila imported from that same country. Head of the department is still taking quotes for the damage. I don't know if it's possible to be hung over a week later, but I still feel like shit. The wind outside is like white noise, the car's heat warms my face. I didn't know I'd fallen asleep until I'm awoken by the radio. Another river crossing. A loner. I call back.

At this time of year?

The man on the other side affirms.

10-4.

Border crossings decrease in the winter, but don't go away. It isn't shocking to have someone make the trek, even in January. A loner on foot is shocking. And now they're going to get evacuated. That's the word we're supposed to use now. Evacuated. *Deported* lost favor after a few months news coverage of families loaded into trucks. We aren't deporting them to poverty in Mexico. We're *evacuating* them from their dire circumstances working American jobs and feeding their families. The flash of a memory crosses my mind. A mother and her two children, evacuated in November to Tijuana. All of northern Mexico is a mess of refugees now. No resources to head south. Vanishingly few ways to cross north. They're probably holding for dear life onto the fabric of a Red Cross tent that the wind threatens to turn into a kite.

I leave the station alone. One car, one agent. My usual partners were suspended after the New Year's fiasco, but I think I can handle a lone crosser. It's a simple job; don't need much more than food, water, and handcuffs. Racing along Route Ninety, my patrol vehicle is unsteady in the wind. Powerful blasts push it left and right by inches. I can't imagine what this walker is feeling.

I like driving alone. I don't listen to music, I just let my thoughts wander. Often they wander to another life, where I'm anything but a Border Patrol agent. Maybe I finish that HVAC apprenticeship and run electrical wire for my cousin's construction business. Or I say screw it all and move to Colorado. Or Puerto Rico. Or maybe New Hampshire. Do I like snow? I don't know. I don't know if I like snow.

The roar of tires on rock and earth runs underfoot as I offroad towards a rough coordinate given for our lone ranger. It's now past midday, which means the sun is getting low already. Its glare is in my eyes as the SUV bounces, so much so that I don't see the figure in blue laying in the middle of the cold road. A plastic bag blown in the wind catches my attention, and I slam on the breaks just before hitting the blue shape, barely caught in my periphery.

The figure's hood flaps in the wind. I call in for an ambulance; even after a car screeching over sand, it didn't budge. Whoever lay under the blue hood didn't just fight hard against the elements, they fought against unconsciousness. Fingernails on the left hand are yellowed, thin fingers purple with bruising. The hood hangs low over the eyebrows while the jacket collar rises up over the mouth. There are no rises or falls from the chest. I pick up the radio again.

Need medical attention for one. No breathing. They ask my position, and I give it.

Nearest carriage is forty minutes out.

I forget to click off the radio before swearing. If there's any chance of saving a life with CPR, it won't be after forty minutes. It'll have to be me. The blue jacket is rattier than it first appeared. Moth holes pierce its pockets while duct tape encases frayed sleeves at the wrist. Inside the jacket is the body of a starved woman. Her eyes and lips are swollen, her face gaunt. Dozens of needle marks in varying states of healing dot her arm from wrist to elbow. It isn't until I lean down to begin CPR that her face begins to look familiar. After lifting a swollen eyelid, it becomes clear enough that I stumble back onto the cold southwest sand with my heart sunk into my stomach.

Brown Eyes.

Border Patrol sent her back to Mexico with no money and no kin. She did what she needed to survive. Probably a Cartel girl. There are other injuries; a bruise here, abrasions there. It's clear why she crossed alone. Escape. Brown Eyes made it just far enough to die alone on US soil. We did this to her. I did. It was only a few years ago that this job felt important. "A few years ago" feels like another universe now. Rip them from home, send them away, catch them again, repeat. Each time they come back a little weaker, a little hungrier, a little more desperate. Each time a few more pieces missing. Or, like Brown Eyes lying dead before me, many pieces all at once. What do we do it for? A few thousand people die so that a few million can feel comfortable?

I don't know how long I sat staring at her corpse praying for a flicker of life. It never came. Instead, I get the flicker of a memory, the same as before, a mother and two children sent packing to Tijuana. I know where the camp is.

Cold air whips my neck and face. It blows across empty, arid ground that stretches beyond the horizon. Maybe I can reach Tijuana. Maybe I can find them, get them across the border, let them stay with me. But right now, I can't leave the body. I need to feel what she felt. Even if only a fraction.

Even if only for a moment.

Tricentennial Blues

Jenna Hanan Moore

Looking back, it's hard to believe I accepted the stories without question. That the Second Republic was founded by patriots who bravely opposed the corrupt excesses of the Old Republic, that the bloodshed following their 2025 rise to power was entirely the fault of the opposition, that life was much better here in the Second Republic than in Pacifica. We were told Pacifica was a failed state. Made up of the breakaway states of California, Oregon, and Washington, it was a den of leftist iniquity, full of corruption and crime, verging on economic collapse. I didn't question the narrative. Not until the summer of the Tricentennial Celebration when my brother's illness changed everything.

Perhaps it was odd to celebrate the Tricentennial when the Second Republic wasn't even fifty years old. But forming the Old Republic had been the first step towards our glorious Second Republic—an imperfect attempt to be sure, but a necessary one. Besides, it's

Alternative Liberties

human nature to celebrate round numbers, and if there was one thing we needed in the summer of 2076, it was a celebration.

Things could have been worse—indeed things *were* worse in Pacifica, as President Turley reminded us nearly every speech he gave—but years of drought had pushed our food prices sky high, our power grid was straining to keep up with demand, and jobs for new graduates were scarce. The future looked bleak.

Senator Stephens, once a rising star in the party, even suggested reinstating Social Security or some kind of national pension system. "Give old folks the option to retire, and they'll clear the path for younger people to enter the workforce," he'd reasoned. Now he was in jail awaiting trial.

Attorney General Janson announced Stephens's arrest at a press conference. "Advocating for the return of Social Security gives aid and comfort to Pacifica, our greatest enemy. Such treachery shall not stand." Janson pumped his fist into the air thirty-seven times during his brief announcement. I know because I counted.

"Damn right!" my father called out, pumping his fist along with Janson as we watched the live broadcast. "We won't go back to the way things were before the Second Revolution. Working people supporting all that dead weight." He scoffed, then looked across the room at my mother. "Are you listening to this, Martha?"

My mother nodded without looking up from her crossword puzzle. To avoid my father's gaze, I turned my attention to my tablet, pretending to be absorbed in the screenplay I was reading for my script analysis class. I'd already earned my art degree, but with no job prospects and little else to fill my time, I was taking film classes to alleviate the boredom.

"What about you, Jillian?" my father asked.

That's when the call came.

Alternative Liberties

My mother took the call in the study and emerged minutes later, her face white as a ghost. "Martin's in the hospital," she said, her voice shaking. "It's polio. His left leg is paralyzed, and his hand is numb."

My father's face fell. My brother's promising career as a surgeon was likely over. So, too, was his summer job picking fruit. The young men of the Second Republic were expected to take on physically demanding temporary jobs in construction and agriculture so we wouldn't have to rely on immigrant labor like the Pacificans did. But the jobs were grueling. Many otherwise patriotic young men of my generation had received medical exemptions. My father was proud that Martin had bucked the trend.

~~~

My brother was in an isolation ward. We visited him via comm screen daily, which was more than we'd talked to him since he'd left for the farm at the beginning of the summer. At first, things weren't so bad. But my parents reacted quite differently to the change in Martin's circumstances, which soon led to late-night arguments when the comm screen was off and they thought I couldn't hear them. Mom was furious with Martin's employer. "They should have closed when the outbreak began," she insisted. My father initially defended the decision, but he eventually admitted she was right. He begged her not to make waves.

Once Martin came home, my father pressed him to choose a new specialty which angered my mother. She wanted to give him time. Martin admitted to me privately that he feigned sleep to get them to stop arguing about his future.

When my best friend invited me to lunch, I jumped at the opportunity. Truth be told, I'd been avoiding Isabella. She was a graduate assistant in the university's astrophysics department, and all she ever talked about was her work. It's not that I wasn't happy for her. I was. But we didn't have much in common anymore, and if I'm honest, I was a little jealous. Isabella knew what she wanted from life and how to get it. Everything I wanted was just out of reach.

"Pity they've pulled so much funding from mech suit research," Isabella said after I described Martin's grim prognosis.

"Mech suit?" I asked. "What's that?"

"It's kind of like a suit of robotic limbs a person can climb into. In theory, it would give pretty much anyone extra physical strength, allow them to do things they maybe can't do now. Could be useful for construction, for instance, or for making repairs to the outside of a capsule during spaceflight. There are still some problems a human being can spot better than a mech unit. But another application would be for disabled people."

"Like Martin."

"Exactly," she agreed.

"Why'd they stop funding the research?"

"They haven't, not entirely." Isabella sighed and pursed her lips. "It's just not the best field of study for a roboticist to go into these days."

"Why?" I asked.

Isabella looked around. "Priorities are—elsewhere," she whispered.

"Could Martin get a prototype?"

"Dunno." She set down her coffee and looked at me. "I doubt they'd have one at the university; they're not that far along. But I can introduce you to my friend Manny. He used to be on the mech suit team. Maybe he can point you in the right direction."

"Oh, could you?"

She sighed. "Of course. Just—don't get your hopes up."

~~~

Isabella introduced me to Manny Carson the next day. His disheveled hair and worn sport coat did not inspire confidence.

"Glad to meet someone who still thinks mech suits are viable," he said without looking away from his white board. He put the finishing touches on an equation, then turned to face me. "The truth is they're much further ahead in biorobotics research in Pacifica. That's why I got out. The party's cutting off our noses to spite Pacifica's face."

Glaring at Manny, Isabella put her finger to her lips.

"What do you mean?" I asked.

"We ain't gonna crack the code unless we work with their scientists," he explained. "Sharing research is fine so long as we don't have to admit they're the ones with the edge. In biorobotics, they've got the edge. That's why I'm working on independent mech units for the Jupiter Project."

"There's no way Pacifica will get to the Jovian moons before we do," Isabella interjected. "We're pretty far ahead of them there."

"For some reason, they decided that with the drought finding ways to increase crop yield is a higher priority than beating us to Jupiter," Manny said, a hint of sarcasm in his voice. "Fancy that."

Isabella laughed nervously. "I guess when your economy's as bad as theirs, you can't fund everything."

Manny shrugged. "Sure, sure. Listen, Jillian, I can put you in touch with my contacts on the Pacifican biorobotics team if you want. But you'll need to be careful. Isabella tells me you're a film student, right?"

I nodded.

"Okay, good. Apply for an exit visa. Tell them you're making a documentary about Pacifica's science program. Say you want to show how far behind they are or something. They'll eat that shit up. You do that, and I'll put you in touch."

~~~

Getting the exit visa was easier than I'd anticipated. Leaving the country was harder. After answering dozens of questions about my proposed documentary, allowing Border Patrol agents to search my luggage, and signing a loyalty pledge, I paid the exit toll and drove ten feet ahead to the border.

The Pacifican customs agent was surprisingly friendly. She asked three questions, stamped my passport, smiled, and said, "Welcome to Pacifica." With that, I drove into enemy territory.

~~~

At first glance, the California desert looked so much like the Arizona desert that it didn't feel like a foreign country. Then I noticed the billboards. Many were like the billboards lining the highways at home—telling motorists how many miles to the next diner, hotel, or gas station—but they didn't light up, and there were ads for marijuana shops but none for gun shows.

It wasn't until I approached Los Angeles that things really started to feel different. The volume of traffic increased, but despite L.A.'s population of twenty million, it wasn't as bad as the congestion in the large cities of the Second Republic. Maybe this was because of the rail lines. Three levels of tracks ran alongside the freeway, and sleek, long trains rushed past frequently. To my astonishment, the smog was barely visible. The skies over Phoenix hadn't been this clear in decades.

The biggest surprise was meeting the biorobotics team. Their lab was on the fourth floor of the Pacifican Institute for Scientific Research. The door was ajar. Inside the brightly lit room, a tall man in a white lab coat stood at a long, high table, his back facing me.

"Hello?" I called. "I'm looking for Cameron Ginsburg." The man turned around and my jaw dropped. Without thinking, I blurted out, "You're Black."

"My, you are perceptive." He raised his eyebrows.

"I—I'm sorry," I stammered. "It's just—I mean, Manny didn't tell me and—it's pretty rare to see a Black scientist in the Second Republic. There's nothing wrong with it; it's just, well, rare."

"Ah, you must be Jillian. Cam told me about you. It may surprise you to know that here in Pacifica, all kinds of people are allowed to do research. Everyone gets to contribute, and no one's overlooked."

"I really am very sorry," I said.

"Don't worry about it. I'm Jet Calloway. I work with Cameron." He extended his hand.

"Jillian Allen. Again, I'm so sorry. My friend works with Manny Carson. He used to do biorobotics research. Maybe you know him?"

Jet nodded. "I've spoken to him."

"I'm here looking for a mech suit prototype for my brother," I explained. "He's in med school, specializing in surgery, but he got polio and now one leg's paralyzed and his hand—he can move his fingers, but not very well."

"You know there's a vaccine, right? Been around for 120 years."

"I know but—" How could I explain that they pulled the vaccine's approval due to safety concerns when I wasn't even sure I believed that anymore?

"No matter," Jet said. "What's done is done. I doubt we'll be able to help, but you'll really want to talk to Cam as well. He's at the dentist. Shall we grab a bite to eat while we wait for him?"

I nodded, and Jet led me to a diner two blocks from the Institute.

"I guess you're surprised," he said after our meals arrived. "We get some of your channels on the satellite, so I've seen their," he paused, "perspective, about life in Pacifica. It's not what you expected, is it?"

"No," I replied. "But I'll bet it's no utopia, either!"

Jet laughed. "No one thinks Pacifica's a utopia. Far from it! But here's the thing: no one expects it to be. We just do our best to try to make life better. People don't always agree on how to do that, in fact, they rarely do. Sometimes the things we try work, sometimes they don't. But we keep trying. Anyway, want dessert? The gelato's pretty good here."

I smiled at the non sequitur. "I'd love some."

~~~

Cameron Ginsburg was there when we returned. After Jet introduced us, I explained the purpose of my visit. As Cameron rose, I quickly realized why Jet wanted me to wait for him. The chair he'd been sitting in, which I'd mistaken for an ordinary swivel chair, was instead a sophisticated wheelchair. He didn't rise from the chair; he rose with it. The base under the seat expanded and tilted slightly backwards as the seat itself tipped forward so it was parallel with the base. Cameron was now standing, leaning back against the seat cushion. He pivoted and wheeled the device toward an alcove at the far end of the robotics lab.

"Then you're like my brother!" In the Second Republic, someone like Cameron Ginsburg probably wouldn't have a plum job in a research center, but after my embarrassing conversation with Jet Calloway, I knew better than to say as much.

"Yes and no." Cameron stopped when we reached the alcove. Then, he pressed a button which released a harness that held his legs in place and stepped onto the floor. "I have muscular dystrophy. I can still move every muscle in my body, but I'm getting progressively weaker."

He pressed a button and a machine that looked like the exoskeleton of a headless robot was lowered to the floor. "This one works with the movement of the user's muscles," he explained as the suit opened, then closed around him. "I move my legs, and the robotic limbs take their cue from my movement, only it does everything I do with strength I don't have. Like this."

He walked across the floor, did a cartwheel, then leapt into the air, nearly reaching the high ceiling. When he landed, he stepped out of the mech suit. "The problem for your brother is he can't move his left leg to operate the mech limb."

"That's where my research comes in," Jet interjected. "I'm working on a neural interface that sends signals directly from a person's brain to the mech limbs. Unfortunately, all we've been able to manage so far is rudimentary movements."

"Allow me to demonstrate." Cameron, now standing next to a different mech suit, donned what looked like a silver bathing cap. The suit took several steps. Its gait was awkward, much like that of a toddler walking for the first time. "It might work better for your brother because he has movement in one of his legs. We'd have to test it with him in the suit to know."

"Yeah, but the real problem would be his hand," Jet explained. "He doesn't need more strength; he needs more precision."

Cameron returned to his chair. "That's a fascinating challenge." He paused for a moment, biting his lip. "I think we could engineer a mech limb for that, but we'd really need to work with him in person. Any chance you could come back and bring him with you?"

"I really don't know," I replied honestly. "But I guess I'll have to find a way, won't I?"

~~~

After that, I made multiple trips to Pacifica, ostensibly to finish my documentary. As a ploy to bring Martin with me, I hired him to narrate the film. As it turned out, he was a brilliant voice artist, and providing narration left him with a lot of time to work with Cameron and Jet.

Six months later, on what was to be our final foray, my brother decided to remain in Pacifica and married Cameron's sister. He took me aside after their simple wedding at the registry office. "You should think about staying too, Jillian. You can live with Lily and me until you figure out what you want to do."

I declined his offer. For one thing, figuring out what I wanted to do with my life wasn't exactly my strong suit. I didn't want to rely on my brother forever. More importantly, for all its flaws, my country was worth fighting for. To do that, I'd have to go home.

Alternative Liberties

So Gallantly Livestreaming

Don Bisdorf

Derek had begged Senator Snow to lose his name when it came time to choose a director for the first Fourth of July parade of the President's fourth term. She hadn't.

He knew he had his own success to blame. He'd dragged the prior year's parade from disaster to triumph. People had stopped talking about him as "the man who tanked a seven-billion-dollar e-sports platform" and started praising him as "the man who saved Independence Day." He'd accepted the congratulatory call from the President with humility, and then he'd fled to a private mental health retreat in West Virginia. But then fall and winter had come and gone, and Senator Claudia Snow had called him again, speaking the four words no American could refuse, not if they wanted to keep their citizenship: "The President needs you." By the first morning of July, symbols of the parade's chaos littered Derek's home in Alexandria—

whiteboards with multicolored lists, laptops left open to municipal codes and e-mail threads, hundreds of sticky notes, and discarded take-out boxes that smelled of pizza and curry. He'd been on the phone, telling the principal of a California high school she had to have her marching band on Pennsylvania Avenue promptly at 6 AM on the Fourth, when the phone beeped, and its screen told him Senator Snow was calling.

~~~

"Six AM *Eastern* time," he told the principal, and took the new call. "Senator?"

"Derek. Why am I hearing that you're still trying to hold the parade in D.C.?"

"Um." Of all the mystifying yet menacing calls he'd received from the senator, this one had started as an eight out of ten.

"The Capitol, Derek. The Capitol's been moved to Palm Beach."

"...Florida?"

"You can't be the only person in the country who doesn't know this."

"Please, hold." He glanced between the two laptops on his kitchen table, then muted his phone. "Taylor!"

His more-or-less girlfriend poked her tousled blond head over the back of the couch. "Uh huh?"

"Have you heard anything about the Capitol moving?"

"Yeah, to Palm Beach. Congress assembled at Mar-a-Lago two hours ago."

"Why aren't I seeing anything about this?"

"It's all over Trumpet."

Derek wondered if there was a word for the sinking feeling he got whenever he realized he needed to join yet another social media platform. A thought struck him. "Wait. Trumpet isn't open to the public yet."

"They expanded the beta and I got an invite. You need to start networking with the right people. All the

Alternative Liberties

big influencers are there, now." She disappeared behind the couch. He was reminded once again who had the brains in their relationship.

He stared at the phone, considering the obvious futile protest—surely no one could expect him to relocate the parade from D.C. to Palm Beach in *three days*—settled on a lie, and took the senator off mute. "The story that the parade is in D.C. is just a cover, for security reasons. Behind closed doors, we're all systems go for Florida."

"Good thinking. All the antifa terrorists will be in D.C. instead. They won't even get any media attention. Speaking of. Why is all the publicity still on X?"

This time he thought he knew where this was coming from. "One second," he said, and muted the phone again. "Taylor, the SpaceX rocket that crashed in Texas. As of today, was it antifa terrorists, or was it Elon's fault?"

She didn't bother peeking over the sofa. "Elon was working with antifa. The President trumped about it just a few hours ago."

"He did *what* about it? Tweeted?"

"Derek, it hasn't been *tweet* for years, and the platform is called Trumpet..."

"I get it. So yesterday, when the President told everyone it was antifa... "

"Bad information from the FBI. The FBI Director's being denaturalized and deported. And Elon. And most of SpaceX. And ten thousand Democratic voters from Austin."

He stared at her.

"Well, the rocket landed in a red district and took out about five thousand Trump voters, so to balance..."

"Christ." He unmuted the phone again. "Right, I have a team on standby, waiting to delete our material from X and roll out to Trumpet. Just waiting for the right moment. If you think now's a good time... "

"Now would be perfect. Glad to hear you're a step ahead of this, Derek. See you in Palm Beach."

After the senator hung up, Derek put his head on the kitchen table, among his sticky notes and take-out napkins, and tried to breathe.

He heard Taylor's soft tread on the carpet, felt her hands on his shoulders. "Want me to pack you a bag?"

"Aren't you coming?"

"Oh, I packed an hour ago."

He sighed, sat up, and met her amused blue eyes. "What would I do without you?"

"You'd watch a lot more porn. And you'd never get the Wordle right."

The security lines at Ronald Reagan Airport were twelve hours long, so Derek hired a driver to take the two of them to Florida. On the way down, Taylor asked a Trumpet dev to get Derek an account, and Derek rushed VIP invitations to a pack of influencers with high follower counts. He sent out a press release, deflected a few journalists, offered empty reassurances to the corporations who'd put their names on parade floats, and finally, after hours of phone tag, reached the mayor of Palm Beach. The mayor knew one snarl from the President would reduce her from elected official to hunted pariah, and she responded to Derek's call with all the enthusiastic cooperation he could have wished for, promising him the parade route he requested. He hung up just as his driver pulled into the shut-down motel the President's team had conscripted for his headquarters.

He got out with Taylor, and she stared at the motel with dismay. Their limousine idled alone in the Loxahatchee Super 8's sun-cracked parking lot. Dust and grime dulled the windows of vacant rooms.

Alternative Liberties

Condemnation notices and public health warnings decorated the check-in office door.

"They told me it would be a Marriott," Derek said.

"I'm going shopping." Taylor tossed her bag into the back seat of the limo and climbed in after it, with a brief flash of toned calves and high heels. "And surfing. And maybe dancing."

"So, 'don't wait up' is what you're saying?"

She crooked a finger at him, and he walked over and ducked down. She put her hand on the back of his neck and gave him a kiss. "Derek. I think you're screwed. I tell you this as a professional."

He chose a room and moved in. His first act as the motel's sole guest was to take a magic marker and sketch a map of his planned parade route over one bilious off-white wall. That done, he took a step back and surveyed his diagram, scowling, reluctantly admitting that Taylor was right, as usual. He was screwed.

The parade he'd originally imagined consisted of three thousand marchers and performers. A hundred vehicles, including floats, balloons, five military tanks and a mobile ICBM launcher. Food trucks. Merchandise booths. Streetside bleachers and banners. In theory, given enough promises and threats, he *could* have moved it all to Florida.

But, for the past three years, the streets of Palm Beach had been underwater. Climate change had transformed the city into a new Venice, and the Army Corps of Engineers had elevated Mar-a-Lago twenty feet to keep it high and dry. The President expected to see his grand patriotic parade sail past on Lake Worth Lagoon.

Derek discarded several hopeless ideas—attaching buoyancy devices to the parade trucks and the marching band musicians; constructing a floating road down the middle of Lake Worth—before the most-practical solution came to him. He logged into his new Trumpet account and scrolled through a feed of rabid early adopters until he found a likely subject. He tapped out a DM.

Just before midnight, Arthur Pearl, self-described Admiral of the People's Navy of Florida, arrived at his hotel door. The admiral, middle-aged and white-bearded, put Derek in mind of Santa Claus by way of Appalachia. He wore a classic red MAGA hat, a green camo tactical vest, and an understandably suspicious squint.

Derek invited Arthur inside, offering him a chair and a beer from the six-pack an Amazon drone had dropped off. Arthur popped the bottlecap and, thawing somewhat, gave his qualifications. "ICE couldn't handle it. Coast Guard wasn't doing much better. President said so himself. Someone had to defend our shores. Friends and I loaded ammo and floodlights into our fishing boats and went on patrol. About a thousand of us now, a couple hundred watercraft. Some are Zodiacs. Got a few speedboats for high-speed interception, couple of forty-foot yachts. Flagship's a hundred-foot catamaran, for now."

The map scrawled on Derek's wall hadn't escaped the admiral's attention. Arthur pointed to it with the neck of his bottle. "Setting up some kind of patrol? Undercover Secret Service thing?"

Derek leaned back in the creaking desk chair the room had come with, and gave a conspiratorial smile. "It's a parade, and your People's Navy is invited."

Arthur's eyes slowly lit up.

The second day of July marked the return of Derek's good luck. The Trumpet influencers had arrived, commencing a rapid blast of selfies and pre-parade gushing. The mayor had given Derek dictatorial, no-questions-asked control of the city's law enforcement, civil services, and emergency responders. Admiral Arthur had taken to his mission with zeal, transmitting endless photos of fishing boats equipped with machine guns, red-white-and-blue bunting, videos of jet-skiers in camo carrying American flags, and a list of People's Navy officers whose garage bands wanted to perform.

Late that night, Derek rewarded himself by crawling under the bed sheets and closing his eyes.

At two in the morning, he woke, He missed Taylor.

He checked his phone. Her Trumpet feed displayed several selfies she'd taken in a Boca Raton club, wearing a new sparkling silver dress, laughing with a revolving cast of equally young and attractive people.

"Good for you," he said with a drowsy smile.

He kept scrolling, and the smile fell off his face.

He sat up and scrolled further, his heart pounding. Then he switched on the lamp, jumped out of bed, and made a call.

A staffer took mercy on him and woke up Senator Snow. "I hope this is good news," the congresswoman told him. "The President is over the moon for this year's parade."

"I can *see that*. He's been trumping about it all night." Derek checked his phone screen. "A multimillion-dollar amphibious float from each of the thirty-eight states, each one with live performers and twenty-foot-high digital displays. Warships from Russia and North Korea flying MAGA flags. The cast of Guns of Freedom 5, acting out the movie's big fight scene on a floating model of the Statue of Liberty?"

"It's ambitious. But if anyone can pull it off, you can."

"Senator." He drew a breath, tried to find the tone of voice that would make her understand. "Where is this coming from? I never promised anyone *any* of those things."

Alternative Liberties

"I'm sure whatever you were planning would be amazing. But the President thought it was important that everyone should see what his vision of America is. It's the first year of his fourth term. The world wants to know what he has to say."

"Claudia, if the President wants to say something, he can tweet about it. I mean X about it. Trump about it. *Whatever.* It's... " He checked his phone again. "Twenty-seven hours before the parade is supposed to start!"

"Which means I should get off the phone and let you get to work. We're all very excited, Derek."

She hung up.

Derek stared at his phone. He scrolled á little more.

Taylor had posted a video of herself making out with Sofia Scout, star of Guns of Freedom 5.

Derek went into the bathroom and threw up.

Twenty minutes later, he came out of the bathroom with an empty stomach and a plan. He sent a DM to Taylor.

Derek: *got a minute?*

Taylor: *you should come to this party. sofia has a hot friend i want to set you up with.*

Derek: *your contact at Trumpet. i need a favor from him. a big favor.*

Taylor: *i'll tell him to give you anything you want.*

Derek: *you're an angel*

Taylor: *so no sexy italian understudy for you?*

Derek: *ask me again after the parade*

The Admiral called him back at dawn. "You want smoke?" Arthur demanded.

"As much smoke as you can. All of your boats, covering the whole parade route in smoke."

"I don't... maybe for security, sure, block the sight lines for antifa snipers, I get it, but... you won't be able to see the boats?"

Derek put conviction in his voice. "The President has a plan."

A long pause.

"Tell the President the People's Navy has his back," Arthur said.

As the sunbeams from the windows tracked across the motel room, hour by hour, Derek had less and less to do. The work had fallen almost entirely into the hands of Gavin, Taylor's contact at Trumpet, and Gavin's team of tech wizards. Derek ordered more alcohol by drone and, by the time night fell, he was thoroughly intoxicated and binging old seasons of The Great British Bake Off. He passed out in the middle of an episode before learning who'd won Star Baker.

His alarm woke him the next morning at eight. He checked his messages. The admiral had refitted the People's Navy's boats with smoke. Gavin had pulled an all-nighter, and his team had powered through their work on a wave of ginseng-caffeine energy drinks. Taylor had scored herself an invitation to the parade viewing at Mar-a-Lago.

At ten, he pushed the terrible desk chair in front of his laptop, chased an antacid with half a glass of water, and started checking his media feeds.

The first posts came from a crowd of bot accounts Gavin had set up. Each fake account presented photos, videos, and live streams of the parade just as the President had imagined it—luxury yachts, celebrities from across the Union, digital glitz, warships. Every image came with an all-caps endorsement of the parade's glory, and every image was a state-of-the-art deepfake, courtesy of Gavin's team.

On the heels of those posts came disappointed outbursts from other parade-watchers, complaining that no one could see anything but smoke. However, it soon became apparent to everyone on Trumpet that many of those complaints had come from left-leaning accounts—also created by Gavin's team, never mind how a crowd of vocal liberals could have scored early invitations to Trumpet—and the orthodox faithful began to shout down any and all complaints as fake news.

The deepfake footage conquered the discourse. The mainstream media squelched their own footage of the smokescreen in favor of the fictional pageantry. Even Derek found himself applauding at the faux Guns of Freedom 5 fight scene.

The icing on the cake was a pair of trumps from Taylor.

Taylor: *everyone at mar a lago is screaming and applauding. you're an evil genius, derek.*

Taylor: *and today's wordle is MACRO*

He read those posts over and over. Allowing himself to enjoy a warm feeling inside that wasn't from domestic gin, he sent a reply.

Derek: *what's the italian understudy's name?*

A silent bright flash lit up the room. Derek blinked, looked up and around, wondering if the flash had come from outside.

It had. A rumble followed, and then a *boom* that rattled motel windows and set off car alarms throughout the neighborhood.

Derek stood and gaped out the window. Then he opened the door and jogged out, staring off toward Palm Beach, where a colossal plume of smoke had begun to rise.

He tried texting Taylor. Then Senator Snow. Then he went inside and started checking his feeds.

~~~

It took him weeks to distill three facts from a maelstrom of panic and rumor.

Alternative Liberties

One: Elon had taken it badly when the President blamed him for the SpaceX crash and sidelined Elon's social media platform.

Two: Years ago, in a rare instance of forward thinking, Elon had put a special satellite in orbit that he'd dubbed *Payback.* It wasn't nuclear, but it was dense and heavy and designed to plummet out of orbit with precision, like a thunderbolt from God.

Three: Although the bomb-proof shelters under Mar-a-Lago had been competently built, there'd been no warning *Payback* was coming, and so only two of the President's partygoers had benefited from them.

One of those two had been Taylor.

He learned this last fact first, when Taylor appeared at the Super 8 near midnight on the Fourth. Smears of ash darkened her face, and blood matted her hair. Beside her on the pavement, outside Derek's door, sat a metal briefcase.

"The bomb shelter was plush," she told him. "I was down there with a Microsoft VP, trying to finesse some inside stock tips. Then... " She waved her hands, miming an explosion.

"Are you all right?"

She peeked through the bloodstained locks over her eyes, tugged them aside. "Scalp wounds always look worse than they are. Listen. So, Walter—that's my VP's name, Walter—he has a private jet ready. Full international clearance. He invited me to Sweden."

And she waited.

Derek looked into her blue eyes and knew this was the moment when he should ask her to stay.

"You should go," he told her, his voice hoarse from hours of shouting over the phone for news. "It's going to be hell here. Now that someone blew up the President."

"No one blew up the President."

"What? He survived?"

"I got you a present."

Taylor tapped the briefcase with the toe of her scuffed, expensive shoe.

Derek stared at it, then back at her. "What is it?"

"The AI server they've been using to simulate the President." He blinked.

"Heart failure, near the end of his second term. The guy was old. But it's not like he was making public appearances anymore. All they needed was to generate a few animations, a few rambling speeches, some unhinged tweets."

"Trumps."

Her lip quirked. "Whatever. Anyway, the blast messed up the President's place. I had to go through an underground data center to get out. Found this. Thought of you."

"Me?"

She stepped forward, took one of his wrists, rebuttoned his cuff. "You're an asshole, Derek. But you've been good to me. Listen. Whoever's left is going to look for someone to blame this on, and my gut says you're on the short list. This thing doesn't just make noise like the President. It has access, codes. You can use it to save yourself. Maybe some other people, too."

He blinked again.

She fastened his other cuff, then gave him a kiss he would always remember. "I'll smuggle you some tariff-free chocolate," she said, and walked off to the People's Navy ATV she'd hitched a ride on.

As the ATV raced off, as emergency sirens wailed, as the lights of fighter aircraft crisscrossed the sky, Derek sat on the pavement next to a case of computer chips pretending to be the President of the United States.

"The fuck?" he asked it.

The case, temporarily unplugged from the world it had controlled yesterday, didn't reply.

Alternative Liberties

Best Pocalypse Now

C. A. Chesse

Here is a picture of my breakfast
And here is a picture of my smile
Here is the latest propaganda
And here is my bathroom's new tile

I agree with you about Hitler
And like this picture of your friends
We all know that Trump will save us
Until the day when everything ends

Here is a picture of my cockroach
And a selfie inside my new dome
We're living our best-pocalypse now
And there's no place–this show place–like home.

Alternative Liberties

Priorities

Pearl Sims

The roll-up garage door was half open. Blue tape, sagging in the middle, stretched across the opening.

I knew what the blue tape meant.

It was ICE. The blue a perverse mockery,

"Please come get the dogs. Please. They're here. I think they're going to..." and the voice mail ended.

That had been this morning.

The screen door stood wide, attached by a single hinge. The once-beautiful paneled oak entry door was splintered, and only a dimly lit living area was visible beyond.

I resisted the urge to look around, instead letting the pull on the leash move me forward. Bart could do that. He was a Yellow Lab. He paused at house's driveway and as always peed on the cement base of the lamppost.

But this time he froze, his nose pointed toward the garage, and he began to whimper.

Alternative Liberties

This was Anna and Rick's house. Why she had called me, I didn't know.

I followed her on Facebook, but her posts had become few and far between. She was a Democrat and our primary interactions had been the occasional political protest. Small affairs, a few of us standing on a streetcorner waving signs supporting abortion rights or gun control.`

Anna went further than the rest of us. Once she she'd gone to jail for blocking the street. I'd remained safely on the sidewalk.

They were more than protesters.

Anna and Rick were immigrant protection activists, swearing that ICE could kiss their wrinkled white asses.

Mostly these days I saw them on dog walks. Winnie was her bulldog and Craig a rescue greyhound. Rick would make Laurel and Hardy jokes.

Treats and barks would be shared.

Butts would be sniffed.

She and Rick loved those dogs.

Now Bart began to whine with more intensity.

"Come on boy," I pulled on his leash.

But he jerked free, ran to the garage door and stood stiff legged. His barks preternaturally loud, echoing in the empty garage.

The street was still.

"Come on boy," I called again.

He continued to bark.

After looking both ways and behind me, I walked up the driveway. I reached down for Bart's leash and that's when I saw Winnie just inside the garage. The little brindle bulldog lay in a pool of dried blood.

Bart began to whimper.

Fear filled my soul. Craig, the greyhound, lay beyond her. Both wore leashes.

I barely remembered how we got home to our own garage. Bart was quiet.

Alternative Liberties

I leaned against my Prius and slid down to the concrete floor. Bart climbed across my lap. A welcome weight. He licked at my tears and I hugged him.

In the corner of the garage, my protest signs leaned in the corner. One, an image of an assault rifle under the text "NO MORE."

I pulled myself to my feet and grabbed them one at a time, snapped the handles, and folded them until they fit in a black plastic garbage bag. I knotted the top of the bag, then shoved it into the garbage can and sat down again with my dog in my lap,

Alternative Liberties

Afterward

David Gerrold

The phone vibrated.

Mostly I ignored it. I had silenced it. Once in a while I still picked it up to see if anyone had called, but I rarely returned calls.

I ignored most emails too, most of the internet. I did not check the news and I did not watch television. I had books to read. I had movies to watch. I had music to listen to. Most of those had been copied to micro-SD cards and the cards had been stashed in several different places, just in case someone decided I was important.

I had food. Not much: rice, beans, noodles, some sausages, some spices. They still made Coca-Cola. I didn't drive much anymore, I didn't like the world outside, so I had my groceries delivered. I survived. And I had a front porch—and every day I sat outside and enjoyed the sunset, sometimes it was glorious. Find something beautiful in the world every day and life can still be an adventure.

My neighbors were friendly enough—as long as we kept the conversations casual. Maybe I could trust them, maybe I couldn't. There were rewards for turning in suspected traitors and the economy was in such bad shape that any reward was tempting.

I could survive. Sooner or later, all of this would end. They'd get around to me eventually. I hoped it would be painless.

I knew I had failed. I was resigned to it.

There was a small village in the north. There was a house where you could walk out into the back yard, walk far enough, and you were in Canada. One day, I drove my son and his family up there. They got out of the car, hefted their backpacks, hugged me goodbye, and disappeared into the trees.

I drove home crying.

Our plan was that I would stay in the house as long as I could, against the day when it would be safe for them to return. But now it seemed like that day would never happen.

And then one day, the phone vibrated.

For some reason, maybe boredom, I picked it up. "Hello?"

It was Matthew. I hadn't heard from him in years. I'd heard he'd gone underground. I didn't know he was still alive. He sounded excited.

"Oh, good!" he said. "You're still there."

"I have no place to go."

"Did you see it?"

"See what?"

"You don't know?"

"Know what?"

"Do you have an internet connection?"

Alternative Liberties

"I think so. I haven't gone online in... I dunno." I wanted to ask why, but there was something undeniable in his voice. It sounded almost like joy.

"Log on! You have to see this."

"All right. Wait a minute."

I trudged into the room I used to use as an office and switched on the computer. I grabbed a can of compressed air and blew the dust off the monitor and the keyboard. The screen flickered to life, working its way through the corporate logos and the power-on notices.

"Are you on yet?"

"I'm getting there." I sank into my chair, found the mouse, and clicked around for a moment. "Okay," I said. "It's on. What am I looking for?"

"National news, any site. Even YouTube. It's everywhere. They're all showing the same thing."

I clicked around for a moment, finally brought up a window with a gray-haired man standing behind a podium. He wore an army uniform and his chest was a panorama of ribbons, what they used to call fruit salad. He was flanked by a dozen other men in uniforms. Air Force, Navy, Marines, Coast Guard, and a couple others I didn't recognize. The crawl across the bottom said that this announcement had been recorded earlier and would repeat until further notice.

I turned up the sound. When the grandkids still had their rooms upstairs I used headphones so I wouldn't disturb them, but after they left I'd dug around for some old speakers and plugged them in.

"—were arrested at 0330 hours this morning in a joint operation, authorized by all branches of this nation's military and conducted as a coordinated effort by the Special Forces of the United States Army, Navy, and Air Force."

Alternative Liberties

He paused long enough to turn the page of the prepared speech in front of him. "A full list of those who have been detained will be made available shortly. A second list of those who are still at large will also be released. Anyone harboring those individuals will also be arrested. Anyone with information concerning the whereabouts of those on the arrest list should contact the operational authorities immediately."

He continued, "Martial law is now in effect. Anyone failing to cooperate with the enforcement of martial law will be arrested. We intend to avoid unnecessary civilian casualties, but our troops have been authorized to use force wherever appropriate. Unless you are employed in an essential service like police, fire, or emergency medical care, stay in your home. Do not go out unless it is essential. Do not gather in any unlawful assemblies. There will be additional instructions shortly."

I turned away from the screen and shouted into the phone. "What the hell?"

"Just keep watching," Matthew said. "It gets better. He tried to escape. They caught him hiding in the Rose Garden."

"Huh? What?" Nothing made sense. I leaned back in my chair, as much distance away from the computer screen as I could manage. My heart was racing. My ears were pounding. I felt weak and confused and suddenly empty. I hadn't felt this way since that horrible morning when I turned on the TV just in time to see the first tower collapse, and fifteen minutes later, the second one, too.

"It's over," Matthew said excitedly. "It's over." And then, "Are you still there?"

Somehow, I managed to catch my breath. "I'm here," I said.

Matthew said, "Don't you get it? They remembered their oaths! 'To support and defend the Constitution of the United States against all enemies, foreign *and domestic!*' They defended the Constitution. It's over!"

"Is it?" I asked. "Is it really?"

"You have to hear it all. General Butler is promising a free and fair election. Eighteen months. Overseen by the military. No collaborators with the regime will be allowed to participate. Popular vote only. And Congress will have to end the electoral college. They have evidence it was rigged."

This was too much. All too much. Too fast. Matthew had to repeat it—this time a little slower. "Don't panic," he said. "There's a lot still happening. They'll be releasing all of their information as fast as they can. The news media still doesn't know how to report this."

"I don't—but why now?"

"He went too far. He said that democracy doesn't work and he was suspending elections in favor of executive appointments. It was so unconstitutional, the generals had to act. It'll take a while, but we're going to get the whole story. Apparently, there's a lot more. The man's crimes were—we don't know the whole story yet, but we will."

I wiped my eyes. "This isn't—I wish we could have—" I stopped myself. "I wanted it done legally."

"It was too late. This was the only way left."

I couldn't catch my breath.

Somehow, I managed to say, "You must have other people to call. I'll talk to you later."

"Take care of yourself," he said.

"Uh-huh."

I ended the call.

Outside, I could hear horns honking. Shouting. Yelling.

I went to the living room, pulled the curtain aside, and looked out the window. Some of my neighbors were out in the street, driving back and forth. Others were on their front lawns, waving their flags. They looked like they were celebrating.

I went out on the front porch and waved. They waved back.

Maybe Matthew was right.

Maybe it was over.

And maybe not.

But, maybe we could build something better.

And maybe my family could come home again.

That would be good.

About the Authors

Mike Adamson holds a doctoral degree from Flinders University of South Australia. After early aspirations in art and writing, Mike returned to study and secured qualifications in marine biology and archaeology. Mike was a university educator from 2006 to 2018, is a passionate photographer, master-level hobbyist, and a journalist for international magazines. He is now a well-known Sherlock Holmes novelist.

K.G. Anderson is a Seattle-based journalist, cat-herder, and practitioner of uncommon sense. Her publications, some under the name Alma Emil, include 11 stories for B Cubed Press. She edited *Southern Truths*. Visit her at writerway.com.

Lou J Berger lives in Littleton, Colorado with his high-school crush and two rescue dogs. A member of SFWA, he has been published in *Clarkesworld*, *Galaxy's Edge*, and a host of anthologies. He is *still* working on his first novel. His website is www.LouJBerger.com. He's on Bluesky @loujberger.bsky.social and on Facebook at https://www.facebook.com/AuthorLouJBerger/

Alternative Liberties

Don Bisdorf is a writer, software developer, and game designer. He and his wife live in northern Michigan, where they look after a hoard of books, a stack of computers, and one very good dog. You can find him online at www.donbisdorf.com

Jason P. Burnham (he/him) loves to spend time with his wife, children, and dog. He hopes his dystopias never happen.

Adam-Troy Castro is a science fiction, fantasy, and horror writer living in Florida. His fiction has been nominated for the Hugo, Nebula, Stoker, and World Fantasy awards and he is a winner of the Philip K. Dick Award for *Emissaries from the Dead*. His more than 100 publications include four Spider-Man novels (including the Sinister Six trilogy). He is also widely known for his Gustav Gloom series of middle-school novels and has authored a reference book on *The Amazing Race*.

C.A. Chesse lives in Portland, Oregon, where she writes eulogies professionally. She has three children and too many plants and rather a lot of books. Embarrassingly enough, she was raised young-earth Republican in the same Baptist school that produced Ted Cruz. At least she learned the value of repentance.

Brenda Cooper is a technology professional, a futurist, a writer, and an editor. She holds an MFA from Stonecoast and is an Imaginary College Fellow at the Center for Science and the Imagination, CSI, at Arizona State University. Her fiction has won two Endeavour awards and been shortlisted for the Philip K. Dick Award. Brenda lives in Washington State where she can be found riding bikes and walking dogs.

Elwin Cotman is a storyteller from Pittsburgh, Pennsylvania. He is the author of five books: the poetry collection *The Wizard's Homecoming*, and the short story collections *The Jack Daniels Sessions EP, Hard Times Blues, Dance on Saturday*, and *Weird Black Girls*.

His debut novel *The Age of Ignorance* will be published by Scribner in 2026.

Loren Davidson has lived in several places in the US, including VT, NY, CA and FL, before retiring to Panama. His Day Jobs covered many occupations, his last as a technical writer. Loren also spent 20 years as a performing songwriter, releasing six albums and performing from California to Key West. Loren now writes short fiction, gardens, and enjoys retirement. His short fiction has been published in places including *Bigfoot Country* and *Every Day Stories*.

Tom Easton has been publishing SFF since the 1970s and spent 30 years as *Analog*'s book columnist. He is also a retired college science professor. His latest B Cubed Press book (2020) is *Destinies: Issues to Shape Our Future* https://www.amazon.com/Destinies-Issues-Shape-our-Future/dp/194947612X/

Jonathan Erman is a writer and musician. He plays piano for theater groups throughout the San Francisco Bay Area, including TheatreWorks Silicon Valley and West Bay Opera. His piece "Take Flight Anyway" was performed by flutist Sara Andon as part of the Los Angeles Film Conducting Intensive's 2020 New Music Project. He has written features and reviews for Film Score Monthly Online and orchestral program notes. Learn more at jonathanerman.com

Voss Foster lives in the middle of the Eastern Washington desert, where he writes science fiction and fantasy from a single wide trailer. He is the author of the Office of Preternatural Affairs series, as well as Evenstad Media Presents, and has had work featured alongside historic classics in the Heroic Fantasy series, as well as by Vox Media. When not writing, he can be found admiring his ever-growing collection of carnival glass.

David Gerrold is a figment of his own imagination.

Alternative Liberties

Debora Godfrey has been involved as author and/or editor in six B Cubed publications. She feels honored to be included in a seventh.

Paula Hammond is a writer and artist based in Wales. Her fiction has been nominated for the Eugie Award, the Pushcart Prize, and a BSFA award. Her greatest joy is discovering the things that can be found in the neglected corners of the world. She reads too much, sleeps too little, and firmly believes everything can go in a sandwich. Her Sherlock Holmes collection, *Eliminate the Impossible*, is out now from MX Publishing.

Stuart Hardy is a writer from the UK commonly known online for the YouTube channel Stubagful where he makes video essays. His fiction has appeared in previous anthologies from B Cubed press and his latest short film *Got Your Nose* premiered at the Raindance film festival in London.

Juleigh Howard-Hobson's work can be found in *Think Journal, Anti-Heroin Chic, Able Muse, Non-Binary Review, Birds Fall Silent in the Mechanical Sea* (Great Weather for Media), *Under Her Skin* (Black Spot), and other venues. She's been nominated for "The Best of the Net," the Pushcart, the Elgin and the Rhysling. Her latest book is *Curses, Black Spells & Hexes* (Alien Buddha). She lives on the West Coast, up a bit from where you first think.

Larry Hodges is a member of SFWA with over 200 short story sales and four novels. He's a graduate of the six-week Odyssey Writers Workshop and a member of Codexwriters. He has 22 books and 2300+ published articles in over 200 publications. He's also a member of the US Table Tennis Hall of Fame, and claims to be the best table tennis player in SFWA and best SF writer in USATT! Visit him at larryhodges.com.

Alternative Liberties

Akua Lezli Hope, Grand Master of Fantastic Poetry (SFPA), is an award-winning creator, wisdom seeker & paraplegic in print since 1974 with 500+ poems published. Her honors include the NEA, NYFA, NYSCA. Author of *Embouchure: Poems on Jazz and Other Musics* (Writer's Digest Award), *Them Gone, & Otherwheres: Speculative Poetry* (Elgin Award winner), she edited *NOMBONO: An Anthology of Speculative Poetry by BIPOC Creators*, a history-making first. She created the Speculative Sunday Poetry Reading Series.

William Kingsley considers himself lucky. He lives in an unassuming village in Almaguin Ontario, CANADA. He does not think Canada will become the 51st state, regardless of anyone's wet dreams. He weeps for his American friends. He has published several short stories and poems; his latest publication is a poem in *Polar Borealis*. His story, "A Place Before The Storm," is, in part, an homage to Hemingway.

Susan Murrie Macdonald is a double stroke survivor who writes speculative fiction, mostly sword-and-sorcery, as cognitive therapy. She has been a member of the B Cubed family since our first book, *Alternative Truths* in 2017, which contained her Darrell Award-nominated story "As Prophesied of Old." B Cubed Press will be publishing her nonfiction book *They Endured* in 2025 or 2026.

Louise Marley is the award-winning author of twenty novels of science fiction and fantasy. As Louisa Morgan she writes historical fantasies about witches and ghosts and other magical beings. She now lives, writes, and teaches in southwest Oregon, where she rambles the paths and byways with her familiar, Oscar the Border Terrier.

Visit her at http://www.louisemarley.com, or listen to her real-life ghost stories on TikTok as louisamorgan75.

Alternative Liberties

Jenna Hanan Moore loves to travel, take pictures, drink coffee, and immerse herself in nature or a good story. Her tales appear in places like *The Lorelei Signal*, *365 Tomorrows*, and *Decapitate* (from the Third Estate Arts Collective). She's the founder and editor of *Androids and Dragons*. She lives with her husband and their small dog.

Nancy Jane Moore is the author of the fantasy novel *For the Good of the Realm* and the science fiction novel *The Weave* along with other books. Her short fiction and poetry have appeared in a variety of magazines and anthologies. Born and raised in Texas, she spent many years in Washington, D.C., and now lives with her sweetheart in Oakland, California. She's on good terms with crows.

Jacy Morris is an Indigenous author. He is a registered member of the Confederated Tribes of Siletz. At the age of ten he was transplanted to Portland, Oregon, where he developed a love for punk rock and horror movies, both of which tend to find their way into his writing. He has been an English and social studies teacher in Portland, Oregon, since 2005. He has written several novels, including the "This Rotten World" series, the "One Night Stand at the End of the World" series, and "The Enemies of Our Ancestors" series... and many more!

Joseph Nettles: After completing his studies in Classics, and taking away the customary longing for an idealized past and PTSD, Joseph now spends his days trying to distract himself from the end of the world by looking at the majestic spectacle of the Alps, where he lives, and occasionally writing trifles he, at least, finds amusing.

Kurt Newton's poetry and fiction have appeared in *More Alternative Truths*, *Alternative Truths III: Endgame*, *Space Force*, *Holiday Leftovers*, and *Alternative*

Leadership. He lives in a fortified bunker in the blue bastion of Connecticut.

Chaz Osburn, the author of *At the Wolf's Door* and *Incident at Jonesborough*, spent 17 years living and working in western Canada before returning to the U.S. in 2023. His background is in the newspaper and magazine business—he's held positions as a reporter, editor and publisher—and PR. He now lives in Traverse City, MI.

Mark Rivett has experience as an educator, digital artist, and application developer. He lives in Ann Arbor, Michigan, with his wife and children.

Andrew Roberts is an old poet in search of a razor. Not to trim his stubble, but to carve carefully into his exquisitely crafted epics. All of which are much longer than this bio.

Ell Rodman is a DC-based writer as seen in the *Midnight Garden: Where Dark Tales Grow* horror anthology, and *Andromeda Magazine*. Ell is an avid watcher of bad 80's horror and fosterer of dogs.

Earl T. Roske is a San Francisco Bay Area author. His Hospitaller Orphan Corps universe is full of stories about Hospitaller orphans providing aid, comfort, and defense to those in need across the galaxy. He is also now a B Cubed Press veteran.

Elizabeth Ann Scarborough: This Nebula-award winning author also collaborated with the Dragonlady, Anne McCaffrey, so she knows from dragons. She's also a Vietnam vet and prefers dragons to war. She's written 40 books and numerous short stories. Currently she lives with two cats and sometimes belts sea shanties with her friends. She's also a bead artist whose work has appeared in books. She did not vote for the current regime, believing it should stay inside dystopia novels.

Tera Schreiber is a practicing writer and out-of-practice lawyer. You can read some of her recent short stories in the *Veneficium Feminae*, published by Amaranth Publications, and in *Moss Puppy Magazine, Vol 7, The Boneyard*. She writes stories about strong women in the mossy Pacific Northwest with her husband, daughters, and cats. You can find her on Instagram at @tera_s_writes and on Bluesky @terahs.bsky.social.

DP Sellers lives in an old house (not haunted, alas) in New Orleans, Louisiana, and enjoys dark urban fantasy.

Merv Sims, his well-worn pink Royal typewriter, and occasional cat Felix, pound out their stories to the rhythm of flashing neon on a third-floor walkup with a view of the Downtown Gospel Mission.

Harry Turtledove is an escaped Byzantine historian. He writes alternate history, other sf, fantasy (much of it historically based), and, when he can get away with it, historical fiction. He is married to novelist and Broadway maven Laura Frankos. They have three daughters, two granddaughters, and three spoiled cats. He annoys people @hntdove on Bluesky.

C T Walbridge is a retired biologist, formerly with an agency that was tasked with annoying multiple industries.

Robert Walton is a retired middle school teacher, classical musician, rock climber, and mountaineer with ascents in Yosemite and Pinnacles National Park. An experienced writer, his Civil War novel *Dawn Drums* won the 2014 New Mexico Book Awards Tony Hillerman Prize for best fiction. Most recently, *Joaquin's Gol*d, a collection of his award-winning Joaquin Murrieta tales, became available on Amazon: http://chaosgatebook.wordpress.com/

Stephanie L. Weippert: Ages ago, a sci-fi convention sent out an anthology call, they wanted slug stories. The idea tickled Stephanie's funny bone, so she wrote her very first story. It got rejected, but the writing bug bit and with her hubby's enthusiastic support she's been writing ever since. A decade later, she has a website at www.stephanieweippert.com, a handful of pieces in small press anthologies, and two out-of-print books she will republish real soon now.

Amy Wolf is a writer, massage therapist, energy healer, medium, and activist living in Seattle. She is partial to gardening, ceremony, and spending time outdoors. Her work can be seen at newversenews.com and at Soundandmountains on WordPress.

Jim Wright is a retired US military intelligence officer and freelance writer. He lived longer in Alaska than anywhere else and misses it terribly. He now lives in the fetid Panhandle of Florida in an ancient Cold War bunker of a house surrounded by alligators and rednecks. Find his Stonekettle Station blog at https://www.stonekettle.com or follow him as Stonekettle on Facebook.

Alternative Liberties

An end note from Bob.

We were watching the election returns. Our ship was taking on water and we were taking on vodka.

We decided to do this book.

The next morning, we looked at the calendar. We knew that the end times were indeed upon us and decided to do the book. The only thing better than an EPIC fail, is an EPIC success. Nothing was impossible, not if you believe in your country, your friends, and your loved ones.

Here at B Cubed Press, we do believe in our country, our friends, our family, and we decided to do this thing. Now that you've bought the book, you're part of the Resistance.

We have a common bond, all of us, in our Resistance to the forces of totalitarianism that have seized the reins of power.

Bob B.

Alternative Liberties

About B Cubed Press

B Cubed Press is a small press that publishes big books about things that matter.

A percentage of every book we publish is donated to charity—usually the ACLU. We are approaching $6,000 in donations. Note that this includes monies from authors who donated their royalties or payment for stories.

We can be reached at Kionadad@aol.com or Bcubedbob@gmail.com.

We're on Facebook as B Cubed Press. Our writers gather regularly on the B Cubed Press Project page on Facebook.

We can also be found online at https://bcubedpress.wordpress.com

Alternative Liberties

Made in the USA
Monee, IL
29 January 2025